HEAVEN
and
EARTH

WAR AMONG MEN

LUZ HERRERA

To order additional copies of this book, contact:
Bookwhip
1-855-339-3589
www.bookwhip.com

We kissed again and everything
will be perfect until our last day on earth.
To E.J

Contents

Secrets Must Remain Secret

Knowing that the world is in trouble, comes to the rescue one of the most amazing men of the moment, one of the super-heroes of history, able to solve the hardest crimes, chasing criminals through the sidewalks of the great city, willing to give their life for others, no matter the danger, goes deep into the night.

Following his instincts can't fail; it goes into the unknown, walks slowly into the tunnel incapable of knowing what awaits him there.

In the distances were sighted some men not noticed who many there were as dark tunnel and night; it should know that everything in this place was different than usual normally.

At that moment came some unexpected, a nice pretty lady go of a luxury Rolls-Royce, one of the most expensive cars in the world, prepared just for her, by the look of the car was armored missile settled and ready for any complication.

Get out of the car with a briefcase, give his coat to his accompanist, my mouth dropped open of emotion, was slender with a reddish dress, with blond hair to his shoulders, walk to the man waiting, to meet them opened the briefcase, was covered to the top with diamonds.

That could be worth more than diamonds? They were given a small red box with white a lath-shaped bow-tied, like a gift for someone special.

My question was why would go, alone with only one companion and with such a load of diamonds, was beautiful too risky to let her go alone if anything happened to her…Well, that would not be my problem, if not catch it, was the first thing on my list, when she received the small box, exchange men went up to the lady in his luxury car, at that moment I faced the vehicle pointing my gun, yell that came out of the car, spent a few seconds and all, three had disappeared, did not see them leave, but as we approached the car was gone, my team captures all but three. The seller, she and her mysterious companion, in the car was only found blonde hair was a wig.

A mysterious girl who was? A mystery too, and that so much secrecy, worth more than a briefcase full of diamonds that was still my question.

As if by magic they had disappeared along with the diamond and so mysterious little red box, I decided to look for clues. But there was nothing, that was the best track… anything, was as if it had been there, like it never happened, interrogated detainees, very subtly clear! What had happened and they were as shocked as we, only repeated, are demons, are demons, no devil frightens me, I said loudly.

In the distance, I hear a melody like no other and a chilling scream, the melody was "kip in real" and the screams were my sister, that said so loudly that my secret identity cold to be rebellious, his voice was sweet, is 18, with slim body but with hips off, long chestnut brown hair, honey-colored eyes, her skin always seemed like silk and white complexion with cheeks like apple, very cute my sister, by the way, to hear their cries and outrageous that she said, let's go, hurry up and be late.

-Wakes up stops dreaming it is late, time to work. Surprise me too much!

-Rays is late, very late.

-If it is it, and also late again because of you, hurry up to have to go school, I have class and then to work, come on, and also because you should drive and let that bike.

-Only if you buy me a car for myself.

She is my sister is older; I have only seventy years, will fulfill the eighteen on February 14 is a special day for all.

But no for me, if you are alone that day, and she has, well, is about to turn nineteen, we are always together is my best friend and accomplice, she has no boyfriend and I…well, let's say I'm at it, therefore I do not want my birthday to arrives, but in the end will come, sings just thinking about it.

She drives a yellow truck, four-door, we both love music, we buy a stereo between the two and enjoyed it, although not always walk with her, she left me at school, go to separate schools, mine is not far from the restaurant where we work, but of her is something far not much but if she attends the college, attends only four days a week and then we are back in the restaurant where we work, I'm back on the bike, which certainly does not have a nice color and green old who bought my neighbors when I was twelve, well not bought only sent to fix, it was Mr. Gonzalez, serves very well this perfect but sometimes make the fun of me in school, as always are abusers but I ignore them because if I do is worse, although sometimes I would like to do something else, will not do it, would be like giving them a delicious snack, I'm not that way I do not like violence, gradually stooped bother me and some of my old friends are no longer friends, but I have new and we get along great.

Always in the park are people living there, who are unemployed street people, every day at the time of release, the leftover food us as we bring it, as this clean, spent part of the night in the park, knowing stories of people who are in it, trying to understand why they are there, but sometimes even they understand.

I do not think we stole the food because it always throws away and it is clean food, and are better than someone else eat to throw it away. To the restaurant come many kids at school are the most and few adults, is a small town but not what we all know, it is old and rare, there is everything is very colorful the name is M.T angel while watching it, I think is not so small.

That evening at the restaurant was a song Chica Bonita, and she came, with a red scarf, faded blue trousers, a gray coat unbuttoned and a white shirt, balance, long curly red hair like fire, was perfect just like my great dreams and only in my dreams.

-Keep in your mind brother.

-Sarah silence.

-What are you waiting for; you get to attend table three.

-No, I will not go.

The door rang again and my sister said.

-Accept change table three and you're the seven, please.

Another time I would say no but we were in the same, was a guy with his companion, apparently his girlfriend.

-Unfriendly arrogant, ahu.

-In your mind Adriel.

-You two move it and wake up. Said the owner of the restaurant

-Yes. Sarah said and then I

-Yes, Mr. Robles.

My sister and I quietly pointed to the orders of our respective tables, went we entered the kitchen talking to someone who needed help with the pantry and wanted to now, Mr. Robles send me to the kitchen to help.

When my brother was in the kitchen, Mr. Robles sent me to attend their Adriel tables, and there he was, too bad with her, had the most beautiful eyes, of all a flirtatious smiled a divine hair and an exquisite perfume, and perfect arms, walked with orders in hand, leave them on the table as usual and when turning stumbled to the other table, I remember missing a few centimeters to the ground and thinking about the pain of falling in front of him, but the unexpected happened, something stopped me as if by magic, something stopped my fall, his arms were holding me, was stunned, wordless, Mr. Robles arrived and ended the spell, my brother was with him, did not even know how they got by me, my brother continued attending them and I could not even say thank you, no time, just listen to the words of my brother.

-Excuse my sister is a little confused with so many people to attend, but I offer something more.

I wanted to tear him apart for saying that, the short black-haired girl answered.

-No thanks.

Unpleasant thought, but it was her companion, after reacting to my failure just wanted not to appear at that table.

They had come just a couple of months to the restaurant, always accompanied him that girl, was not hard to imagine that it was his girlfriend, he never was alone, the silence was interrupted.

-Friday will be your birthday. Sarah what will you do?

-Well, my friend to work and I have class early Saturday as to whether what I will do is sleep.

-Do not be boring; look, let's dance for a while, maybe meet a cute guy.

-Enough, no guys at the moment.

-I forgot, no boys.

She replied mockingly, she is my best friend Monica we've known girls friends since then, and we are almost neighbors, she studies where my brother, her parents paid the school are lawyers and earn quite well, but I think she does not like and who travel a lot, she hides that, prefer this alone but I know that miss them.

Time passed more slowly than usual, was time to close almost everyone had left, the last was the guy who saved me from falling, would have preferred that he had gone first, close and went to the park-like every night this time there was plenty left, but from something for nothing it was fine, we finished early and in the distance, I heard a strange noise but fails to see that it was.

Adriel interrupted by a blow of his bike in the truck that scared me, the was rising, only was the night it was okay, it was just paranoia, went home and the next morning there were only a couple of days of my 19 years, time passed.

Sometimes though that my dreams had been left behind, who never be realized, never had time for me, just work and taking some class as was paying at this rate, I will have forty never finished school, every night dream strange things I tell my best friend, my brother and Monica, spend hours and days go by and life goes on unchanged, was strange sometimes because I feel what others feel; I am sad to see them, I suffer from his suffering, would do more to help them, get them out of this life as difficult but I think if I can't with my life unless I can help someone.

I do not understand because I feel this pain to see them suffer, sometimes ignore them would turn around, but I can't be ignored, so obvious, my brother is the same, and every time I'm sad that it is, as if we felt the same and we are not twins, I think it's because we have good feelings and spend so much time together that we are inseparable, we are a team together, we've never been apart, so it's not as if we were would be, although that someday will be, we must make our lives one day apart, at some point we will choose different paths.

As if by magic, the case in which I, the detective who was considered by people a superhero, his extraordinary case was still unresolved, and I had gotten out a hand the most beautiful girl I had seen in my entire career of detective, was out of my reach had escaped, the detective who never leaves unsolved case was still on, with the case of the missing girl mysteriously as if by magic, is it something evil, I follow a trail to a bar called Blue Star, where at the end of a corner with good lighting expecting a gentleman with a lady, I approached them.

-Ray, Sarah, do not wake me up again, that's just late for work, the house is falling or your hair is on fire.

-That's funny; it's time to get up.

-It's time to work, but there is no light.

-I know but promised to help clean up the park and you will help me.

-I forget, but that's ok think anyone go so early to help, do you think would serve the flyers to distribute.

-I hope so and if we will only be those of the moon and we.

-Great.

Indeed, those of the moon are those who stay in the park if they fall asleep that in the light of the moon, not by choice, of course, this time I drive.

To get to the park there were more volunteers than we thought, the park was not very big if that would be fast, unexpectedly there was the girl who took away the dream, and the gallant who like my sister, of course with her friend that would not let for a moment, but there were both, as I gathered the trash next to some trees behind the bathrooms along there was a man saying thanks to the end I found you.

-Sorry, you speak to me Mr.

-If your kid, this is for you.

-But why, I can't accept it, to notice that.

-Of nothing it belongs to you is called the Blue Star.

-Yeah, right, like the bar of my dream, and why, is not a star is a... rectangle and is purple.

-When the time comes, you will discover.

-Adriel where you are? Hear my sister scream

-Herewith this gentleman.

When the flip was gone, I looked in the end, but I could not find it.

-Or maybe not. I said quietly

We picked up the garbage bag, in the end, Mr. Robles brought us coffee, it was very nice of him, the guy who liked my sister brought biscuits was unexpected and rare, well, but I m very happy with the work we do, in the end, had withdrawn almost all.

-Sarah see you, I'm with my friends.

-Okay, see you later.

My brother walked with his friends, my beau was withdrawing from my truck after helping up the bags and was approaching in his black sports car enviable even poke to see the brand, to see the car was more than obvious that it was a good car, as he approached his car in the back seat, bent down and pulled out a gray bag had no brand that I had known, took out a box no very big with a purple ribbon, looked good, strange but good.

Suddenly started coming toward us, but increasingly approached as if in slow motion, I love watching him and my heart froze for a second seemed like it was coming to me, but did not believe it when I had it in front said.

-This is for you.

I froze felt he was talking to me but did not know if it was true until my friends woke me with a small knock on my arm.

-It is for me!

-If clear to you, happy birthday and you know you did a good job today.

-Yeah, well, we did all, but thanks, did not have to bother besides no today will be tomorrow, and as you heard.

-About that, it's easy; your friends do not cease to say.

-Ah.

Silly to ask that, he was right, look to the other side, they were they kept glancing.

-Thanks, but do not think I can, is that we do not know and do not know I could not.

-If I know, but tomorrow I can't, also is at midnight and can't see you at the midnight, if I wanted to be the first to give you something, and apologize if I bother you the other day at the restaurant.

-As you know.

-Well to hear your friend say.

Clear that uncomfortable me, if it was not because they were all it would have run and put to mourn.

-Yeah… well, thanks for the other day, saved me from falling, thanks but I can't accept.

-Well look is a simple gift… because I did not know you could like it, and I was my grandmother, has barium years and I think it is appropriate for you, please accept it you liked it.

Behind me, I heard a mocking laugh when he said that was his grandmother, I felt somewhat uncomfortable and he also.

-Is fine, but with a condition.

-If.

-What is your name?

-To that condition. It is good just Alan, and yours?

I gave a little laugh, as someone gives you something without unknowing your name.

-Sarah.

Do not hesitate to say without many rodeos.

-Princes.

-Excuse.

-Princes, that means your name princes, well nice to meet you, princes, you enjoy your gift, see you another day.

Was very attentive to him I forget that we are not alone.

-Friend if you want us carries the trash to the recycling.

-No, I take it girls… he is Alan.

-Is a pleasure, although we met in the restaurant?

-Yes of course. Answer Monica

We said goodbye and walked away. Suddenly heard more laughter from those who were with us, including Mr. Robles, my brother did not miss all this it was close and did not resist to mock, well, we went to the restaurant, the day ended and we returned home and at twelve with a minute I hear a song sounded strange was like a music box, but know where it came, went back to sleep and woke up missing just minutes before work, ran to wake up my brother, but to my surprise, he was already awake.

-Clam, dress up breakfast and then go to work.

-This crazy is very late.

-If well, talk with Mr. Robles and said it could be late just for today if you talk to him, but that said let's calm, do not run.

Was rare that I fell asleep but my brother never lies to me with something that interests me, spent two hours, as in the morning there are few people in the restaurant; We headed straight, our day like any other, at evening was so full that I did not have a time to breathe, I did not have time or think today was my birthday, however, some remembered me and more when asked who had given me, especially is a golden box.

My dream come true, or my worst nightmare, what are the chances that someone will give away something on the day of your birthday with the excuse of apology and without knowing you, and also the person who you like the most, I think any, even with my interest had not been able to open my gift, forget the previous day in the restaurant, leave it on the counter and saw every time I passed by there, but I was too busy coming to see it, I was curious but not I dared to open it.

As he said did not appear that day at the restaurant, had to do more important things I guess, but his gaze, his laugh sometimes thought that looked at me, but was part of my imagination was clear that also a girlfriend.

The day in the restaurant is almost over, we started to clean all; all my friends gave me some gifts and before going congratulations to me and sang happy birthday, while attended.

Enjoyed a cake in my honor that I only had time to blow out the candles and split, not tried it, but my brother saves me a little, ended almost at midnight to clean everything for the next day, I came late but no my brother, and do not want to leave all the work for him, of course neither wanted and was happy to stay late.

Missing a few minutes to go, there was midnight just when I was born, October 13 and it was Friday, that's fascinating, my brother approached, I had not said congratulations even this morning, carrying a small red box a pink ribbon.

-Happy birthday sister, you enjoy it.

-Okay, very nice where did you get it, thank you.

-Let me put it myself.

Wow, was a necklace of pink ribbons, and hanging fascinated me, seemed worth very little truth, but it was divine, with three purple roses on a stone in the center of each rose, on the side of rouses decorated with more stones forming a rectangle on the outskirts forms of chains adorned with purple diamonds, really was very nice.

-Where did you get it?

-Secret sister, and also hear it called Blue Star.

-But is purple and not a star.

-I thought the same thing, but then I understand, and if you're the star.

-Yeah, right, thanks.

-Now the next gift.

Finally opened the gift I desired to open, it was easy too, just remove the ribbon and it was all.

-A sphere… a snow globe with an angel inside.

-Cool it was his grandmother, what would give you that? It's silly.

-Shot up It's cute and also with this beautiful piano music I love is… perfect.

-Hey, mine is better and I bet that more expensive.

-If, I love you brother thanks a lot, "ugly" and if your gift is very nice.

We were getting sentimental, gave me a big hug, and birthday gifts with the others were a couple of CD, cards for shops, and a pass to the book fair, that was great I love reading and may choose some, only that it was tomorrow afternoon in the library, great I have to work; yeah, well, luck for Sunday will also, I have to go do not ever lose it.

Close and we headed home; it was strange felt someone watching us, Adriel thought the same, but we see nothing, finally at home and to sleep.

I approached the lady and the mysterious knight, before I ask a question, listen to say, we will be close, "take care of you and our sister, she is the key to all this"

-Adriel awake, we're late again.

-I'm getting tired of this when I will finish my dream?

-In those, now you know who the mysterious woman is?

-No today, I only dream that I must take care of you, that you were the key to all of this.

-If I am the great key for you, "superhero" and since when you dream with me. She laughed mockingly

-Ha, ha, let's go.

Sunday morning dawned cold as usual, what is expected in October is always called at this time, it was time to go to the book fair and let the town down, I leave the truck in the restaurant, the library was not far away, I started to walk after a few minutes go to store to buy a scarf purple color with pink, I found cute, even though I had some at home not resisted buying that, to get to the library I was not surprised that it was almost empty, started to cross it and look some books, I found one and not resisted to open it, I remember something, the book was a meaningful name, find mine…

-Actually, if it means princes.

-Good nor surprised me, that he knew that, look for his own, Alan (Iris Gaelic) "handsome, cheerful"

-Of course, is handsome, gorgeous.

-Now talking to myself, it was pathetic.

-Hi, what a coincidence, not seen you since the park.

Scared me, he was crazy, never spoken to someone in the back; his face hid a small smile.

-Thanks for my gift, I was wondering when I'd appreciate it properly because with my friends was not enough, well not know who you are, less would have your phone, well thanks.

I left like a fool, so many tanks, but not so much, I wonder if would be hearing me talk alone, if course he did, as no listen.

-You do not have to be thankful; it was nothing thought you would like to.

-If I like thanks, I know the song becomes known, I thought that somewhere there was listening, but I do not remember, I believe was called a white butterfly.

-Seriously.

-Yes, not surprisingly.

-Yeah, I will continue seeing some books and then we see.

-If clear… wait, you said we'll go.

-Well, Kalinda comes with me.

-Of course.

Keep watching, find the name of my brother, Adriel (Hebrew) "Of Gad's Majestic" hum… I look around where he had gone, but do not look, I think he walks very fast and silent as a ghost, though more often than ever before began to daydream wanted to see him again, even far from once more, finished viewing the book of names and headed to the area of fantasy books, then to the supernatural stories, I chose two books, one is light and darkness and the other the sun and the moon, both of fantasy, by the two, did not sound so interesting but sometimes they are and were cheaper and more with the card they gave me, I kept touring the library, started reading a local story, was that some twenty years ago there were some disappearances, thought that some jaguars, but over time a forester saw a group of people, then a very strong light and then nothing was just a story of someone who was hunting, but nobody paid any attention, the disappearances stopped.

Was about to leave when I looked at him, this time alone without her companion, was sitting at the table in front and when I look at it approached me, greeted me, but rather said goodbye, he said he already retired from there, who had been sufficient between stores, told him I almost withdrew me, but wait until he away first, and not just because he did not want to think to follow him, if not for not wanted to look at my pay with a card from the library.

He retired with the girl and paid for his books, carrying about ten books, read them all, took out his wallet and her a card like mine, I smiled to myself as I was a fool, he did not care about that stuff, feel sorry or something, paid all with that card, not even suffered, was worth more than mine; I sigh deeply, they left, I finished reading the newspapers and back in place, after that I pay my staff and went to my house.

I was watching television entangled in a blanket of Scooby-Doo, drinking tea I was falling asleep, were about eight-thirty, the neighbor's dogs became agitated, someone attempted to enter the house and made disasters, try to run to his home but too late, the intruders were gone, and surprisingly were not injured, that thought, surprisingly, Alan and his companion were closing in, while the intruder began to take another home, take a few seconds to understand that it was mine, I ran over there but they stopped me, call an ambulance for Mr. and Mrs. Gonzalez, then running after them into the house, to reach the entrance for a moment I thought it was the television that makes these noises the scandal, looks like it was watching a movie, they knew very well fight and had not 3D TV, well I interfered at that time.

One ran behind me, try to fight him, but was not able to do it, I fell on the couch, that was convenient, batter that on the glass table, the man just wondering where the blue stat was and the wanted.

-I do not what you mean.

Grab my throat and I remembered that I had given my dear sister, and cry not between me, as I could not say anything, but apparently, they listened, Alan tried to get him off, and then vanished into the darkness, but it seemed there was no unharmed, I remembered that my sister would be in danger for my birthday gift, I started to call her, but only voice mail answered, Alan told me she's fine.

-At bookseller remember silence phone.

I start to leave the house and they behind me, not even ask what they were doing there.

Did not worry about her, wait for the ambulance to come by my neighbors and then got on the bike and get started down the street, as no even over a minute and saw her yellow truck approached, it was fine, return to the house while she stepped out of the truck, and the other house ambulance and some patrol troops were still, and began asking questions and check my house the same way, she asked what happened, and did not know that answer, she runs to the neighbors Gonzalez and they were well, back to the house and was a disaster.

-And you do here Alan and…? I ask

-She is my sister Kalinda.

-Oh, your sister, nice.

-But they do here? Ask my sister.

-We passed by and stopped to help, right Adriel.

They made gestures, no to say anything, but never lie to my sister that would be the first time for a few more.

-Yes.

-You better come through some things and stay somewhere else just in case.

-I do not be better than me and my brother; we stay here, besides not where we could go.

-Sarah just for today goes with your friend Pilar.

-I think that just for today okay.

The sad look to convince and it worked.

-Well, just for tonight.

We picked up just enough and went to with her friend Pilar, all the way thinking about the four guys who were at home, and as they fought Alan and his sister, and has a strange name but I like the name, of course, I could not even think straight, just it has been my fault that the necklace had my sister was the cause of Mr. Gonzales they were exposed in the hospital and my sister in danger, and could not say, could not tell her how I got the necklace, not what was happening with her beau, they offered to take us, but we do not accept, on the way my sister talking to her friend Pilar, she was happy, although Alan's car was still very close, I thought they lived further up, arrive at the house Pilar, Alan's car stopped.

-Adriel happens? You look like a liar, you know that.

-I'm rather surprised, how it got your boyfriend and knew where you were.

-Or that, I have the answer, I found him in the library, and he came out first then me.

-Since when you go out together?

-Do not go out, I found him there.

-Timeout, you find a dollar in the street, not a person.

-I was there and him too, that's all.

-Yeah of course!

They reached the door, opened us Pilar very worried, and hug my sister.

-You are right? And doing here has been already your boyfriend.

-Not, and is a good question.

-Come in.

Kalinda went to check, made sure there was no one else; he just looked not a word.

-We go anything we can talk about.

Said that while gave me a call and walked away.

-Hey, since when are friends? Asked Pilar

-We are not.

-What happens? Pilar asked again

-That would like to know.

-Where you go.

-To sleep, it's too late.

-An explanation.

-I would like one. Angry answer

The next day in the restaurant waiting to see Alan and his sister, as expected, they did not show up, we got home and cleaned up the mess and my sister was listening to the snow globe and then fall asleep, the passage of week everything was still quiet, but I never took his gaze to my sister, not let my impatient restlessness, but it was obvious she felt that something was wrong and was just concerned about not knowing anything about what happened, third the week of October and it was as if they had disappeared those brothers.

She wonders what had happened, did not know that answer, I also had questions for them, although he only gives me a cell phone and sends text messages, asking how we were but did not answer my questions.

We start to think that maybe it was a robbery like any other, but why so much interest in us, in that we were good, and even sought the necklace that I give to my sister, I could not take off and leave it to the view where someone could take it and we get rid of the problem.

Fair on Thursday, as the last few days my sister fell asleep early, and within seconds entered the house two figures coming towards me, I could not move from my place, then distinguished them were Alan and his sister, came to talk with me, I had so many questions, not even leave me to speak, explained that the four of them were looking for the necklace.

-Their names are Duff darkness, Petulah the search, Lowell Small Wolf, and the girl Ophelia Snake.

-That means that also have some gifts, like us.

-And why they want the necklace? And why not give it, and that's it. I paused.

-Wait, gifts… what are you talking about, what you smoked?

-The necklace belongs to you and your sister; we have always cared for but had been lost for a few years, and when we find we take care to give them to you, only you know who it works.

-Then not caring forever.

-Something likes that.

-And what does the necklace, why it is so special?

-That just knows that you and your sister, it only works with you, I told you so.

-The old man gave me, you sent him.

-Is a friend.

-The way they are looking for?

-Do not just look, but it just needs you equal.

-If, so is the necklace holds the power to destroy and create, but only you can use it.

-Create and destroy you believe that, and in this case is too much responsibility for us. Looked up and agree with me

-If, my name is Kalinda and means sun and I have the power to control the temperate of thinks more than other thinks.

-Other things? She was referring to her powers, she is better in one than the other, will be useful to remember

-If we have the same powers, but specialize more in which we play.

-See you later, just do not do anything silly. Alan said and walked away to the door.

-Leave us alone and if they return.

-We would know immediately.

-How are soothsayers?

-No, I put a tracking device on the cell phone that I give you and a camera in the snow globe, so we know you are okay.

-Spy on us, and as you place the camera in the snow globe that is ridiculous as this.

-It is not, well if a litter, my sister did it to care for you, we could not follow all the time, she came up, it was safer, and without wasting time.

-Seriously the snow globe.

Kalinda said if his head before leaving, but his cell phone rang a step back to the door.

-We can stay, all change.

-Great all change and lay down.

They spend the night in the house, I fall asleep and they took turns to keep an eye on, I woke up and they were in my bedroom, my sister woke up and I ask if everything was fine; they said yes, that my sister was bathing.

-You spy her in the bathroom.

-No, heard the shower.

-Or if, and do not indent to go, remember my sister got up.

-No, you will come with us.

-I don't think so, I rest today, and she is about to leave for work.

-Is true, I think that is about to leave.

-As I said.

-Is about to knock.

-Adriel it's time to go, I can enter.

-Not.

-Why.

-Is that I'm… naked.

-Oh, see you.

-Sarah Take your snow globe with you.

-What, why?

-Because otherwise, I throw it away, I already desperate the song, and if I see I throw.

-Naughty.

In the end, it took, feared that I throw, she left and then we left to go to her house, I really did not know where we were going, but was far or so I thought, at one point my thoughts were confused, I feel it is part of sleep.

-I thought we were going to your home.

But it was not his house, was the monastery.

-What we do here?

-We come to see friends.

-Here!

All was quiet in this place, in a room where some tracking devices, computer equipment, a large plasma screen, I get used to playing video games on it, I thought between myself and looking silly.

Containing different parts of the city on one side of the restaurant, well inside, but no my sister, of course, she was not always nearly there and hindered a vase of artificial roses battered, that we had tried to replace, but eventually always forgot, the strange thing was that she always had roses at home everywhere and any flower liked to put in water and no matter which flower was, she loves flowers, nature.

When out to walking in the front yard, not a large chapel was, the monastery was brick color near orange, but it was beautiful, was the more peaceful place I had seen, my sister invited me to come for some time but I did not, and she was right and what she said not mistaken is beautiful, the other side was a few doors down the hall you could hear some strange noises when the opening was crazy, a retreat of the Pacific, was training martial arts and was coordinated chaos when I retired Alan talked me.

-I'll teach you to defend yourself boy.

Sure at the time I needed it, was too hard is easier on television, but I will try, Alan was very tolerant the others mocked but enjoyed it, I could not say the same, I was hitting really; when thought it was easier, was the opposite was worse, the only thing I thought was my sister, was all I had, I do not lose, but I do not hold much after a while went back to the monitoring room, they wanted something more on the screen, ask what we're seeking and said the heart, a bracelet a necklace or something else, it was weird all.

-What's that?

-We would like to know.

Answer someone who had viewed but did not know his name

-We have not found that there is no way, it will only found by the chosen one.

Observing the screen where my sister was, just looked at her without saying anything, he did not realize that I watched, for an instant.

-Why you're not going to see, she likes you.

His partner looked at him weirdly.

-Hum no, it just works.

-If of course, and then it is your job to see if she's OK, can I ask anything.

-Yes, do it.

-Have you ever fallen in love, maybe you already are? Remain silent a moment, but answered.

-Well, long ago I fell in love, with someone very special, but she fell in love with my best friend, got married, had two children, but she died when her youngest son was a year old, never stop loving her and she knew it, I always look like a friend and only that, the day of his death could not do anything to save her, she saved me and all, just asked me to watch their children, and I have done without the knowledge.

-Still, love her? How much time has passed?

-Several years like 16... I think.

-That? But you, who?

-If, well, I am immortal when she died year's longer meets, I stay at that age, forever twenty; some of us here are immortals as my sister.

-You should forget it.

While we saw the monitor and my sister appeared, about to make a call, "he told my daughter" might be impossible, before saying something's cell phone rang, it was her, was worried about not having called her, I always did, I told her I was okay, watching television a while, as I watched the huge screen, I was no lying and then go for a walk, it was quieter and hung, looked at his hands and then hid in his pocket, fails to see that it was.

-And her children where they are, they are well?

-If, they are near me all the time.

-Some day they will know that you care, they have someone who knew his parents.

-I do not know, but I hope not.

-I think it's not fair they need to know about his mother, she wanted to know how it was, I did not have my mother and I would like to know more about it, look just saying that if you know anything about it, they deserve to know what has happened, I would like to know how it was, and of course my father.

-Relaxed, they resemble its mother, she was unique and they equally, and sometimes the truth is somewhat hard, and the secrets must remain secret.

Time to go home, it was dark, we were near the restaurant and was about to close, we hope that it will close and go home, of course, diving faster than she, so I have come before.

It took more than fifteen minutes to arrive, I was worried he explained that she stopped because felt bad, but then get better and continues, just was sleepy; it was more than fatigue, it looked bad, tired, and sad, fell asleep in the room so fast that she no even take off the shoes, removed them, Kalinda, I cover it with a blanket.

He just stares at her did not take his eyes off, she spoke asleep and when Alan gave the name he approached, he touches his forehead with love and tenderness as if he loved her as more than a friend, a lover, a father who cares for his daughter, was a profound and powerful look so full of love and pain.

I did not want to keep looking was strange, Kalinda went to the kitchen was uncomfortable, was silly for her to say his name, and I wonder since when, and he seemed not to care, as if he had listened before.

Then he left the room immediately, he went to the bedroom of her, I followed and sought in the drawer of her bedroom, he takes an inhaler from a music box that was our mother who did not work, he took him to her, I tried to give, I was surprised, I did not know she had asthma, she concealed me, it was not fair, she was sick and did not tell me, we had no secrets, but that was one of them.

-Do not bother she did not want you to worry and almost do not need it, she knows too well controlled, it is not dangerous, not for her, only that she needed at this time, but it is fatigue, and so it was late, but she's fine to exercise a lot and that helps her.

-As you know that?

-The snow glove, we have seen using it a few times, the weather here is denser harder to breathe, is very cold.

-How much have you looked? He did not answer.

-I hope my sister never finds out that the observed.

-Will not tell.

-Of course not, my friend is your problem solved it you're… seriously you are in trouble.

I fell asleep after that, they were still whispering and guard. Sometimes it was pathetic and very cold and spoke as we know very well.

I sat next to them; give me a reason for the content of the red box, the torturing continues all day if necessary.

-You are a pathetic detective! Is time to go, or will arrest, "not" so it seemed.

Capture you were easy, I just had to pretend to be your driver, if you do not tell the content never see sunlight, just white walls, he said nothing but, after laughing so much to see cartoons, like the coyote trying to catch the roadrunner, he decides to talk, asked to stop his torture, the box contains the key to another world, the soul, the heart.

-Adriel come on, wake up is too late.

-Well, is time to go to work!

-Yes.

-Turn off the cartoons and let's go.

-Sure glad, are torture.

-Yes, but are fun.

-No for two days straight.

I give my comment laughter, which sees cartoons for two days straight, "and the guests disappeared before I woke up"

-Adriel hurry, as it takes you!

My brother takes so longer rather than I to change, another day at work like any other day, went out eat with my friends Monica, Carolina, Sonia, Jasmine, and Pilar, we had a great, I had free the rest of the afternoon, I asked for a litter rest, and had long since gone out with my friends, Carolina and Sonia were already married, but they always have time for an afternoon of girls, Carolina has a son named Marcos, was four, but the child was very naughty, very nice indeed, we joined that day, Monica was the sister of Carolina and Jasmine, Pilar and Sonia were sisters, Sonia married but had no children.

My brother was working inside the restaurant, although a little cold toward us we ate out, like some others, my brother paid more attention than usual, but did not care, in the shop next door which was antique, were a pair of men, who had ever seen, it seemed that only mattered to me, maybe curiosity nothing more.

-There are two strange men, we are looking weird.

-If, and look at it, Marcos does not say anything just keep eating. Nobody seemed to care, also not reveal much, but give me the impression that something looking or someone, we spent about an hour in the restaurant, Sonia has to go home for obvious reasons, Pilar went with her, had things done, Carolina stayed a little more like Monica, but eventually Carolina and Jasmine leave because Marcos was impatient and was too cold, I stayed a litter longer with Monica, she is 17, arrived at the restaurant redhead that my brother liked, had days we have not seen, came with her boyfriend and friend I guess.

I did not know them very well, were too quiet and abusive to the others, and that bothered me, I will stay in town until my brother closes, and deliver the food as every day, we took a walk.

Today the restaurant closes late, my brother did not realize when we left, were beginning to darken, I untie the disbudding coat and scarf around my neck, which had bought a few days ago, the necklace that my brother had given to me remain uncovered, Monica observer, praise him a lot.

-Hopefully, your brother gave one, but is gaper with that redhead, that's courage.

-Relax, you're cute, he well realizes that you have much time.

-Thanks. Say happily

-I welcome you as a sister?

-Definitely.

-By the way friend this is silver and very expensive, they are real diamonds, where get your brother.

-Are you sure of what you say?

-Of course, I'm sure, think not what I say.

-In that case, I also want to know.

-If of course, keep walking.

-And now it is called the redhead. Monica asked

-No, not really.

-Too bad, hopefully, have a horrible name.

-Hopefully yes.

We laughed for a while, we passed shop fragrance, was the very sweet aroma of jasmine and roses, we stare to try some and I chose a fragrance of jasmines and a pair of candles flavor of amaranth, to the bathroom, she chose candles rose, we left the store and I realized that the same people of this afternoon we were near us, we kept walking faster, but Monica did not want, and I have to tell my feeling and she believes the same thing, that fallow us and walks quickly over to the restaurant, but.

Was useless reached us and caught Monica gave me the impression that it was not just a robbery either, Monica tries to move, but failed, she began to scream for help, but it was as if all had gone, I told her to calm down while I was asked what they wanted, she obeyed, and they came to me, they untied the scarf slowly until he uncovered my neck and the necklace, I understood they wanted the necklace, try me backward.

Fortunately defense classes I took during these last year's help me, I started to defend myself, were very good indeed, they fight as if nothing, but try as I could defend myself, not help much, although I knew something was not enough, try to free for my friend to run, but was in shock and did nothing just screaming, well was something, but they were better than me, I was caught, he removed the necklace and my bag, I knew it was a woman and two men, was no difficult because she was wearing tight clothing that showed off her hips.

-Lets us go. Say Monica

Did not respond took us with them, Monica was scared, but well, she was calmer but was still screaming, they screwed Monica, they put something in her nose and mount and she was unconscious un a few seconds, put her in a black SUV that looks like a suburban, just as they tried to the same with me, someone called my name and said. Are you okay Sarah? But enough to smell a little ammonia and I was beginning to be unconscious.

Saw only shadows listen dropped the necklace in the middle of the tire, and I tried to find and finally grabbed it, I wanted this to end and everything went in our favor, I could see Monica and tried to reach him but I could not, a figure grabbed her and took her away from the car, I grab the necklace tightly against my chest and was still wished it was over, all around me I could see the silhouettes of those who still fighting, and suddenly anyone placed me in his arms and we disappeared amid the darkness, just thinking about Monica and who had, and all because of me not to let it take my birthday present.

-Sarah Danika, wake up, are you okay?

Only one person knew my second name which was never used, and it was just my brother, but from where he came, it was who took me out of that fight, and when he learned to faith, he does not know.

-Sarah your home, you are okay.

-And Monica where she?

-Is in your room, I think it affects you more than you, but will be fine, a little dizzy as you but good.

At home, as fast we arrived, I felt it was only a few seconds, for a moment thought I was dreaming, I could see Alan and her sister, but

I think was a hallucination, I closed my eyes and leaned back on the couch, and I thought to be unconscious.

-I think I just saw Alan and her sister.

-So is, they are here.

-Are here… why?

I got up quickly, but it was nonsense, they were, not even from the hour they watched, I lay no without asking why they were there.

-Well, whimsical if you had not been away, you would not have found, in your thought to face with them, you are insane.

-Kalinda now leaves her alone.

-If you defend again, it is a fool, does not even know how to take care, how you expect to do their work.

-Kalinda, keeps quiet or you leave.

-Great I go out, I'll be outside.

Why she would be so angry with me, I did not know, but I'll find out, I mistook the phrase, you defend it again, that Monica woke up and left the bedroom, sat next to me without saying anything, just saw my brother and Alan at that moment someone came.

-Are Hewett, Dylan and Samara will help us reach the monastery, here it is not safe.

Sure, I did not know where to start, Monica began speaking.

-Who were those guys, they wanted?

-Wanted Dani and the necklace she is wearing, they are the Hokon brooders those who choose.

-Choose, what, and who is Danika?

-Hello friend I am Dani, Sarah Danika.

-Seriously is cute.

-Jokes are horrible. Alan swallows saliva.

-The good thing is their meaning, I looked the other day, and it is "Morning star"

-So, if it's nice, I like your name. Kalinda interrupted us.

-Finished already.

-That temper.

Monica said softly but I think she hears that, and Hewett laughed.

-I tell them, choose who lived and who died. Hewett told us.

-In fact, choose the strongest and take away life. Samara entered in that hasty, something was saying.

-They came and are almost here.

The Hokon was on the way, we had to leave, but was a little late for that, they went everywhere with eyes on me and buy a necklace, which by the way someone places me while unconscious, Monica hid behind me and Adriel, we begin to defend, the most awkward was my brother and Monica, but he knew things that I never saw that done, Monica tries his time to defend, but better got help from Dylan, Alan took my hand when I fall on the other side of the couch, he was pulling my hand towards the exit, I struggled with but it was silly and useless, he walked away with me.

-And my brother and Monica?

-They will follow us, will be all right, and came with Samara and Dylan.

-But!

-No, hurry up to the car now.

Getting into the car accelerates so fast that I could not say anything more, scope to see my friend and Adriel out, I tranquilize, he stepped back to see that they only came and went with us, but missing others, he looked at me closely but he says nothing, and I did not ask, I felt safe being with him, it was dark and not a well distinguish road, and another car followed us.

-They are Elmo and Curran, I think something happened.

-We headed to the monastery Alan? My brother said

-Yes.

-What did I mess!

-No, well, yes… later sister.

Slightly away from the house we stopped, Alan comes out of the car went with his friend, spend a few moments do not listen to what they said, but I asked my brother what was happening and did not answer, that exasperated me and I get out the car and started walking back home, they also get out Adriel and Monica, did not stop to look.

That was what they were doing, I was scared, but Monica was happy with my brother that looks after her, I kept walking, but I would expect him to reach me, told me not to put up resistance, because, in the end, I had to go, I wanted to yell, but I'm not that way, everyone watched us, take a deep breath and got in the car, I seemed like a silly whimsical, as his sister had told me, he showed a slight smile at my angry face, but ignored, my brother and Monica were in the other car, gave me the impression that did not want to get into my anger, it is better that way.

He drives and I recognized the way, the road leading to the monastery, he when straight and then go on a road with, trees not too large, stopped opening the window and put the password to enter, the door opened, no wonder most had entries like this, it continued down the road a couple of minutes, so I gave him a small smile.

-Is that broken!

-Is broken?

-Enabled with the car, but broken by playing it, we wanted to settle voice recognition, so now only open like that.

-Clear only acknowledged the car.

-Is so, then the arrangement?

-I can know what kind of trees are.

-Are cherry, some fruit and some are just red flowers and other white.

I indeed loved red flowers, after that stopped the car and the garage was open, he put the car into the garage, he opened a closet that was full of weapons and electronic equipment and cables, star to charge a brand new white Hammer higher than the usual, I loved that it was shielded, but as he gets it.

-Like this?

-Sure, how does not like a hammer in his garage.

-Yeah, well, it's just a car, I don't like it very striking, but the occasion requires it, you like it!

-Very striking, of course, I like it, and where are we going?

-We will overnight in this place.

-In this mansion, but my brother and my friend,

-They are home to Kalinda and Dylan.

-You say, Kalinda and Dylan.

-Yes, they are spouses.

-A… Will that be fine?

I say to myself husbands.

-Yes, tomorrow we will see, today will stay at my house.

-Your house?

-Yes, welcome to my home.

-Your home is a mansion!

He smiled again, that disturbs me.

-I think I deserve an explanation, don't you think?

-They want the necklace you've got, Cyrus he calls himself the emperor of the sun, and Tansy she's the one he sent to you.

-Who she is?

-She is immortal like some of you met today.

-That is true, it is unreal there are no immortals is a myth.

-Think I'm lying, it is unreal but we exist… really exist, and as you'll see will not allow them to stay with the necklace.

-Well, why did not leave, I'll get my brother, my friend I go home, you care for it.

-Your offer is unacceptable, also they need you and your brother, you are the only ones who know how it works, I wish you never had to be in this life would give my life if necessary, we tried, but did not find, try to keep you out, but we could not change your fate, although we try.

-Do not know us, as you give life for a stranger that you know nothing about him, and as you say you tried. What you're talking about?

-Forget my comment; it's time for you to sleep.

-It seriously.

-If, been a difficult day.

-Your day was hard, mime was awful and you say complicated.

-I regret that seriously.

-You should, and why did your sister say that you defended me again.

He took a breath mockingly.

-She thinks it was a mistake, let alone in the library, but convinced otherwise, and do not agree with me.

That is not to defend, know nothing about this, she was crazy, but I do not know any of this, and if I had been invited to go with him, I would have accepted, as that was what I wanted, that's silly, agreed with his sister, in not bringing me.

-Or that day, what were you following me? He turned away and said nothing.

-Since when?

He did not want to answer and I was terrified to hear.

-From the first day that showed up at the restaurant.

That was my terror I was a fool, I did not know if I was angry or confused, he tried to say more, but the words would not come, or did not want to say them nay.

I hope this was a mistake, but he looked very sure of everything, even I knew how to use this medal what can I do, but for me, it is nonsense, how it works.

Could not sleep, had so many questions, he sat on the couch and he left her bedroom for me, there was more, but I do not know why I keep some other, the door remained open, I was tired and it was starting to get cold, he lit fireplace and sat on the sofa, I think I slept about an hour, woke me up the human need call me, when I left the bathroom to pass by him, had fallen asleep was a blanket that was in the foot of the bed, I sat next to hem covered myself with the same, it was big enough for two, his breathing was so warm so clam, like a dream, I was sure I loved him, but it was so cold, so indifferent, who did not understand it, was nonsense to say that love him, I will say that I liked better.

The following morning I woke up in his arms, he was awake and did not seem to be uncomfortable, tried to enjoy some more about this company, I pretend to be asleep a little more, sometimes tried to take a look around the blanket, to see him, but after a while pretends to open my eyes, because I thought he had already noticed.

-I wake up! Thanks for the blanket, was very nice of you.

-Sorry I did not want to bother you, it's just that I sat for a while you were sleeping, wanted to enjoy the fire, and fell asleep.

-It's okay, it was a pleasure.

He said it was a pleasure, every time I'm crazier, was so close to him that I could hear his heart, I wanted him not to go, that will not rise, he was with me for a long time, I stared into his eyes a few seconds, my face closer to him and was about to kiss him, he walked away.

-Sorry.

-There are things to do. He said

-No sorry I should not have stayed so close to.

Ignore my comment and walked away, I said if I want a bath and took me to the bedroom next door, and said to pick some clothes, what I would like.

Heaven is a huge closet.

-That room was someone special person, and leave it all at home, keep it just in case, and Kalinda and Samara filled it with clothes, they love the clothes.

-And who does not!

Good is a huge room with many things, he leaves, look at a couple of minutes, had all kinds, but the one that caught my attention was the old clothes, which was at the bottom, took more than half an hour watching the clothes, were beautiful dresses of all models very elegant, but just take a pair of black pants, a shirt and long coat, and my scarf of the previous day and other days.

I went to bathe when I went out to breakfast was ready and waiting for me at the breakfast table, I not wearing the coat her house was very warm, best said his mansion, when I sat he ate too fast, I forgot for a moment I also have to eat, he watched me for a moment, then get started to eat, he apologized and started to eat more slowly.

I did not mind looking at it is too delicious to resist, I thought that while eating a cherry, I wonder if it is his cherry orchard, when we finished breakfast, clean the table, and wash the dishes, at the end I started pacing around the house, he was in the garage preparing to leave, I was still hanging around the mansion, that was easier for me to say home, is bigger than I had thought, last night I could not see it very well, most of had no light, I opened the double doors and going was fantastic full of books, all kinds sizes and colors was a library at home.

-Fabulous.

And by the window was a desk cover with books were very pleasant to be there, had its fireplace and some nice cushions in front, I start looking at books and chose one, and I settled in front of the fireplace that was still off, but it seems perfect, leave the doors open and get started to cool, since the heat of the room did not reach this place, so the fireplace, I thought, then go colder and lit.

-It is designed to turn on when it's cold.

Breathable deeply believes that I am silly, but I did not answer.

-Is great, sorry is that… sorry, just caught my attention this book.

-Okay, it's time to go to the monastery.

-Well, let's go I have to see my brother.

-No, it's best you stay here, I'll just go for a moment and he will be not there, is with my sister and they are okay.

-I will stay alone.

-This place is protected if nobody can find you here, so I'll go a while; just do not get hurt yourself.

-Why the monastery, you are going to pray or something?

Laughed a bit, with what fascinates me does it, but felt he was making fun of me this time.

-I look at some friends there, please don't leave.

He turned around, and I just said if, with my head, I followed him and hugged him.

-Thanks.

I told him for everything he did; he left in his black car left the Hammer in the garage, I went snooping around the house and into another room was a weapon collection and seemed to have a century it was interesting to see how everything was so well off.

In the center a place to train with them, was great I guess he trains here, the old weapons were in glass cases, all clean, take a few that were available to me and among them some swords I had never used any, but I knew how it worked and try not to kill myself, as he said.

Step noon and did not show up, finished using the room as it was sweat and decided to go to take another bath, I thought to look clothes, but decide to go bathe first, and as I left the bathroom, I was entangled in a towel to the clothing room, that has not only clothes, furniture had sawed boxes, had seen antique lamps among other things neat and clean.

I started to try on the dresses of a century ago, they looked newer than they were, very careful I wonder who would really be, his sister and Samara, where no event old-fashioned, very elegant.

To end on a corner was a cupboard close, the doors were mirrors in which I looked at me, as I looked at the dresses, there were fashionable clothes a bold too, but most were black, the color was not very nice, but still wear, I preferred light colors but this looked good, I continued with others, spend about an hour and a half and I continued with the dresses, there was a grade red, looked great except for lace, too elegant I dared not to wear it was too bold but beautiful, well I tried it, when suddenly I see it through the mirror, approached, I could not say anything, the buttons were following unbuttoned, I wanted to take it off, but it was impossible, my back was discovered, he approached started motionless for a second, but it made me forever.

He pulls my hair back, his hand was cold and gave me chills, and at the same time I felt that my body was shaking, I knew it was because he touches me with their hands, were soft no too common for a man but were nice, my body trembled as the zipped and arrange the strips, I end up very fast, could almost swear that was even looking just touching, I was thankful it was over.

-Well, as see me?

-Just in the measure.

I gave some grief, but since.

-Whose was it?

-A very special friend, it looks perfect.

-Thank you, what time is it?

-Around three in the afternoon.

-Heaven you came too late; I take a long admiring the dresses.

-Not really, get a while ago, but did not want to interrupt. In my mind, I thought that if he had seen me naked.

-Do not listen when you arrived, sorry.

-Not, these dresses need to out for a while, also we will eat something, keep your dress, and you look good.

-I'll not stay with you.

-Why not?

-I feel uncomfortable.

-No one, can have it because if you want.

-Okay, thanks.

I kept the dress on that came Hewett and Samara, I felt like a fool in fancy dress, just wanted to take it off, they made no comment, just threw a strange look, I just pass saliva, they ate with us, Samara price the dress and never took his eyes off Alan.

-Alan will go to the library, right back.

-Sure.

Samara left, Hewett and Alan went to the room, spent a couple of hours, only came to say that there was no danger, all was quiet, it seemed that everything was normal, after that I felt weird in that dress for lunch, clean the table, I would go to change pass by them I think you do not hear me they were looking television.

-You're playing with fire my friend and you'll burn. Did not answer just look at him in disapproval?

-I have to say it, it's disturbing to see that dress, are identical, why left her to use.

-Is my decision and do not to give you explanations?

-Well, I'll shut up, besides I have to go, my cousin does not like seeing her with that thing.

-Hewett none of your business.

-Of course, if we care at all, you know that my friend.

-Enough, I do not want to talk about it, be better for you to go.

-If as you say, goodbye.

Walking backward slowly disappearing, listen when they came out, went straight to the huge room, that I use more and more, I thought that was mine and looking for some clothes, was such that it was difficult to choose one, this time I approach the big mirror, but had a serious problem, as I would take away the dress, not as buttoned, did not even know where to start, with the ribbon was somewhat difficult to try to unzip it, but it was all tangled more complicated, I grimace of despair, it's like a ghost does not listen when he entered, not a single noise, was just beside me with a great smile.

-I help.

-If you please.

-It gets somewhat worse; I'll have to cut the ribbon.

-No, I'm sorry, there is a beautiful dress does not cut it, go another way must be another way without breaking it is cruel.

-If it is, but is that, or leave it forever.

-Okay, but I promise to repay you.

-Wait here.

Stepped back opened a drawer of the dresser that was beautiful, and take scissors, I close my eyes as he approached me, he pushes my hair as before and like at first did not take long to break the ribbons, the dress was unbuttoned while I held my hands to keep from falling.

-Can open your eyes is not as bad as you imagine.

-Thank you.

-You're welcome, wear something comfortable.

-I look at him to come out.

Did not, he looks at me like a fool I take a coat to cover me, he helped put on my back, since only take with one hand if the dress would fall, when I place it fears it with one hand and drop the dress came out of him, takes the dress and put it on the small couch that was there.

He took the dress, and I felt bad about it, I threw on some comfortable shorts and a shirt because the house was warm, I went out fast, did not want to spend more time with these dresses, I just thought that I had ruined the dress, I look for a couple of minutes and I did not see, but then appeared, as usual, did not listen he asked me if I had been using their weapons, and I could not deny it, but I do not apologize because I did not know what to say, we walked till the hall where they were.

-You like guns, you looked.

-Are interesting, although not as useful.

-I will show you, come on!

-Seriously.

He gave me some instructions and between, I thought it would be fun.

-As you learn?

-William's teacher taught us.

-Fencing, seriously!

-Sure, is very convenient sometimes.

But the shock is taken very seriously, for a moment, confused me, hit me according to his slow, try to keep up with, but it was so fast that it was impossible to follow, I stood a little scared that also stopped him.

-I'm so sorry I thought you were faster.

-Its kidding right.

-Of course not, you should be faster you have to learn to defend yourself.

Expected that the harshness was not for the dress!

-I do not feel comfortable with this, will be better to finish.

The fighting continued for me not to leave; I was more scared than before.

-I'm sorry.

I did not answer, was very strange, I was terrified, I just wanted out of there, I went to the bedroom and picked up my things, which fortunately were few, and I do not think back what I wear and do not think, he is crazy.

Seeing how well do not know why I like so much, but not what I think is terribly live with him and stressful, and speaks very little I would not stay longer, I'd rather be alone than in bad company, in that I talked to my brother, maybe he would be better than I, try several times but not answer, then I went to the door and he was right waiting, I throw a look of disagreement, but he did not care, just stayed at the door will not let me out, I think my despair was so great than a tear came out of me and rolled down my cheek, and he took off and let it go.

Walk a little and heard some shots, I was not sure they were and did not want to flit, but I did, he had gone mad he was throwing and hitting things that were at the entrance, I follow the road and after a couple of minutes my tears were more intense, I was scared he was angry I did not know what to do, I sat awhile in the entrance, even the road looked, just sat and cried I was confused, scared.

I just want to go home and forget it was cute, forget that I met him, I do not how much time spend sitting, this time heard his footsteps getting closer to me, did not look up I knew it was him and was in front of me, just looked at me, and after a while, he put on his knees in front of me, all he did was hug me without saying anything, time went and I stop crying, was better, but still scared I could not ever trust him but were comforting her arms were strong and were perfect.

Way too cold and it started to rain, I was so tired I did not want to even move, I felt strange he lifted my face, the rain was intense shooting in our faces and wiped the tears, of course, it did not work, but the water felt good that my body seemed to need her, we want to keep sitting there without moving just looked at him and he looks at me.

Finally embraces him and my tears often confused the rain, but my face pain continued, he took me in his arms and I was too tired to protest, too could my thinks were thrown, and took me in his arms back to his house, it seemed that I would end not to cry, till fall asleep.

I remember even when we entered the house; I think that if the entry was away.

He walks away so slowly that his arms were so comfortable, I just felt a kiss on my forehead, and hear sorry, and thereafter will not remember, I was so tired I felt cold and wet even after sleeping my body was shaking, I was so cold, and my dreams, remember our fight, then I realized that he must be better.

I woke up the next day, breakfast was ready; I was hungry, and he leaves a note.

"Sorry! I'm back soon, do not go"

I was wearing different clothes, it was scaring me that he has changed, but eats breakfast and bathes me, a change of clothes, and my wet things were on a table, they were already dry.

-Hello, how are you today?

-Better.

-Came with me please, you do not have to fear, just come.

-Is easy for you to say.

-No… you know it's not, I will not be wrong again.

-Once again, your weapons are scary.

-I just want you to help us, you can't leave because we need to stop this, we can't alone, but you have to be ready, I will be patient with all this, I promise to understand you more and I hope you'll understand and trust me, please.

-Okay and how is my brother?

-He is fine, is getting prepared, it is more cooperative.

-Likes to be hit.

-Girl, no but understands more than you.

-I'm a fool?

-Clearly not.

My face change, accept, would help you, as my brother did the same with Kalinda and her husband, I had really knows what's happening, I did not know how it worked the necklace, just thinking about discovering because me and my brother, and he hit upon our hands, could not concentrate in the fight, he was too strong against me, beat me again and again, his gaze was constantly changing, sometimes I thought I would like, and sometimes I felt despised me, his look changes too fast, as another person.

I was furious with his mood swings, could not continue training with him, had to go out sometimes, whether I felt better and rested a bit, he controlled his emotions but his eyes betrayed, how is it that I could like?

Is so cold as if his soul gone out; I felt his pain and made me feel like him as if my soul was gone.

-Have to concentrate.

-Yeah, right.

-Stop thinking just feel.

-I feel, and what about you.

-Think I have no feelings.

-I feel you, the soul is different, that is not you, something happens, and you do not want me to find out.

He remained indifferent; I do not ask more.

-You're wrong.

Had no intentions of continuing, he left to the room, after that I kept thinking and how were my brother and the others. I was worried as we got into this, as it happened and if it was fate, nevertheless had hope that everything will be over quickly, I needed to return to work, ending the day, I was grateful for that.

The Silver Cascade and the Ice Water

We will hike, you have to prepare will be cold, so go get the necessary, we go to find the heart and not know exactly what it is, whether we know it when we see it.

The Hammer was ready, and he was already in the garage it was fast, went up to my things, and he finisher of carrying up some ropes and we went, I thought soon to see my brother and my friend since had not spoken with them in a couple of days, was the first time I spend so much time away from my brother, and I missed a lot, though I knew he could take care of himself, I felt that I had to be nearby to protect him, give my life for him, is all I have, I would take care of him, the fair fee frustrates me and least hear his voice, the road was long and I was very sleepy and I fall asleep.

Panic around me, I felt in a bubble could not move drowned, look skyward and saw an angel in from of me, there was no pain, only peace, my body covered with calm, with eyes wide open thinking I was in heaven, all blue the sight fascinated me.

-Awake almost there.

Was very sensitive to wake me, but still, I get scared.

-How long I slept?

-No much.

-We went to the waterfalls.

-Yes, hopefully, find something.

Drove a black jeep Kalinda, and one more following us closely with Elmo and Curran, would know more friends this weekend, or the brother of Dylan, my brother came with him, they are all families, Dylan accompanied us, of course, was the husband of Kalinda, could not be alone, Samara and Monica join us in another jeep with Hewett this was yellow color, it was Samara, Alan told me as we arrived, he knew everything, Hewett I did not know who was exactly, but he was a friend, arrived and we went down first, as with parked first, we accompany another friend of Alan, do not ask your name, so even told me, Mr. Anselm, he was older than the others, in fact, the only one, all the others we were young, and still, the boss was Alan.

Apparently, all agreed with that, and is also told us that Anselm was not immortal, he said, of course, was not as comforting, Monica ran first to greet me that my brother, told me that she had told her sisters would go on an excursion with us all weekend, it's smart to tell lies, least I.

I know it has always been and always came with it, but not fool us because we already know her, plus it's great their company is super fun and cute, then huge my brother as if had a century without being watched, all down with a backpack but me, till my brother and Monica, then Alan down one for me, but it was not that one I bring, not left me to carry mine, this was a bit heavier, Alan grabbed my hand and start to walk down the path of the falls, I had visited this place in the summer, and is somewhat slippery at this time was even more dangerous fall, this day has rained a little.

But they trusted in themselves and we had to do it, we divide into three groups to look, Monica, Elmo, Alan and I went to the largest, Kalinda her husband, and Anselm and the other group was Samara, Hewett, Curran, and my brother, who went to the last.

Did not know how to search just knew it was a heart, the way was long, had walked before, but still tired, according to the records of the waterfalls there was nothing more than the narrow passage for tourists every year visited them, was different that day, they could and no one there, was too cold at first, but as we went down better with movement.

-As we know what we want if we do not know what we are looking for.

-I know it when we find it.

-Alan, to the rappel ropes are, if I do not think there is no way we need them. Monica wonders

Was true, for what we wanted?

-May have to look behind the waterfall in the background and there are only two ways to get there, descend, and summing.

-Great freeze us. Hewett said.

-I hope that none of the options we use.

-I hope Adriel. Hewett said

Laughter could be heard through the headphones, all we could hear what he said any of us, the others had already reached the cascade, but we handle the biggest, looking across the top of the waterfall was said to have a secret passage to somewhere, but found nothing, perhaps was in the forest surrounding the waterfall.

-Do not think it's a good idea to come down. I said.

-I said the same thing. Elmo answered

-The water should be frosty, but we have to go down.

-Cold, freezes on me, my friend.

But still down Alan y Elmo to look behind the waterfall, the water reaches them quickly, the water was stronger down than it seemed, it took about twenty minutes and had to return to cold, as they were wet, had special clothes was not enough, I was glad it was not me that was down and had started to give me cold, they had to leave, the night has almost covered us and the cold was more intense every moment, when they reached the surface change clothes and we camped, we had to keep looking for the heart, was exhausted like all, the night was quiet, one of them perfect for camping with marshmallows and horror histories.

-As you know is here?

-Mr. Anselm told us, this is a good source.

I did not want to question that, but hesitant, the man was something different.

-Are you sure and if you're wrong.

-Well, if have make a mistake, no problem, we all seek to find it.

-Why it is important?

He did not want to answer and asked again, Monica approached me, the fire needed more wood, and Hewett and Alan went for more.

-How did it go to his house?

-That is insane. I replied to Monica

-What he's cutie.

-Yes, this crazy.

-I do not believe it.

-If it is, but was a good time. She hit me with his elbow

-And how about you.

She does not answer gets to the tent, I did the same and after a while, everyone was inside.

I thought of the beautiful redhead of the restaurant, who had just a few days ago talked for the first time since I saw more than half a year ago, gave me his phone number, for when I wanted to say hello, did not have much time if I could not even ask her name, also gave her my number just in case I got to talk, that if I had time to do, I was sleepy but even if wanted to sleep I wanted to watch for any event.

My body cold as ice, motionless as a corpse lost in time, thinking about my life as a detective, that made him difficult case from the beginning, still breathless and the lady mysteriously and his companion would not let her alone for a moment holding the red box, I had not discovered the content, I had not even been near, heard a voice saying the heart, is the heart, it is in the forest, that voice blew me away, the box contains the key to the heart, did not understand, at that moment, my cell phone rang.

Though it was rare because I believed that I had no signal in the woods, but it was clear that Alan had given me this, that was something different! It was six in the morning, was the girl of my dreams, well the one that I wanted in my dreams, was very early, but it was to greet me, know how I was because that day we were not goodbye, and then she left the town and could not speak, I told her that I was in the forest and no more questions, I think cutting the communication and that was it.

Nobody had heard my conversation, but they were all out of their tents, ready to begin searching again, started but despite our efforts, none could find it, nothing; when suddenly in the evening, they tried to get the necklace, were more this time, I guess they knew that we are a lot.

Another girl was not the companion of the meeting at my house, I guess it was the white rose or Tansy something like that, I could not see his face I knew it was her, I knew how to defend more, "well" better than before if, but still needed some help, they were more than us, but it still does not beat us, we're better so far they caught me and Monica, my sister and Alan ran to meet us, when we let go of my mistake took away his necklace, managed to take this time felt it was my fault again.

All were furious and the angriest was Kalinda in case she always looked angry, everyone knew what it was the end; Alan approached others.

-That necklace is useless if they are not with and the heart. I wonder who has the heart, "that many objects"

-True, but still did not have to take it.

-Elmo I agree, but there is something that worries me most, as they found us. Alan said

-That means they are closer than we thought, who knows more than we think. Anselm said

-It may be, apparently not know about the heart, did not ask, or even try to get it. Hewett commented

-Is true we have an advantage in that. Said Elmo

-Do not think it that way, they know, only that they want us to find first, they want the job easier, just take off our hands.

-Alan is true, as happened with the necklace that took just now, that dirty, both look and they stay with it.

-That's low very base.

-As they know we have not yet?

-Good question Hewett. Said Curran

-Better return.

To say, Alan, picked up everything and went to the monastery where someone was waiting to enter, seeing hem hug my sister, I was surprised, but not the others, it was William's teacher, with coaching, not a chance was, it was planned, there were many trained to battle, were more than just training controlled our mind given his soul and that stuff.

Spend the night in the monastery, Alan kept thinking how wrong he was to believe that the heart would find in the cascades, he was sure this would be the right place to keep looking, I do not want to question maybe just not looking well and we would have to return to find in that place.

-Perhaps the informant was wrong. William said

Informant, I thought how good it was that my sister and I had to work the following Monday, despite change we have our live, friend, and everything else and Monica had to go home, where we continue with our lives like any others, after all, we're human, we can only continue with our lives.

Spend the day as usual, no news, but still, we wonder where could be the heart, suddenly I saw her again I had completely forgotten that had not been spoken since the day of the camp and the signal was cut, the woman of my life, the redhead, as they called their friends of my sister, we talk a little bit about where I had gone, throughout the weekend, when I asked, she said she had gone to get something in another town and spend all weekend there, with relatives, but gave no details, my sister covered me for a while, as I was talking to her, finally asked her name, and she said it was Rosalba, lovely name.

-Rossy.

-No Rosalba please, I'm sorry, but I like my name.

-Rosalba is fine, nice to meet you I hope we continue to see.

I had to return to work, we have to rush when closing time comes and clean this all, and we have to stay longer than necessary, Monica waits for us no longer away from us, she is in danger of being aware of everything, we can't leave alone, had to go all the way plus I liked his company.

Just before closing, we find serious problems, Hokon tried to regain my sister, this time the boys arrived fast enough to help, unfortunately, it seems we had to stay longer than planned in the restaurant to clean the disasters.

This time also accompanist the white rose, as always, we could see their identity, excellent fighting well, almost struggled with Kalinda, and always seemed to win, but most of the time the fight ended before knowing who won, fell from his pocket of Alan something that looked like a medal, outreach to pick it up to put it in my pocket and continue our fight in the restaurant, increasingly seemed harder than the previous, adrenaline ran wildly through my body, was worse than we thought at any time felt afraid of what would happen next if there was an after.

Did not know the result now, and less than after at the time, unfortunately at that time reached the restaurant the owner Mr. Robles, very bad time to stop it was witnessing this incident, unfortunately, that was the situation, we now have to defend Mr. Robles, thought they would get hurt, even though we tried we could not defend all this was the work of Hewett, Alan, and Dylan was just them, the others not yet arrived, it was also strange that Mr. Robles showed up around here, rarely does.

Our enemies took advantage of people who wanted more, we wanted everything to be fine, but this time something change, but we tried we were not strong enough.

Monica was the change, unfortunately, took it away, Alan stopped me before I had committed a folly, my sister wanted to go after them, but Hewett stopped her, she struggled with, but she can't get anything, we had problems we could not stop them, not only with them if the police, someone called, and Mr. Robles was badly wounded, the ambulance had to take to the hospital and again we were involved, we said they had kidnapped Monica, to keep them busy, plus it was true, believe us because his parents were lawyers, certainly had enemies and having told his sisters.

But knew it was more than kidnapping, his real-life was at risk, but we could not give details of what happened, who else would believe us, we went to the hospital, we needed to know how was Mr. Robles, spend the night in the hospital, almost leaving the doctor told us that he would recover and come out in a couple of days, we were better for him but worried about Monica.

-We can go see it.

Ask my sister who was eager to enter.

-Have a few minutes.

-Thank you.

We went anxious to see him, looked good, to have spent what happened, he said he wanted the restaurant clean, for when he back, we're just as cantankerous, was always very good to us we know from childhood, we promised that this would be, we also see how it went Messrs. Gonzales, unfortunately, they had gone wrong, but were better soon and go home, we went to the restaurant to begin cleaning, it was a disaster, we had to end but we kept thinking about Monica.

-This is a disaster that will take all day.

-And all night, Adriel is best to start in the kitchen.

-No, it's your turn in the Kitchen.

-Well, but will not help you with the bathrooms.

At the beginning I fell asleep in an instant, I even notice that it had spent about one hour sleep, I woke up the music that was, woke up and heard a few laughs were the friend of my sister who came to help, and also some people that we give sometimes to eat in the evenings, some of them had a knack for fixing things.

Monica sisters were not here as they should be waiting for a call from the kidnappers or something, although I do not think they call them, I felt bad about it, sometimes talk to my sister on the phone.

-Hey guys finished drooling table.

-That fanny.

Was great that would end up faster, not everyone thinks they are good, but my sister thinks that there is always goodness in people, only to suffer sometimes forget that there is hope for them, and we must not lose faith, just need a chance.

Some if more cruel, but even so she accepts them, but I'm always near just in case, decided with their help remodel a bit, but it would take more than a day, we were so tired we decided to close, anyway, not finish today, we went to the monastery in search of Alan and the others, but only find Elmo and Samara they were in charge, while the others returned led us to a room that will rest.

Told us they were trying to find Monica, we could not do anything but wait, I knew more things than my sister knew, and as I had slept little and when into the room where his surveillance equipment, where it appeared some parts of the town the most visited, appeared no trace of them, in no monitor just like normal images of every day, had already completely dark and my sister was not in the room and went to look, was with his teacher who was trained, seeing it I realized it was better than I. Behaved different after a while, looked at me and smiled the teacher sent me to change, for me to train with her, but she was best that I, she has more time studying, the teacher and I tried to win, but it was certainly better than I, but no better than him, end up falling and she laughed a little.

-Have to be outstanding in all directions, feel the wind calm down, place it together with you be one.

-Join the monastery with us.

The teacher gave me a blow on the head and Sarah laughed, Alan suddenly appeared attacking, I wanted to interfere but the teacher stopped me.

-Not interfere, I just said be careful in all directions.

Seemed to be tired and losing, but she did not give up, the other was next to me watching the couple fight until the teacher sent them all to train, I started laughing at myself but he saw me.

-You equal, you're not an exception.

-Why me.

My opponents were too strong, well, I fight with Elmo, he seems more friendly, I think I do not quite so fast, and I'm wrong, it was worse, would not let me breathe, I was dead, turn to see the teacher and I could see a small smile but he was mocking.

Next look at Kalinda fighting with my sister, had changed partners was more entertaining.

-Looks more like a pornographic seeing these two.

Elmo throws a look of approval to Hewett; Alan did not share their comments and glanced at Hewett of disapproval which suggested behaving.

-Is true are sexy. Hewett said again

Heaven, I had never noticed that my sister was sexy until they said, and he was right, at times distracted by their movements seemed to fight and not to train, but my sister was so concentrated, and that when least expected Kalinda received a blow that was not expected, in fact anyone my sister won to Kalinda but as expect she do not accept.

All stopped and we were serious Hewett praise Sarah, and she was just silent, be turned his hand to Kalinda but as expected she does not accept.

Someone calls Alan and he calls us all, and went to the monitor's room, he hurried, when I enter the monitor had canceled the restaurant's it was obvious that he did not want my sister knew that watching, he still had problems with that, I do not want not to think when she finds out.

In the larger screen lyrics were a gold color, which they say, "came together" at the entrance of the church, was sure it was related to Monica, by the way, this church was built of stone and is beautiful, despite what it said at the entrance, was not as exaggerated letters were more like vandalism, but they were unusual in the church as the highly respected, some had to go, of course, I wanted to be there and know what she will be fine.

-I can go.

Alan replied to my comment.

-It's dangerous, but if you go Elmo and me.

-I want to go as she is my friend.

-No, you'd better stay; you are more secure here than with us you stay with Hewett.

-I feel like he wants to eat me. Said silently

-Okay.

She said, but all heard what she said was right on Hewett and looks weird, rarer than Alan, some showed a slight smile at the comment very sneaky, she sighed when he saw that all listened.

We headed to church, not knowing what might happen, it was completely dark we went on the jeep of Elmo and some weapons, not only expected to pocked knives, cross-shaped some round with symbols on them as if they were enchanted or something, someone was more rarer.

I did not want the church to remain at the restaurant, would be catastrophic, was no so far from the monastery if we got in a couple of minutes, we parked at the entrance go down without much noise, we knew they were waiting, we opened a large wooden door, when we were sawed behind us, then we open door glass through them only watched the lights of the candles, medium altar Monica was sitting on the stairs, some tears in his eyes but it strong as ever endured what was happening.

We realized it was a trap, appeared behind us our enemies, scared just thinking that these evil people dared to enter a place without respect, made us walk to the front in the first row of seats, on the right hand was an unmistakable figure, the white rose, I ran into Monica wanted to know how she was.

-Monica.

-I feel fine!

-I'll get you out of here, I promise.

-I'll be fine, you're right?

The White Rose began to laugh.

-You think that turn-up.

-Clearly yes.

-If of course, who would get it, or rather will have the same fate as the two.

-Leave her and stay with me.

-Clearly, I'll have you too, do not worry about it.

Alan continued to observe the surroundings; I wanted to know what the plan against a White Rose was.

-Alan dear, to you I'm just Rosalba.

Alan was left without breathing for a moment, but continued as she took off his mask, his mysterious identity is rebelling.

-But you, is not possible, you Rosalba this Rosalba.

-Of course, it is Said Elmo

-Adriel would not believe you and I, Alan sweetie missed me.

Is not possible that all this time, I've been in love with the person who did more damage to us in these last days, and Alan knows, it is his love as she put it, truly had something to do, well, I'm not surprised the two immortals but had questions, Alan would know about it, his expression said no, but was not sure.

-Come on, do not make that face.

-Sure Rosalba, let's leave that for later.

-Of course sweetie, now let's see how we managed.

-You want to change the girl.

-You know the answer dear Alan, I want the heart and you know where it is, true.

-Do not know, we have sought but not found.

-Be creative look, try something else, is that you get close do not lie, I know you're lying.

-We do not.

-Good in this case continue with it, take her away.

-Not, leave it, take me through it. I told her

-Tempting offer, but I'll take her, then go for you, dear Alan then we see.

-We must do something.

-Alan honey, I want the heart and give you the girl.

-Let it go already, or.

-Or what? Alan knows what's good.

-Alan?

Did not answer me, nauseous just listening to their filtrations towards, as possible they went out together and I have like, my heart despised and I think never love her, but knew that Alan did, not know she like me so far, but we had to think a way out of this nightmare, they closed the entrance to leave, and unfortunately threw a chemical numbing gas and toxic poison according to Alan, not even question it, Alan said that it crated hallucinations, hysteria a fiver, we had to get out of here, we look at the main doors but nothing, at the right was smaller door, beat her to open it without throwing, it was one of the exists in a corridor, with tall glasses which looked at all down there.

Though the glass looked like Monica boarded a van, I looked like Monica ascended into a black suburban, and the White Rose smiled, for me at this time was the Black Rose, I was confused my heart had never hated anyone, while in the room next to the corridor were still trying to get out, obstacles we encounter fight against them, this time they were no better than us, beat them more easily, even though we ran after the truck failed to stop, it was frustrating that time, so close and so far away, without knowing where.

-Alan you were right about this.

-So is Elmo.

-What! Already knew this and did not tell me, as they could?

-Suspected child, watching it since you speak in the cascades and found us, she has never been interesting and suddenly as it does, is not it strange.

-And did not tell me and you Alan is dating her?

-Long time ago.

-And the restaurant when you looked, you lie to us.

-Of course not, and I do not have to say anything about my life kid, she is past and did not know who was.

-Time to go back to keep looking for the heart.

Elmo said and in fact, Alan was right, was not to tell of his life.

-Monica what will happen with it, we must be seeking.

-We will make it, but we need what they want.

-How we will make Alan, since we do not find it.

-Continued to seek, we find it.

Elmo patted my back something strong.

-Will bring it back boy.

-I hope.

I said something annoying as if he imagined must have a plan not only prove that she was, she was responsible for all since arriving at the same time as it was no coincidence that the two looked the same.

-We got a go we can do nothing out here, we must warn the others.

-And we expect?

-Patience, boy.

-I do not think my patience lasts long.

Would like to see the face of my sister when she finds out what there was between Alan and Rosalba, was a problem for him, was in serious trouble, so I thought I remember the monitors and imagine that they saw everything that happened outside and knew that we do not get to Monica, knew of our failure, but what happened inside.

As I went in the truck saw the look of Adriel was looking anxious and looked how I walked away from his sight when accidentally drop a tear, slip down my cheeks, for a moment I thought it might be in love with me, but deceit me, everything was to recover the necklace, and nothing happens to her sister, but her eyes said otherwise, think it was beautiful, but it was just an illusion, for a moment I forgot I was in trouble, could not see anything through the truck, but if I listened to very angry voices, from that let go Adriel, if they already had, it could change for me as he said, but she said she would have anyway it would eventually be, would be very easy to catch.

Give me chills in his comments so cold and cruel, and think that knew he liked a lot of bad redheads, I did not know what to make of all this, after all is a very strong feeling to want someone, how he might choose her or me, if he loves her, there would be no hope for me, to get off the truck and the redhead pushed me and I fall, made fun of me, but was worse to hear her than fall, I looked up never let that she had his way to see me without hope.

-Take it and tie them well feeding do not want to die before the exchange.

-Of course, however, will not last long.

-Of course.

-You never get away with it, Adriel and his friends will destroy you and you know it's true.

-Silly girl, of course, I go out with mime, to him do not care about you, he will come with the necklace and you not worth it, but you are good bait.

-You're wrong, he's my friend, but I see that you do not know that you do not have any.

-Take it and not be fed.

Spend too much time here, every second was eternal, too much time to think, and who choose Adriel, I wanted to think it would be mine, spend the night thinking about him, I slept a little bur still dreamed with him, spend a terrible night, the next morning came for me, I went to a room with large windows, but thick curtains covering them, which prevented the entry of light, the cold was terrible.

Started to get hungry I felt too weak to continue, in the center was a table covered with delicious food and the smell was exquisite, it sat most of the voices that I had heard during the last days, knew them all, was like a reunion of witches, black clothes all very trendy and the girls looked good with expensive coats, and taught me with cold and hunger, that nightmare, I sat at the table was not tied up and offered me to eat at first did not try to touch the food.

-You better eat dear; if that turn in to Adriel, he will say that I will tread you badly.

-And it is true, but does not plan to surrender.

-Sure, but do not have to know, right.

-Will does not get away with it.

-We did it and well is that Rossi behaved something wrong, but so is she, my apology.

-If she is, he will come and shatter.

-Look girl he never does anything against us, I assure you.

-Do not know he is the best.

-We know, he is the indicated, you'll see.

-Even so, I trust him.

-Cause we just hope to came and will, now eat girl.

Started to eating was hungry, the food was delicious for a moment I forget who was with the enemy and kept eating, I was kept there by the man who appeared to be the leader of the other, rather than trying to accomplish by knowing where I was, could not know, trying to understand what was happening what were his plans, but never talked about it, everyone knew what to do to keep me listening, I was so tired, lay my head on my arms closed my eyes, and want a few tears in my eyes, thinking about my fate if they still had one.

Anyway, I thought this was a trap and all would end as they planned, but I had to go because I wanted to see Adriel again and my dear friend who will always be so, here and him beyond distance beyond my dreams, and wanted to see my sisters, began to fall asleep dreaming with my friend, but was not asleep at all, listening to their voices that hear soften exchange with me and Adriel.

His plan looked better than I thought I had to admit they were good with that, after a while, my fear vanished calmer my heart was left to be accelerated, I knew that would come out of here I had to trust my friends they will come to me and everything would be fine, did not have that mourn for fear, my fear was gone while the voices began to fade and began to sleep, the last thing I remember is his voice man saying that everything is ready, put his hand over my mount and I fainted.

She was tied to a chair, looking at me with eyes full of tears, her eyes telling me not to worry that everything would be fine that she trusted me, his look change by more love than pain, that I was a consulate to see me one more time, she will be happy, but my soul was filled with fear of pain, courage, just like running to her out of that dark place.

-Wake up brother we have to go; it's time to seek for the heart.

-Of course, we should talk to Alan, what will your plan.

-Adriel came here brother; we will recover it and will be fine, I promise nothing will happen.

-Know everything will be fine.

-I leave you alone I'll walk a little.

I need to think a little, also had to go home for some things, including my diary I had not seen it for days, not written in, is like my life well in fact is my life, I write, but is the only one who knows my thoughts, walk a while in the halls of the monastery, past the chapel stop by, and see it was impossible not to enter, is small but very nice, enter and stayed for a moment I sat on the back, I did not kneel, I do not pray, just looked at the few pictures that had in it, it feels strange being there, after a few minutes went out, I keep walking, reaches a corner where you could see all around, the fields, the houses that under my gaze away were being more small.

The cold breeze caressed my icy cheeks, it was later every moment, my heart was pale inside I could feel it, my head was spinning just thinking that my friends come out hurt because of me, in the back of me said I could put an end to all this, there was something in me that could end it all, I heard some footsteps approaching, it was Alan and my brother, as I did not return they came for; for a moment they looked what I, they were watching all around us.

-Is there somewhere, just have to wait, there will be a time I know, was just a matter of time.

-Danica I think so too, all we have to do is waiting, we have no choice, and we can only fool them.

-I thought it would look.

-We will but do not have much time.

My brother was silent   looking down as we, calmed down and then went inside, I think for the moment we only had to wait, walk around with Alan, and asked him to take me to my house for the thinks I needed, I was no sure if it would be a good idea, but he agreed to take me, if not I would go alone anyway.

We spent in silence, staring at the road, and I observe nature, we reached the road facing the house, we passed in front of the house of Mrs. Gonzales, they were well had returned home after the incident, we go off the yellow jeep at the entrance, walk together to the door, hesitate for a moment but reactions and entered in the house, which now seemed quite cold and alone, it was my mother, but did not remember much, only in a dream not know it, it's real or just a dream, I remember in the forest and beside it a flash of light, and I was at his side holding hands and my brother the other hands, but it was only a dream or perhaps a nightmare.

I went to my brother's bedroom for their thinks first, and then by the mine, I opened my dresser and took out my inhaler the replacement for asthma and in the background was my diary, take it out put it between my bag black color, I wore a cream-colored coat and went out with my stuff, but before leaving look at the photograph on my desk when we were kids, my brother and me, I remember that my mother takes, just my brother and me, and take more of all together, but not know what happens to them, I was with my father and one of his friends, I don't' remember him, but I do remember that she gives a picture of it, and one to my father, never knew what happened to my father, not even remember very well, and my mother did not to know how just know she died and no one to ask what happened to them.

We left the house to go into the jeep Mss. Gonzales was in the hallway, I said hello and smiles at me, I was sure that they are well, now back to the monastery and give the things to my brother, and Alan said we need to go home; I accept, he had already accompanied at mine too, arriving there he began to search the books to read.

-What are you doing, I can help with anything?

-I'm looking for something to help us find the heart, and prefer you to go to rest; I want to do it alone please I need to be alone.

-You know that everyone is looking for and if I'm here is because I have something to do with all this, you said yourself, you need our help you should share with us, any way you will have to, but that's ok, I withdraw.

-I did not expect to make you feel self bad, just which I prefer to look for myself.

-If it's okay, no problem and I have already withdrawn.

He took my arm and looked at me tenderly.

-I will not let anything happen to you, neither you nor your friends, I promise.

-If I believe you, tanks and I hope that.

He let go and I left, I think that was what he most wanted at that time because all we were promised something that day, but apparently it was more difficult than we thought, keeping a promise is a very sacred and dangerous, difficult to enforce, all promised to take care of and nothing hurt us.

I went to my room, well his room, was so comfortable it felt like mine, I approached to the window and look for it a while, the starless night, looking through my things and take my journal, I started to look through and stopped in the day that I met Alan, first was not special, attended only their order and I found it charming, a new person how to enter the restaurant, which had to be attending as any other, and accompanied by his girlfriend, now it is her sister.

I started to write the last thoughts of the day while listening to some classical music, of course the mp3 it was all I had at the time and did not want that he listens, the melody was on the piano, this music sometimes makes me feel better but when I was afraid this night was very dark gloomy and I was sad more than other times, and still did not understand Alan's behavior was so cold and still not trust him, I still had something to fear or if although liked, I started to write.

At the same heart pounding on my body knowing that would be the last hours of peace, as a body can endure so much pain so much anguish, as the heart can survive that as is vital for life, to keep breathing, love is more difficult more intolerant at times just want not to feel.

Torments fall on my memories, dreams and reality became one, the fantasy is real, evil is worse than I thought, and I think there is still goodness in the hearts of people, but sometimes we can't understand the capacity of people to harm others, is painful to think you've lost the battle before you get started.

Sometimes life is cruel and whimsical, sometimes rough and tedious, every day we began a struggle for survival, to feed the soul sometimes die from lack of faith of hope, but that is the hope, in our opinion, is never give up and less before you start, you never stop fighting.

The tunes still and I continued writing, in the other room could hear dropping some books.

My friends are more important to me, but how to protect, if I was scared inside, was still a child as innocent as they were saying, believed that everything would be fine as long, but I'm still afraid, everyone told me that my heart was still a girl but never trade it for anything I want my heart still believe that there is more gentle love that evil, believing that there are faith and hope.

The maturity has nothing to do with what; the heart feels provided they understand what is right and what is wrong.

Friendship to me is the best in the world, all have friends I am lucky to have my brother and tell him that he's my best friend and have everyone else around me to trust me, my friends.

The sentiment I feel for Alan is different of friendship, but I felt something more for him, desire to kiss him know that I can love again, but I fell that is not what I want or do not know, something that prevents me feels something, are hiding something it is not loving what he fell from me, his gaze at me sadly reflects anxiety, wanting to hug, but not love me, it is different the feeling is more of protection, seems to be guilty but I had not done anything, maybe it would be better if I stay away from it, some things are better not knowing how, not have to mess with some feelings and less if they are not ours, but? The desire to feel his body close to me, I'm crazy, it's so warm that I forget that is so cool with me.

Halloween

The next morning I woke up thinking it was a few days for Halloween, Alan knocked on the door brought me breakfast in bed, thinking nonsense, but he leaves on a table that stood by the window with a couple of chairs, swear that I do not saw yesterday, was something else, but I give no importance except the breakfast he accompanied me.

And at the end asked him to take me to the restaurant which had days closed and we had to finish the little remodeling that we had begun, he accepted and went with me, seemed not wanted to take off my.

My brother was in the restaurant, it was not much just redecorate the front, the Messrs who lived in a street painted drawings on the walls, very beautiful were works of art, they had talent, painted in colors more friendly, they may have the light, have life, put a bright yellow roof whether when entering reflect more light to the entire restaurant, at the bottom of the drawings was white, were at the entrance was more cultural, in the other a blue sky, white bows and red, decorated with paintings.

With the help of all ended that day and opened the next day, we've made the last preparations for Halloween, despite what happened to Monica.

Prepare a party for Halloween night, started putting some decoration and ghoulish sounds, among other details, the week passed quickly.

On Saturday we dedicated to search for the heart, which is supposed to be according to Alan had read the ancient legends, shine when the heart find the right person, well when touch my hands or my brother, this is crazy and hard to believe, but according to them it was all true, and although we did not understand it or maybe they got the wrong people.

Traveled the road from the monastery to the church because according to the witch said it was close, and we were on our way to an ancient shrine on the road, some people left candles, relics, flowers and went to visit that place, including some medals, looking under rocks without disturbing the altar, there were some people bothered to see us, but this was important, but in the end, we continue, we could not find anything, finally decide to look around the church, we separated to look, I look at along with Elmo, he remember the words of the witch said, my brother stood in front of the altar, stood motionless a few minutes, he did not move, we continue looking but unable to find, I guess it was not there the witch was wrong, did not know what my brother felt, Alan and the others entered, he was speechless watching my brother, took his arm but my brother refused.

-Tell me, when will you say, when you will, she needs to know.

-Relax child, here is not the time.

-If it is, this time is perfect she was sitting here and I could not do anything about it, I was so close, tell who she is.

My brother was furious Alan looked at me, what happens between them, since when they hate it that way, and yet my brother to face.

-Rosalba… she was my girlfriend many years ago, as she is immortal, it was long ago, ended for quite.

-And therefore not had the courage even to try to save Monica, that's your excuse, is no fair. My brother said

-Not so, we have to protect yourself; you are important.

-She did not.

-Not say that.

-Who is Rosalba?

-Is the girl with red hair, she planned from the beginning everything was a trap. My brother said

-Wait! The girl who flirted you with her, a second she is the White Rouse, Rosalba is the one with Monica and who is Tansy too, they are the same person or.

-Alan will be true that they are the same person. Elmo asked

-I hope not.

He seemed confused; I think that had not thought about it, well he did not have that.

-Seriously did not know Alan. Ask my brother

-No, she did not care anymore; we will do what is necessary to save Monica.

I get chills thinking they were together, but there was more, I could see in his eyes, and Elmo knew it, and my brother with the witch.

Until now I knew he would not be mine and was aware that he had someone else in his mind, but she never, well it was pretty and provocative in those clothes, but that does not matter much at this time, it's just past and do not back on, if he said it, I will stop worrying for Alan and his girlfriend.

What mattered was to get back Monica but did not have what they wanted in returned, we're thinking to make another offer, the minutes passed the better we leave the church, and headed back to the monastery, was not very far if we get immediately.

I went with William, the maestro's great, not much of it, but it is young to be my teacher was so upset about not being able to do anything and wanted to get all that anger, a new feeling for me as I had ever been so angry and stressed out, began to cloud earlier than usual, the cold was worse than other times, but it seems to be perfect, the maestro Olalde that is his last name was great, new techniques taught me more perfect than before, more accurate, he asked me if I believe that anything can happen.

-Anger is something new for you, impotence is nasty, but you have to control it, is not all bad but you off enough.

-Course I'm not angry.

-And why you think that this so the weather, look at the sky is completely black, as a storm was approaching so.

-The sky changes it is fall, this place is always cloudy and you should know.

-And when it snows in spring, is normal.

-Yes, in this place it is.

-Careful what you ask.

-Always say that.

-Well, continue.

-I have another question teacher, why agree with all this; I thought that the seminar was only a few people praying and that stuff, why many of the seminarians also train?

-Fighting evil with our prayers but that does not stop completely, faith ends, and demons always find a way to destroy this world, of course, I'll help, and besides these demons are human, and not stop our prayers will not stop, just learn to defend ourselves.

-True evil sometimes wins, but I believe in justice.

-I believe more in God's justice.

I began to calm and the sky began to change, not taken away the clouds, but the color black change was now more white, could but no longer kept gloomily, that afternoon it was normal like any other could day in the Mountain.

Ended, and we will have to get everything ready for tomorrow the Halloween night, I stayed in the home of Alan as the last days, according to him to be more protected, felt that it was my babysitter, did not want to continue that way, I thought I say I would return home, but for now, think I thought about what would happen tomorrow, and what I would dress tomorrow, had not bought anything, so I thought I'd dress like any other day, I was very concerned that my best friend would not be with me.

Walk around looking at the collection of books that had many, had already read, but others had not even heard mention, some were of poetry and mystery were many, others very old but all in very good condition, looked after them very much, in a corner of the room were some magazines and newspapers, I started to look at them and found one that caught my attention, it was the same as had been reading in the library a few weeks ago, about the strange light in the forest years ago, the date was the same in which my mother had died, this time I paid more attention, it was at the same time, that both the heart and the necklace had disappeared, but it was foolish to think that all this had something to do.

I kept going through the newspapers, some unsolved murders, where something strange no fingerprints, no blood nothing, as if had done a ghost, shadows without witnesses, the strange thing was that nobody had claimed the bodies, no one could explain, perhaps had not family but it was strange.

Leave everything as it was and I went, but before I go to the room to tell him until tomorrow, before bed I started to write, could not describe how I feel at this time, this time writes on the table by the window looking out, sometimes I looked out into the sky, thinking how nice it would be a star at this time, in a night so dark, so sad, it's been several days that Monica was kidnapped, but did not know anything about it, the last time was in the church.

Thought to imagine that my brother started to feel something for her, would be a great, but more painful discovery at this time, I knew that Monica felt for, she believed that my brother was cute and playful, she loved that, he was always cheerful, though these days is changing, we've all changed.

The brightness of a star comfort the pain, I feel they are my life I feel it is not only solid rock, is something else, that glow is like the brightness of the soul, angels shining in the heights protecting us.

Thinking that life has special, what sense would live to suffer, the star would be perhaps the soul of a person, which is always to guide it, is beyond my dreams, beyond life, that would give to be a star, to shine as she, be light in the sky, be the inspiration of love, sometimes I felt that someone beyond watching me, that as a star is my friend. A star is my guide, their light is my joy, and I'm your joy, as I am protected by them.

This time could not be aware of me, for a moment I thought I should do something with all that was happening.

Life just beautiful needs to know who to live with, it is hard and rough, but not everything can be perfect.

Knocked on the door the only person who could do would be Alan, I closed my diary and told to came in that was open, when he saw the diary entry but his eyes showed no interest, carrying a large box as a gift the box white simple.

-I hope it's to your liking, is a gift, see you at the party.

-Sure, there we see.

-May you rest, till tomorrow.

-I will thank you till tomorrow.

Accept it because it did not have to say no, I'm using everything he has, I lay dawn leave the dairy on the table, trying to remember something about my childhood something that would serve me who I am, I had never tried to remember, was happy as my life was, not to question me not trying to remember anything from the past was good was bad.

But that was before someone watching over me, before being left alone, we know that someone cares about us, and we never lacked anything and never bothered us social workers or something, and never question anything we got, the house was my mother, that person told us that sometimes we had money, but when we grew up never saw her again, she opened an account for us, were deposited the necessary and we never asked where it came.

Closed his eyes and started to remember things from when I was a child, I remember someone reading books, fairy tale stories interesting, but not in my mother's house, but one with many rooms like this and a large library much like this, only this has no children's books I remember being at the window watching the stars and my brother by the fireplace, playing with someone I do not remember, he walked towards me, look me in the eye and said the star guard us, they crate our destiny, of course, sometimes we can change it, clear that sometimes, belong to them, one day like all off as you be up there, you're special you can change things like your brother.

Just I reminder that I had forgotten, but being in this room, I remember it so clearly, but can't remember who told me, not who he is, maybe it's just my imagination, I do not know, but it's so real right now, that may be true, always full of dreams of premises to myself, that has faded over time, have been lost dreams and promises, loves and nightmares that are returned.

Finally came the day of witches, not even know what time I fell asleep only is a new day and it's time to start, look for Alan to say goodbye, but I did not find it on any side of the house, he let the

Hammer so that I will take with me to the restaurant.

Will finally give me alone, went up things including his gift, I was sure it would be a disguise for the size of the box, was not difficult to know, I went to the restaurant and I thought I saw a patrol in the distance the road, when I approached, I trough to know him, the same officer who collects the interviews and evidence in the house and the restaurant and which was looking for my friend.

Just pass me by without much curiosity, driving cautiously and would have not to excuse to stop me, fallow my way and the patrol car headed to another street, arrive at the restaurant about eight o'clock in the morning did not open I started making arrangements for the night of the party, those who worked here came in a while, but I had many things to do I start to accommodate the tables so that they could dance, of course, was a restaurant and work more here, but Mr. Robles always left me in charge of everything, it seemed as if I order here, the only responsible for carrying money to the bank and deal with the accountant for taxes.

I did not care much, appeared about ten o'clock my brother, brought Elmo and then go, he just came to leave my brother, he came with a pirate costume on hand, but very nice, made me laugh, I thought for a moment, do I imagine that he came dressed, but not, I told him to help me, this day we were just us, our friends had already done enough with the remodeling and almost all of today's decoration was ready, Kalinda came with the yellow truck I had already forgotten her, brought her to use my brother, and had made some arrangements, did not know what arrangements and do not ask, she hated me, and of course that would come those who work with us and arrive on time.

Now it is the day to pay them, whether they came early, sound settled into the corner where you could see everything, there a top that we had reserved for occasions like this, but this was the first time we use it, Mr. Robles was still in the hospital, we advise of the party and he gave us permission, as long as we hand over the profits, we agreed and everything was fine, perfect, the phone to my brother rang, he was in the bathroom, and if I answer, was someone who did not expect, was the witch, I knew she had the phone for the reason that they talked before.

-What you want witch?

-Relaxed, talk with Adriel of course.

-I am what you want?

-I want him, by the girl.

-Will I'll give you something else, not him. Move away and enter the broom closet.

-Listen, you have the heart.

-If you spy us, you will know that we have not found.

-Of course I know, we'll see after midnight in the restaurant and I hope your offer is better.

-Sure it will.

When I left the broom closet my brother was looking for me, conceals find the broom with a silly grin, I put the phone in place, erasing the last call, to not notice, it was evening, opened about three, if some families coming to eat and stay a little to the party, in fact some were coming by snoop, but it comes out, some if they stayed, actually they were our most frequent customers.

Indigent people would not come, but still gave me time to bring something to eat, because at this time had a shelter from the cold, they helped me a lot in the restaurant, I escape for an hour or so to share with them, my friends arrive at nine, my brother was already changing in the office, when it left seemed to be someone else, was great the costumes were perfect did not cover his face so that showed his charming smile.

-You, what time think going to change?

-Well, if I do not have a costume, do not buy anything but Alan give me a box with something inside, I think it's a costume, if not for what he give it today.

-Please let' see, show it. Tell my friends

-No, I will go alone and if I like, I'll put it, if no better so I stay.

-No, we know that you would not put, so we'll go with you, and there is not but.

-Okay, in a little while we will be ok.

-Then we will.

Time went on, looking out the window, but did not arrive, I was so sure he would come, well, in that case, it would not interfere with my plans with the witch, still, miss him, wanted to see him in a costume, or maybe he was and I did not recognize but it could be, is unmistakable is unique. Therefore, I would know, I could not go wrong, but he did not reach, was desperate to see, but ten thirty came and not appeared, then the plan with would go well whit the witch and he would not be present to stop me, look for the girls and take a few minutes to find them because we're too many people, but I found them, we went to the office, always remained close and more that day, the box that gave me Alan was in the chair, all were curious like me, but I dared not, finally to open we were silent and strange motionless it was strange that could not breathe.

-Is excellent, beautifully!

-Carolina is more than that.

-Jasmine is right… good pull out and tries it, if you do not want to change your dress; the widow dress you would come good.

-Sonia quiet widow, you look divine.

-Well, try it, what are you waiting for? My friends were anxious.

-I'm not sure, if well, besides he even not come; maybe not the time.

-No, please is a day off look different, do not play, this is a perfect time, the dress is fabulous if no change.

-Like you Carolina!

-Well, just saying.

-Okay, but not go dressed like that.

-Of course not force you.

-Girls do not cruse fingers.

-Hmmm.

The dress is fabulous, was better had ordered to make some arrangements, this time was combined with black with an opening in the leg higher than normal, had fixed the cleavage of the back, the tangled ribbons were gone, was a huge scot that my back could be seen, and ribbons do not throw, place them in the hip, was great, I loved the dress most beautiful red dress, that have a few decades became more modern, the front left little to the imagination.

-Is perfect you look beautiful. Caro said

-It had been put before.

-Seriously.

-Yes.

-As any princess.

Sing and I would think the same, inside was a box separately it was a crown was not so striking, "perfect" a white mask covered with stones like diamonds was fabulous and put some gloves that were as soft as a feather or better than that. It covered almost the whole arm but were indicated, at the back was mostly bare and the front or say the dress was super bold and beautiful at the same time, something strange, my friends help me with a little makeover, but I felt that was too much, could not see me only had a small pocket mirror, not it was risky, I was petrified but even if we thought that was the most beautiful gift I've ever had does not end there, there was another box, my friend Carolina opened and was speechless.

-And say that does not like you!

-Show us. Said Pilar

-O by God!

-What it is? Ask them

-Is crazy. Said Carolina

-I think the same. I said, seeing

-Know how much it could cost, he is now so old to have a fortune or their parents are rich or he is a theft.

Was a diamond necklace with a red heart in the center, the necklace was too large would notice all, was a fantasy, not wanted to touch, but my friends put him on my neck and not only that was the complete set of diamond earrings and red heart like the bracelet.

-You know you only need the ring.

-Yes, of course, taunt.

My friends get out first was almost eleven, but it was a good time, tonight would be long and early morning, hesitate to go with the necklace, just need the bracelet and earrings if I put them on and finally came out after five minutes, my friends waited outside, nevertheless, also Caro waited for me, but was worried about his sister Monica, leaving the office everyone stared at me, I think I know why.

All its heart Carolina thought Monica as well, and everything would be fine and also I expect it that way, I went dancing with my brother for a while and forget that we put a mirror next to the sound and when passing by knowing how beautiful I looked at, the dress was perfect, but the jewels were equal, that we started to scare me, I dance with some friends.

-We can dance lovely?

-What, who you are?

-I know, we've hardly spoken, I am Hewett remember me.

-So, I remember, yes of course.

Is true, we had not spoken and he tried to find the heart, we dance awhile, was very nice to be with him, although he flirts a lot, and it was very handsome in the same way, I think all were and although some of them were seminarians or priests, then it was almost midnight there were only minutes, maybe the witch was already there, but his instructions were to speak with me turning twelve, she wanted to enjoy the party I supposed.

Then I saw him dancing with someone, they were all, from when they were here and I did not notice it, gradually ended the melody and another began and approached me, but I continued dancing with Hewett, without thinking came to me and offered me his hand to dance, but Hewett doesn't let me, he just stood there a moment and laughed as Hewett, after a moment took me with him and started dancing, he approached the young man who was preparing the music, and the melody began as a waltz.

-Let me dance with you this melody.

-I'm not sure I could.

-Just trust me, please.

-Okay.

-By the way, you look divine, you know.

-Thanks to you.

Dance at his side for a moment I forget all of us watched with unconcealed but I do not care, I did not care, just me and him in the middle of the dance floor, after a while joined his sister and the others, of course, they knew the steps were so easy to follow and not knowing the song of the kings, only they dance, we looked so rare, no one knew as they danced this Waltz alone, his friends of Alan, was looking fabulous all but ended up, maybe it was a long time, but for me, it was hard too fast, began another song and this time most dances and I react.

-Be right back.

Without another word I ran to my brother's coat and remove his phone, was a little after midnight, and I figured she let me finish the waltz, my brother brought me a fabulous white coat in the same way and I take it and headed to the office just in time, was the witch.

-Having fun with my dear Alan, if you know he went to bed with me, sure!

-I know only slept with you. Establish her comment

-Know maybe we will not make the deal, best annihilated I get your brother as a gift he is a good option.

-If you do, you will never have what you want, where is she?

-We are I the party that you prepared, you know Alan is great and god is still dancing as always, with my finished with a kiss.

-Is not about him, if not for the deal, I'll do it without changing anything.

-This will be a pleasure, outside in five minutes, I'm dancing.

-Witch.

It seemed that everything would be chaos, I was nervous everything was suddenly cold, place the phone I the left pocket of my brother's coat, I noticed something at the bottom of it, was no stranger could be anything else, take it and without seeing what I got in my pocket, I kept walking slowly, playing with it, I headed to the bar, so I could go out the back and no one notice, take the snow glove that had given me Alan and with one hand waving, I was nervous, but I was curious to know what was in my other hand.

Before heading out the back door, take my hand to know what it was, I stare at my hand one second, and then opened my hand, was something strange, it was a chain with a hear one of those continents photographs inside, I opened it to find out who it was and began to glow with an intensity I could not believe what I saw.

I knew this was what they sought, and was in my power, inside was a picture of a beautiful woman with curls it seemed to me, and on the other side one more, two children it was strange that I could not believe, look at the women and children, holy Gad is the same picture of my brother and myself that we had in the house when we were kids, I remember more than anything in this world, at that time slips from my hand the crystal ball, fell to the ground in slow motion as I could hear the shake off the water and the snow inside, the music slowly fading to finish, fell to the ground and got out of there quickly, how got my brother or maybe always has had, I did not know but because we had not noticed.

-Would be the heart?

I thought of what Alan said, as only shine in the right hands, so do not shine with my brother, they were his hands, was mine, I knew this was what they wanted, but why are we, suddenly I had a plan and work, knew that if I exchange for Monica they had their plan as well, almost like with a spare, but this change everything is better, still it's time to play and win.

Place it back into the pocket of the coat, on leaving them waiting for me in costumes, that if get to see at some point as well as Monica in the sexy witch costume that looked great, I did not recognize, though all she was well that made me feel better, more than I expect, everything was fine, I know I had the advantage against the witch who was dressed an as an angel, that irony but she was with someone other than their friends Hokon.

-Change of plans will go for a walk.

-We had not been in that; it would be right here.

-Plans can always change. Said the witch

-Okay, we will go.

We left in the black suburban perhaps the same that which had seen before, after a few minutes near the road not far from the restaurant, but on a lonely road, I knew I would be disadvantaged in this place but had to deal with, we all got off the truck.

-Well, let her go now.

-Sure, away from my sight.

-Gladly witch.

She gave a blow before Monica to stay away from her, I could not even move, but she was well, approached by my, untied, and told her to leave but she hasn't obeyed.

-Let her away from here and have what is yours.

-Think it's that easy, and it will go on foot.

-Of course, she will go away from here do not hurt her.

-I would not be so sure.

-Go away, Monica.

-No, do not ever leave you, do not even dream it; you know they still will not let me go, they kill us.

-Go Monica obey and go.

-No you never would you do.

-Of course, I would do, now get out of here.

-I will not move.

-Too sweet, but the party is after the princess, you're ours and take care of Monica.

-Of course not, not without a fight before.

-Great follow your game and then we go dear.

I start fighting with their companions, while the witch delighted in the fight, the dress was not a problem the opening of the leg made me easier and helped me with some tips, use a little wider of the dress hang some of them, Monica also looked at, could not do anything plus she was a little weak for the days captive, a few moments thinking about Alan they would be doing, the three companions are almost unconscious, she intervened, but they kept on, not by much, never kill anyone but I'm stronger than before and defend myself.

-To them, you can beat, but no me; you're still a weak girl.

We fought it was stronger than I thought, but would not let me win, it took about the moments and the fools woke up and joined the fight was harder than I thought, but I had to treat, and what I knew the heart had a power that they wanted, only I must know how to use it, they threw me and rolled a little, so I stay a few seconds.

-You better give up and came with us that was the deal, you for her.

-Change of plans anything can happen.

I pulled up under the coat to the heart and put it to me, brighter than before and I knew if I would help the witch stare.

-Impossible as you got it deceives us.

-Let us go, and you are not hurt.

-Never, that thing is mine and your equal, plus you do not know who it works, get her.

-I think not.

The Hokon were not immortal only one of them, the others were followers of the witch came tried to put their hands on me, but this time I felt stronger than before, around me was a glowing light and out of my hands a power inexplicable, that I could only feel, I did not know how it worked but I felt, when they tried to hit me and went into the light that surrounded me, I close my hands strong and they vanished as if by magic, the light blinded them and made them all just became one with the wind, I watched from afar as the witch away in a hurry from there.

-Sarah.

-I'm fine, how are you.

-Scared.

Monica was beside me but she was not hurt, she was fine, but did not know how to stop it, felt my heart beating more and more each time, but could not stop, I hear felt like it went off the chest, dying at that moment I did not care I knew we were safe I Monica shouted at me but could not distinguish what she said.

Approaching in the distance about five or more shades, felt I had to continue protecting Monica even if I died in the attempt, that was my feeling at that time, I could not let him take her I had to relieve pain and keep fighting for her, belongs to my brother, the shadows drew closer, one faster than the others, ran towards me, try to defend myself, but he hugs me and for a moment to hear it scream, could not see who he was, knew nothing about, all I knew is that Monica would be fine, but had to stop this that hug me.

Nothing happening to him, hug me so tingly that I could not breathe, the air was missing, I could not move, I was tied at his arms, thought as he stands the pain if felt my body was burning, I wondered why he did not hurt me I'm not damaged, I stop fighting I closed my eyes and when I reopened after a couple of seconds I saw it, was Alan the one hug me, I do not want to hurt him, I closed my eyes, but it was so hard to stop this, it was hotter than me, I had wanted to kiss him, saying I was sorry, I could not stop and suddenly hear more voices but did not know who they were.

-Do it and kiss her or kill you.

-Do it now Alan.

Suddenly he was kissing me, that silly advice, of course I was dying to kiss him forever, but it was silly that someone would suggest, I close my eyes again the heat began to slow down a little and slowly felt my heart calms down and the light faded, I felt a warm tear that rolled down my cheek warmer than normal the heart beat more normally and his kiss was more fascinating, could not stop kissing him.

-Cut it out. (Someone shouted)

I felt that my body was asleep slowly and fainted, so leave it alone, I felt like my body faded away as, if I had taken his life, I fainted, I would not know what would happen after, just knew it was a dream, I felt trapped as if I were running in the woods, but I knew I could not be true it was a dream or was dead, only if it would explain.

-Alan is enough, let her already.

Good heavens his kiss was warm, but something told me that if I continue could die as she, I did not want to try, but it was almost impossible to stop kissing her, was addictive, but finally let her, promised that nothing would happen to Sarah, as promised to his mother, but my kiss was killing us both.

This day should never have come, I felt that my body was fading but it was impossible to separate and leave her, his power was more than I supposed, had embraced the so strong that I was hurting her, his power was immense, I had held up before and with the same intensity, had to be his daughter, inherited his power, I made a promise to his mother and was breaking it, in that I knew I love her and would not let happen again, she gives her life as his mother, I start to feel like my heart stopped beating as he paused, as I was gasping for air, around the salty kiss, I knew she was crying, she had to stop, I knew did not hurt me, I felt like I die slowly.

No matter if I die as she is saved, I do not care, since his power too much for me, it is impossible to control, felt like we vanish the two, she had stopped kissing me, I felt like was killing me, I realized that we were both being unconscious or killing one another, but was the only way to reduce their power, handing some to me, the two were unconscious but I kept remembering.

From the day she was born until now was forbidden, she could be my daughter but was not.

Was the most loved people in the past, his mother, but I try not to feel anything for Sarah, this was stronger than me, my heart betrayed me, I love her and would give my life for her, Hewett was right, they are so similar, was disturbances, brought the dress was her mother, though physically the same, his heart is different, I began to see her since we find the first necklace, I had been away from her, the news I heard from my friend who posed as a social worker was enough for me, not to hurt my heart, having her around, was too much pain.

Until right now is that I should avoid, but my heart could not, every day was torture, each passing moment she remembers me to her mother every moment, but they are different they are not the same, I know how to differentiate my love I have for her mother and now I have her, I was so nervous that she will remember who live in my house as a child for a while, was easier when she was small.

Was irresistible not to see it is beautiful, and I love every smile more each day, each moment, it was not that I had to ensure their dreams, where she pronounced me asleep, but it was fascinated to know that dream with me, was the one, my inner fire, my complements.

The temptation was stronger than me, at this point to read his diary in the last pages were said that she loves me, she mentions that he loves me, but it is impossible to be close, my heart is confused; it said to herself, I felt a huge pressure; soon to beat more strongly the heart, I felt alive but was not conscious to know if she was ok, that was all that mattered at that moment, but my eyes do not open, although I felt my heart beating, my anxiety was intolerant do not know who to wake up, it was as if something will pull me inside and yelling at me that I must be asleep it was the best, hear a voice in the distance, I could not tell who it was, was an angelic voice so sweet and tender, that made me feel comfortable, despite the pain the burning of the body, at last, I saw her my beloved of the past.

-Is not time yet.

-Lucy, you know I love you, and I love her, who to avoid or destroy.

-She needs you, come back.

-But you and her, I do.

-She will follow his heart.

Breathing missed me for a second, felt chokes I got up hastily, was unsettled, was my sister who was with me, but my vision was so real, the first thing I did was look for her, note that I was at home in the living room to be exact, Elmo took me by the shoulder and stopped me.

-She's fine is unconscious you took enough power, could be died bout, or maybe all.

-She stopped herself; she knew that is hurting me.

-Yes, she felt it, is strange but stopped, well she is strong.

-I know and Adriel?

-This with her and Monica.

-We are all well.

-And the other sister, and your husband?

-Are in the monastery, ware to check that this entire okay. Said Elmo

-I'm sorry I could not hear the phone for the music, I forget for a while I'm sorry. Said Kalinda

-Should not be neglected, even a second it is also my fault.

-We should all be vigilant. Said William

-She saw inside the shrine, she knows she is his mother and they, as obtained? I thought you had it. Said Hewett

-I do know, neither knew that was the heart that we were looking for, it's confusing; do not know who she got it.

-I do.

-Adriel, who?

-I had it, you threw in the restaurant, put in my coat but never opened it, I completely forgot to return it.

-I did not realize it.

-Stop lying she is my mother, as you get it? I hope for an explanation.

-Yes she is your mother, it was a gift for you, and that someday it would give.

-She is… we are the children of your story?

-If you are, and I have never left alone.

-Would have been better looking at her now, this is a lie.

-She will be fine.

-I will walk a while.

-Wait.

Elmo stopped me, was right, was not the time, I had to leave him alone, was a very cruel lie to learn, Dani did not wake up, one more of my unknowns as she reaches such a high level, no one else could ever less control and also those who tried died, went out after it entered Adriel, I kept walking behind the house just spinning, as reactionaries it with all this information, a new world for her and her brother, would be the same after this, in case she does not entirely trust me, I had made some mistakes, I hate to hide the truth but could not do anything, that will do more harm.

The world is spinning all the time as our lives revolve and change all the time, it could change ours, it could control the power that was given her to care, as you try to change the world and not as able to achieve, as many time tried to do good but always know that evil exists.

You can't always change people, but you can try and eventually, you'll notice that some will never change, I continue circling, they still unconscious, had to rest, finally came to the room where she was, looked so much like her mother was like her, with the same dress she wore on the day back, I a party in which I met her, she looked as beautiful as her daughter now, but his daughter was much more, as it seemed to his father too.

-Need a rest sister.

-Okay Hewett.

-And Adriel was gone already, and Alan?

-It was with Elmo leaving Monica home, they also have to explain where they found, and Alan is outside, I think.

-That will say.

-Easy, she was found walking on the road, and she did not remember, so do not question it will continue.

-Okay, you can go to rest, I take care.

-But you need to rest too.

-Yes then I will, you can go I will keep in touch.

-Okay, not a good idea, but I will.

-Goodbye.

-Hewett careful you know you play with fire like Alan and do not want to see a fight with our brother.

-I know, but she is beautiful, do not think, also there's nothing between them, I can try.

-Both are wrong, you know, but I do not want to fight I better disappear.

-Well said, sister.

My sister walked away upset about being alone with her, I sat on the sofa beside the bed, as she thought that not wake up even that much energy had used his body as she knew she was doing, but had no answer had to wait to ask what was happening, I remembered the kiss they were Alan and her as she walked away, was not wanting to hurt, do not take all the energy she needed from him, if give you energy, it was strange, that's why she is unconsciousness.

Still tired, I approached her and see the heart was in his chest, I dared to take it, I opened it, I remember the day that my brother gave it to her mother and she then places the pictures in, was so quiet evening at home, was taking photographs of her two children and I will take one of her, then store the camera in a wooden box with a lock strange, but I said this box was a secret special ever, special thinks, then closed and placed in a strange medallion in the lock, that was the key, then placed it to his daughter as a necklace either and she said I only knew that it was for the necklace, which would serve us someday I keep it in a larger trunk and never happened to that special wooden box she sent to do, shut it and not know what happened.

Just spinning around the room, and I did not know what to do, I was tired, but fine, the hours passed and she was unconsciousness it was too long, the next day was almost over darkened, no one had been, just Alan and I, we were, Alan talks on the phone, I sat in bed watching his breathing, I moved a little to her, her body smelled a rose was an incomparable perfume, but it was his body that smelled so delicious, I sighed and put out a little but returned to it and I approached her mount slowly, I was so close and my heart was racing, angel face made me not take off, could not but had to follow my instincts, something I could not detach myself to any more had to follow my instincts unexpected, cried out my heart and my soul was in accordance with my desires and emotions, without feeling my lips touched hers were so pale, his breathing and his taste was fruity and the smell of her skin crazy, it was crazy to be close and not to kiss her, his kiss was so spectacular that no words can describe it, his aroma making me crazy could not stop I felt his hand caressing my face, lift the look and she opened her eyes I slowly away from her.

-I'm sorry, really sorry.

-Hewett but what you are doing?

-I felt sorry, really sorry not happened. I paused and asked

-Well, what do you remember?

-A, Alan kisses me and not you, or was you.

-No, it was.

-And where it is.

-Resting.

-And you.

-I look, I'm taking care of you until the return of your brother and Alan and certainly should do not take long.

I lied, he was outside.

-If thanks.

-Forgiveness by…

-For which Hewett? Ask Alan

-I do not know just came up and happen.

-Okay, forget it.

-A question which was better mine or Alan.

-I do not remember yours.

-Ouch, that hurt.

Before saying anything more I pat her hair and approached to me and I was still on it, I had not moved an inch of her face, she kissed me back, more than just a kiss, his hands caressing my skin and I hers, it was hard to resist his touch, his hands were so soft that my body shook with each touch, she kept kissing me, leaved over my head, I followed kissing and caressing get to hear his heart, which was faster than before, I felt that my body shuddered, forget that Alan was close.

-Are you okay Hewett?

-Sorry, what were we.

-Stay away from her brother.

Rays was hallucinating, I'm crazy just amazed by her kiss, and my sister did not want us to have problems, Kalinda was right I'm playing with fire, Adriel entered into it.

-Sister woke up, how are you?

-Well, I think.

We watched for a few seconds her and me.

-I can speak a second with you.

-Of course.

What happened, what I'm thinking?

-Just happened brother, I approached a little and it happened.

-You know that if unchecked, it could have killed you.

-Like you, and still kissed her.

-I know I've done it before and will stand more than you.

-You do not know.

-Enough is enough to not want to hurt.

-Afraid that falls in love with me and no you.

-No, perhaps it would be best she knows what she does, just do not want something happens to you.

Return to the room where she chatted with his brother, I stood at the entrance, she saw me that his brother had obstructed his view.

-We take Monica home after everything that happened had to rest.

-Clear as is she.

-She is fine, her sisters are happy to have, the consent to much these days, you can talk tomorrow.

-If clear, I can speak with Alan, please.

-Dani you will be fine.

-Yes, I'll be, you know Hewett kiss me and kisses well.

-I see you were in good company eh.

She lied, she was aware of my kiss Alan also heat it, I look him smiling, he swallowed

-If something like that, you can tell Alan to come in.

-Alan.

-Do not shut, that I could have done.

-Yes, but I miss the show, he is crazy watches over you as if you were of him and already have competence.

-Shut up.

-What happens, are you okay?

-If, can I get up.

-Of course, you are great.

When I got up, I run to hug Alan and my brother, Hewett stared, Hewett hangs his eyes and was about to leave the room, similarly hugged and kissed him on the cheek, Alan did not move, I thank then all three, Alan smiled at Hewett and walked out with my brother.

-Know what happened to me Alan, and please do not lie to me, do not do more.

-I do not know, I do not know.

-Please.

-Did not know that was the heart that was looking, so that is why Rosalba said it felt close, and as for what you did, not know, very few can have so much power and control so fast.

-I did not know what happened.

-If you thought when you were alone, you could have died.

-But no.

-I do not understand how it was done?

-I do not know, just felt I could do the first time that the necklace shines, I knew I could save Monica.

-But that was no your plan right.

-No, she for me.

-It is serious, you are wrong, you know.

-Neither you nor anyone else had a plan, I miss her and it was my fault, I couldn't leave her, stay and do nothing.

-Try to find the heart and if we were looking for her, you had to trust us.

-It would, you lied to me, you had told me, you had this and you did not tell me, she is my mother and we are; do not think we should know.

-Maybe.

-Just maybe.

-You know I'd give my fife for you.

-Do not have to, but I appreciate it.

-Do not ever do it again, do not let us out your plans are a team.

-Thank you for going to me.

-Always be for you, just trust me. Let the room be hungry.

-And my brother.

-Is out with Monica.

We came to the window and see them walk out, as the light of the lamps illuminating the garden, had lights everywhere.

Walk a while as she told me what happened when she was captivated, but did not remember much, she was scared a bit, but happy to be good, she thought for a moment that will not survive.

-Monica I'm sorry I could not do anything, sorry for not helping.

-It is okay Adriel, we could do anything we were in the hands of the witch, and sorry I know you like her sorry.

-You do not have to, do not hang your look, was nothing.

-Sorry, I do not speak it that way.

-Look at me; I do not mind your comment.

Without thinking I take her hand in mine were cold and trembling.

-She is nothing to me; it was crazy that way because I want someone else.

-Really.

-If you can't tell which at the witch.

-Good graces.

Their hands away from mine and we kept walking, take it back, she do not reject my hand, then went back to the house of Alan, arrive the door was open and our hands we were still together, Elmo is a smile came out to watch us, we slowly let go of the hands simulating a little, they came as we walked Monica and me.

-Where is Alan?

-Where else with your sister.

-How is she?

-Fine Monica.

-I'll go see it.

-If I go with you.

-And that angry face of Kalinda, what happened?

-You'll see why keep walking.

-Hello sister, how you feel?

-Perfect, let my fruit is mine alone not true joke grip.

-And he doing there?

-Explained Alan.

-Anything it's just that he did it again.

-Again.

-Yes.

-You misbehave sister.

-Therefore the face of Kalinda is somewhat upset.

-And so how long it takes.

-Few minutes.

-If it's true when I went out was fine.

I said and just give me something to laugh, Hewett sees sleeping on the table like a fool, and he deserved it.

-I can't leave her alone for even a minute.

-Do not exaggerate it is assumed that I scolded you, know you to me.

-If true.

-Monica good to see you, you look great came hug.

-Thanks, friend.

-I missed a lot give us a big headache.

-Well and you say after that scare, I did not know what to do but I'm glad you're okay and you know the witch ran away.

-I certainly do not remember that part, was great.

-Clear was great to see her face in terror.

-What about Hewett e Alan.

-Don't worry about, being right.

But would not say the same of Alan's face was too serious it was logical that he was angry.

-You stay with them, Elmo.

-If I stay in case they need something.

-No better to go to the monastery. Alan told us

-Kalinda and her husband.

-They are good and it will be passed to Kalinda.

-Okay, see you.

-Goodbye and take care of Moni's child.

-Clear.

-Moni goodbye.

-Good-bye friend.

Arrived in half an hour, after the park I take some time off was very cold, but then I saw a light approaching it was Dylan, with a lamp on hand came to pick us, had spent more time in the care that I thought the cameras had been watching me, and sent to him by me, I get off the truck before it hit and give me a sermon, however, gave it to me, Monica walk hand in hand through the halls aimlessly did not know where we were.

-Boy we've all been through tough, but we all end at some point.

-Dylan heavens, not the sermon that everything will be fine you can't, try something else.

-Cleary I will try, we all tried.

Did not know where we were going, we got two huge doors seemed a dining room, but later another smaller door and then later a longer one, entered a small library, I began to read a book just pass the pages.

-What's new in this?

-Read and learn.

-Good great.

Cleary without wanting to read, Monica went with him, the first page does not contain something interesting, just words that I did not understand the five page note anything odd picture of a moon reflected in the water with bright stars, suddenly it seemed that they were moved into the third dimension, I close my eyes for a second and then look again, moved and the stars shone more intensely than before, as if came alive, I closed the book and put it aside but my curiosity turned and follow, past the pages and read but not understand anything, it was like a kind of a tongue twister, I think it was Latin, try to read everything I could, but was giving me sleep, but each time I got tied my eyes closed, I do not like reading because my eyes burned.

Never let the things you start, you think and you'll know the answer, passing through a dark street a light at the end, was the mysterious woman and his strange companion was more gloomy than before, was the entrance a palace there a huge dining room, dark and ugly curtains for my taste, for quieter than they realized my presence, they tied me and took me in front of a strange old man but it seemed the leader, Fear has not just removed the heart to live better, a light shining in my hands realized and there can't leave without a fight with the mystery man, the voice kept saying, do not give up you're something else you're a superhero, we need, you can finish what you start.

-Wake up, come up.

-Rays are killing me.

-Arise now we'll go with more than just lecturing.

-Dylan I have to sleep more, I'm going crazy my dreams are better than real life.

-If good, still have no idea what might be real.

-Well, I going.

-I wait outside in the strike, do not delay others already started, and just need you.

Rushed out into the yard, but before leaving Elmo was waiting for me just before the exit, walk slowly toward him and he stopped.

-Elmo something happens.

-No, it's just that we lack many battles to be waged, many more.

-Why do we fight?

-Fight for ourselves.

-What do you mean, and are doing here?

-You see, most of us are immortals, but there are ways to die, sometimes easier than you think, we now have fewer of us that we were many years ago, sometimes new is born immortal, we can't explain why we are, only one day we'll find out, not everyone is immortal young age is different, you became immortal, does not deteriorate your body stays the same as if no time went on, there are also people with the same powers that are no immortal, sometimes even stronger than us like your sister, she is a risk that can't control her strength, she absorbs their power to touch it, is kept in the lives of others, so it becomes a deadly weapon, something that could destroy us if someone controls it is a danger, of course, you can always change.

-What about me.

-We're not sure I think that has to do with your dreams, appears to be real, serious like seeing the future, but creating it yourself, it is strange but if it just wants you to understand, I lived long enough to know that everything in life can change and you just have to control.

-And if I can't, and who are you so sure about that.

-Sure you I can trust you.

-You.

-Your sister already knows all this Alan told she to now, this bitter, but she has to calm down or it could end the life of all if she wants, but it can only end up with what she desires.

-Thinks she is a problem.

-A problem even for her, of course, Monica is among us, it is not clear like you say she is a difference she can only control the water, unlike your sister who controls everything.

-Let me see, Monica has powers and I did not know.

-Discovered clear what being locked up, it helps her not die she is immortal like us.

-It's a joke right.

-Clear that they tried to kill her, did not give food or water, and had sedated her body resisted that become immortal, but discover the control of water.

-Great, super.

But still, with many questions, I was more confused than before I'm the dumbest of all without powers, as it was improbable my dreams mean something, good dreams are rare always meaning something I like dream to dream, but not if they came true, some are nightmares.

-And you what power you have.

-I well, you see, it's just a little something from nothing.

-And we are waiting, where we.

-Just outside.

-Of course, have a few visits, then came more as time passes and we need.

-We need it.

Unanswered and I came out behind him, opened the door and went outside, I saw him was on the other side, well it is fast, but I did not know what happened, where many people all around the courtyard forming a huge square, how they could be so many people were there, knew several of them, were the same that we in the class teacher who taught us to fight, but others not, walk and put me next to anyone who I did not know he was.

-We seem to complete and continued the testing.

The teacher was in the great courtyard, the wind blew hard I could not move from the could but the rest was as usual, they carried black coats as if everyone had agreed, for a moment so far failed to distinguish who was who, a storm is coming but it was too early to know what time, as I slept, was early morning, the teacher gave the order to fight, Elmo was good that barely touched the ground, the teacher yell a name.

-Andrew.

Too fast for him and seem as strongest, appeared Elmo would soon give in, but suddenly the new uttered something.

-Aduro. (Bourn)

At that time that he pronounce beat Elmo with such force that sent him flying till the other side, he writhed in pain, and I stay private for a moment and then Elmo.

-Aqua ae. (Water)

Stood, I could hear some laughter, but he hit back from afar it was like a whirlwind to hit him again, but it was water, got up quickly but it was incorporated Kalinda were two against Elmo, to continue the fight, after showing that he had, giving way to one of the students of the monastery if had looked on at times, also demonstrated a good ability to fight, then it was time for Dylan against the student, but then Dylan against Samara, was terrible, Samara was very fast for him but although he gave a good fight.

We were very attentive, but I died laughing and shaking like a leaf, then it was the turn of Curran they had more energy than others, were more cruel than others end up with everything, they had apparently all had powers or something if, I did not know what was happening then, the teacher named Monica it was his turn, advance one step but who that was beside me and pulled me back, she had never fought so would it hurt her.

-Without consideration.

-Of course teacher.

I twisted stomach, I thought that hurt Curran seemed crueler to my consideration, not afraid to hit a girl, Curran began to attack Monica but she evaded him very well, the teacher was around.

-Monica without fear attack your opponent as you see, your mind knows what to do.

-Sure I will try.

-Try is not enough.

Finally she attacked him weakly and he returned the attack aggressively as expected, she struggled as she had seen but he was too strong, she fell many times more that I could count, but she did not surrender was still fighting, in one corner was a small puddle or rain the day before, she toke advantage and made the water dirty hit Curran so hard that he fells across the pavement but incorporated and the counter attack with the same movement, she eluded by chance but it was better.

-Is good. Made fun of him

-Adriel's your turn, child.

I approached thinking that Curran would destroy me and would be nothing left of me, he began to approach me with a smirk and suddenly walked away from the place, left in from of Monica and without thinking she attacked me and I fell like an old rag, I woke up and I hear laughter behind me, for my fall.

-Come on kid.

-I do not want to hurt her.

Began, she learned very quickly my movements, the more I attacked but defended it from me to the point that she thought the girl was not weak, I thought, she attack with the same water that Curran and sent me flying, laughter follow me around flying like the wing, I get up again and I remember that she was sickly immortal, then the real game started I remember a word of old book.

-*Terra-ae. (Ground)*

While the attack she fell to the floor.

-Are you okay?

-Do not trust.

Got up and continue, did not realized what I had done, but she continued with his water play, me with my memories of words, as if by magic and tried to remember what it said the book, I repeated in my mind but only remember that world, and the teacher stopped us.

-Sarah it's your turn, good job Monica.

-Hello brother, Monica beat you up.

-Hi Dainka thought to be home of Alan.

-If well, Hewett is fine, in fact that the other side with Alan.

-Let begin sister.

-Clear just be careful you do not let unconscious.

-Not a chance, I do not you can kiss Dani.

-I do not need.

-Do not use your powers Sarah.

-Of course teacher.

A blow but she did the same, and against attest, she was too strong for me, although she was not hurt me, she tried to control himself, but is stronger and more dangerous really has too much to control, but to me it is easier for her because I am his brother and do not want to hurt me, she really has everything under control, but really what would happen if she gave herself completely and would destroy everything as it was, if really a danger as Elmo said, and what we could do about it, kill her.

She knows what their limit, suddenly entered the master and I try to withdraw from the fight and then watch and said continuous, we both against her, this time it was more difficult for her to win us, but his strength increased as she defended, that they came about to fight in pairs, without looking at who, just simulating a real battle, but really if it was a battle, real blows were heard and felt real for training, almost fainted but still, I found myself with Alan and Monica, the two together attacked me and as one of students alike, but help of my sister, arrived in time take off the student, the teacher and Alan against it and like Monica, whether we knew that she would be better controlled but it seemed that only had so much energy, does not even know who to use his power and did not know what had, that was my impression, do not look exhausted but if I was and Monica as well.

-Use their power, try to use them to control it, remember everything is within you.

If clear it all sound a cartoon but real, Andrew hit me and I fell and approached Monica to help me but Alan attacked and shot with me; my sister was in front, I did not even realize how close it was, Alan and she throw a look of hatred.

-Not you see that are on the floor, she just helped him.

-I know and that is why attack should never lose concentration, can die if they stop.

-If it is just a practice do not have to hurt.

-Not only that is real and they have to learn.

We got up and went backwards doing with the teacher, try to get me I but the teacher stooped me.

-Know I think we will continue training.

-Sure with pleasure.

Start the fight, she seemed to be comfortable not a hint of exhaustion in his face, in either of he, had spend a little but when I turn my head on my shoulder, everyone was on the shore, did not understand why they did that, was so fast, the teacher told us that we should go the same way, he look too strong for her and he had already won before on my sister, but although this time it would be different.

He was quick and that was good but every day she grew stronger, through she was good and not easily upset, the power she had was stronger than her, one could say that the power control her, a defending noise was heard, as grinding that bothered the ears, look the teacher and everyone was on the floor with ears covered except Monica and me, noise does not affect as but we listened, it seems that Alan had a shield that shone and seemed not to hurt, but I did not know, the longer it took, non understood why nothing happened to us but the noise was louder and louder and began to hurt as and the teacher told us all something.

-Feducia(trust)

Everyone understood, except me, and apparently it works and did not bother them more, and while they continue to fight, the teacher said I had confidence and if it was, the noise did not bother us again, he said we had to endure his power would be better for us, we practiced with our partial shield.

-Great you learn fast Sarah, let's see how good you are.

Fell to the ground the noise end, too much air and leaves flew everywhere, Alan began to use his power, was indeed very strong and fast, my sister was in trouble, continued their tight, now I understand that we are on the edge all, they are very strong, but Hewett had told me that many here are, Alan including.

-He is teaching your sister, she did not know what their powers, whether she is learning and we also, are all strong but she is more, just do not know. (Hewett told me)

-You give Sarah.

-No, not yet, *aduro. (Bourn)*

The wind stopped and Alan remained in the ground, I could tell he felt pain, but trying to get up.

-*Rutilo. (Flashes)*

-Can't be, as possible, we had never seen him do that.

-Hewet what did you say?

-Did not know he could.

-What?

-Observed.

Could only see him stand up and his hands came out some light some flashes that hit my sister, she fell.

-What happened? (I ask)

-Well done Alan. (Dylan yell)

-He won teacher.

-*Quippe. (Undoubtedly Hewett)*

-Brilliant.

-*Recedo ere. (Withdraw)*

-Control it girl.

-Not control you Alan, you're great.

-Thanks girl.

-Well he actually controlled, I think it will not be so difficult William.

-Whether it seems Andrew.

-What are you talking about? (I ask)

-Nothing.

All went, my sister talked to Monica and me with Hewett, the only that was annoying was Kalinda, apparently she does not like the idea of endangering his brothers, she thinks my sister is a danger, that can destroy us all, but I do not think that way, I trust my sister.

-I can speak one minute teacher.

-Kalinda clears what happens.

-I think you should not be risking much to my brother she is a danger and you know it.

-You know that can't happen, we need someone to teach her and can control and Alan is the strongest of all and it has shown.

-But teacher.

-No, but it can be controlled.

-I do not think; she is a danger we must end this.

-What are you talking, they want to end my sister can't do this.

-We will make what we can, that not you see, that this killing us.

-You will do not hurt.

-Clear that we do not do damage to your sister she is special.

-Teacher.

-*kalinda consisto-ere. (Enough is enough)*

-Do not do anything to your sister, I leave.

I could not say anything to my sister I was too sad about it, they do not believed in her, but I do, still talking my sister and Monica and I approached Alan.

-It is true what it meant Kalinda.

-Are you talking about?

-She wants my sister die, that's the best.

-She is wrong, I would never let something happen to your sister, she told you.

-Heard her talk with the teacher.

-Is best that you bring home Monica, and see you later.

-Kalinda we need to talk.

-Yes of course, what happens?

-In private.

-Clear right.

-In what were you thinking, not should say nothing, when you learn to be too quiet.

-I'm not mistaken, I do not want anything to happened, and she's getting into with you and Hewett that is not done.

-Are you talking about?

-It makes you fight and the two are in love with her.

-Do not know what you mean.

-If you are and you better forget it, once you die, I will not lose you again, this happening again.

-She was your friend and saved us all.

-She kill you and almost destroyed everything, it will be the same.

-Do not know.

-Better die.
-No, never let that happens.
-Alan.
-Enough Kalinda.
-Sed quanion (Why, why)
-Quia promisio-ons soror -oiris. (Because I promised, sister)
-Interrupt.
-Iterum. (Again)
-Certainly not Sarah, we're leaving.
-Something happen Alan?
-No nothing everything is fine.

Star to change the climate the air was more intense water seemed to fall with more force every time, we say goodbye to everyone and went to his house, and he has always remained locked in his books, I know I like to read but he was obsessed with the books of the past, and leafing through every time, trying to find an answer to what happens, and I just spun throughout the house which I found very interesting, almost do not ask Alan about what happened, but was a little sad I never want to hurt someone still giving hanging around was s little desperate.
-Sarah, Are you okay?
-If I'm okay, just miss my home and my friends have time do not go out with them.
-Well, you can talk and if you can get away with it.
-You will be watching.
-Know that if.
-If I guessed.
-But not only that you care, that's right.
-Is true, I can ask you something.
-Depends.
-Depends.
-If I'm not be angry, if you can ask.
-I do not want to hurt someone but.
-But what?
-Men who tried to hurt Monica they disappeared.

-You want to know if they are dead.

-Yes clear that if.

-Well I think are not, only went or rather that send them to a place not too sweet.

-Where?

-Is known by various names but they are in the abyss.

-Hell.

-No really, no they can emerge from the abyss of hell can't leave.

-They return right.

-If so we must be ready, you should be ready.

-I have fear, I will not kill anyone especially you, do not think I could bear.

Late in answering, I would save her and all, she's strong hold over the powers, know where to get the strength to live and not be crumbled, but I was afraid at the moment, and if she really kill us all, which is what the bad guys really wanted to do with her, with the necklace, the heart and his brother, who she had to deal with all that, it was his destiny of all, she could change everything, despite the efforts of others, some if it withdrew to a safer place for not knowing how far his power could reach or mine, to where I could get mine, could equal mime I close my eyes and concentrate.

-And Sarah you must do.

-Do what.

-You can control your power.

-They are afraid to me true.

-Some do.

-And you.

-No... well if a little, but I believe in you.

-Thanks I fear I have the same.

-I Know you know very well hit me, you're great.

-You won.

-For a little, just barely.

-Your sister is angry with me.

-*Sicuti! (So it is)*

-As you said is Latin a.

-Yes it is.

-And you said.

-So it is.

-So it is that.

-*Sicuti means so it is.*

-Clear, I could teach you.

-You know what you should know.

-Only a few words, is nothing.

-*Postquam. (Then)*

-Of course.

-Later on.

-I learn.

-And I believe that if.

-How old are you Alan?

-The same as you, well one more.

-Since when?

-Not long ago.

-Okay.

-Well for some twenty years.

-Then you forty years, are old, my mother who old she was.

-I am an old man that's what you think.

-Yes, you could be my father.

Swallowing that was the most feared and do not answer.

-I'm sorry I did not bother you.

-Okay I'll tell you that, well she had more than me.

-Greater that you.

-The same age only long.

-As much.

-Long time but do not know how much she never said.

-Joking right, and my father?

-No, never joke and your father was no immortal was the same age, but speaks no more of it, back to the monastery suck everything will be better.

-Everything is normal for you.

-Not all, you is something new.

So silly, do not answer, if not that distressed and change the subject, I should not say anything.

-Not want to go to the monastery I go with my friends, strange school and work.

-You can't, not yet…

-You must learn to control yourself.

-*Postquem. (Then)*

-Learn quickly and not heard.

-True.

-Well tomorrow I take you to the restaurant and can do whatever you want later.

-What I want.

-Clearly if.

-Fanning waterfalls.

-If as long as I am around.

-Go to another state.

-I would go with you or would send someone else.

-To scream in the middle of the street.

-You scream.

-Have time I do not.

-And you scream in the middle of the street.

-Only once.

-When.

-Time ago.

-I will be rid of you no way, be watching me all the time.

-So its girl I can't leave you alone and you know it.

-Would not be better if I died and everything is over.

-Is a joke, I never will leave you alone, I promise to be near you always.

I hug very strong she understood the significance of the hold close.

-Really thanks for everything.

-Everything will be okay Sarah, do not keep watch.

-I do not believe you.

Nothing is Forever

While the next day he took me to the restaurant as expected he would leave me his Hammer and left with Elmo, he would not watch me, trust that I did not make a nonsense, I finish shift at the restaurant, my brother came later, if they would come out later, my friends came and get out, we walked, felt the heat of the sun sometimes went out and warmed a little, but the clouds covered their at times, stranger was always very cold and had been cold, but the sun had risen and was very nice, the aroma of the forest was unmistakable, warm paradise full of flowers of new life, still walking this time alone in circles in the same place at prices warm the day, I thought it was just my imagination, but I enjoyed it thought it were.

Hoped that this is not over, it was so beautiful I was not a monster not a weapon demolish as Kalinda thought, and some of those in the monastery, perhaps I could create life, we sat on a rock to watch the sun coming through the holes of the tress, that beautiful scenery hides this place before the world, but it was hard to climb even for me, close my eyes for a moment and then sighed reopened and I lay on the ground, was warm and seemed to be among cotton, the smell of flowers was spectacular still on the ground when suddenly a shadow darkened my sight, I closed my eyes and clam and when I saw that unique smile that eased my hear and I smiled too.

-Know the teacher would have given anything to see what I see out.

-You saw it, wait you see?

-The sun the heat is great, you change the climate.

-Wait what… only thought of one day so.

-That's all you did was great, wanted to stand but could not, did nothing wrong, just the opposite and see that your friends enjoy it, how you feel?

-I was scare but not anymore, I feel calm at the moment I understand what I am and my friend do not fear me, they like the sun and look at his child is happy.

-I thing you know everything will be better if you can control your power.

-What are you doing here, I though you would let me alone all day.

-Thought to, but did not believe that nobody would notice that there is sun in this part of the forest and knew it would be you.

-I trough you mind.

-To change the weather is great I like the heat I would not miss. Was approaching, he sat staring at my face and I his, while the forest still warm, then lay down next to me, we were looking at the sky and everything was perfect and I felt so close to me.

-You really are extraordinary your smell is equal to the woods you know.

Did not respond and knew it was not the first that said it, but I smiled a little, just like his brother.

-I brought something special look open it.

-It is.

-Do not ask just open it.

-More gifts.

-Yeah well, you liked this one more.

-Indeed.

-Like you certainly do not mistake me.

-Is clearly an album she's my mom and us, you and your brother.

-If, like me…

-I know that is not the time, but I have hidden much about your mom, but it was hard to say something like that.

-Love her very much.

-Look was long ago, never can forget about people, but you can lived with his memory and continue.

-What happened between you?

-It's just that she fell in love with someone else, and I her, we were only friends, but she always knew that I loved her but did not tell, she knew it could not lie.

-Who is my father?

-Forgiveness but I'm not ready to tell you that, maybe then I'll tell you it was my friend.

-Was.

-Yeah well things change like the feelings.

-Feelings can change.

-If they can change everything can change.

-You've ever changed.

-If more than one.

I got up and put my face in front of his and look into his eyes, he did not move it seemed he was not breathing; caress my face and look at my eyes, finally got up and hugged me with great force.

-I love you girl and do not know how, thought this is not good. Do not answer just closed my eyes and a few tears rolled down

my cheeks and sighed hug me more strongly than ever, but could hear his heart racing, no matter that my friend were nearby was just a hug, he got up quickly leaving me on the floor and stayed crouched for a moment, I got up and now I hugged him, but he became very distant as if someone or something forced him to leave, perhaps the bother but I did not nothing, I love looking at his heir, looked at him and continued with the distant gaze, waking among the trees and disappeared for a while just told me to stay there with friends and not let alone.

-Sarah what happens?

-I do not know Monica, just said to wait here will better be ready.

-If, I will say to the girls do not away.

-Yes you tell them to come and eat something; you better are near. The girls could understand what happening and my brother arrived at the time not say anything he was comfortable enjoying the warmth as well as all of us.

-And that you have this where did you get.

-Was a gift from Alan?

-Sister know I do not think that is right whatever gives you and me who.

-You're right…

-Also is yours take save.

-Said she used to stay at home sometimes but they we were friends, spend time with him and left many things there, things that when married could not go because they are present and were things she did not want to go with it but wanted a lot and even de dress belonged.

-Is strange that my mother spent much time with him.

-If I know.

-May be different. Monica said

-Different like, I'm not sure. I paused

-Sure friend do not wish for.

-Yes, but Hewett he's great and he think I fell something and do not want to hurt him.

-Yes and not think about is regret, wait you actually taste your kiss friend.

Should not comment on that it went wrong are totally different.

-I do not want to complicate anything I did not know he was doing… but.

-Do not do, he kiss you, not you to him. Monica kept saying

-No matter.

-Yeah right forget it.

Pass a while and Alan retuned from the forest, was still perfect color loneliness were the ideal forest, while walking unbuttoned his jacket and his shirt a little, the sun beat on his chest and my friends watched me and laughter were notorious but not scandalous, I settle for a better view check also her eyes smiled seemed to know what I was thinking, sat beside me and I felt somewhat uncomfortable, it seems to me to kiss him at that time, approached me and whispered.

-Deserve another chance.

-If true, I love you but have feared do not want to lose you.

-You will not lose me I will always be for you no matter what happens I'll be around forever.

-Promise.

-Clearly I promise, forever.

-Yes, but you know I am not immortal and someday I die.

-Not think about it Sarah, for now is far from that.

-If true.

But not believed knew the end was near, he smiled and asked.

-Afraid.

-No, I am not afraid of time, but not to fear of loneliness, say as you can live without someone, when you're really love, if I were you and you were to die, die with you.

-Would do the same thing would die with you.

My breath stopped my thoughts became words of pain.

-Not happen and maybe you're immortal and do not know.

-As you say?

-Yes well, will not check it through a dagger or something really.

-Of course not, but it would not be a bad idea.

-Just do not think about those things.

-A that you went to the forest.

-It was just a friend.

-It's all good.

-Actually yes.

Eventually returned to normal the lives are beginning to agitate around us, the temperature began to drop and it was getting colder my concentration was over.

-Nothing is forever Sarah.

-I know, be better to leave.

Was foolish to continue, we had to return all was cold and we had to put on our coats as well him, we start to walk.

-Were you going?

-Home.

-If good, will be more difficult if you go out there I think it better to the other side will be shorter.

-You laugh.

-I do not.

-I want to go home of my mother, I did not want this.

-That.

-Good, I want a normal life I want my life.

-Can't have everything in life.

-Already know it is what I have to do but meanwhile I want to continue with my life.

-We'll talk then I'll let you in your home with your brother and I hope no mistake I'll go to the monastery.

-Thanks.

Was so foolish that I could not change her mind, live it at home his brother came later and Monica seemed to stay with them and Hewett, do not looked like a good idea but there was not option, I went to the monastery had new news, sad for everyone but I learned something new today.

-Teacher.

-Alan what happened?

-She is fine, we all are, and I had a meeting with Gregory.

-No news.

-Yes know how they do.

-What find out from his brother of Andrew?

-Is dead, they murder.

-Holy heaven and you know why?

-Know they took away his energy powers to give them to their leader to whether to continue living.

-Is worse than I thought, wait a minute.

-Send for Andrew please Vanessa.

-Course teacher.

A second spend and Andrew came.

-*Notuis-a-um. (My friend)*

-*Quemadmodum sed. (Happens)*

-Your brother.

-*Quomodo. (How)*

-They killed.

-*Virtus-utis notua-a-um. (Strength friend)*

-Thought so but was hoping that it was not real, you know that plan.

I put my hand on his shoulder but nothing could comfort his pain, his only brother was dead, understood his pain as he felt, ever go through the same thing, no words you can say to someone to comfort his pain, the pain never goes away always remains, time does not heal the wounds, the pain subsides but the memories of the heart still, the pain is always immensity of the memories, you can never compare the pain a person feels when he loses a love one.

-Andrew will stop them.

-I hope so, many of our friends are dying have to do something.

-We also have another problem.

-You talk about Alan.

-Teacher… Gregory mentioned that think releasing a demon of the abyss.

-Which devil you know.

-No, nor when.

-We must prepare.

-Teacher does not want to say anything to the boys.

-Three of them will not know but everyone else will.

-Okay teacher.

-Filius-ii, potentia-ae is-ea-id aeteher-is eter. (Son, force he is in heaven)

-We will do.

-Find ways to overcame.

-How, we know that the devil is it can be anyone.

-Fedes fidei filius-ii. (Faith son)

-Benignus-a-u, (Okay)

We left I had to get home to Sarah, my brother still did not know that we faced, not even we knew, was considering leaving to do their stuff but I think it will not the best time for that, I can't leave her alone, to be near her, this time would came faster I driving a motorcycle, would come in a couple of minutes, between without knocking and they were talking together and watching a horror movie, my brother was having fun, to be a lot to not have a normal life deserved this good time, not tell anything right now, Matias was his friend and was dead, I do not think they heard me.

-Hi guys.

Everyone screamed and hugged each other like crazy; popcorn flew and outreaches to catch.

-Alan never touches.

-I'm sorry I thought you had heard through.

-You have not noticed that nobody listen when you walk, especially me.

-She's right.

-Of course.

-Want to sit with us? Asked Monica

-Yes of course, if accompanied.

-Alan wants something to eat?

-No.

-If clear right beck.

-We just want something.

-I'll go. <<I say>>

-No I'll just go to the kitchen, be well let me go alone.

-Which is what they desire?

-Just bring some nachos has been years that not eat one, with much cheese.

-Do not overdo my sister Hewett.

-No this fine now I bring.

-With you friend.

-Clear.

I stay near to the kitchen door and listen to what them was saying, talking about us.

-I thought there would came, would leave you alone for a while.

-I know I thought so too.

-This is hot the two brothers want you.

-Do not laugh.

-Is not joke and its crazy almost killed us in shock.

-Never heard, if it is true when it comes is like a ghost.

-And you, what happens between you and my brother?

-Nothing.

-Nothing, not deceive me he will like you, and something happens.

-Well do not know I feel I like, but not know what happens.

-Speak with him.

-Not leave it, I want to, I want him to tell me I wish he say so just that.

-We are ready.

Left the kitchen I was sitting on the couch with the kids, spend time and the movie was over, went out to talk to my brother and told him what had happened, is very depressed,

Matias was his friend were know for some time, and had spent much time investigating the disappearance until he disappeared, my brother's fault it for not being around him when he need it, but could do nothing were in different places, also had to talk to Sarah but I dared, so I asked my brother to take care of her, I turned away for her and I would go with the boys to find the way to destroy the demon that beset us, I asked him to let her go to school as she wanted to continued his normal life, he accepted.

I felt silly telling her that I loved her, but the thought of my brother close to her and I confess and I regretted having said it, though she said as loved me, but is having fun with my brother and he had every right to be with her, I do not interfere, and is my brother never fight with him, I'd better go and I forget some of her, left the house without saying goodbye to them, it was too late, Hewett would stay and live with them, be well with him I got on the bike I went the monastery, and I asked the teacher to let me go with Andrew he refused at first thought I would commit a foolishness, but eventually accepted I had no intention of risking my friends, I was very aware of what was, we would go three, would accompany us too Curran.

-Are you sure you want to go brother? Ask my sister

-If I am.

-Is for her?

-No it's me.

-I do not understand!

-There is nothing to understand.

-I do not want to lose you.

-You will not lose me, I'll be fine.

-I hope, when you leave.

-In half an hour and Kalinda take care.

-You take care, you better came back soon.

-I will.

-Alan does not do anything stupid and caring for my brother please.

-I'll do, nothing will happen to your brother Dylan promise.

-A hug brother.

-Sure came here angry girl, I promise to be well okay.

After for a while I noticed that Alan was not there, ask for it and Hewett told me was gone, had important things to do and it was all he said, I went to the room trying not to get angry, locked it and put my head on the door a few seconds and them to bed without looking at anything else, in light of the moon and stars through the window, then I lay down just when I locked out the window to see the stars I saw hem sitting in the chair beside the table with his book in hand, I am a bit scared after seeing him there, had made no noise, thank goodness I did not say anything while watching me.

-Hello how are you?

-Well I thought you'd gone.

-If I left and I'll going, just could not leave without saying goodbye, are waiting for me, look down there.

-It is true is Curran and Andrew.

-If they are and know you better open the door.

I opened the door but he kept on starring at me, and then the book, well I didn't know what to do so I went towards the bed and I sit down, it was late so I wouldn't lay down, I was tired but not much. He started reading out loud and I lay in bed putting a lot of pillows behind my head to be able to see him, and got closer and kept reading, I didn't pay attention after a few minutes. But then I started to listen like he was inviting me to listen, I closed my eyes and started remembering where I've heard this history before. It sounded so familiar about a treasure in the deepest of the sea where all dreams comes true. I opened my eyes and I told him that I've heard this story before, but I can't remember where.

-Close your eyes.

And he continue with the reading and I started remembering my house, It was cozy and peaceful, and all of the suddenly I saw my brother and a women beside me and the lecture continues, and then I looked where the voice was coming from, and then I saw him reading to us and then I opened my eyes and looked at him.

-You remember, right?

-Yes, but how?

-The thing is that your mind erased those memories purposely and it doesn't want to remember, all you need is time and everything will come little by little, and then you'll have all your answers.

-Why you were reading?

-I liked to read and your mother likes me to read to you guys.

-But why I can't remember my dad?

-He wasn't near us when we would read. He wasn't jealous because your mother and I were best friends. And your mother and your brother liked me to be with them.

-Did you guys ever fight for mom?

-I'm not going to lie if we did, it was my friend and lied to us, at the time they were looking for her, and she had the power as you.

-What do they want from us?

-Look, there are some that don't have that power and they want it from us.

-How would they get the power from us?

-Killing us and taking our hearts from us.

-That's the only way they can get it, that's why they want to kill us, some of the immortal have disappear lately. And some people that have some kind of power and some friends too.

-And do you know who the one who wants it is?

-When your mother died we found out when it was too late. He pretended to be our friends, but later he died.

-Are you sure about that?

-that what we think, if not he would be too old and I hope it doesn't happen the same...

-And don't you think that if he's not dead, he would be strong?

-If he killed he is strong. But he can't be immortal and getting old slowly.

-If he is not too old, what about if there is some one new?

-If is true everything could happened.

-Yeah, that's how it is.

He got silence and hugged me, I closed my eyes and started listen to my heart that got faster and faster.

-You should get some sleep, is kind of late and I think tomorrow they are going to the hospital for Mr. Robles.

-That's true, it takes time to hill.

-Yes, that's how it is.

-Well, where are you going to sleep?

-You don't mind if I stay here, promise not to bother.

I fixed myself without saying anything, I took out some pillows and he was about to stand up but I hug him so he could stay. He stood up and turned off the light and he lay by me and hugged me but I couldn't sleep, I had another question for him.

-Listen who's my dad?

-I knew you were going to ask that question, I'll tell you his name. He made a pause and looked at me and then he put his hand down.

-So, what it is?

-Well, his name was Patrick.

-That's quite name, what happened

-No more questions go to sleep.

-But I want to know.

-It's better that you know, even though you know, you wouldn't understand.

-Serious.

-I told you mother that I would never tell you so go to sleep.

-Okay, only one more.

He stood up and looks into my eyes he hugged me and gave a kissed in my forehead.

-Okay, what is it?

-I forgot

-Okay, go to sleep.

-Okay

In the next morning I woke up, but he wasn't in bed and breakfast was ready in the room.

-I think I can get use to all this.

-Sure Sarah.

-Monica, what are you doing here?

-Well, I came here to wake you up but somebody got here first, who brought it Hewett.

-I don't know

-You don't know

-Alan stayed here last night well until I feel sleep.

-Serious, and what happed?

-Nothing

-Nothing, I don't believed you

-I'm serious, he read to me and then we talked for little bit and I fell asleep and this morning I wake up and he wasn't here.

-Well, hurry up finishes your breakfast.

-Of course, I'll catch up later.

-Yes, take your time

I got ready to go for Mr. Robles to the hospital we got in the Alan's Hammer, Hewett went with us to the hospital and my brother and Monica already saw us. When we got to the hospital, the doctor Hugo was waiting for us, he was checking up on Mr. Robles. He said that he would be out of the hospital after all the paper work. It's not necessary for him to stay, especially when he doesn't like it here. We signed the papers to go home. Mr. Robles like alone so we didn't know where he want to go, but we didn't asked him either.

-Well, this are the last papers of the day, he has to return in a week to see how he's doing, and if he feels bad, come right away.

-Of course I'm not coming back to this hospital doctor Hugo.

-Did we treat you that bad?

-No, but it was a long time being in here.

-Well, we'll see you later.

I went out with the doctor to ask him if he really was ok, and he responded that he was ok, but it was better we take him with us. The doctor knew him and he knew that when he gets alone, he gets depressed. Before we took him to the house, we took him to the restaurant to see the new changes, I was hoping he wouldn't say anything like he use to. We parked the truck in the parking lot in front of the restaurant, and my brother parked my in the back of the restaurant.

-Surprise Mr. Robles

-Well, what do you think?

-Welcome boss

-Sarah, what happened to my restaurant? What did you do with it?

-I told him that we made some changes.

-I did tell them but this is too much.

-Well, we all helped

-Mr. Robles, we all helped so it wasn't that expensive

-Monica, you too? He thought about asking

-Well, yes

-Everyone helped, even the neighbor helped a little

-Come over little one

-Yes, sure

-Good job

-Seriously

-It's great I've always wanted big minors in the back, and speakers instead of CD player, thank you everyone. We all hugged him and welcome him again, although I was surprised too, it couldn't been worse, we ate, and he looked happy with all of us, and everyone pay for him, it wasn't a party, he won't give anything, he needed to get back what he gave in the hospital in the restaurant my brother helped in the tables, there wasn't may people, but as it was getting late, the restaurant got full, and the music perfect and the environment too. I started helping my brother, I haven't work for days, and he serves it. He didn't let home helped him; he said that in another time. We stayed there until 10 o'clock we still needed to decide where Robles was going stay. We all help during cleaning. Hewett kept talking with Mr. Robles; it was only my brother, Monica and I the last. The rest of the workers were gone already. I got a lollypop from the candy jar and started eating it.

- Lollypop is delicious sister

-Yes, of course, I'm sorry

-No problem, but share.

-Of course

-Well guys its better if you guys take me home, as you can see I don't have a car.

-Talking about that, I think you should stay with someone.

-No, I won't be better than in my house…

-Don't think so, you should stay in my house and Adriel would feel better if we have you close.

Hewett looked at me, he didn't agree with the idea.

-I don't think it's convenient.

-You, see this guy agree with me.

-What I mean is that, it's dangerous to stay the three of you alone, after what happened

-I don't think nothing would happen, we know how to take care of ourselves, and you know it.

-Sarah, it's not a good idea it's dangerous

-No, he would go with us

-I agree with my sister and I want to go back to my house

-You guys can't be alone was.

So mad that he didn't noticed that he raised his voice and no one has seen him that mad.

-I'm sorry, it just that you guys shouldn't go back alone,

-We know that's why Monica is staying and you too, and we all be more at the house will be fine, and each one will have their own space.

-Well you guys decide you should take me home place.

-Don't be a Childs Mr. Robles, you will go with us.

-Ok let's go. Monica said

Hewett didn't say anything until we got home; he got out of the truck and opens the door. He was faster than me. I couldn't say anything and behind us was my brother. I open the door; the house was a little cold. I turn the chimney and he was still in silence. Mr. Robles was resting. I went to my bed, it was my moms, I did several turn and then I went out and into the kitchen for cup of milk and then I walked for a will but return to the bedroom. I lay down and I saw the moon, and then I fell asleep.

-We see you at the school Adriel.

-Of course.

-And Hewett.

-He left, he had some things to do and Mr. Robles is or he is with the neighbors, and win be there until we get back

-Great he will be busy talking to them, since they have a lot to talk about.

-We see you at the school.

-Good bye friend.

I took Alan's Hammer, I use it for everything, and I got into the class room early I had a lot to turn since I missed a lot of days, I got into the classroom and Hewett was there, I got surprise but not a lot, I sat down and he sit down by me but I ignored him, at the end of

Class, I left in hurry to the classroom but he was there also and in all of the classes

-Hewett, Are you following me?

-I didn't want to go to school

-I don't believe you.

-Alan wanted to keep an eye on you.

-Seriously, where is he at?

-I don't know

- Of course.

-That's I haven't talk to him, I might call him later.

-Well, I have another class and then I'll go to the restaurant.

-What a coincidence, I have the same as you.

-Yeah right.

-You know what I want it to be near you is like being a teacher and student, but is more fun like a student, look at all the girls.

-Great go with them.

-I would do it alone.

We and the days the next few days were the same. Life always changes, always different from what we think, but is fabulous, even though it has pain and suffering and responsibilities. How can we choose the best, if we know that we can't escape from things that we know we never will.

I am a machine of destruction perhaps I should never have known which was my power, nor know his limits, sometimes not to hurt someone's best to stay away, it will be difficult but it will be better, difficult at first, with the time everything might change some day, some moment.

Every moment every minute marries second it will be warm, but for the time being it will be bitter, every day that it spends is a normal day one day as that had before meeting Alan, not even and Alan ordered my things with Elmo almost Christmas was the covered street of ice and some days with snow, but almost all the time was not looking at it for three weeks it was in the school and in the work as earlier everything was normal.

My brother kept on going out with Monica they were inseparable almost it was not going out with, so attached to her who for moments was thinking that he had forgotten about me, I did not believe that it would be so quick, thought that it would be some day but not so fast, mister Robles had returned to his house it was much better, sometimes he was visiting m neighbors misters Gonzalez, my brother with Monica was looking happier than I, although it was accompanied of Hewett and sometimes it was going out with my friends, was not the same he was missing I was not known that it was happening.

Had Elmo gone out of the village a few days ago, they had murdered immortal some to the surroundings and they were investigating more closely of that, I wanted to help, it is only that had bothered so much and did not know since, what it was so bad to be angry? Here also it was quite well, was well we not have any problems, one week before Christmas, while walk on the park, manage to see a well-known car, it was so similar to that of an old friend, but I it do not believe that, there can be others it is only a conscience, the whole day happened and when I finish our shift in the restaurant.

We go to the refuge of the destitute persons in this time. The government was obtaining them a place for them, but he needed volunteers to serve was assisting it. This day was so tired that I went out to taking some fresh air, it was snowing there, out look at the light of a car, and it was approaching towards me I did not put attention kept on breathing the air.

-Please get up.

-I think you are crazy get away from me, disappears.

-Not do it and you know it'll follow you until you decide to talk to me.

-What do you want?

-Talk.

-There is nothing to say.

-Know that if, perhaps an explanation.

-The excuses do not work for me and you know.

-Yes I know but please I need you to listen, not come to fight.

-And your girlfriend's car.

-And I'm not with her.

-Are tired of you.

-No, I do it.

-Yeah right, out of my life but never go near my.

That came in my brother was worried about me, realizing the person who was in the car, was furious and run, he got out the car and said he need to talk to us, but my brother angry do not let him, he said that if he approached me he would hit and send him to jail, I agree with them.

-You better leave and never come back.

-Sarah forgives me.

My brother did not stand and hit him in the face, as expected knocked him down and stated bleeding, my brother stopped, it could kill it he gave another blow.

-Away from me and do not follow me.

-I've been fallowing.

I sighed and took my arm only.

-Come inside, let it.

-If not worth.

-Are okay?

-Kidding me better than ever, ever want to smash his face to you ex, you're fine beautiful?

-If I am.

-Sure.

-If, hey good blow.

-Thanks.

-You know you could have killed he is not like us.

-Yes I know but I gave him slowly.

-Slowly left him bleeding.

-Richard comes up to you if you tell me.

-Yes I will, but I'll be fine, super hero going home.

-Do not mock.

-Clearly I do not toddler.

-That told me not long ago as growth.

-Know you grew up without noticing.

-Do not get sentimental, smiles sister.

When I got home I seemed colder than I thought, stranger, I felt like I do not belong to this place, I felt unfurnished and even although only had about my brother, I knew I needed something and today's meeting was strangely weird, the past returned, reminded me how stupid I was when I was near him, and I still am, to love him, but his departure was like a suicide to my heart, Richard left without saying goodbye, like Alan's departure, saying nothing, know you're busy trying to save his own, but it's hard to say goodbye, goodbye is not complicated like Richard and Alan did the same they left, what is different is that Richard went with his uncle to another place not to say he has fallen in love with someone else and had married while being my boyfriend.

The boy was older than me with six years, I was only sixteen was a fool, spent three years he left with her to his uncle's house to escape my questioning, only after a call sorry just happened and not like but pass, good the past is past, now wants to be daring to come here, which is intended you better not follow the thought of that is my past.

Understanding what Alan said about the past witch, pastes a sigh, and missed more.

-Sister wakes' not thinking about that dumb.

-That of course not.

-I know you think about Alan.

-Good if a little.

-He loves you, it's just that he has worked to do and you know.

-If it had been dismissed but it is so hard to say goodbye, I could have gone with him had been able to help.

-Sarah even knows you do not control your powers well and you could hurt yourself and him, do not bother but true.

-That funny, but he should call and Hewett tells me nothing except that this well.

-Really quiet sister, he's fine and you'll see that he call, I will ask her to marry me.

-Are you talking about?

-I love Monica want to be with her forever.

-You feel good you're too young to get married and you know it.

-I'm not so much… well yes, but almost be eighteen.

-True but knowing her and wants to marry immediately and you say yes.

-Good I need to find out.

-If it is when you will ask.

-This weekend.

-Are you sure you do?

-Clear, but I want to know something you're not mad at me.

-Because it would be, she's great she's my friend and also loves you and you to it, that's what matters and I want to be happy, you know.

-If it is.

-Well ring what you will give.

-Yeah, well that will have to wait, I need to work more, to buy it know.

-If good then go to sleep now because tomorrow's work.

-More events.

-If I go to sleep.

The next day was awful day, the air was too strong, ruffling my hair, work in the restaurant was slow accused of could, not much to do, it was all calm, too calm, I thought of my brother, he would ask her to marry him, I was sure she would accept right away and ask him when you marry, what was my wedding gift to them.

The weekend came, as he thought the request to be his wife, and was not angry, a little sad but it was all in the background was happy for the two.

-Sister and I go; you could change the climate a little, only just a little.

-You know I will not.

-Good.

-Where would you ask her to marry you, in the restaurant?

-No, I still do not know, depends on the day.

-Question, will go to the monastery in the evening, you will go?

-If I will go I need to keep taking classes.

-If, especially at Richard, Hewett and then Alan.

-Do not play with me.

-Okay, by the way I thought I live here with you.

-Seriously you and Monica.

-If you do not mind.

-Of course not, okay.

-If.

-If, good if not a day had find the kitchen on fire, but that's ok you can live here.

-That fool makes plans and not even if she says yes.

-Kidding do not know her, she's dying to ask it, is excited.

-You think.

-Clear and I know and you always liked.

-Well I have to go; I was spending all day with her.

-See you at the monastery.

-Clear, we are beyond.

My brother left, I went to my closet, high in the corner was silver box with like diamonds, had never opened the box, my mother was, was close and since childhood saved the box stayed there, never look in all that time, but I think it was time to open it, put it on my bed and clean the dust, and I remembered something strange, the box resembled the silver snow globe with diamonds around it, but no, it was strange but did not have the key to open it, and the box had no needed so that one or some combination, only had a double heart shaped, for a moment

I thought I was silly and weird, but then maybe, just maybe it would be possible to look at the necklace she wearing, I opened it I took it off and look at the picture of my mother and mine with my brother, I remember that was taken at Christmas, the heart was so beautiful that I kept appreciating, forget for a moment the box, but then I looked away and I got it, place the heart.

Perfect fit, but not opened, the heart was written friend forever, I read aloud while pushing inward.

The box was opened immediately, the first thing that was strange was full of photographs and papers were indeed quite care, perhaps the sealed box and there were smaller box without a lock, was wooden heart shape also, to bring with so much of hearts, opened it and found a beautiful treasure, were the jewels of my mother were very beautiful, it included a necklace of photography that was in the heart, looks more beautiful than in the picture my mother, diamond was with figures of leaves, well with all this I would be a richer person, of course I am to locate an things of my mother, I feel good and that's what matters, among his things I found a ring very special, with a note of it had taught me one time and showed me where I keep it and said it was from us.

"Good use it was Grandma's"

Was a perfect beautiful sapphire, place it on my finger, I kept it on my finger was stirring things of the box, there were many photographs of her and Alan together, even Hewett and Kalinda strange were friends, Samara was even in them, still looking and everything looks normal, at the bottom I found a picture of my mother on her wedding day, then he was my father, but did not recognize it, I've never seen, not even in my remote memories, deep down there was a tiny little box with the name Alan writing.

Very nice box like all the memories I was, the more the checked seemed to be no end, many necklaces so many surprises to discover, the box also does not belong to me if not him, his secrets were tormenting me each passing moment.

And his prolonged absence without fixed return, I was still waiting for his return, I was no worse wondered why, as if he had disappeared, sometimes listening to his voice that comforted me, saying that he would eventually return, do not hesitate to it, everything would be fine and that everything would work out better than we expected, sometimes seemed so real more than a dream, but it was only imagination, things look finished, save all, just stayed with grandmother's ring, put it on my finger was fabulous, that would be the gift my brother would love, even thought Alan the box he would not be in the monastery, I left the room and was watching television Hewett, greeting me and continued to state for a while.

-Sarah you want goes to the movies? Has much to not go and these days there are good movies.

-Yeah right, we can go after going to the monastery.

-Yeah well I would like to go elsewhere before, you come with me.

-Okay.

-We go.

-Already.

-If, better if we go once.

-Okay let's go.

-Where we're going.

-I drive you'll know when we get there. Handling about forty minutes we arrived.

-Seriously.

-If we go.

-I do not skate, one time I try and hit my head, it was very painful.

-But I was not.

-Incidentally it was my brother.

-We will be fun.

-Clearly if.

We enter, had a lot of people, rent skates, he put them first and I had no intentions of wearing them, but convinced me and I accept, he entered and skated perfectly fine, in the distance there were children learning with their teacher and it looked fun, he retuning for me and enter the not let go even one moment, I fell several times but not completely caught me, and I was having fun and the as well, told me that by far not much fun I do too, we spent time skating and without realizing it, his hands were very soft and warm, I liked being with him, it was fun and was always inventing things.

Time step and fort all, no sorrow there was no pain, I felt happy after even learned a long time to stop, and then we went for a drink and my day is starting to ruin, Richard was there, just the other side of the track stared, but did no approach, for a moment I thought he was fallowing me, but I remember that he like to come here but never brought me, he looked here with his wife why not invite me, I began to feel uncomfortable but did not want to ruin the day of Hewett, was having a great time, back with the drinks put them on the table and gave me a big hug and thanked me with a kiss on the cheek, I smiled and he also I was happy and did not want to ruin everything, some time passed and finished our drinks and told us to leave, it was nearly noon, and said if I wanted we could go to the monastery, asked if he wanted to go elsewhere but said if tomorrow, after a while the movies and elsewhere tomorrow, and if I wanted to go with him amused me much by his side, but before we went up to Hammer, look Richard again coming out of the place, we went and stayed serious for a moment, and I notice and wonder what happened, to turn told him to look at the man over there.

-If I see it and that's with the.

-Well I think that is following me.

-Why you think that?

-Well, do not tell my brother that we saw.

-I know.

-If I went out with him long ago.

-Long.

-Well, three years ago.

-And that with him?

-I look on the other day, he knew where I was, and my brother fought with it and thought it was gone, but I think not.

-You may want to look back with you.

-He married when he was still my boyfriend and I feel that following me.

-Think so.

-I feel uncomfortable with that.

-Do not worry you know that I will care and you can with him.

-I know thanks it's just that's I got a little scared and had long since felt.

-Then I'll be on the lookout.

I thanked him and gave him a kiss on the cheek and talked all the way remember how well we had together, and that day was not over, the road was still frozen and drove slowly, arrived at the monastery and had already begun, arrived late, and got off laughing, they observed us.

-My sister is furious.

-Your sister.

-If, Kalinda is angry look at her.

-Really kidding.

-You speak of do not see this furious.

I froze, I heard you said but I thought it was brother of affection; they were not actually brothers, Monica told me that with the two brothers wanted me, but I did not listen, as they all say brothers, I understand that this furious Kalinda.

-Joke, really.

-You did not know we were brothers.

-Not.

-We live together and do not know.

-Wow would I know, never said anything.

Is sister how was still angry, had not seen her in to the time his brother was gone and I felt bad about that, we stop to laugh, this time only fight with Hewett and Dylan, they taught me new ticks, as Alan use against me the day that he wins me, and I ended up closer to my brother.

-And you say to Monica?

-No I have not found the right time.

-I know I have something for you but you'll have to go out there.

-It's cold.

-I know but trust me.

-In five minutes.

-Clear.

Talk to our friends, helped put a table in front of the statue of the angel who was there and put flowers around, I was cold but it would be fixed soon, Monica went by, I made sure that my brother came out first, Elmo took him and leave a note with the ring on the table, he had read, Elmo sent me a massage to confirm that all would be well, climate change not warm but better less cold windless, all quiet walk with Monica down the aisle of the chapel, even side was the angel with everything ready we finally arrived.

-What about the cold and not so long ago.

-I told you continued.

Finally arrived and my brother looked nervous but accompanied by all around him, even Kalinda was present, despite everything she was romantic.

-Sarah's going on?

-Pleasure only my brother, you know I'd do anything for him and for you my friend.

-I know.

-And waiting forwards.

Approached my brother and despite the wet grass was the hope kneeling with the ring in his hand, that all we could see, she approached and knew instantly that this was, managed to fall a few tears, she was in front, we were all silent.

-Monica I love you and want to spend the rest of my life with you, is that we are still young but we'll do well, I love you and want to be with you every day, and every one of our strange days, agree to be my wife.

Froze looking at all, and she looked at me, I made sings that if, she turned to look at him stretching his hand.

-Clearly if I want to have strange days, if I want to be you wife.

He placed the ring and the snow began to fall, and a little rejoiced with great emotion and looked, but I had nothing to do with it, they kissed so passionately that took longer than they thought, Elmo until interrupted, all applauded and toasted them with hot chocolate.

Looked hoppy leave them alone at his table with hot chocolate and a good meal for the cold weather had change to be better, the table had an umbrella so that snow left them peaceful to eat and talk, the rest of us retired and after a while I had to go see them, Hewett promised to go with the movies and had to leave.

-Guys sorry to say that I have to go and the cold will continue.

-And snow.

-Know I had nothing to do with it, is the nature.

-Yeah right.

-Is seriously, just wanted to warm them, see to continue snowing, see you guys in the house.

Help them to pick up everything and we left, they had much to talk we went to the movies, the movie ended and we follow with another, finally we left unfortunately ruined the moment, there he was this time approached, Hewett handed it to look and grabbed my hand and we started away but he followed us to the truck.

-You want Richard?

-He's your boyfriend?

-If I am, offered you something.

-I want to talk to her.

-Good speech she hears.

-Not, alone.

-No, he can hear what you have to say.

-I do not, or you fear me.

-Do not touché it or you'll regret.

-She can tell me.

-Off me.

-You heard her away from her.

-Okay, I just want to talk that's all.

-Well, I'm listening.

-I just want a chance.

-Kidding right.

-No, please be true.

-Away from me and I told you, do not want you near me.

-I still do not believe you.

-Never want you again, nor a million years.

Took my face and kissed me, in that I pull Hewett and told to let me go, he turned and hit him, but nothing happened to Hewett.

-Made a big mistake.

-Child away from me, she will come with me.

-You never taking her.

Again took me by the arm, but was terrified that it might depart from me over, I was not hard, looked at me and Hewett threatened to call the police, do not let it hurt but his eyes burned with courage but did not wanted to go in that beat Hewett could not contain herself the most it gave a few punches, that left him unconscious, had to call the police for an ambulance to came by, we had to make a report of what happened, and asked for an order of restriction.

Spend more time than I thought, was very could then come over and hugged me, look at my could increased and would not let me alone for a moment, I felt pretty comfortable, when the ambulance was leaving Richard had awakened a few seconds looked at me shame-face, and then took him away, he'll be fine, spend a nice time with the cops, finally let us go, Hewett opened the truck door and climbed the closed, took a couple of minutes to climb until all the policemen left, then up, we went home, I was still could and kept something thoughtful but finely spoken.

-Are you okay?

-You were right on, I was following.

-I think so.

-He will come out and I do not respect not approaching you know.

I keep quiet anyway knew he was right, and did not know what I would do, we can't hit it every time it gets close, and not was a good idea, also did not know what he planned the witch, had been very quiet, Elmo had brought no new news about the murders and Alan, well I did no not know anything about hem, at least not me.

Finally get home, my brother was already asleep and not wake up.

I went could and did know why not go away, the fire still but still had could, I retire to my room take a hot bath and put on something comfortable I slept, but was still could, Hewett stayed awake talking on the phone, when finish he to my room are without touching let him in.

-Are okay.

-Yes, but I have a cold.

-If perhaps you are giving hypothermia it passes in a while.

Way to my bed and sat down and not wearing his shoes had left the room, told me that he spoke by telephone with Elmo, wanted to investigate more about Richard, had to have a good plan to stop approaching me again.

-I am giving you problems Kalinda be furious.

-Do not panic, it's not your problem.

Then hug me for my could without my avoid it, he gradually introduced in the covers and hugged me, I also actually hugged him, it was so warm that my cold I did not care, his face so close to mine, his eyes shone were beautiful blue sky, truly reflected the sky, but what is happening.

He is the brother of my beloved, this can't be happening, I enjoy being with him and could not stop, my mind could not control it my actions, and happened we kissed for a long moment, forget that I love his brother and began to stroke we kept kissing but my heart began to react had to stop, I had never been with someone and this could not be, so complicated, I love Alan and I have betrayed.

-No wait, we can't continue.

Did not want to stop, but I tell him again stopped?

-You're right, my brother would kill me.

-What?

-Yeah, well before going on told me that he was aware that this could happen.

-He knew it.

He knew this could happen, did not trust me and not mistaken, my cold still did not know what to do, I was confused and it was so fast, but that hug allow anything could happen, it was no so innocent was guilty of everything.

-Yes, it was that he wanted to leave you do your life, would not hinder you.

-Hinder.

-Yes, he hears what you and Monica talked on the kitchen, which not let you not for a moment.

-This should never happen, look knows it's my fault but I can't be with you.

-I know, is mine too, but let me be just today till you're better just need to recover today.

-Understated.

-Yes, I know you love him; you think that I've noticed as you missed all this time.

-It is and not because he does not speak, I do not understand.

-If it is difficult, if not had promised and broke my promise, he is on a dangerous mission and we know nothing of it for days, we are concerned.

-Might not grab his phone signal there.

-If perhaps.

-You know what was.

-Yes, but I will not tell.

-It comes to me right.

-Go to sleep.

-That was the last thing you heard from him.

-Elmo went to look.

-I thought he had gone to investigate a death.

-Is so were other friends but Alan was with them.

-Know where he was.

-I think if I, but will not tell you unless you give me another kiss.

-Really kidding.

-Not.

-But you tell me everything.

-Not.

-Where it is.

-Girl okay, but you fall asleep, I think the town is called the Aurora or something.

Did not have to keep asking was everything I needed to know, but I was worry worse before knowing all this, my patience ended.

La Aurora

Fell asleep very fast, contemplates his face and was afraid to foulbrood was to happened in my absence, I know my brother takes care well, but that's what worries me, I have to go be better that way, kissed her on the forehead and said goodbye, I had to leave my friend waiting for me, down by the window of a jump and they smiled and went, we had a long way to go, we had been to see some friends in another town, about two hours from here, not for away, was a small town, maybe they could help us, even though we were saddened by the death of Matthias and among our most remote though wanted revenge, as we walked away not stop looking at his window.

-They are well indeed.

-If I know.

-But if you want to stay we understand.

-No, I'll go with you my friends.

-Sure, some music for the road. Curran said

-Alan knows we had arrived faster running.

-Yeah, I know but we needs things, you're going to lad the Andrew.

-Clearly not do it.

True, if we run arrive faster we would avoid the traffic, despite the time we arrived at the agreed time, if we had not gone to see Sarah would have come sooner, our friends were waiting for us, their names were, Kyra, Hank and Pitter, were grown that reason would know how to help, greet us we had time we watched.

-Boys as they have been?

-Good Mrs. Kyra. Answer Curran

-But pass are at home.

-Clear thanks. We answer the three

-Something to drink or eat.

-No thanks so we're fine lady Kyra. I said

-Know we're coming.

-We know but we have nothing Alan.

-That's child we know some places can help to investigate. Pitter said

-Okay, you tell us and we will go.

-Go with you.

-Be dangerous Pitter.

-The same for you.

-Yes, but we want anything to happen. Commented Andrew

-Andrew sorry about your brother.

-If thanks.

-But what they do is wrong should not play fate, revenge is not good.

-Yes but make me feel better lady Kyra.

-Do not think so son, you think your brother would be happy listening to you says this?

-No, I think not, but it's just.

-Sometimes nothing is fair and less hatred and revenge.

-Yes that is boys, need to be aware what we seek is a demon and feeds on hatred, of their fears.

-If it is true we know Mr. Hank.

-And do not know what evil is and before were angels, are very powerful. Replied Mr. Pitter

-Kyra where we started. I ask

-Our destination is in MT. Bachelor.

-We'll leave at first light, to rest guys.

-Because in a mountain lady Kyra?

-You live in MT. Angel is protected can't get there and this mountain is too high to be able to summon a demon spirit, is very far.

-Great colder, we need Sarah. Curran said

-Sarah son that Sarah.

-If Pitter that Sarah.

-She must get away from this place do not have to take risks.

-Are you talking about?

-Do not know she has the power to open the door to demons.

-Pitter explained you say?

-Already said, what else I can say?

-That's what they plan to, let out all demons.

-Do not know but if she can do it.

-Rest, soon to dawn.

-Yeah right. We all said no encouragement

-Alan that's true.

-Apparently if Curran.

Andrew commented that we were in danger and Kyra was right demons feed on our fears our anger, dawned and we were more than ever, we could not know he planned, we went to MT. Bachelor, the road will be long but we needed we climbed the mountain, we knew did not separate, very risky.

According to them every time we got closer, but there were signs that someone was nearby camp was terrible could and I just thought Sarah, if would be fine, a week passed and still no news, all was crazy, if had power but we were human and though we were immortal could and pain in our body wreaked havoc.

Wanting to surrender, arose more questions than answers, I do not had communicated with my brother since we started up the mountain, should be worried, but it was better than anyone knew we felt the suspicion that someone is within us was betraying, was terrible to think about, that we consider a friend a brother and someone betrayed us, I wondered how my brother would be Sarah if something would happened between them and forget about me, the days passed and we managed to find the door where the demon would come out and did not know how to stop it, no matter how fast we went we could not find, two weeks after our forecasts were scarce, we must hurry, our friend were the ones who suffered the most, who are immortal but also were suffering diseases and always there are ways to kill us.

-I think we should return Alan. Said Curran

-If truth be back tomorrow.

-Guys we have a problem.

-Mr. Hank what happens?

-We have a blizzard; we have to find a better shelter, tents that will not help us.

-Be in a hurry. Andrew said

-Curran together all you can and let's go. I said

Blizzard reached us too late the winds too strong to walk, but still, after a few minutes Mrs. Kyra found a cave, was better to in, and it was covered with snow not matter.

-Enter no choice.

-Clear.

-Is everyone okay?

In that torches were lit.

-Wow, we thought would never come.

-Rosalba.

-Hello dear, those were expecting.

-Alan is a trap.

-And noticing thanks Curran.

-Guys enough. Kyra said

-And look brought us snacks.

-That is what they want?

-You'll see, get them.

The blizzard we had weakened slightly but still we fight them, we had been watching, wanted us to weaken and they are succeeding, finally caught us all, they were more than we do, everything had been planned.

-Honey, stops fighting is not worth, not strain yourself.

-That's what you want?

-You know.

-Opened the door to leave the demons.

-No, just some and my brothers that you loved Sarah sent to the abyss.

-You fallow. Andrew cry

-Later, bring to Alan.

There was not too deep well in the cave; you could hear the water running, my friends could not move, could not help me.

-No work, you can open it just Sarah.

-Silly, Sarah could get everybody if we wanted but I just want some.

-Are you talking about?

-Of you, you take him out.

-Never.

-No I'm asking, I'm ordering, hold him well.

-Never will open.

-Want to bet, look where you beloved Lucy died, she gave some of their power, are part so it, so if you can open it.

-Not true.

-Who may not know that you are strong but they, tell me how it is that they age and all present that day remain the same.

-Is impossible.

-If she was not destroyed anyone so you could live likes their children.

-Then so not open it.

-No option; or you open or kill them.

-Even so, the kill.

-True guys I need more blood they can.

-No waiting use mine.

-Do not do it son. Kyra yell

-Shut elderly… good where we were, so blood.

Cut my arm and left him bleeding for a long time, began to weaken over every moment and confounded all.

-Aer-is, aqua-ae, ignis –is, terra-ae, anperio aperui apertum, ia-ea, barathrum resusito Nerilim Asmadeo, Apollyon agreman iste frater fratris. (Air, water, fire, earth, opens the abyss, raises the hell's Angels, Asmadeo, Apollyon, Agreman and my brothers).

My blood was still falling and the demons started coming out in the distance my friends still fighting for freedom, as Rosalba was distracted looking at the abyss my friends took me to that place; we were all together and uttered something Kyra.

-Fulgo fulsi ia-ea fedes fidei, feducia-ae scutum is-ae resedo luz lucis. (Faith shines with a coat of withdrawal)

-No.

We left there, I heard that scream Rosalba, Kyra use all his power to get us out of there and translated us to where we left the trucks, we got all in one, we could not separate us, Kyra was exhausted and attended her Pitter, I would not stop bleeding, Curran stood me his shirt to stop the bleeding, and Andrew driving, everything was chaos, we could not go to the hospital was far away, we went to the cottage we had rented for the entire month and there I attended and Kyra was better.

Became unconscious for two long days, we returned home from our friends in the Aurora, apparently followed us when we got home we were waiting, we got caught again, we walk to the forest for a long time, this time we separate and took our friends and us on the other side.

We had nothing from them, they took us to a house among the woods, just hoped they were okay, three were unconscious, woke the next two or three days and did not know I lost track of time, but I kept thinking of my friends who had not seen, was worried about my brother and Sarah hoping that the demons had not been for her, were presented, which continued to torture me more than others, but not killed me or them amused, Rosalba was not, had left, they were in charge of caring that do not we escaped, we were tide at three, after a while she back but only for a day and then had to go, but before.

-Hi Alan, are comfortable?

-That's what you want?

-Torture and pleasure that you friends do not know about you by the way you know what your brother do and beloved girlfriend.

-Of these caring.

-If I think so, send one of the demons with them.

-Witch.

-If well, I know, but you want to know what have done.

-No thanks.

-Well just look at the pictures.

-Is his bedroom, a demon can't enter his home.

-I know, do not get a demon but a friend of yours, or rather our.

-Are you talking about?

-Well look at another photo, they look good together and see this from last night and look at this is this morning sleeping together and not even wake up, look at them they look divine.

-God is my brother and her; they want to, I do not care.

-True then you joins us? No answer me now, can you answer me tomorrow I get back, really I have more things to do, have fun with my brothers, and you dear Andrew, your brother begged us not to we kill, did not want to join us, was a coward.

-Not true, he was not a coward, had the courage to die rather than serve you, that makes him a hero, I would rather die than join you and you demos, I'm better than that.

-Well it's you choice not mine, see you later guys.

-Alan ignores her, that's what she wants from you.

-If a friend, find a way out of that. Andrew

-Alan. Insisted Curran

Did not answer, did not want to think more about the pictures of my brother with Sarah; just close my eyes and began to wait for the end.

Woke up scared, knocked on the door, Hewett was still asleep beside me.

-Come on in.

-Sarah, Are you okay?

-If, in a moment Monica.

-Hewett's slept with.

-Yeah…well not, it happened so fast, it is not what you think, nothing happened.

-So you tell yourself.

-No really, nothing happened and it's not like I tried, I love Alan nothing happened and what about you, you slept with my brother.

-If, in my dreams he wants to after the wedding.

-A good idea.

-That silly sleeps like a child, look at him.

-Is true Hewett is tired.

-What has happened last night?

-Tell you later.

-Well, but I want details.

-You'll have them.

-Okay.

-Get out of here.

-I'm coming.

-Hewett awake too late.

-Five more minutes.

-Awake.

-Okay, what is happening Sarah; Sarah I'm doing here?

-Calm nothing happened.

-Is true, because I wake up.

-I know how to find Alan.

-Are you talking about?

-Yeah, but I need your help.

-No, I will not.

-If you will is your brother, I just want a favor.

-Okay I'm going to change me, I'll wait outside.

We moved quickly we said that we would come out as the day before, but did not ask questions.

-Now what?

-Screens used vehicle traffic control certain.

-As you know.

-Not think that is obvious.

-Continues.

-I need to go to the monastery and review.

-And we did and found nothing.

-I will.

-Okay let's go.

-Just act normal.

-Normal I'm breaking what I promised my brother.

-Look this is the home of your friends true, we seen them come in, but not out, there is a forest behind Elmo found them in this part.

-Yes, we looked there.

-Incidentally remain in there.

-No, we would have found impossible.

-Accurate, but sought in this part?

-There was no reason.

-Well, I have one, is that are still there.

-As you know.

-Can't leave this river, only if they return, and we have not seen unless they can fly if there were left to walk, they are still there.

-Is enormous not find them.

-I will go, if you want to go well and if not do not stop me.

-You are a fool you'll wait for me I drive.

Drove around the town a bit and then headed to the Aurora, arrived at the house of his friends, there was nothing walked around the house a few minutes.

-I told you they walked.

-As you know.

-Marks look the trees are burned resisted, and this is his truck.

-Could bring in theirs.

-If not, feel they're here, they're in danger.

-We are in danger.

Follow a path that was not on the map, it took a couple of hours and then we walk had passed to Alan's house for some of its weapons, we took some, Hewett was worried about not having warned it was better so, we walked for a long time in the woods, we could not find anything, till after a few minutes, I found Alan watch.

-You were right, they're still here.

-Yes I fell we're close.

-Know that we do not have a good chance to get out of here alive.

-We will, look there is a cabana or it is.

-Yeah, see this guarded.

-They are the Hokon.

-If so it seems, we should bring binoculars infrared, help us if they are in.

-We need to approach.

-Sarah wait, foolish.

-Know what to do, come on.

-Clear.

-Petula I will go to check on the prisoners.

-Ofelia care that are reminiscent of Rosalba.

-Will review and return only.

We listened to what they said we were too close.

-Hewett you wait here and I'll take them.

-Wait.

-Now what?

-A kiss.

-When we get back.

-Only four that can happen… Sarah is crazy.

I want to the back, not care, scope to look at the guys, they were badly and more Alan, try to enter through the top but they could not leave, if I had to find another entrance was a door but the witch was with them, I had to do something to get his attention.

-Apeio aperui apertum. (Open)

-Are you doing here?

-You fear that I win.

-No, I will not have to call them myself, I murder you.

-Try it.

-Sarah.

-He Andrew can awaken.

-Clear.

-Good start.

We fought it was not stronger enough for me; I had to win and get them out of here.

-Tera-ae. (Ground)

-My turn witch, comburo-ere-ussi-ustus oboe-is-ire. (Burn and dies) The unleashed but they were not very happy to see me.

-We got to go get up Alan.

-Are you doing here, you're crazy.

-Then thank me, let's go.

Andrew and Curran took him, he kept looking at me serious but had no choice, they had, Hewett looked at us but it wait till down, help them take them.

-You're with her, will kill you.

-Then you do brother, we got to get out of here before they realize.

-As we found.

-Andrew was she and not as.

-Quickly the truck is set away.

-Come on.

Andrew was exhausted so that helps with Alan, but he did not want to help him, even so I did, we realize that had already been realized, followed us closely, almost we reached the truck when we reached, fight with them, but they were not alone, almost dusk

, could hear the noise of a stream, we were running and stop for a moment, I felt lost, I stopped and listened to the sound of the leaves, something was not right, was different, I do not felt confident, look around and was in silence, others looked at me.

-There is something I do not, truth.

-If it is the reason that you should not be here silly girl.

I did not move and in the distance a pair of eyes look red as strong as hell itself, approached without making a sound, does not know who he was, but the others if they did, terrified me your eyes.

-Hello dear.

-You are?

-And you realize right, you never will take them alive of here.

-Want to see that if, you are?

-I have many names but right now mine is… Apollyon.

-Clear, of course.

-Alan did not you tell what has happened.

-You see, I could not talk.

-Sure fleeing from me.

-You're not real; there are no demons, no more.

-If well thank Alan for that, he let me out.

-I think not.

-Well, we were, thus I was told you were beautiful but look more beautiful than they rumors and smell delicious.

-Leave it. Alan and Hewett yell at the same time

-If I do not do anything, not yet.

Took Alan and threw it against a tree and did not move, try to run with but I could not, he did something with his hand and stopped me, we were all paralyzed and others were suffering, Hewett said something and let go of me, try to fight him but was stronger, actually was a demon, the demon of the abyss and shadows, now as the Hokon returned, although one was dead, and threw me and fall along with Alan.

-I told you, you were a fool to come.

-Never have let you know that you were in danger, I had to come you had given up.

-Are you talking about?

-If you give up, you wanted to die.

-How do you know?

-Not believe me.

-Well, we will not leave of here.

-If we will do, the truck is close I'll get out of here, if I have to die trying.

-Your will not.

-I smiled and help him up.

-Just trust me, said it was a demon, right.

-If it is and I let him out.

-Well I have a plan I hope it works.

-Will you do?

-We should approach the boys.

-Yeah well we expect.

-You go, I'll distract.

-You're crazy, I will not let you.

-Trust me, they are suffering.

I distracted while fighting it, he approached them and releases them with little power he had, thrown me very close to them, I get up and I smiled.

-Pretty will you do now, but not out of here although Rosalba wants them alive, I prefer to have it as a snack.

-Did not will have, come back where you belong.

I hag Alan and gave the hand to Hewett, the others understood and approached us, looking at the Alan's eyes and shone like two moons in the dark, unable to move this very devil, I had missed a lot.

-Not hurt you trust me please hold.

Just take some energy from them and forest, the moon shine a little more than usual, and my body shine too, smiled at Alan and see the devil and told, redituros ad barathrum (come back into the abyss) was not immediately struggled to stay, I concentrated more and shine much of the forest, as all knew that shadow demon feared the light and would have to return, I come back, I released the guys stand in front of them protecting them and saying again to return to the shadows, finally vanished slowly, mixing with the light that made him back, my power increased and controlled it very well, the devil vanished and after a few seconds my power is retreating, we were all fine.

-Sarah you did?

-Then I tell you, let's go still follow us the Hokon.

I gave them my weapons, and that I had no used, but they were weak and would need, approached and also had weapons we heard shooting, lift to Alan and hid behind some trees, they were shooting, we drove away slowly and soon we reached the truck I drive and Hewett was fine, we went to the main road, and for a moment we thing we no longer pursed, but suddenly heard and felt a blow to the truck, they were chasing us, they would not care about traffic, we were chased, for a moment I almost lost control of the truck, they were hitting some cars ahead, and prayed to God that the people in those cars were good, we continued and we were shooting, for a moment scream, but the bullets did not enter.

-You would not believe I gave the truck just luxury do you.

-Not clear that you did not.

-Still almost got it. Hewett commented

-Whether I fell not, they have us.

-You can lose them Sarah you can get rid of them.

-Andrew I thought you did not like violence.
-This is an exception.
-Well hang on; Alan's something in your vehicle to help us.
-There grenades.
We look at it for a moment.
-Really kidding!
-No.
-Good something else, we will not use it on the road.
-Yeah, well let me think.
-Make it quick.
-Well, not anything I did not believe this happened.
-If good and now.
-Fix it tomorrow.
-Kidding.
-Stop hitting my truck.
-Yeah right I try.
-Watch out for cars. Curran cry
-I see.
-Careful. Curran cries again
-Already saw them, you do something.
-Hardly see them, just bring s few bullets.
-Well not fail Hewett.

Almost crushed us a truck that transported gasoline, just a few inches to beat us and close my eyes and stopped the truck, did not know what to do, I opened my eyes and suddenly he stopped the truck alone, they looked at me.

-I did not do anything.
-Closed your eyes almost crushes us that thing and closed you eyes.
-Andrew would repeat that came in front with me.
-Well I…
-What happened? Curran asked
-As stopped? Ask again
-I was not.
-Yes I know you close your eyes. Reproached me Hewett
-Well where are they? Asked

-No see them. Andrew this time

-Well need pass the truck. Nobody sees anything.

-I'm coming Alan.

-No start.

-Hurry someone approaches. Hewett screamed me

-I can't turn it on.

Not turn on the truck and approached several shades and we did not have bullets for the guns and were exhausted to use our power, we left the car and approached the shadows, Alan was placed in front of me protecting me, and the rest looked worried.

-Perhaps are crazy destroyed the road and the truck.

-That who is?

-I can't let him leave a second because disobedient children.

-Dylan is you.

-And who thought it was. Will said

-She destroyed the truck. Alan said

-You owe me a truck girl.

-Alan was not yours.

-Yes, but I will help fix it, you owe us a truck. Came everyone; except Kalinda.

-We have to leave the police arrived very soon.

-The news, we all know Alan's truck.

-If good his bad.

-Dylan takes Alan's truck. William said

-If teacher.

-Monica arrives at a time and Adriel in other trucks to leave.

-How they came.

-We run girl. Elmo said

-That?

-You will understand then.

-What happened with Hokon.

-Already left.

Alan was still without even looking at me, Dylan could turn the truck and took her, we walked away as they came, my brother finally found us on the road, each carrying a black truck, enough for all, and then went up to Alan and then others, Hewett went with him end I had to go in the other truck with Monica, in the distance we hear sirens patrols, ambulance and firefighters.

The return trip I made eternal, and I could not stop thinking about what happened, finally a while we reached the house of Alan, they were already there, reached long ago, when we enter were in the bedroom, where I stayed ever attended him a doctor of the monastery, he was worse than I thought, he look at me just a moment then turned, was still angry, that came in his sister turned to me with his angry look.

-Perhaps went crazy as you dare to go alone without saying anything.

-Do not would have believed.

-Watch nearly killed because of you, you are a threat to us are dangerous and disobedient.

I did not answer anything, I found it that way but I would not tell, she went with him and I got out of his room, Hewett went behind me.

-Do not listen, is upset because she was not who found him.

-She's right I should not be near you.

-No, she does not, she's scared, and you know we need you.

-I know he'll be fine really.

-Yes it will.

-You could take me home.

-I do not know I would like stay with my brother.

-Okay not have to stay with me, just take me.

-Yeah okay I'll tell my brother.

-And I to mine.

However take the keys to the truck and my brother's coat, which is next to the keys, I put it on and went home, everyone was mad at me, I do not turn away from them, I will continues to help but would not stay in his house, I would stay at the mine, in that his cell phone rang my brother, I look was Hewett, I answer did not want to follow me.

-Hello.

-Do not wait.

-I'm sorry I had to leave, he's fine.

-If well.

-As you know I had the phone of my brother.

-Is not you brother is that Alan is his coat.

-That? No, was with the keys to the truck.

-You can check it them but of my brother.

-Yeah well, that you want.

-Just to know you're okay.

-If I am, I have to go home.

-Well we will go after a while.

-Not be better to stay with them.

-Do not bother to me I help you do not forget.

-Thanks for that but I want to be alone.

-I'll be not trouble, remember that live there and pay rent.

-Do not pay rent.

-But I can afford it.

-Yeah right.

-Than we will be thereafter.

-Clear goodbye.

I drove home come quick, I went to my room I took off the coat and take out the phone, see and indeed whether it was Alan, and had several missed massages, would not see them but some Rosalba was saying, and I had to see them, were massages from photographs, opened the first massage and I appeared with Hewett, day of last night when we kissed, I kept looking and had all that had happened to Hewett, was terrified for a moment, why? Who had taken? No one had entered my bedroom except Monica, but can't been her, I then dial her phone.

-Hello.

-Monica.

-Sarah something happens.

-This morning someone broke into the hose to find me or Hewett.

-Let me think.

-Tried recalls.

-If on the night I speak Mr. Anselmo call, wanted know if they were at home and I said yes just arrived.

-Heard when we arrived.

-If I could not sleep was contemplating my ring is fabulous, by the way thank that you gave your brother, was your grandmother.

-You're welcome was my girt, but tell me in the morning.

-To whether Mr. Anselmo also found him in the room before you wake up, I asked it wanted to Hewett and said that if I had gone to look for his bedroom and did not find.

-What else he said.

-He had things to do and then would look.

-Thanks see you in a while there.

-Come back here.

-Yes but do not say anything.

-Of course.

I hung up and I had to go home to Alan, not much later, between and everyone looked at me, wearing my coat and in that other hand his, was with Kalinda, Curran and Andrew were better.

-How are you Alan? Ask

-Well.

-That girl doing here. Kalinda said

-I came to return the phone to you bother and his coat.

-Great leave them there and you can go.

Alan did not stop her as before let her say what she wanted, did not say anything bad not yet, I sent some of the photos to Hewett along with a massage no to go in his brother's bedroom.

-Need to talk to him alone.

-Will not let you.

-I need to talk with Alan, he wanted to know something he wonder when I found it and I'll tell you, now out please or force you out.

-Do not you dare?

-Kalinda out please.

-But brother.

-Please and do not listen.

She looked at me waiting to hit me went off leaving the leaving the door open, closed and look at Alan, he still did not look at me, did not care much what I had to say, I was angry look and after what I did, feared I do something to her sister I supposed.

-Alan knows I said I knew where to find you, but can I ask you something.

-That is?

-Well, before my question I'll tell you why you hate and tell explanations.

-Not want.

-Know.

-And well.

-I said I would learn Latin but that's aside, what you know about angels.

-They are spirits that God created and something helps us.

-Certain you're right.

-Say that an angel told you where we were.

-Something like that, you know my intuition was what made me go to that place, the night I stay with your brother in my bedroom, I had a dream, I look to thee giving you up, did not understand why but now I know and know it is not fair that you risk that way, you could have saved you friends and just wanted to die, I feel your pain suffered when you did and not to were fighting.

-You know nothing of what happens.

-Yes I know, and I'll tell you, hear the voice of someone in my dream makes me believe it was an angel and they can give us dreams, metaphors some sings like this.

-My watch, I think I dropped not even remembers where or when.

-Well it's the power that binds us to the realm of spirit intuition, matter to trust our intuition, knew who died if they were less your brother, I knew it and for that reason I did not say anything, trust my heart, and what you thought would not let you die just because you looked slept with your brother, just stood there, not allow it, if it has been another reason I had understood and there was not a reason.

-How do you know?

-Indeed, to get you phone your friend sends you messages Rosalba.

-For if you do, then looked.

-Course I did and not blame you for being angry.

-I know all that happened, my brother told me on the road, did not have to repeat it.

-If I had to say is whoever took and sent to you girlfriend.

-It is nothing mines, waiting know who sent them?

-If it is it's one of your friends and also advised them where we were at the falls, it was not the call of Adriel.

-Who is?

It was hard for me to say but I had to, I was not wrong.

-Mr. Anselmo is the sending.

-Not true, he could not do it.

-If he did and you can check his phone calls and see.

-Someone else knows.

-No, just you.

He got up felt better, took the phone and talk to someone and ask where Mr. Anselmo and could not account for them.

-You can tell the teacher to enter.

-Yeah right, was all, I have to go home, till then Alan.

-Wait… thanks.

-No matter you not have to thank goodbye.

I left his room and went the leaving room and told the teacher to come in and then I went with my brother and Monica.

-Friend happened are okay.

-This photograph.

-Who took it, you said nothing happened.

-And who do you think, who was in the house before I woke up.

-He was!

-Mr. Anselmo was.

-They will do, you told Alan.

-If I already did and Alnsemo was not found in the monastery.

-Sarah I'm sorry but nothing happened.

-Know but that does not matter, this proves nothing. Hewett approached me.

-I told my bother I explained everything and believe me I think.

-Okay bur no matter, I have to go, and he's fine.

-If his wounds heal faster.

-I go guys, stay or leave with me.

-As we go I'm with you.

-Hewett not have to go not proved necessary.

-If they are beyond all my stuff.

-Okay let's go.

We went, Kalinda was in the other end of the leaving room and said nothing, I ignored her and went, arrived at the house.

-Sorry Sarah was my fault friend.

-It was not, is both.

-Really sorry.

-I equal.

-But he loves you and you know it will pass.

-I do not want this anymore, okay.

-Clearly not a word more.

I went to sleep, which by the way the room was still not fixed, I could not even do that day, I just wanted to sleep, to forget what happened, I do not know because they do not understand me, because they do not believe me, I knew what I did was not wrong, they would be dead now if not for me, nor that I give me credit but save them, I trust in me, that I am good person and I can be better, but understood that it was no just that, I was the kiss with his brother, Kalinda did not know and when she finds even be worse.

Christmas

Woke up scared again, knocked on the door Monica, beginning to believe that it would be that way every day, it would be revenge for that did the same to my brother every morning, we were on vacation and also tired, even though we were on vacation had to work always worked, I told her to enter.

-Sarah today is Christmas Eve wanted you to help me cook, you know that I do not know and I wanted to learn, you will.

-Know I have to go to work.

-I know but do have to go, you can stay.

-I do not know, I do not want to celebrate.

-I know but you can do it for me.

-Not.

-For you brother. Makes a sad face

-Okay but takes away that face and let me sleep a little more.

-Done.

After a while I got up and went to the kitchen and Monica was still a mass in the kitchen made knots and almost crying, I had to help wash and clean everything and start again, the only thing that was good was the turkey, but everything else was a disaster.

December 24 is the darkest night of the year; we celebrate the birth of Jesus Christ the son of God, who came to earth to save us and crucify for not believing in him and we realized that it was when he was dead, it was late, but it had to be, I wonder if it was his destine, had to comply, if God had wanted different what had change, we know that he rose again the third day, and ascended into heaven to the right of the father, I understand the this in charge with his father, we all controversy as a God born in a very dark night like that, and animals in manger, well anything can happen and I think not one knows exactly when he was born, some historians say that Jesus was born on another day, was chosen on December 24 that is a dark night, the darkest of the year and against there was so much evil wanted some light on the dark night.

No matter what religion we have or what we think of the past, the important is that we believe in one God, no matter when was born, when we celebrate his birthday, we have faith in him, believe in one Almighty God, to serve and fourth we must obey, evil will always be present, we temptations and sometimes we can't control, evil exits but also avoid the good, we can decide, we can't change the past but we can change the future.

I believe in God almighty creator of heaven and earth, and the things that happen have a reason therefore pass, but we must remember that we can decide between good and evil, to do right, be defeated or never stop fighting.

We can defeat evil there is always light in so much darkness, between such evil, there is hope at the end, the feelings are part of life, are emotions that God left us to have, created us perfect, his thinking, but we have corrupted the gifts he has given us, we have change the lives our life Convenience over the years have change, excelled evil to us is overcoming, is destroying us, parents killing children, children killing parents, brother against brother, everything is a mess and we can't stop, or rather do not want to stop doling evil.

Christmas Eve a night of peace faith night, a night with a ray of light, a litter faith, holy night.

Way? That is life without God, without faith, without love? My life would be without God?

-Sarah how good you are staying the desserts, they look wonderful.

-And taste great, we laugh

We celebrate Christmas Eve, the day that Jesus was born but can also celebrate Christmas Day, with gifs from St. Nicholas and dinner at night that would be two days to celebrate.

-Almost everything is ready. I said

-That well, they have all day in the kitchen. Grumble

-Brother should help.

-We're doing and we tried all and give the go ahead.

-Yeah right and how this all.

-Perfect.

-Almost perfect I bet the turkey did Monica will do us harm.

-Hewett for you there will be no turkey or dessert. Moni said

-No turkey, dessert if truth Sarah?

-There is only dessert if you eat turkey. We laugh

Our friends would come and Gonzalez and Mr. Robles, Hewett would be with us liked the house and had made friends with my brother, and my clear mine, would not go with his brothers, he was more disobedient and wanted to avoid scolding, just speaks for how this, and there was no novelty.

Our friends were arriving, everything was ready for dinner before we thanked God for the food and let us live another day, Hewett was still tormenting Monica with turkey as he ate, but if she cook realities well, just liked to bother her, no one talked about what happened at Aurora, just at work, school, kids, my life was normal one more day, perfect but it always ends, the hours passed I finish one more day of Christmas Eve, Christmas came Hewett and my brother looked like children, us to wake everyone.

I think if this revenge by lifting early, the tree was full of gifts that everyone put, were many each will buy something for someone, the little ones were super happy, they received more everyone brought something and his father of the little Marcos so consented too, and indeed were his cousins by their father and were enough children, we leave room so that our guest will use them, we were in the room, the distribution of gifts still seemed to go on, and some punch and coffee were served to awaked, share hugs and smiles, everything was perfect it hat snowed a lot and could not leave the little ones from the cold was terrible, played around the house.

To imagine how it turned out, the night came and as well as over, midnight offer, share more hugs, the little ones slept though all parts of the living room, were exhausted and it was time, were a tremendous chaos, was happy to celebrate other occasions had other work all day and was sad that I missed my mother have liked to share this Christmas, the next morning everyone went had to visit their other friends and we had to clean.

-Monica they clean.

-What, not myself.

-Sure your idea you clean your party.

-No fair who help me.

-I have to work.

-And I equal.

-And you Hewett.

-I, I have something to do goodbye.

-Leave me alone.

-Goodbye my friend.

We said goodbye an she stayed in the house alone, did not believe that never ends, we said goodbye and she stayed in the house alone, did not think ever ends, walked and thought that if she wanted New Year's party, I hope that after this is canceled, snow covered the entrance but nothing that could not be fixed, my brother would take me because and he was still using my truck, occupied more than me for Monica, the streets were clean had been cleaned for machines, but were still slippery, my brother had put nail wheels in a while but sometimes it was not enough, we had to go slow, it took something to get in there, let me in the restaurant and he had the day off, but also do not want to be in the house and Monica had to clean alone, not that I would not want to help but do not finish, whether that stated the day many stores did not open from the cold and snow, not many people who attend and some of the guys who worked there left early, I stay to close and later I picked up my brother, arrived on time as he said, when we got home just as I thought Monica had not finished cleaning, was in the courtroom, was a disaster, had not even settled and all tired, actually looked strange, my brother almost laughed but she looked so strange, before he could do about it entered Hewett he looked at her if not restrained began laugh, we all look at him and she broke to mourn a little, my brother hug and calm down.

-I said I?

-Men never understand.

-Monica not worry we will help all cleaned.

-All, I will no, watch TV.

-Hewett clear, watching TV and cleaning at the same time. Frowned, finished cleaning the house, Monica bathroom and

sat the couch and fell asleep, we kept watching TV and talking for a while, then we went to bed, my brother took Monica to her room, then he went to his own and next day started again.

Spend the rest of the week working, had to, was not rich or anything, had to continue my normal life, not going to the monastery, there was no reason, they continued for some sing of Anselmo, but found nothing, Hewett sometimes smuggled me without me to ask that his brother was fine, and if he wanted to tell me more paid no attention and him already said nothing, really understand what was happening, no felt the desire to know, if I could not be with him, her sister did not want me to come to him maybe she was right.

Ended the New Year and Monica ask not celebrate the day at home, did not even know it got that day, like the other day I had to work and if that day was kind of busy, but not enough even then I wanted and it would work, my brother took me to work but asked him to let me near the library, had long since visited her, after that walk in the park, not matter how could that was what I could stand and arrives to work and every start as usual.

-He Sarah what time finish.

-Hi Monica maybe about ten or earlier, not much to do for that.

-Well, I have planned a dinner tonight to celebrate the end of the year and New Year.

-Want to celebrate, I thought you were chastened.

-And I did, it's just being on Alan's house, invited us but...

-But...

-I want to you cook some delicious desserts.

-What, no, I will not too late.

-I know you can, do miracles.
-Not true.
-Well I mean you're very good and fast for thought, please.
-Not convince me, I'm working.
-But there is almost no one if you have time.
-Good I will but came for them.
-If you talk to me, you go right?
-No, so do not ask please.
-But…
-No, no but do go.
-Okay not insist but you should think about.
-Monica good bye.

I hurried to finish the dessert and talk to her just her want that, I did some more just in case, other than those she had tried and few more for the guys were working, the smell was very nice to sweet, talk her that to be ready around eight and arrive quickly.

-Are fast.
-Ready and waiting for you to call.
-Yeah well I helped raise them.
-I can only slightly.
-Not.
-Just a little bit.
-Not beg.
-Please bother you all the time.
-Almost you go.
-Please please.
-Well I save a little to you, knew that you will not resist.
-You're the best.
-I know.
-Yes, they are delicious you know Sarah, Alan will love, he wonder about you, he is better.
-I'm happy for him.
-Do not be like that he is worried about you.
-Because it should be.
-He misses you and you to him.

-No longer misses.

-You can't lie and you know it.

-Enough Monica no follows.

-I'm sorry I know you just want to help.

-Not go, true.

-No, you're right I miss him, will not go by that I can't stand her look.

-Are you talking about?

-He not talking to me, looks at me with anger, could not stand to be there watching it and not even close.

-I understand, well I have to go.

-Remember my brother to have to come get me.

-Sure I remember.

-Beware.

She left and went to finish my stuff in the restaurant, near the ten boys retreated to their desserts I gave them and thanked me and give me a hug for Yew Year, everyone was happy and finally left me alone, my brother will be here soon, but did not hear the truck, take the phone and I had to talk to him.

-Hello.

-Hello and come for me.

-Sister not in a while but I am going.

-That of which you speak you forgot.

-Not just that I time went.

-But I closed it and I'm alone.

-Scare you?

-Of course not, it's okay to call a taxi will arrive sooner than you.

-Well you take care.

-What?

He hung up, I had to talk to a taxi whatever would be better and let him have fun, was not taxis it too late, someone finally answered, came in a minute I hear the sound of a motor sports, that was the only thing I had found, I heard parking in front, if was my brother stationary behind, I take a minute to turn off the light, take my bug and went out in what turn to close, hear the door opening, a taxi driver never comes out, turn quickly.

-Hello sorry I'm late, came slowly snowing. I do not reply or move; he approached.

-Hi are you ok?

-I'm waiting for a taxi; I think I'll wait inside.

-No, wait I'll take you.

-No thank you and call a taxi.

-Not coming.

-That.

-Curran was the one who answered.

-Not true he could not be.

-If he was.

-Interfered the phone,

-Only when it I arrived it was late.

Not possible but I suffer more that what he believes, I look standing there in front of a yellow sports car, four-door, no sure what mark it was, but it was cute, I stared at his eyes that were a delight, I was fascinated by his eyes resembled her brother blue as the sky, his eyes fascinated me but did not want to see him, does no to tell.

-Well I can take you… you will not answer?

And across the street was him, had already left the hospital and jail, was still paralyzed watching I had forgotten him completely.

-That is what you see Sarah.

-Alan anything, no matter, its okay you can take me. He looked at him

-What here.

-I will not, do not go.

-Know who he is and what he wants.

-What?

Walked away, my heart racing, beat faster, did not know what would happen, was about five minutes and then left, did not know what happened but he left and came back Alan, was more frightened than before, wanted to go back inside the restaurant, but follow me still.

-Are you okay…? Sarah, Are you okay?

-I'm fine as you know.

-My brother told me about it.

-Your brother tells you all the truth.

-If we have no secrets and needed help.

-I can know that you told him.

-Do not worry, not bother you the more.

-Thank you.

-Sarah just wanted to go with me for him truth.

-If true.

-Then let us go I have cold snowing remember.

Go into his car was very hot, we spent quiet most of the way, quiet almost to my house, but he continued.

-Wait, you went home.

-I know I'm taking mine.

-Alan did not do it I have no desire to go. I told the truth

-Thank you.

Go on the car very quickly opened the door, I got out of the car and followed me to the entrance, opened the door he entered, I thought it was reviewing the place.

-And well, which do now?

-We do? You have to go home now.

-Did not think that leave you alone, right?

-Why not?

-Today I have to look after you, my brother was in my home well everyone is at my home.

-Not have to take care.

-If I have to.

-Was fine, you can stay, I'll go to sleep.

I walked into my bedroom and said something.

-Your brother is waiting has something to tell you.

-Will do so tomorrow.

-It is important.

-Alan let me you'd better leave.

-That's wrong, he is you brother should be with him.

-I'm always with him.

-Then go.

-Not this time.

-I do not understand why you bother with.

-No with.

-Truth is with me?

-No.

-What happens?

-Off me.

-I did not do this I'm sorry.

-If only took my arm but exaggerate slightly.

-Alan I'm just tired is all.

-I understand, well I'll stay on the couch. I stood with hardly breathing.

-Yes… are you no want to be around you, you would not understand.

-You're right, I do understand.

-Know what I feel when I look at you and you see me with a look of terror, I can't be around you and look at your eyes, I feel that you despise.

-You're wrong.

-I'm wrong.

-If, as you say that I despise.

-To no.

-I'm not.

He tuned again.

-I look at it I should not go wrong for you, but I had to do it and it was wring what happened to you bother but nothing happened.

-Sarah knows, and I'm not upset and not have to repeat what of my brother.

-But.

-You see, you do not understand truth.

-What I do not understand, will better go.

-Sarah wait if I'm angry a little you kissed my brother clearly hurt me I thought there was something between us and everything ended.

-Know how to end something that never started, just saved my life with a kiss, when I knew that you wanted we were nothing.

-You said you loved me.

-But if you leave and do not understand.

-I understand. Take my hand approached he looks at my eyes look

-Sorry never ask something very important, I just thought... I thought we had something.

-I also.

-Sarah wants to be my girlfriend. No answer

-I get it; I know I should be prompted for before.

All was silent not knowing what to say, that was what I wanted the yes but not answer.

-Okay never mind, sorry I can't go, I have to take care, rally I have to stay.

-Tell me, my brother it is important to what he had to say.

-If it is, for him a special day.

-Your brothers are there really.

-It it is.

-You can take me promise to be good.

-Go.

Take my bag again but before I remember something.

-You can wait a second.

-Yeah right.

I went to my mother's box opened it and take the box containing the name of Alan and put it in my bag, I would be where I felt better and had a chance, but this is silly and miss my chance if I wanted to tell him if, but I was afraid, I left the room and went almost was eleven thirty.

-Thanks Sarah.

-For which.

-To go for me, you were right wanted to die.

-Okay, I had to go.

-I'm not upset, I'm glad you were I'm upset with me for putting you in danger like that.

-Endangered by that?

-Forces you to go for me, for a simple confusion.

-Would do it again.

-I know and I will not let you do it again.

-But I mean if you do not have to do it again, will not let you alone, sorry I could not see you before, but as I did not feel really good.

-Not have to.

-Sarah stop saying. Stop the car was furious

-What happens?

You know very capricious a girl and not want to see, sorry for leaving you but every day that passes away the only thing was you thought, even in my dream only was you, so I can't promise anything, because we do not know how to end this, we do not know the plans that they have, I like what you do not realize that although they are crazy I love, you're just being yourself, think back you was all I wanted, I thought that frozen place that had to returned to you, at the time when I fails quit was that, I believed the witch, what was between you and my brother, instead of understanding that it is terrible to know that.

-Alan.

-Let me finish, you put my patience, I gave it wanted space, you can defend it so I prefer not to interfere between you and my sister, the two I care, and if ever interfere fixed, do not tell me not to worry, if all I do, everything I do I do for you, look into my eyes and tell me if I lie, do not tell me to stop taking care of fighting for what I want, what you mean to me is more than you know and do not tell me not to die for you, that I will, die for you, risk it all, close your eyes can hear what I'm thinking, search my soul if lie, you can look inside my heart.

-I can't do.

-You will.

-Of course not. I will not play with this.

-Look at me is not a game, you and me against the world.

Take my face with his hands frozen, nothing made me shiver that his kiss I had wanted for so long, he forced my mind to see his soul, everything I had thought while he was away from me, as glad to see me go by and as he blamed for that, in his mind he blamed for everything, I could not hold back the tears that rolled down my cheeks, I could feel his pain and anguish memories for their friends and the Sirs who killed the witch, to know how much he loved me and I him, it was if we were one heart finally stopped him, but could not with such feeling, not wanted to see more of his memories.

-Nobody planned this just happened we can't blame us for everything that happens let me know if you love me too.

-Alan… if I want to be your girlfriend. Laughed and kissed me again

-I love you girl.

-I love you too.

-No matter what everyone say or what may be with you.

-Together for all eternity no matter what happens I will be with you always.

-I was afraid.

-Fear that.

-When I went for you I was afraid.

-Come here.

Hugged her and she was crying of course she was scared was normal and there is nothing that can change that, but she save my life and killed a demon, drove very well to be safe, although that ended the truck, dry her eyes relaxed.

-Is almost midnight we have… we go to my house, us to will be waiting.

-Yes we go.

-We'll be fine.

-Nice car.

-Well you finished my truck and being repaired.

-You did not have another one.

-If that is for me.

-What.

-If I have another, this is for you.

-I think not.

-If you finished the truck and your brother used yours.

-Will give me a car.

-If it is yours, you like.

-You know if it is yellow.

-I knew you would.

-But I can't too.

-Not again.

-While I accept that.

-Great are almost there.

-Rather already we. We got

-Something else, I can hold your hand.

-You know I will feel strange.

-I already fell strange. Fears his hand

Entered the house there was music and chatting all, were in the dining room, Monica had fallen for him like my home, seemed like a mansion, like all of them, for me it was just a house, we all looked and Sarah blushed, in itself it to and more right now.

-I said he would bring… way to go brother.

-Hewett you owe me twenty dollars.

-Only twenty to my bet, me two hundred and he win, they will let you bet more against.

-Shut Dylan.

Bet if he could bring it there was cruel to us but it did not bother her, and knew them.

-Sister takes long, just in time for the toast.

-And who will say something. Nobody wanted to do

-What about you Sarah.

-Well I do teacher.

-Well I toast because we are together…Look at all… I toast to life.

-So is sister.

All toast, Alan would not let go of my hand or a moment, finished the toast and continued with hugs, pass all jus missing Kalinda, but hesitate for a moment I remembered what Alan said, I did not want to be angry with her, so I went I gave her a huge everyone stared, as if expecting something else, did not take long, and Alan came over and too my hand again, walked and talked with everyone, for a moment look at Kalinda and chatted with Hewett and approached me.

-Alan I can talk to Sarah.

-Sister and talked about this.

-Please.

-Alan is fine already back. We move a little

-Well in question?

-Know my brother loves you and does not want anything to happen they are all I have of course and Dylan.

-I know and I did not want to hurt him.

-I know I'm sorry, I wish I'd been the one to find him, I think he was scared of losing him.

-Kalinda I love him was scared but I had to, had to go by.

-I really appreciate it very much, for taking of my two brothers.

-Hewett is very good friend and I also saved me to.

-Then it happened, do not than me more.

-I will not.

-And we're not friends.

-Clear, we are sisters in law.

-True. Smiled and return with Alan

-What she say?

-Women's things.

-Do not tell me.

-No.

-He all, Monica and I want to tell you something.

No attention until Alan hit the round thing like a cast bronze plate.

-Adriel continuous.

-Well, we had something to say.

-If anything to say. Monica interrupted

-Continues friend.

-Monica and I are getting married.

-We know. Someone in the back shout that knowledge

-If they do not know when.

-If we get marred this spring after turning eighteen.

-Monica you not you birthday years are immortal you stay in seventeen.

-I know but we have to wait until it is legal, the age account.

-Good great friend, brother I wish the best for the two which anything you want. All congratulated and applauded

-What are your plans?

-Think a simple wedding at the monastery and Sarah you to take of the food and be my maid of honor.

-Seriously. Look at Alan

-Sure.

-And Hewett be your brother…

-Alan wants to be our godfather. We look at it all.

-Which is the same as Hewett?

-Not this time.

-Well of course I do.

-While we have a wedding to plan.

Alan hug me and time passed more quickly, did not want to be away from him, I told him if we could go to his library and said yes.

-Happens.

-Well because you gave me a car and I have nothing to give you.

-Not have to give me anything.

-I know but his is yours. Remove the box from my bag.

-That is?

-Do not know I found it has you name and in think it's a good time to give it you.

-Where you found it.

-In my mother's things, but open it when you're alone.

-Not want to see it.

-Not, bring a note saying only you could see it.

-A note eh. He said laughing

-If.

-Where this.

-Forget it, but I told you were saying.

-You know you should not read it.

-Curiosity.

-Well if you had not read you would have opened the box.

-Of course not.

-Good if. And laughed

-You say with me.

-I'll be with you forever.

-I mean here in my house.

-Do not think so.

-Well keeps it for later.

-If we go.

And had fun but were tired, Alan offered his house to stay and did not have to stay in the living room each had their own room, his house looked different no dust with all the lights on, and had mare life, I think there had been long time that way, I was tired I stayed in this bedroom, as the last time, he stayed me for a while and then left, it would stay in another I thought, I woke up around ten o'clock in the morning, had not woken anyone believed that the teacher was with some of the guys in the training room, my brother was still asleep, ask for Alan and they sent me to their library, among untouched, in fact it was open, he stood by the window, was lying on the couch with a book on his lap, I approached.

-Hi good morning.

But no answer, looked outside and I moved closer look, he was asleep, I spoke not, take the book I sat next to him, and star to read the book he had, angels, was reading about angels, would be so I said, side on the floor even more books had me up and look all about angels, are many have read all, were many rightly still asleep, I started one with a very old dough.

Angels are believed to act in our live stimulating the minds and imagination, we whisper in your ear, the good word and shape our perceptions of the world. Teaches us that we know, the precise place to be, also the life that leads to it, the answers to our questions lie within us.

Angles are those who inspire us in a divine and are the angels who raise our spirits, angels help choosing a healthy way I integrate, lead us towards those beings and situations that promote our development and spiritual psychotic.

Yet know what we can't see or feel about ourselves.

Names were many angels, I guess everyone has one close, Alan was still asleep, leave his books aside and turned to approach him, I sat on my knees on the couch watching it, out there the snow was still falling, I think all we would stay at home and no one seemed to want to leave, was also huge so we're comfortable, I much this is the best day I'd like your house, I just walked through the halls but will on another time, I could not stop looking at the snow.

-That beautiful out there.

-No more than you girl.

-I woke up.

-If something like that.

We watched a second; he did not move from there, it looked very comfortable, he also watched the snow fall and gradually stopped, be started more slowly when the end finish everything was covered with snow, was fascinating to live there and look around, it was a beautiful white and all quiet, I wanted to go out and play in the snow but cold embers, I felt anxious.

-Sarah we leave out.

-What?

-If we take your coat and let's go.

-Okay.

Left the house laughing went outside and walked, the snow was deeper than I thought, but no matter we kept walking, we went through the woods away from the house.

-Where we go.

-Just keep walking.

-Is difficult.

-Walks, not carry you.

-I did not want that, well yes. He laughed

Walked up a creek now frozen and covered with snow, some animals around that are not scared to see us, he was very quiet, but nevertheless I could not same for me, I fell one time and left me, not to me if I got up I was standing, was a divine light, the light that came was perfect but it was too could but not matter.

-Keep walking.

-Be long.

-After these trees.

-Are you sure?

Just kept walking, he said nothing, he came first, I stayed behind again, I fell and when I woke up he was standing looking at something, just saw him.

-Look there.

-Is impossible.

-No, is divine, made by Gad.

-Believe in God.

-You're not.

-Sure.

-Every winter I come to this place.

-As your secret place.

-Now, the guys know it, everything's perfect.

-Sure I can see my house. He smile

-Well, he would see only that everything is covered with snow and everything looks the same.

-Is true all the same, We are all equal, there should be peace, look at all those people ending what God created, this place is perfect.

-Is a mountain course is perfect.

This place can't be truly perfect, all clear across the lake and a view of the world, as would the little Marcos, when we took him to the monastery, wow I can see the world, I wonder how it will look in the spring, at this time was dangerous to be up here but I did not matter much.

-Frightens you will be here.

-A little but I'm with you and the view is divine.

-So it is. I threw a snowball

-Seriously.

-Because no.

-Know that I shall gain.

-I do not think.

We played in the snow, ran and laughed, the cold was no problem, everything was quiet, we ended our little fight, and we walked into clearing, and as each day went with it instantly wished never ended, that day out forever eternal.

-You think Sarah.

-Want to know what I think.

-Clear, you see I can see in your memories unless you let me.

-I like that the day will never come to an end.

-Why you think that.

-Look everything is beautiful, everything is perfect, and who would want this to end.

-Truth is I do not want it to end.

-You see it was a day forever.

-Do not want this moment to be over, but I disagree with you, do not want this day to be eternal.

-And because no.

-Think.

-I do not know.

-If this day off forever, if never end, I lose tomorrow, and if this is wonderful you imagine the following can be better that this.

-Better yet.

-To you many days left to enjoy, just think about the days you can continue, if we are together, discovering something new every day.

-Be with you and have many days like this if I could desire and wait for a sensational morning.

-Best of all this is to be with you.

-Whether it would be wonderful.

-Yes, the first time someone accompanies me.

-Really.

-If.

-Let me see and endless day or many with you.

-If it is.

-I like the idea of many with you. We kissed

-But even if I will enjoy it as if it were the last of them.

-Clear that's fair.

-Back.

-Yeah right, you want to run a little.

-Know that I can walk with difficult and you want to run.

-Trust me and trust you.

-Teach me something new.

-Sure, you just watch. He ran

-And saw nothing.

-Uses wind, give me your hand.

-I can't.

-Have to can.

-Like it's so easy.

-aer-es. Throw it in the snow

-Sorry.

-You do not have to do that.

-Sorry just thought that.

-Do not think feel not trying to kill you, just to feel the wind and you can do it, it's simple and not about power and only know how to move.

-Teach me how to be silent like you.

-I think not.

-No.

-You can't, and then I taught.

-No, again.

-Okay pay attention.

-But do nothing.

-I just feel it.

-Good. Wait but nothing'

-Not help me.

-No, learns to walk.

-Okay.

Still trying and still falling, he enjoyed not even disguised, was.

-Enjoy it.

-Every moment as if the last.

-Ha ha.

I throw more snow but this time use my powers.

-That's cheating, buurum-I puella-ae (well girl) —mons-montis moveo-er (mountain trembles)

Moved earth and I fell from the tree a lot of snow, trapped, he them removed it I just felt that the wind took her.

-Sarah, Are you okay?

-What was that?

-I thought you learned.

-I believe that not everything.

-You have much to learn.

-I should think so.

Continue playing until we get home, as I said Monica his castle and even when we got we keep playing with the snow, the others were watching us, Alan threw one to his brother and he's returned, my brother also joined the fight, two against two, then Monica and Kalinda equally, and as expected Dylan joined my brother and the others are distributed around with Alan and others with Hewett, snow was a war which is sometimes used our powers to put more interesting, he left the house and accidentally hit him with Andrew reached the snowball, all stop throwing snow and watched Andrew apologize, the teacher did not answer but instead if joined us throwing snow falling from the trees, the teacher look it as entertainment because we made practice in the snow, but we took it as fun, besides not want to leave the house of Alan, was a rest so much pain continued throughout the afternoon practicing.

Following day was better as he said his side could expect fabulous days, showed me part of his house where there was some places in, had a great room that was closed in the background an amazing white piano, the room was round all covered with white, even the roses were white, everything was white curtains without any frames just as white as snow.

-Is yours you know haw play it.

-No.

-Not know.

-Yes but not mine, it was my mother she plays for me, well said for the three.

-That happened.

-She died grew old and it was time to leave.

-And your father.

-He had powers but was not immortal, taught me everything but just get his time to die.

-Sorry.

-I'm sorry too.

He breathe deeply it was hard to talk about it; the pain is always present even thought the time.

-Spent a lot of my brothers and I with them, listening to my mother play was fabulous were very happy.

-We like what we?

-Sure.

-Alan knows who to play it?

-Only a little.

-Can play something.

-Maybe.

-I can play something.

-If I can play it.

-Know how to play the piano.

-Just did not think I hear that music without knowing touch.

-Well you can play.

-Just do not make fun of me, but I' no expert playing it.

-Just treat well.

-Berceuse de Faure, something sad, something else.

-Have such this.

Copin waltz in flat, caisson-Le Calibri —Cleary, this is, sonnet in 1 in e minor cello or Bizet.

Were some who were on the piano I imagine that he or someone else liked.

-Not come, dance something.

-Like.

-Just wait.

-Listening to music.

-Sure just listen.

-Mayer (Short Trip Home)

-Is sad but very good.

-All were sad.

-True.

He leaned out his hand, took a rose in a vase and was offered it to me, I smiled and took his hand, he pulled me towards him and in his arms, still dancing.

-Who taught you to dance?

-My parents, dancing all the time, this was their space, this I my favorite song.

-Is beautiful.

-You like.

-Sure, but it makes me mourn.

He look into my eyes and kiss me, was a wonderful moment and very special.

Music was heard throughout the house but no one came, continued as more songs as Mozart Beach and others, but not only those listening liked modern music and equally loud, heard of any but continued dancing other the rest of the days following, and reading in his library, looking all over about angels, I just wanted to read and be with him, sometimes he read to me apparently was fascinated by books, he saying it was like another would who might travel, loved to learn and I thought only I liked reading but he beat me.

It was strange to think that will be there and it had to end, but I thought about what he said, I had to let time pass and wait for tomorrow, our love grew stronger every minute and we could not be away from each other, could not stop loving him, would not stop loving, our day did not end in the snow, after that freeze, Hewett and Andrew left the water running and was so cold that froze, managed to do several things, one could say that works of art, everything was frozen, it was too slippery but still left, it was interesting to practice on frozen, but when we fell was more painful than the snow, was like falling on pavement, still trying to walk without being heard, like a shadow but I accomplished nothing, I learned many things, sometimes hear stories about how they were before become in what it is and how they missed their parents like me, but it had to be.

Special Occasion

Unfortunately the holydays ended we all had to go back to our old life, I to school and work, but Monica had a wedding to plan and had to help.

-Friend look this is what I need for my wedding.

-I thought it would be small.

-Of course I will, look.

List

-*Wedding dress.*

-*Place.*

-*Bridesmaids clothing.*

-*Suits.*

-*Invitation.*

-*Cake.*

-*Flowers.*

-*Banquet.*

-*Decorations.*

According to me it was what I needed for my wedding and my friend Sarah would help me, I was nervous and did not know where to start, had many plans but did not want anything over the top.

-We have to go see the dress.

-You know where.

-No not yet.

-Alan and I were good thinking something… no if you want, because the godfather is trying to help.

-As help me?

-Is a friend of the person that well, you remember the dress that he gave me?

-How cold I forget!

-Well that person can make yours.

-If to do so if it is just as great as yours accept.

-This afternoon you can go to take the measures and then just wait.

-If you're the best friend thanks.

-Know.

-You need something more in your list.

-That?

-Music.

-True.

-Star, a long way from the day.

-Time flies Monica.

-If true that we will first.

-Let me see you list, ready dressed, place know where.

-If the ceremony will be in the monastery and the reception your brother asked Alan who was at his home.

-Well said.

-Well.

-Said no.

-Of course he says yes.

-Good place ready.

-Your dress follows Sarah and Kalinda and my sisters.

-If who will choose.

-I clear my wedding.

-I do not want one horrible.

-Of course not I know who to chosen.

Time passed and the date approached, we agreed that in the spring, that everything comes back to life, everything blooms, I like when the trees are still flowers, Alan was the perfect house fascinates me, and had enough space and only so many trees would buy some white and red roses there are more than just these but all full of roses love those colors, and maybe some carnations, chosen colors of the dresses for my friends and blue with an opening something bold, but looked good and Sarah did not say they were horrible costumes, so that would be, the boys were together for their suits and have fun as well, everything seemed fine, Hewett would take care of the music and the cake Sarah, I would continued with the invitations and decorations, it was not much, if everything was ready, we were several times to test the wedding dress, was running perfect, like everything, my parents would come that day, and everything was fine and we had not bad news of ill, everything would be perfect, I spend valentine's day we celebrate each one separately, Adriel took me to dinner and dancing, clear a few gifts, Sarah told me they did not, but the pass very well knowing Alan, not that I did not like what I did is that it is well, it is considered perfect, my wedding day arrived we would celebrate in mid-April, would be great but was nervous.

We were all gathered at Sarah, Hewett one began with a bachelor party Adriel, he was already planning to do end where would, would clear Alan's house this.

-Clear that we will do nothing.

-Why brother, of the Monica's do tomorrow.

-That! Not true.

-Clearly if I will.

-Way to go girl.

-Thanks Hewett.

-And we will not have Adriel.

-Sure.

-Great, will be tomorrow.

-Boys behave yourselves.

-That will make Sarah.

-Anything that you do not Alan.

-Nothing you we do not. Stared at each other

-And what would be the fun.

-Can do anything else.

-And you.

-Otherwise.
-Well then it's a deal we'll be good.
-Clear that we will do guys.
-And that wicked smile Sarah.

Not answer every one returned to his things, the next day his sister Monica come around three o'clock, had planned many things and did not care Monica wanted to have fun, I think I we do pass very well, we play games and after a while I get the humorous, Monica placed in the center and blindfolded and us around, we prepared that we'd danced to it, we did it to play strange parts, we all laughed and then the boys came and danced with her, and thinking it was us playing, his sister Jazmine recorded everything not miss it for the world show it later, after a while she took off the blindfold and saw the daring dancers yelled, but then got exited and did not mind just had fun.

Forgetting for a moment that would make the boys, we'll worry about that later, after it was over all were asleep in the living room hugging, I was late and do not woke, Alan Adriel came, and the whole house was a mess, Monica gifts were everywhere, many of them were interior sexy clothes, and some toys his sisters were tremendous, and you can imagine, one of the guys stayed with Pilar, of course nothing happened respected, stayed bad soldier.

-What happened here?
-This means that my friend ignored the rules.
-And you want to you behave well.
-Alan if I'm good, you witness this.
-Clear if the teacher already forgotten.
-It was your brother's idea to bring those girls.
-Yeah well we wake up we have a dinner to plan.

Climbed the music volume all that was, passed the twelve in the morning, we woke up all scared and with a terrible face, we were looking at the mess and then them.

-Girls broke the rules.
-We did not.
-So and so. Did not answer

-Pilar, what happened.

-Was my fault it's nice.

-While all clean.

-And what is this?

-Do not tell me you do not Alan. Pilar wonder

But blushed and turned around, we laugh and we started cleaning for dinner with Monica's parents, the boy went but Pilar invite him to the wedding.

Nigh came for dinner, everything was ready and it was perfect, wishing the best for them.

-Alan and you they did last night.

-Just talk girl.

-If as no.

-True and remember you're punished, broke the rules.

-Your equal.

-Not true.

-I know you brother do not forget.

-Well if it was better than yours compared.

-Yeah right, ours was better.

-I doubt it.

-Have proof.

-They were recorded.

-No, well yes.

-Hewett also.

-We will discuss later.

-Sarah and I'm the best man and you maid of honor, we could pay their honeymoon.

-As they do not believe it is a good idea to leave things as they are.

-I think otherwise.

-I do not understand.

-Apparently everything is fine and I do not pass anything and only a few days will not be much.

-Already talked to my brother.

-No, that's up to you.

-That's not fair.

-I pay you will say.

-And to think where to send?

-To the city of sin.

-To Las Vegas.

-Why not.

-I think not.

-A better idea.

-There is a reason to send him there truth.

-Is true there is.

-Which is?

-You really want to know.

-Sure.

-A demon is there and we have to kill it.

-That the risked.

-They will not know we're there.

-We.

-Clear not leave you her alone.

-Good we come in handy some heat before it hits the summer and ever go.

-Heat is good.

-If it is, it's fabulous.

-All set.

Good it came the day special for my brother and my best friend, revising that everything went well, we were in the house of Alan, everything was perfect, I went to see my brother before it started the ceremony, all of them were ready but Monica even not was, and took advantage for postponement is a bit.

-Are ready brother.

-Do not know I'm nervous.

-Of course you are, and I like.

-Sister a hug.

-Yes but before the wedding gift from Alan.

-That is?

-Your honeymoon good for only two days with all expenses paid.

-And we can go.

-Sure, everything will be fine, well be only two days, it could happen.

-You day.

-I say.

-If you say that could happen, something will go wrong.

-Not this time.

-We will be unattended.

-If.

-Do not believe you.

-Okay no, but I want you to enjoy this day, you better leave, we will be in the church but you must reach before. We hugged

-My mother would have liked to this day.

-I know but I'm brother and all will be well.

-Time to go, make sure you do not miss Monica.

-Of course.

I went to see my friend and almost finished it looked beautiful like a goddess, finally was ready and left, Monica looked nervous and I was happy for them, we finally got it down to the limousine, wait at the entrance while checking if everything was okay, it was clearly that my brother was anxious, I finally went with Hewett walked and Alan, together, then the other, then we hope to get Monica, watched my brother and sensed that he had wanted to go with her, but stand it waiting, gave his father and brother and my brother off the face veil she had a big smile, all stated, Alan delivered the rings, was the best man and everything was perfect as planned the priest had marred.

His kiss did not end with this story, but is started another story that will never end, it will be for all eternity.

After the ceremony her parents of Monica took a lot of photographs, and when leaving the expected with great applause, fell bubbles and red rose petals around her, just as she wanted.

We headed home Alan this time I went with him, clear that the couple had to go together, the banquet was ready and the cake was perfect to prepare them, time passed and the night came, they danced their first together as spouses, clearly dance with my beloved and his brother, took not one so I had permission to dance with, although I would like to stay with Pilar they seemed, and I think that ultimately meet and danced together, her friend went bachelorette had another job, the night ended, we stayed with Alan, my brother and Monica would go to another day in the afternoon, she did not know so she had to pan his luggage and us alike, we said goodbye to them and wish them luck and that we expected back at last they left.

Disagreement

ave to rush to get there before them.

    -If well Alan but does not seem fair that we do.

    -Is for good reason.

-If that kill a demon.

-If so is.

-All go.

-If all.

-Know how to kill a demon.

-The teacher has a plan.

-I'm included in you plan.

-You are the best weapon.

-Alan I'm a weapon?

-Was just an expression, do not bother.

-I told my brother that someone will be watching.

-That you say?

-Because he's my brother.

-Okay time to go.

Only carried a small suitcase was only a couple of days, but was worried about all this to jeopardize my brother and I said nothing of what was happening, so that not to worry, before we did not have lie, but lately we hide things to each other and that made me feel bad.

-Really know how to kill a demon.

-Well teacher has a plan.

-Know what is.

-No truth said he preferred it to be secret.
-Why?
-May not want to Rosalba finds out.
-If you do not think so.
-Well, we will do in the meantime.
-Locate that is our job.
-Will not be easy.
-Yes, but after the others arrived to help.
-Who takes care of my brother?
-Some of the monastery.
-I fell this is crazy.
-But if I just have to trust the teacher.
-Yes but it is still crazy.

Arrived at the airport, Monica was radiant loved it and it was my wife, although had been too early I know it was what I wanted, I could not stop loving her, we board the plane to Vegas, known as Sin City, my beloved wife was equally excited, but concerned about Sarah, I had a feeling that I feeling that I was hiding something not very good to lie, it did not make long to arrive at the airport we picked one the casino hosts, Alan and knew them and planned the trip, I expect myself to choose something, but the person who picked up said everything we ask him would get it for us, dropped our luggage was not much and shown to our room, knew we were honeymooners we got the key and left and of course I gave them tip, the room was perfect with champagne await us and the bed had heart of rouse petals and also throughout the room, load my wife to the bed, the kiss her and the champagne service, dinner and some music in the light of the candles, everything perfect not stop admiring the beauty of my wife, as also kept kissing her and the rest be better than imagine it ever left the room all night.

I woke up and looked at my wife still sleeping like an angel and just thanked God for allowing me to be with her, I do not wanted to wake up, talk on the phone to ask for breakfast to be deliver, I was waiting beside the bed and she woke up, gave me a good morning kiss and hug me, she was happy to be with me, had breakfast and she wonder what we would do.

-Go around the city.

-Town.

-If I made a reservation and awaits us a car outside the hotel.

-Rather it is a casino.

-If true Moni.

-Then I go get ready and go.

-I'll wait here.

-Not have to wait turns around in the casino and then I go down.

-Are you sure.

-Clear.

-Do not delay.

A walk down to the casino and I found my host, and told me everything will be ready.

-Yeah well just missing my wife.

-Why not play while waiting.

-No thanks I do not take much.

-Well, if you change your mind beyond this.

-Thanks indeed.

I wait but not down it takes an eternity, I want to play to pass the time, I played only in the machines and did not even know they were doing, Alan's crazy to sending us here, but being with Monica changes everything, finally come, looked divine wearing something low-cut dress with her hair down, it looked weird look that way, or rather think than ever, where we live it's cold, so always wore pants, or do not know I think I had not noticed before, I went for it and we went in the car it had while waiting for us, the good that Alan would pay for everything, according to him, was a gift for being the best man and also Hewett, well we went to explore the city.

-We do after; I do not even have time to look around the city.

-I think so.

-Not true, we only have until tomorrow to see it.

-I have plans, everything will be fine, trust you husband.

-Ok.

The car stopped.

-We go sir. The driver goes out and opened the door

-Let wife of mine there to get off.

-No possible I will not.

-Or if you'll do mine beloved.

-Do not know that I'm terrified to fly and want me to get on a helicopter.

-Will be fine you're with me and never let it happen at all.

-Maybe you can fly.

-Hopefully not proved necessary.

-Not matter. Take her by the hand

-While I accept this, but I'm terrified.

Ups, she really was terrified scream when we took off, I held very strongly firs close his eyes but then had to open them or all would be lost, both paths did not last, but ours was different, would take us beyond the city.

-How are you?

-Terrified but I have fun love.

-Great.

Las Vegas drove around in a half an hour and headed to the great canon, we took several laps was impressive, and scary for her, but was excited, was still terrified, the helicopter had permission to land in a safe place in the canon, we got off and took the food there in the top, it was breathtaking spectacular views, Mr. reserve fuel carried and placed him walk while not far away, enjoying the wind that's why we had to return, but not before watching the sunset together and with a champagne and clear our afternoon ended with a kiss, but not end our adventure, we also returned by the Hover Dam and arrived in the city at dusk, it looked awesome, when the helicopter landed and our transport is waiting for us and drove us around town, as I had asked go somewhere else, we finally arrived.

-Really kidding.

-Of course not, we will be fun.

-Not have enough magic if you want to see more.

-Clear not would go to see a magic show.

-Some fun.

In spite of everything if we enjoy the show, we had dinner and then headed to hotel and back in the room still looking at her, I could not stop see her, watching her face her look was perfect, as she smiled at me across the room overlooking the city, my way so slowly without saying a word, I felt a lump in the throat, did not know what to say she just looked at me and walk.

-I'm happy to be you wife.

-And I more.

We kissed again and everything was perfect time again, the next morning was our second and last day in the city, go back home tomorrow, but would spend a wonderful time, this time she chose the places to visit, we spend some time at a pool and went to a concert, we were tired and went to bed.

Fallow trying to figure out what secrets kept the box, asking some who had owned before. Just know it was dangerous, that contained the secret of the heart and in the wrong hands would be the downfall of all we know in life, a soul for the light of life.

Walked towards the dark castle corridors hoping to find the mysterious lady, but deep down I know I wanted the danger, that could be my death, but a voice inside me was saying continues, do not stop is your fate.

I had to follow the dark corridor, was brave but not enough, in my heart I was scared, even though I was the best detective in those times, although it had been unable to find the answer, the black clouds covered the sky they did even more dangerous and desolate. As every hallway has an end, the end comes but nothing, only solitude, my soul felt empty, I know something would happen.

Fail in my search, if it would be the end, it would be my immortality destruction.

-Awakens love will make us late. I woke up scared

-Are you okay?

-Yeah, you are?

-I'm not sure.

Alan and I arrived in Las Vegas as were planned, we headed to the hotel where we would run, was in the outskirts of the city, it was not anything fancy, we would be only a few moments, each had a room.

-Sorry not very elegant.

-Okay we'll do next?

-Look the devil.

-As we find them.

-Just go to walk and that he seeks us too.

-If we are looking for because it did at home.

-He can't enter the mountain, is protected.

-And that we come from?

-To find it.

-And why?

-Okay he really took a vacation like not really controlled and is known will come.

-As he know?

-By rumors.

-Leaves and playing with me, tell me what happens.

-You bothered.

-I'm upset.

-Honeymoon of you brother. I look angrily

-He knows that your brother will come, it is waiting.

-They made you, they left as bait.

-I told you you'd be upset. He paused

-But I promise you will find before.

-I lied to my brother I came I put it in danger.

-Not, so you just have to spend two days.

-For two days.

-Give us time to find it.

-I have to tell my brother.

-You will not Sarah ruining their honeymoon.

-No matter.

-Are you sure about that. Let the phone

-While we will look.

-If well.

-Where we started?

-Go there just to walk the streets and see that look.

-Not have a plan.

-Is true, not yet.

-Alan God is my brother.

-I know but just have a chance.

-We expect.

-I need to get the teacher and others.

-Why, by you plan?

-If it is so, he knows what to do, to look after you brother will be fine.

-If I'm not.

-Well let's walk.

-Okay let's go.

Was angry with him, out of the hotel he wanted to hold my hand do not let the, he swallow saliva and kept walking, and not say a word, just looked around me, I could not believe that the used me, and I had deceived, even though I loved him could not bear the thought that he was lying and put my brother in danger, walking through the stress all looked normal among so many people, like to know who will be the devil and which will by that he had not said the hell out of the abyss, or how many had been nevertheless sometimes discreetly watched him, his eyes were lost in people, as if he knew where to go, and I walked fast beside him, sometimes I was a few steps back, and walking while continuing to waiting for me, at some point I wanted to return, started to tire, her noticed and stopped without saying anything, the evening come, we went to eat but was no hungry just itched the food, he took his phone and made a couple of calls, after a while we left the place, entrance in the blue car we expected a two-door convertible model Snyder, he said we climbed and I would do not want to keep walking more, I was exhausted, although I liked walking seemed silly to me not knowing where to go around.

I did not comment the car, I figured that's what calls were made, he kept his gaze distant and I was still angry with him and do not know what to say and imagine that either, he do not speak all the way, arrived at the hotel late and others not yet arrived, I went up to my bedroom and he to his own, wishing for their look and behavior would say he wanted to go with me to my room and talk, but I went so fast and I close that time did not give him anything, this time to listen through the door as he walked away, the wood creaked strange the ever to a sound maybe it toward to listen.

I sat on the edge of the bed, waiting but did not know what I expected, there was nothing to do, my small suitcase was still unopened and not touched, not even a book to read and time pass, look in the canyons that were there, the only thing I had was a Bible I began to leaf through even I read, I lay down in bed all silent and all heard was the clock on the wall, listening to every second pass, as he was listened silently stronger, spend much time listening watch with my eyes close and was about to sleep.

I finally got up and stated reading first page was the creation as God made everything and how old was the first men lived, were too, some nearly seven hundred years, and follow but skipped the pages.

Reading a new chapter of Timothy and the last sheet was saying because the purpose of the commandment is love from the heart, clean and good conscience and a sincere faith. Ti 1; 5

Bible is endless mystery and is best not to discuss it, everyone understands his convenience, I think.

I closed and I turned on the television in the news channel and I fell asleep.

Knocked on my door not too hard woke up, I was confused for a moment where I was I had forgotten, I watch the clock up on the wall, with the noise of the TV did not hear his tic, tack, was nearly nine, very late and were still knocking on my door, I finally got up, and opened it.

-Hi Sarah are already her, sorry to wake you.

-If once I.

-I can pass and wait.

-No, I have to change; I'll be right Alan please.

-Okay, do not delay.

-Of course. I sigh

I close the door and rush to change, I just got a T-shirt and jeans and went out of the room, not much later, the not left me waiting in the hallway, walk next to him, even though it was quieter was angry, walked another room this was bigger than mine, was where the teacher and the others gathered.

I thought everything would be fine and that my brother, and so was everything was fine, they said they have a plan but is still would say it.

Finally ask what his plan but just looked at me and the teacher came to me and mentioned that I would say until the time came, his expression of all was the same as mine, disagree, apparently no one knew the plan, in that case we were doing here, well said and tour the city in search of something strange and they knew each some friends that we could ask, of course I had to go with Alan, we spend all day walking the outskirts of the city, at time I thought it was a waste of time, but we found some people who had known a person a little different.

-He knows we're here and when he wants it appear, just have to wait.

Remained silent, spent the day, the night came and the next day arrived, it had not wanted to eat well lately and I felt a little dizzy, not come out the room, I was lying, this time not hear he knocked, he entered without being heard as before, this was his custom, was with the lights off, all in silence, listening to the clock go the minute, listening as they passed the hours wanting the day to end.

-Need to eat something.

-No thanks, you should knock.

-If I knock not you let me enter.

-Maybe.

-Are you still upset, but he's fine, are having fun.

-I hope but not change the fact that I lied and you to me.

-Know and I have no excuse but you have to eat.

-And then I do not want to tour the city.

-Okay, you can stay here.

-Leave me alone? He looks and sat on the edge of the bed

-Of course I'll stay here with you.

-Get bored and also have to help them.

-I'll be fine here.

-Great can stay.

Good, I ate what I take this delicious, then everything was still as if her were not, and went back to lay next to me even, close my eyes and looked at me without saying anything, I could hear his breathing close to me, I put more attention to him that the sound of the clock, I straightened and looked at him and then I slept on his arm, hugged me and I could hear his heart beating so hard, now the only thing I hear is his heart beating, still without saying a word, the day was almost over, I was tired of lying down, to him not seem bother, I got up and looked out the window, looking at the city I all its glory so light and wanted to go for a walk at night, he stood up next to me and looking at me as if he knew what I wanted.

-If we can get your want.

-Would walk.

-Just something more, enough girl.

-What you mean.

-Stop tormenting me, I can't stand your indifference.

-I do not; just do not know what to say.

-Just say you're mad at me, whatever but says something.

-I really do not know what to say. All was silent

He took my hand this time even though I did not want to take her I let, but then I let it.

-I have to change.

-Clear.

Watch his face with intentions we got out, I made a gesture and smiled, but did not get away, grabbed my things and went to the bathroom which was fine for me, but according to him was not enough, I later something out of bathroom, I usually change into my bedroom but trying to change, for fine output, not wearing fancy clothes, just normal that used at home, hem whole time it looked good and I felt uncomfortable to go if this place with him, but no matter, and the other day we would leave home, and we would go for a walk alone, I wore a black jacket and finally come out.

-Well, come on.

-If it's okay, just a question back tomorrow.

-If…do not know, will tell us in a while. Walk

-I'm sorry I lied, but I did not know this would happen; the teacher did not want to tell.

-Does not tell us the hope his plane works.

-If I like.

-Never question it at all.

-Never is wrong.

-And if it does.

-Good question.

Walk a while in fact very little, got a call and had to go, they were all together, we to his room and all were there waiting.

-Happens something teacher.

-Yes, we will be better tomorrow and do not leave the hotel to any of us.

-Is seriously, better be yes.

-I can know what happens.

-The devil has found us and you better be ready.

-What about my brother.

-He is safe.

-Quis cognosco-ere,-novi-nutus de abl angelus. (You learned about angels)

-Antistes otitis. (Teacher) Looked at him strangely

-De w abl angelus. About angels

-Postea posume loqutor loqui locutus antistes otitis. Then we can talk teacher

-Quippe quemadmodum si. Definitely yes

-Sarah goes to your room you should rest.

-Are you talking about? He took my hand and walked to my room

-What's going on, who wants to the angels.

-As you know.

-Not much just understood that word; it is easy angelus, angels.

-I do not know.

-Why you were reading about them, you mean. Enter

-Not, looks do not bother, wait it was just a question.

-My brother back tomorrow.

-If, he returns tomorrow.

Finally after several days hugged him, her gaze shifted it looked happier, stayed with me, we were hanging around waiting news and arrived the other day, I could not sleep, read me a book the carrying, I like to hear, his voice the way he reading it reassured me, the morning came and I think finally slept.

When I woke up it was almost two in the afternoon, my head ached and everything was spinning there was food on the table, but he was not, to arrange and if I ate, I thought that if I had given something to sleep much, were very late, finished and headed to the room of the master, perhaps had fresh news, and what time we would go we.

Touch were to come in, and then enter, they had to leave for a time, and the teacher came out, had several books and found one very old, and I opened it and started to read it as I expected.

Invocation to the Angels

Angels can help us in many ways and at any time. Follow to the next line.

The powers of names number three.

I read some words and understanding.

Single invocation.

Facing north and south. Center.

Crystal. Mirrors. Pure oil.

Spring water. Meditation. Help ritual.

My heart sped up, I felt that my breathing was cut, I closed the book and put it in place, I could not believe, surely I'm confused, they were not able to, they can't, no air was still, I approached to the window was open, I take the air, I could see the street and I could see the teacher and Alan talking or rather arguing, he raised his eyes and can see, I leave and ran to the bedroom, where he entered did not understand what he said, was still dizzy, he approached me, I downgraded more I even realized that run just look at me, I felt something strong air, close my eyes, I was scared, I felt his hand grab mine and pulled her the pain in it, pulled strong, I did not open my eyes, do not know was dazed, still felt strange.

-Sarah opens your eyes, look at me. Do not open

-Reacts.

-Hurt me, let go. I tried to removing his hand from mine

-Girl opens your eyes you're doing.

Finally opened them, looked at his eyes, was something far, was still dizzy, I wanted to let me go, but look at the anguish in his eyes, I closed mine to open a second and I realize how wrong I was, the I was hurting, but it wanted to save me, holding me with his hand towards the window had fallen, react.

-Alan that happened.

-Hold on do not try to let go, give me you other hand.

-Hold me do not let go.

Then I went up with no problem, hugged him, I still scared, did not know what happened I do not realized I had fallen out the window.

-What has happened, because you could not get on?

-Because you were struggling, wanted me to let you go.

-That it is possible not what was happened.

-Girl silly, why you did it, you were thinking.

His eyes filled with tears, never seen him so scared, he hugged me and I to him, still on the floor, followed a little dizzy.

-These better.

-No, I fell something wrong, I think I have nausea.

I get up, charge in his arms ignoring all those who were, the teacher talked and ignored him, took me till the room and I learned back on the bed I do not felt good everything was spinning, try to get up but I could not, he came to me and sat down and hug me.

-What happened?

-Maybe something I ate, Alan I will be fine.

-Scared me, never ever do that girl.

-Arrived very fast, I saw you down.

-Ran.

I kissed was happy to be with me, I think I would have died if not for him.

-Sorry, not that I spend I did not even realize that I fell, I'm sorry.

-No need to apologize.

Follow frightened and I lay down and him next to me, it took away the nausea, I turned to face him.

-When we're out of here, I do not want to be.

-We can leave early tomorrow.

-Are you sure.

-Yes I am how you feel.

-Good, we can go.

-Where you want to go.

-Please just go.

-Are you sure?

-If.

-Well let. Go out the teacher looked at us

-Where they go, they can't leave.

-We will turn around.

-I can drive myself.

-Okay, you know where to go.

-Not be difficult.

Gave me that keys, we jumped and drive out of town, was impressive as we were leaving behind, would disappear, no one imagine that there is.

-Well I wanted to see the star in this place they look closer, or so I had heard.

-Is true and you can stop?

-Okay, where.

-We will follow that road, not yet dusk, whether we can see the sunset.

-True.

Finally stopped would spend the afternoon admiring, I was better because I knew that my brother would be home by this time.

-What happened to you at the hotel?

-You know your truth.

-What you mean.

-Know they want an angel.

-Did not know until this morning and I disagree.

-They will.

-I do not know.

-We do?

-Wait.

-I'm scared.

Looking at the horizon the sun disappear, disappearing heat reflecting I a reddish, Alan kissed my forehead and hug me, the evening came to an end. I knew we had to return at any moment and deal with what they wanted to do.

-Wanted an angel to the end with the devil, do not know how to end it.

-So it seems! He was saying as he sighed

-Think they have not already called.

-No.

-How are you so sure?

-Because for that they needs you.

-To me, that.

-Remember that my blood bag demons.

-If and. sing again

-Well to get an angel it takes more than…

-More than Alan.

-More than just about pure ingredients, pure blood needed.

-Blood.

-Your blood.

-My blood.

-If so it would let you not.

-Is a joke really, then can't remove it without my blood.

-If they have to be blood, the more pure it there.

-And my blood is.

-If it is so pure and powerful that not only one but many would leave heaven.

-Know what you say is crazy, I'd rather die before having and angel as a slave, would not be fair, they are free spirits only obey God, not man.

-Know and we are here, we'll be fine.

-And what will happen when we return.

-Not be able to do anything, just have a try and was finished soon.

-What you mean.

-Know at this place come the stars feel that you are closer to then, closer to heaven and you can get an angel this day, today only half spring.

-Hopefully good finish and then return.

-Clear that it.

The night came and it was true, the star came out was really fascinating, almost felt that I could touch, watching them, they were like a sea, millions of them everywhere you turn around were infinite, we lay in the shade of the car, to some could but not enough I could still stand, time passed, all in silence, we were in the desert in the middle of nowhere, well knew that the city is close as a couple of hours but still were in the nowhere.

-One more day with you, you were right. He looked at me and smiled

-Get up Sarah.

-Happens.

-I hear someone coming.

-I see noting, as you know.

-I'm sorry, I feel the sand moves.

-I fell nothing.

-But I do and someone is coming.

Looked neither heard nothing, least felt anything but fear at that moment he looked a little anxious.

-Not far from me.

-That I would.

-Just do not go away no matter what happens.

After a couple of minutes, looked in the distance some lights approaching, we were there standing in the middle of nowhere and someone approaching, I wondered who would be.

-We found.

-Who?

-Well, for their driving is the teacher.

-That trying to get the angel?

-I'm afraid so.

-Would let you not, we got to go.

-Is late, it is not the only thing that follows us.

-The devil.

-I'm afraid so.

-We do?

-The devil took a while more.

The lights came up, there were four sports cars, parked in front of us the lights of them got out, they were our friends and the teacher, Kalinda and Dylan fell glad to see us or Alan.

-Guys who like to find them.

-Teacher.

Alan took my hand trying to defend our own friends, was enraged, light cars reflected the shadows of them approached Hewett, and was place to one side of me, like Alan did not agree with what the teacher wanted to do.

-Kids to understand the devil is close, what we have to do is the best, we need help.

-Enslaving an angel, does not seem fair.

-Life is never fair girl.

-I will not, will not have my blood, it'll give you the never.

-Serafina, brings things from the car.

The girl under the objects, I had read in the book, placing them in the shade of the car, than placed one by one and put them in from of me forming a six-pointed star, wanted to get away, the scent of things to me known, it had smelled before.

-Please teacher do not need, find another way, brother agree with.

-Not think there is another option, not that I approve but I see no other way out, the demo can kill us all.

-Dylan and Andrew I guess you agree.

-Alan no I'm not, Sarah saved my life I believe in it and I'm on your side.

-Andrew thanks and you guys.

Suddenly approached some cars but were some of the boys of the monastery, and had seen earlier in our fist training, they agreed with the teacher.

-Friend we are with you.

At that time Curran, Dylan, Andrew, Samara and Elmo were passed on our side protecting me, except Kalinda; Alan was puzzled by his decision he hated the idea of fighting with her, but not for that I would leave them to use my blood to bring an angel from heaven and enslave.

-Not a good decision Alan.

-Is true not want to fight with you, are family, we're good people.

-If we are good people but we must stop this madness.

-Madness is what you try to do.

-Sarah understands there is no other option.

-Should any, we will not became like them, so their plan, they drew a demon us an angel, not their war not of an angel.

-There is always war between good and evil.

-Yes but this is a war between humans, and you know, not between God and the devil, we are responsible for what happened, if God wanted to send an angel to help and would have commended.

-But the demon kill us all and not just one, are two demons.

-Then so be it.

-Girl bad decision.

We all got in battle position, Alan I step back from it, but I do not right that I will fight to each other, walked slowly backwards pulling away a little of them, step by step slowly without making any noise as I Alan had show me, all eyes were on me, I walked away thinking that would be best, I pass a car side Alan, he do not hear when stepped back, was attentive to what they did, ready to attack, but cautions because he did not want to, listen Samara tell she would take care of her cousin Kalinda, as Dylan hesitate to do something, then I felt a great chill happened near my fast, I did not fell anything but second was a little more away from everyone.

-Too late when Alan and others rolled their eyes filled with surprise.

-Alan warns you, it's too late now, said the teacher.

Alan walked slowly towards me; I knew right away that passed, was the devil, like the wind fast and quiet, I had caught, but between my thought was not too late but behind him and approached the brothers Hokon, and more evil of which we had thought.

-Let her go. Mentioning Alan

-Child never fools.

-Let me go demon.

-I will not, will have to see how all your friends die.

-They are stronger than you think.

-We'll see. The demon speak in anger

-Destroy them.

Although all were friends we protected each other and Alan nevertheless took care of her sister and brother, she thanked him with her eyes, happy to be around him, the teacher had to fight the evil, had no other option, sometimes look at me.

-You should to pay attention to it and bring the angel from heaven now too late for them.

-Never too late for anything, and tell me what devil you are. The demon laugh,

-I am Agramon, the demon of fear.

-And tell me Agramon you to be you afraid?

-Well you better start to fear.

Fortunately had learned a lot this time, at one point I get free, and stated to fight with him, was very strong as expected but was not willing to give in to, and ends with one of them but was stronger would beat him also, the only thing what I feared was a bad anything happen to my brother, and is safe, followed by fighting with, Alan trying to get to me, but it was near the left but could not do anything, had to defend his brothers and friends and was difficult decision.

Them or me, the devil hit me and nose bleed, remembered that a single drop of my blood could get an angel from heaven, and try not to get close to the star drawn in the sand, caught me again, was trying to hand myself but did not.

-Beautiful pity, they'll want you alive.

-That would be that.

-They want to open the portal.

-Want to get more demons.

-Dumb for that would wants.

-That's what they want.

-The heart to open the portal.

-Clear want to conquer the world. The demon turned to laugh

-That are misinformed, they do not want to conquer the world, well yes and no.

-What you mean.

-Can't control the world without first conquer the heaven?

-Are you talking about? What to conquer the heaven, that's impossible.

-Of course not, think beautiful if you can open as portal that will lift an angel from heaven, sure you can open on to enter heaven.

-There is no such of portal.

-Clear that if we'll open.

-Is not the only thing that wants right?

-Exact not immortal like you and your brother, he wants his immortality to rule the heaven like a God and never die.

-A God it will be impossible, the true God never allow it.

-That's the point when the portal is open not only take us to heaven, if not God will be vulnerable, maybe not kill but I we can lock them up.

-Never happened before I would die.

-I will not let you.

Still fighting, this time I fell on the car of Alan, I do not noticed that my front jab is bleed and was falling inside the star, I did not realize I was in it, my heat spend up, the demon could not get closer to me, that what terrified, Alan try to reach me but could not, the teacher stopped him, it was too late, the portal of heaven opens to bring and angel, had been completed, I thought it would not open that was closed, and all lit up around the star with me inside, I could not move my body lay still close my eyes and felt as if time stopped.

The light was intense even with close eyes, the feeling was calm, so peaceful the air felt warm, the sand revolved around me could see everything happening outside the star and nobody could get into it, heard a voice in my inside me that said you have to leave the star.

But it was more powerful than me, I was saying to myself that do not had to let go of the angel, try talking saying, if you can hear me angel, would not come as a prisoner did not want him; him to stay and the heaven, struggling to hold him, the stars shone more brightly I could touch them with my hands, I felt I was in heaven, I closed my eyes and wish someone take me out, hear outside that Alan was saying that resist that do not let him out.

See someone coming toward me, everyone watching him, run very fast, opened his arms and achievement into the star, I thought it was the Angel that I had let out, went out of her hard and being outside of the star yet was still lit, react and see that it was my brother that I had taken from her, stretch out my hand to the star and said nothing still on the floor I thought it closed the portal, use the sand to cover and destroy the ritual, which to me is wrong, trembled a little and broke the objects, look a light and heard a voice that said thanks, then vanished, my brother I get up from the sand, I was still upset, look the devil and I follow to continue with our fight.

-You know, if there is something that you fear.

-You're wrong not afraid of anything.

-I fear me. Looked at me with disbelief

-Sorry, so not belong to this place come back into the abyss.

Alan was still trying to get close to me, when he finally managed to take off them all over, was approaching I look with a smile that was fading fast, he could get neither he nor anyone, place a barrier between them, as hard as diamond, only the devil and I, Alan screaming that I did not, was afraid that I died, the demon was stronger than me, looked desperate, my brother could not get in, they'd be them safe from harm, Alan was still trying to get in, trying to break the barrier with his powers but he did not, I was still fighting with the devil.

And did not have to say a word, just had to think, just as the last demon light shine it toward my once again, this time controlling me and know what to do, he also attacked me with his powers but managed to avoid them, my hands were burning but stand the heat, it was if my hands had a shield, finally as well as send and there was quite an uproar fluttering, the demon became part of it disappearing, finally ending at whether our small fight, the demon back into the abyss from which he had come.

Sand finally calm, everything became clear and after that let alone the barrier and just looked at my friends, did not see the bad or the Hokon who had been here, just when I remove the barrier on my Alan did not hesitate to go for me like my brother, Monica and Hewett, I fell to his knees, somewhat depleted because the energy had been too, my brother and I hug him, but was a little dizzy, I get up and Alan broke a part of his shirt, I had forgotten that bled and it was worse than I expected, not only was my head but my arm too and not even sense, he tie on the lift blood and let out.

-Brother how you got here.

-Monica this morning when I woke up I felt I did not have to go, that something would happen and you I was talking about you and not answer.

-But how did you know where to find me.

-Friend was not difficult the light looked from afar, we knew it was you.

-Thanks brother saved my life.

-No, you to us.

Hugged her, when I looked up all looked scared, that I thought, but the teacher who came to me and asked forgiveness for not listening to me.

-Now if I wanted to go home I'm tired.

-Okay, everybody go home.

-Happened with the bad.

-Were only shadows and went along with the devil.

-Shadows, they looked so real.

-If they were so real.

I looked around and all looked so peaceful desert, as before everyone arrived, the stars of sky shone even more and the moon was so big even say it felt to be watching her in front of me, we walked to the car.

-Sarah destroyed another car.

-You said Dylan.

-If you look, you owe me another car.

-Was yours.

-Clear that it was mine.

-Sorry I already owe you two.

-Alan will not lend you another one of my cars.

-Well and do not lend you my dog. We look a bit confused, a dog by cars.

-That… he like being in my house, it's my dog.

-Give it back.

-No, give it back my car.

-A dog, Alan.

-If not just any dog.

-Good then you will know.

Everyone jumped into their cars, but Kalinda to wait for, Hewett went up to the car and climbed back it would go with us.

-You do here.

-Please, will not go with my sister.

-Okay. Climbed each in his car

-The police.

-If you brother is right everyone saw the light, send someone to investigate.

-If brother will believe that were aliens in the Nevada desert, near Las Vegas.

-Yeah right as they were to believe.

-Are okay Sarah.

-I think so but it hurts the wound.

-I take her to the hospital.

-It is necessary.

-Indeed.

- Alan brother that we could not get in with her; only his brother.

-I think we're no as pure as they.

-What happened there friend?

-I do not know, I just thought not to leave out the angel, and I did not believe but I hear him say thanks.

-Really.

-If true Hewett, maybe it was my imagination.

-It was not, I also listen and I think the teacher and you brother well.

-And I do not?

-I do not know brother.

-Great have a fried angel sister in low.

-Like you said.

-Sister in law, you are right.

-Look at Alan.

-If I think. I hold his hand

-Again what you did was silly.

-That?

-Refused to let us get in.

-Cold not enter you have hurt the same.

-Even so, I was silly very risky.

-Sorry I cause fear.

-Kidding fear was terrified like all Sarah. Hewett grumbled and Alan wanted to hit.

-Sorry.

-Scared me I thought you would die, because you do.

-That was the right thing.

All silent for a moment, one step saliva Hewett hit him in the back.

-Do not be grumpy brother; she knows what does trust her.

-True trust me Alan.

-Clear that trusts you.

-Hey brother think the teacher wants another angel.

-Do not think so, I think this scared.

-Really sorry guys, Alan you said you need my help, I'm giving.

-I'm not sure what you mean.

-Is a joke really, I thought you needed us.

-The need but not dead, we have to look after them.

-And what is our purpose, we all have the same power, but we specialize only one, that gift is stronger than the other powers, you can use all that I do not.

-because you power is unlimited and you can destroy the world.

-I'm really dangerous?

-Sometime I think so.

-And what about you are as strong as me.

-Is different, you learn the more you will have more power and have no limits, we have them, we know what is ours.

-And?

-And you have no limits do not understand.

-Understand that I am the only one who can stop a demon and you get an angel thought, so do not trust me but discover the courage to stand for what I do, I know I can help, I can control myself.

-I do not agree with you and I'm on your side.

-Enough guys think there is no more to say.

-Hewett sorry.

Arrived at the hospital emergency room, the two was accompanied me, my brother arrived after, I cleaned put staples and gave me pain medication, back to the hotel for our things, and went home, Alan do not talk to his sister.

Keys

Rosalba hello, I have a sister that news.

-A great Patrick.

-Well tell me, but remember this just for you that's my name, but I'm Cyrrus.

-Everything went according to plan, you were right was in a safe place where not notice my presence, the portal to heaven is real, could take an angel and return to heaven, the power of her is enough for our plans, but they already all know, the devil told.

-No matter Rosalba, the plan is in place, how many keys have.

-Blue star only, but get the heart.

-You better do it soon, time passes quickly.

-Clearly if I will… as you know the portal works.

-The portal opened twice.

-As you say.

-The third day the resurrected and ascended into heaven, body and soul, will look light shine upon him from heaven.

-Jesus Christ.

-That's right, if we can ascend to heaven as well.

-And the second time.

-Do not know and I gave you the first clue.

-True his mother, the Virgin Mary.

-That's right; she opened the door once more… well let's do it.

-Something else, you need to bring one more.

-Not think it's enough.

-Never enough.

-Will be harder to find someone alone.

-Take away the demon with you.

-But.

-I need another body to take more away his power, I deteriorating more quickly.

-Okay I hope will be sufficient until the time comes.

-Never enough.

-Should be, since we would have to kill more, almost a day the portal opens.

-But until then I want more.

I disagreed, we keep killing immortal for his power, was much even for me, but my brother was right, every time deteriorates faster.

Send the demon in search for one, was difficult to find it but brought it, he did not even know he was immortal, just had some kind of power and was all, output did not want to see his murder, maybe I would hurry to get on with my plan.

Know how to find the brothers and knew what his weakness of them, I have to get the keys, blue star was the first, then the heart, the brothers and the last Alan, but had gone out to before without knowing who he was, at this time was the enemy, the finish with all my family, my brother told me they were friends, killed my parents and I her to his wife and murderer, was my enemy at this time.

When I knew disappeared from his life be hating, bur for the single was one distraction, but we have still a demon, the strongest of the three, walked the halls of the castle and remembered that his wife was her kid prisoner, among traveled a bit, stay in this place and as stand therefore not died, could not be unless you had powers to be like them, well easy to figure out, take my phone and talk to my old friend Anselmo.

-Yes.

-Anselmo, the wife of Adriel like us.

-I'm afraid if, pretty.

-Nice.

I hung up the phone, my plan improved even more, summer will be here soon and everything perfect, to the old Anselmo well as he wanted to be immortal but that will help us, but I do not last long, this old and rundown, but we serve.

Had more to do than just kill, I did not like that idea, I just wanted revenge for the death of my parents and this was the only option, no matter that I perish, he is right.

But did not wanted to live with him in heaven, it was not for me, I like my life here on earth, I belonged to this beautiful, I'd go with although it was just what he wanted, did not understand my decision to stay if I could have everything in the heaven, but the truth I have everything on earth, is that do not I have a family but I have everything else and I wanted to stay on the planet.

May not be better than in heaven, but I like it, is that Patrick think that heaven is paradise, but if he make a mistake or is the same as here, like say a phrase, "thy will be done so in heaven and on earth" that if equal, also he it wants to change want to do their own will.

Walk back with him, I had taken a decision to although not agree.

-Are you done with the boy Patrick?

-If you can take him… Rosalba something happens.

-Well I been thinking about what you already had commented earlier.

-That was it.

-That still prefers to stay on earth that is my decision.

-I had told you, you better, everything will be fine.

-I know, but I like living here and that's my decision and I want you to respect.

-Say you are regretting.

-No brother I gave my word and perform it'll help you open the portal but will not go with you.

-Think we'll see mom and dad.

-Know but maybe that was his destination.

-No. Cry on

-It was not, died because of your friend Aland and pay.

-If pay but do not want to go with you.

-Think about it, for our parents and for me, I want you by my side.

-Already thought and it is my decision not yours.

-Okay I'll go and follow whoever entered, anytime you can go with me.

-Thanks for understanding.

I left there and on the way I found the brothers Hokon, I thought they had gone along with the devil.

-As made it out of there.

-We went before, when they were about to get the angel.

-If we escape, not with you help of course.

-If you had good lock.

-Yes, we had it.

-Where they go.

-With Cyrus.

-Well, then we see.

-Precious curse.

-Keep your hands off of me.

-Do not bother just playing.

-Do not mess with me Donovan.

-Okay, okay not touches you.

-Sorry but this so hum, baby.

-Rossi's fine.

-Rosalba.

-Rather the white rose.

-Do not refer to me about is how, those days are over.

-Clear as if it was erased.

-We all know you like that; to your friends they do not know you and are Tansy same truth and that such Alan your friend knows that you will same.

Hit so hard tree with my power that gave the wall, take to Duff and pull a knife gold funded miss marble handle, place it on his neck, he looked at me with huge black eyes, almost pleading to let him go, that knife was my father, it was the all I had of them.

-Cyrus shame that need, otherwise I would end it with you.

They retreated, true Tansy and I were the same person I knew long ago when Alan had killed my parents a Tansy I became the white rose, sometimes as abducted her friends and gave them to Cyrus, as Rosalba was still tender with Alan, I do not go soon to his side, I did it suffer, he told me about his friends and those he destroyed Tansy, from time to time until I get tired and left.

Is better although I am and I can do it without hiding it, Alan paid like their friends.

News

We arrived everyone home by end of a few days so intense that at first they were boring, Alan under my suitcase and help my brother with Monica, while Adriel down his suitcase Alan left his in the car, entered the house very quiet and sad about the absence, Hewett was in it but in his bedroom, and seemed be his home, left the room eating nachos, I think it was his favorite food.

-Have arrived.

-Hewett you do.

-Eating, you want to Alan.

-No thanks. Monica took one, was bringing hunger

-Monica, Are you okay?

-Yeah, I'm just tired, I sleep.

My brother took her to his bedroom for him, we realized we could be with him, I had sound too but Alan was not going to if I had to ask.

-Will you do Alan?

-You want me to go.

-No but I want to get some sleep.

-Well guys I also go to sleep.

-Hewett goodbye. Said goodbye with a blow to the shoulder

-I can stay Sarah.

I hold his hand and pull him to my bedroom, he not protest kept walking, takes my pajamas and went to the bathroom to change, I got a little comfortable, and when I enter the bedroom he looked put the window.

-Everything is fine.

-Yes.

-Want to talk about something.

-Like.

-Your sister.

-I do not want to talk about it.

-Good not talk just listen.

-No.

-Well is your sister, do not walk away from it, that's all.

She sing and lay down next to me, close her eyes and as usual I stayed on his arm, it was not long before dawn, when I woke up he was as usual reading, it was about nine o'clock, the breakfast was set aside bed.

-What time you woke up.

-A couple of hours.

-Do not sleep.

-Course, only I could not.

-And prefer to read.

-If it relaxes me.

-Relaxes you, also you get stressed.

-Clear that if.

-No noticed.

-We have to take care more this time, because they will come for you.

-If true, you think if they can get into heaven and control.

-Anything can happen.

-I know, and then stop.

-If we will.

-Are still mad at me for what happened.

-I'm just unfocused, you put yourself in danger, do not think.

-Think clearly, but just pass at the time was what I needed to do, what I had to do.

-It'd come back hopefully not ever.

-If that wanted to. Knocked on the door

-Come in.

-You have to watch the news.

Left the bedroom take the juice Alan had brought me and I take on the road till the living room, Hewett and my brother were already there.

-What happened guys?

-Wait for have to see this.

Breaking news, last night in the Nevada desert from the city and present a strong wave of light as bright as the sun, on e of our reporters was flying over the city and he capture these images.

We were looking at the images.

Was true managed to film the light in the desert and all happened down there, we never saw the helicopter, perhaps by noise, the reporter continued.

We also received release after the flash of lights, we capture a few cars moving away from the scene, unfortunately we do not know who they were or if they were from the government or other organization, some claim that the government was trying to clean up some mess, but others say that could be Aliens.

Hewett was drinking juice and when told that he laughed and juice came out of his mount, not wanting me laughs at that too.

-I told you.

-If, as we extraterrestrial friend. In that Alan's phone rang.

-Hello…

-Okay go to there.

-Who was Alan? Hewett wonder

-The teacher saw the news and wants us to go.

-Brother I'm not; I'm watching the news, look we're on all channels. No one wanted to go

-Well, come with me Sara.

-I have another choice. He looked at me

-Okay I accompanied them.

We went to the monastery, led me to where he had their screens, teacher and Kalinda was waiting for us there, he did not speak to her sister and took my hand, I think if he felt better and I too.

-Teacher happens?

-Got a call from out friend Ernesto, CIA and told him to call then, soon to.

-Of the CIA.

-If we have friends there.

-Clear, it should not surprise me. The phone rang

-Hello, I will put waiting loudly.

-Alan happened in Vegas.

-Hello friend, I think you know.

-Yeah well as clean up this mess, we are blaming that, we received hundreds of calls.

-Well you will know you are an expert and you know that we need your help.

-And once covered in the accident that caused you friend Sarah, the kid rescue.

-Know and thanks, but you'll have to help once again.

-Just one more time or will I have to do more.

-Do not know yet but will have to be prepared.

-Already know what they want Cyrus.

-Fortunately if, Sarah achievements make the devil told her.

-Need my help.

-If this time we need, we want you satellites locate it.

-Know what you ask, it is impossible to find them, they are well hidden.

-There is always a trace a clue.

-To tell you the news?

-I have an idea.

-Sarah I guess.

-If you like movies sir.

-Clear that if.

-Well that's a perfect answer.

-Want to say it was the filming of a movie.

-Bingo.

-Is a joke really.

-If you are who you say there will be no problem.

-Insinuate that I have no power to deal with this situation.

-Of course not. We look and laugh.

-Well so be it and you'll help Alan.

-Thanks Ernesto.

The call over but not even told what the problem was maybe already know.

-He knows what Cyrus plans.

-Not have to know to help.

-That?

-He knows us and handle it as a terrorist threat or something if.

-I rather kike the CIA, and while we do?

-Nothing but wait.

-Well I have to go back to school tomorrow and I have a lot of homework to do.

-Don't have to go.

-Also if I have to go to work, unlike you of course.

-Think I can't work.

-I did not mean that, I have to work on things that I have to pay but if you do not know maybe work.

-Clearly I can, give me work with you and you'll see.

-Work with me, has to be with me?

-Why not, I know I could do it.

-Well, tomorrow I wait in the restaurant, one thing you did not think to go to school too.

-No, Hewett has that job.

-If very good so might think that he like.

-If I think and also likes your house.

-If he enjoys all that maybe if he like, you can take me back I have homework to do. My phone rang

-Hello.

-Sarah knows the answer to question seven.

-Hewett, Are you doing homework!

-Cleary, if payment classes that serve something.

-Well as the way we will do together.

-Good.

-Alan if he likes school.

-I am happy for him, before he did not like to try out but declined, this time I hope the end.

-If I also hope to get to finish it.

-What you mean.

-What if we die before.

-You better not think so yet.

-Well but happen.

-Let's get your home; you have to help my brother.

-You can help us.

-I will of course not.

-Why?

-Because it is you task.

We got home, Hewett was waiting with the books, started the task, Alan was still reading his book and did not help us but still finished and went to sleep, Alan went to his house and not later would look up to him in the restaurant.

✿

Brothers Forever

Friday 13

That day in the restaurant were people than before, you could hear the door open and close at every turn, at times I thought that Alan would enter but he could not, well we have a new helper also, people keep coming, as the day was a little hot, it was a perfect day continued to open the door but it did not put much attention.

-Hi Sarah I'm ready to work.

-I thought that you not would come.

-I was so late.

-Well I have a perfect position for you, come with me.

I smiled and bring it to the kitchen with our new maid, my smile strange and also smiled.

-Well you will learn to cook with it.

-Kalinda does here.

-She also wanted to work, well have fan, he's Jonathan were the cook will tell them to do.

-Hello Jonathan.

-He Alan.

-While I have things left to do.

Output, the doors closed behind me thinking that there was a remote possibility that destroyed the kitchen, they are not so peacefully settle their differences, the end after all are brothers, follow up to the counter where my brother and was heard tired like all, I gave a pat on the back and gave me a smile, he look confused or something.

-Something happens.

-Do not know is Monica.

-That goes with it.

-This somewhat rare.

-It is always rare.

-Is true.

-Brother as time passes the more will understand.

-If I think and how are Alan and Kalinda.

-I hope there are well.

-If you do not ear they run the kitchen.

-I do not think so.

-Want me to go to see them once in a while.

-If it would be good.

-Sister even I could talk to you but you knows that the guys are right.

-About what?

-You have to trust everyone, let help.

-You know what they would do.

-If you know but I do not mean that.

-If.

-Not actually trust everyone, but we can help you could have died in that desert.

-Did not want to leave hurt, I could do.

-If protect us but you are not alone, is the work of all, I think I'm just saying do not bother.

-I have not bothered just afraid of losing.

-Never I will lose I'm with you every time.

-Have a life to care more and have a family.

-Are jealous of it.

-Of course not… well maybe a little.

-Do not be silly.

-His words resonated with much love that I do not bother to say silly, he had reason.

-You'll always be my sister.

-Clear that if.

-I mean I will never leave, brother forever remember.

My memory back in time when we were children, while he was learning to ride a bike no more than seven years, he fell on the pavement, ran to help frightened he was bleeding, had beaten strong, but not crying, his face reflected pain but scruffy, not up, continuous lying, as I screamed for someone to help, not knowing what to do was afraid, rather than embraced and comforted it was backwards, he said it was fine and not him nothing would happen, we made a promise that we would be always together, brothers forever, the end did not was of great importance, he was fine, cleaned the wound and continued playing.

On this occasion did hug and remind myself that I have to be afraid, he would be my brother and would be close and it showed in the desert, was there for me.

-You're right I'm a fool.

-If you are.

-Good keep working… thanks brother.

Rarity looks with my brother but do not talk.

-Friend you better move guys have much work.

-That'll help.

-Well you cook, your sister does well.

-Clear what would, be better than her. She did not answer, not take long to get used in the kitchen, I wanted to prove to Sarah that I can do it, my sister was on the other side, several boys separated us from, going more harm to her that to me, she sometimes had to help wash the dishes, I was still angry even Kalinda or acting that way against Sarah and not lean on our decision.

I really was having a great time, Jonathan was very good appreciation by to have a taste of food, for two months shut myself in my house several years ago, actually have a job but me and Ka, everything was fine, sometimes I stumble her but without speaking, later to be near us play both.

-Should not be here Kalinda.

-Sarah wanted to help me asked.

-I asked her.

-If. Swallowed.

-Not have to be so indifferent to me Alan.

-Not what you mean.

-Is what you think and I know did wrong and I'm sorry.

-That changes tings.

-I can't change what happened that I know but… but do not let it happen again.

-As trust you, you knew what they were planning and did not tell me.

-I said I was sorry.

-And I listen but that does not change anything.

-Not have to change; I just want you to understand me.

-You want me to understand.

-I was afraid that do not know, though that would be best.

-Desist in listen!

Kept walking up and moving around but she still did not stop talking.

-Sarah says it was scary and I understand, that does not hate me.

-She does not hate anyone.

-Yes, but nod at me.

-But I do. I finally said

Spend time before answering again.

-And I understand.

She walked away and left me was right on but fear makes us do things wrong and silly, we all had fear that day and we were wrong, after thinking about it for barium time.

-Kalinda you know you're my sister and I love you as such, but you continual setbacks ruin everything.

-I know but I want a chance.

-Clear are my brother and you give it another chance, do not waste it.

-Thanks Alan I love. As she hugged me

-Will have to make merit.

-Clearly if you think that this count.

-That, helps Sarah, maybe.

-Perhaps only that, look at me I'm cooking, washing dishes and just say maybe.

-If maybe. I smiled

-Have to behave better.

-I will.

Adriel then went and look at us surprised.

-Did not know they knew cooking, are excellent.

-Well guy you be surprised what I can do.

-And see that everything is better with your sister.

-If at after all we are brothers.

-I agree with you, help you.

-If why not.

Jonathan was happy us help you, I understand him and very few did, we had fun cooking up a point that apparently we were all friends, they made jokes about us and the time passed very quickly toward long time since I live with other people different from my old friends.

-Adriel not thinks its good idea.

-Are you talking about I'm great.

-Do not think so buddy.

-You are right it burs everything I cook.

-Put more attention.

I think not much amused but we of the, but we ignored and still trying again and again.

When entering the kitchen I is amazed, Alan playing with his sister, throwing small lettuce leaves, Jonathan and like others were laughing and it was rare that Mr. Jonathan laughed, everyone was delighted with our two visitors, Kalinda although the idea was to show that could help me trust her, but she did it for his brother, but then said wondered if Alan had been my idea and said yes.

Not look at me but I approached some would say you no longer had to cook more almost close, but I like to see how much the boys enjoyed it, my brother throw a piece of lettuce without knowing that I was watching him, unfortunately it fell to my, still contained water and accidentally paste a cry, not very strong but they looked.

-Sarah I'm sorry I did not want... I stare at them all.

-No longer have to keep cooking and we will close almost have to clean everything.

I went out everyone was silent, I was not mad but I went out laughing stay close to listen.

-Alan was my fault.

-My fault.

-Your fault boy.

-But I Mr. Jonathan.

-You turn to clean, I almost leave.

-Great K.

-No brother I clean my thing and you do your thing. Me laugh and enter.

-All clean up.

-Okay. All responded

-Adriel you too where you going.

-By a broom.

Between all ends up faster, well almost we were still joking, Hewett came to look wise we were all there and came with Monica, and although it was late all together and a little tired but no matter had dinner together at the restaurant, Hewett as joker as usual, had a good time back home late, the days continued in the same way, except for Kalinda who was no longer working but Hewett was with us every day, and Monica that did not get away from her husband and he was very fond an her close, the time passed quickly.

Monica's sister to take care speak to small Marcos, as his birthday approached the child, for some people would be the worst day of all but his mother Carolina and was special for us because the little one comply years, and it was a great day, but the little on was tremendous, had a very strong imagination, her birthday of Marcos will be on Friday May 13 and wanted so much, he already had a list for his party, wanted a huge cheese cake decorated with a track about where to include Mater and Lightning McQeen cars the movie was not the only thing he wanted a huge trampoline and many gifts.

On Thursday, one day before brought him to the house and take care of all, Hewett and I were doing homework and Alan was in the

Kitchen with Adriel, Monica entered the bathroom couple of minutes and leave it alone, just to hear very well, I hear the keys lay with the cars, which were but did not know I could do with them, in a moment did not heard the sound of the keys, I heard my brother talking, the sound of the microwave was clear and look at little one out of the kitchen, approached me with a smile I do not break a plate, an angelical smile.

-Marcos you do little one?

-I'm not small I'm big.

-Well that makes a child your age.

-I like science.

-Science, good choice.

An explosion was hear in the kitchen, not as laud a bomb, but enough for the pictures to move, hit a coy hear, the first thing I did was hug the little Marcos, was scared and crying hugged him told him that would be fine, Hewett ran to the kitchen, Monica left the bathroom and hurried in search of Marcos, she shouted in despair, then yell that was with me in the leaving room, it was rushed and I gave, then I headed to the kitchen where Hewett was raising my brother, he was closer to the microwave and the glass I had reached a little and covered his ears like Alan, the look seemed they were fine.

-What happened?

-Apparently the small Marcos was experiencing.

-That?

-Yes, look at the keys in the oven exploded controls keys.

-Controls keys.

-If you look put those, everyone inside.

-He had reason likes science and how we did not realize that he entered.

-I walk like a ghost.

-Just like you Alan. He smiled

-Okay, let's get you cleaned brother.

-Take it and bring it to the room where was Monica, was a bad idea was scared she and Marcos, I return to the bathroom, and clean it, it was a good idea to go to school to study medicine is useful.

-Do not complain you will be fine thank God you were no so close.

-If that is naughty Marcos.

-If, you know he told me a few second before he liked science, but this.

-Is true what I knew Monica told.

Everything was fine; Alan had cleaned up the mess but the little Marcos was still scared.

-Little Marcos do not be scared, already pass.

-Sorry.

-No, come here.

Hug and console him, my brother hugged Monica to cry out as if it was talking to her sister negligence or not, until it was decided to tell.

-That was great little Marcos. Commented Alan

-Is true.

-As if such a thing happened to you.

-I do not know. While shrugged

Pass all so fast, but everything is fine, and then began looking cartoons, after a couple of hours I get her mom, I received but did not tell anything.

-Exploits the kitchen Mommy. But did not understand

-Mommy did science.

Carolina ignored him, the little one always said that, and we just we looked at, she headed to the kitchen said she was bringing a little hungry and is said was fine but we were still silent; no one dared to tell her anything.

-Sarah and you microwave for heating food.

-I told mom exploited, did science.

She looks at everyone and no one answered.

-What happened to Adriel guys?

-He cut off.

-And the microwave? Look at Marcos

-You made little Marcos.

-Mommy science.

-Sarah. Not answer

-Sister went to the bathroom and let him play whit the keys and place them in the oven and exploded.

-He did you?

She took his hand; left the food bowl and she look at all.

-Should take more care, we'd better leave.

-Waiting sister.

-Only I have to go, I have things to do and my husband waiting we see in his birthday tomorrow.

-Okay sister.

Disguise his annoyance but not enough and more with Monica, but it was not his fault, it was an accident, even so we all feel guilty about it.

The next day we went to school and then I went to help Carolina with the party of little Marcos, was still serious but not both, the guests arrived, everything was perfect and my brother arrived Monica, Caro received them but was still upset with Monica, his sister came and Hewett arrived with Pilar, indeed make cute couple, all gave gifts to the little Marcos.

Romp with huge trampoline and then your cake as he wanted, then opened his gifts, my brother was a set of tools, according to the totally safe, the science was Alan, mine was a game to assemble, after opening all the little one went to play with friends and new toys.

Us we were having a great time and everyone equally, except Monica but she did not leave, because it was his sister, after a while all change, it was light throughout the house.

-What happened? Carolina said

-Marcos where are you?

Everyone look outside and inside the house, when Alan try to reestablish the light, lineally gout it, we speak Alan.

-Alan happens?

-I think I know what happen.

-Marcos. Said Carolina

Marcos had unscrewed the lighters all in house and also where things are plugged, fair with his new gift of tools, which my brother had given him.

-Carolina that will make you think the volcano that brought Alan.

-Do not joke Adriel.

Carolina was not altered, but it was headed to her sister and hugged.

-Thanks for caring, though it is a problem.

-Sister is not a problem, only is just too curious.

-If it's true I'm sorry I bothered not your fault, forgive me.

-For they are the sister.

-It's true I love you.

-I love you.

-Sister forever.

These pictures and had seen before, were as close as us, cried a little, his other sister arrived and joined hugs, my brother looked at me and I to him, Kalinda also looked at his brother, and they are also good, better than good, after that we all gather to outside, the little Marcos was asleep in the arms of his father, he was tired, Hewett began talking.

-Well to know we're all had a few days' strangers but this was fabulous. Everyone laughed

-I want to make a toast to what I see and what I have learned these last days. All took a glass of wine

-Know that our friendship is stronger than everything and everyone and today was demonstrated, all the promise we made this month. We were looking

-If I know everything and we promise… was that we would be together, "brother forever."

And we all gave a nod and offer, so then I applaud, it was true all cherish our family, our brothers are those who unites all what I do makes us stronger, on other side of the table Kalinda hugged his Samara cousin who had been upset; Andrew look you out a small tear for the loss of his brother, but had won more my brother and they did Hewett always feel like brothers, clear Elmo, Dylan and of course Alan too, and knowing that he felt was best, and continued enjoying the party of children which ended up being an evening of friendship and brothers who will always be brothers, regardless of differences.

For a moment we all got sentimental, for Hewett's words, but then everything changes, and back to normal, continues night we danced a bit and after that we said goodbye to Carolina and her husband, my brother told her that the volcano was careful, she laughed and then hit him on the shoulder.

-Good just saying.

-Sister we're leaving, well's see tomorrow.

-Clear, drive carefully.

-Clear mom.

-Do not start.

-Already well cared Monica. Finally we all went.

The Gift

In early June, the weekend ended and we were all in exams to Hewett was not worried, but my brother if he was, Monica was no worried, but she a little dizzy she was in the kitchen drinking a glass of water, his face was pale as cotton, and look strange.

-Ails you friend?

-Do not know, I think it's the fatigue I have no slept well these days.

-Already you have.

-And that is?

-Girl guesses you think. I laugh a little

-As time has passed since you married.

-Six weeks.

-And well you feel bad. She did not understand

-If and.

-I think that I will soon aunt.

-She dropped the glass and stood still paler.

-Sorry maybe did not have to say.

-No, okay just had not thought of.

-And think. Hit a cry of happiness

-Do not tell your brother.

-Course not fainted from excitement.

-And I will do?

-Well I find out for sure is to go to the doctor if you want I can make an appointment.

-Would you do that for me?

-Of course.

Together we cry with emotion and embraced, the boys heard us but ignored because they knew we were that way, we calmed down and left the kitchen laughing, they went getting ready to leave this time Monica was left with me, Hewett and my brother went every man for himself, in the way she was coming down paler than before but of emotion.

Call the clinic but she gathered up the other day at noon, we had to wait, calmed and each went to class, she was scared just hoping to do well in their test.

The next morning we went together again for the first class, we looked in the parking lot and headed to an appointment, this but nervous and I felt like, we waited a couple of minutes.

-Friend can come with me I'm scared.

-Sure.

Finally called, we got up at once and there was no problem for me to come with her, grabbed her arm and walked, had the feeling faint, but not, in the end started to look, ask questions and then the sent to your test, we waited in the room for ten minutes spinning.

-And if I am, as you tell your brother.

-Good question and find the time.

-And if it bothers, he wants so much, after the hell I'm scared.

-You need to calm you take care of you all.

-I have fear and if I am not a good mother, you saw what happened with my nephew.

-All help you and of course you will be good mom, you're great. Finally entered the doctor, she grabbed my arm so hard that it hurt, but did not say anything.

-And what happened. Dr, smiled

-Congratulations are four weeks pregnant.

Monica passed out before the doctor finished his sentence, I hold before it fell, lie down with the help of a nurse, I do not want to be weird since, so wait for him, and when recover and woke smiled.

-What happened?

-Friends are pregnant, and you fainted.

-What a fool I am. She began to mourn

-No, everything will be alright not being sad.

-I'm happy but scared.

Hugged her and then calmed down, the doctor gave instructions on how she should take care o and then we went, no longer take to school, the pass to stop with Carolina, she will know more to tell, since it is already mother, she surprised to see us so early in the day, we came never more than weekends in the afternoon.

-All good girls?

-If only this little tense and would not leave her alone.

-By that alone.

-I think I have to go back to school but you better get her back tomorrow.

-These good sister. Gave the results sheet

-I knew it I knew. The embrace

-Congratulations and Adriel already knows.

-No not yet. She reply

-And when you think to say.

-I do not know.

-Well I let them take care of her if I return later. And went

-Sister we talk about.

-If well.

-And you would like to have.

-I have not thought of.

-Do not worry you'll be fine, you have a great husband.

-I have fear and if he does not want.

-Do not be silly worship him.

-As you know.

-Just know.

-And Marcos.

-Is sleeping, this is still tired babe.

-And if I neglect like I did with my nephew.

-Take care of you will know, nobody knows it but you mother instinct will help you know what he need.

-But do not know.

-You do not know.

-Did not tell my Adriel.

-Are crazy.

-But will tell him later when ready.

-And when will that.

-Not only do not tell promise.

-Okay but do not think it's a good idea.

Gulp was scared, did not know how to tell my husband I was pregnant, spend all day with my sister and my nephew, I felt bother enough to return home, speak to Sarah for to come for me, said if just had to finish a few things in the restaurant and would come for me, wait after I arrive, greet Carolina and Marcos, and after a while we went.

-How you fell Monica.

-Better but I have something to ask you.

-It is?

-Well do not tell you brother.

-Of course not, you have got to tell you.

-Yes but I will not tell yet.

-What you mean.

-I prefer to wait.

-Not have to, he'll be happy to tell you but of course this is you decision.

-Thanks.

We got home, Monica went to rest and I left me in the living room, after that I get Alan had time not come home since the incident with the oven.

-Hello and that face.

-Is nothing only Monica.

-Then if it is something.

-If good is terrified that she is pregnant and does not want to tell my brother.

-Huh… well it's you decision and you have to understand.

-I it do, and tell me what brings you here, today is you day off in the restaurant, thought you might resting.

Anguish which I wore wires face but was safe perhaps.

-Happens.

-Nothing just get's nothing.
-Not have found a clue.
-Not one.
-Well and your friend Ernesto.
-Nothing is hard to find.
-Monica had said in a kind of castle, how difficult is to find a castle.
-Not easy to be well hidden.
-You stay today.
-No, just a while.

Sat next to me on the couch, and leaned back on my shoulder, his breathing was warm and listened to this heart also, I put my head on hears and did not move, was comfortable but exhausted, ought to have been looking some information, I did not move, did not want leave, I liked having him around, was on the TV a comments even with what happened in late April, but were only very small, they had believed that it was a shooting of movie, I hardly believe how people think but so is.

He kept learning on my shoulder and I looked like I was asleep, try to watch your eyes were close, I stroked his hair somewhat curly and no resistance at all, I loved to her hair and she kept touching it, spend an hour and finally got up from my side.

-What time is it?
-Not too late.
-I'm sorry I fell asleep.
-No need to apologize, you just slept an hour.
-Then.

And returned to lie down without falling asleep, and follow stroking his hair, this time television was still just looked music videos, I liked the dancing, some were good and others not so may good, I got up I turned towards him, I was sitting on my feet on the couch, I looked into his eyes something passionate kiss without saying a word, who do not have time to and I was not required, after that put his head on mine and we were silent for a while, the took my hand with great affection and looked up, was somewhat confounded as guilty for kissing me, and I felt same way, when you look at her beautiful blue eyes that shone like a star, we are looking at us and again put his forehead on mine.

Spent minutes to myself were seconds, he turned to kiss passionately, this time to kiss a lot better than before, and did not take off, this time I hugged him and hug the waist without even thinking similarly and was on his lap kissing him intensely, everything was still beyond the limits that had never allowed anyone, beyond the limits, I remembered but could not stop, myself I take my shirt that I had no matter what Monica is in her room, anxiously looked at me and continued touching me and kissing me, beyond the limits, I went back to remembering and push it slightly, the effortlessly walked away from me again and kissed my forehead and hugged me without following.

-Sorry I think I altered in more. I put on my shirt

-If we alter of more. He laughed

-Well, I think it's late.

-Want me to leave.

-No, of course not, just thought that maybe you have already bothered.

-Because I bothered.

-Well you know provoke you then.

-Life is like that sometimes we cannot handle.

-Clear, as you do.

-That, controls me.

-Yeah sure.

-It's not easy you're beautiful, but it is a difficult decision for you and I understand.

Difficult decision, you have no idea.

-Are you talking about girl?

-Well if it is difficult, I do no…

-You do not… wait, never?

-So do not ever, not want to ruin it.

-Ever.

-Do not make me repeat myself.

-Not sure, I get it, but it's strange, because you are.

-I know, I have almost twenty years but.

-I can ask why.

-No… but I'll tell you it's just that I want it to be perfect and had waited for the right person.

-You think I am.

-Yes of course I just do not feel its right.

-I understand.

-You will not go right.

-Of course not.

-While not happen again.

-Good.

And turned to kiss me, this time was more careful not to provoke, and I was still sitting on her legs but then I take of the.

-I'm sorry but its better that way.

-If true.

-Well you should rest more Alan.

-I can continue to sleep with you, I promise not to bother.

-I never disturbed.

Settled back again, I think I was the one who caused it, he did not do anything and I was the one who took off his shirt, not him although I would have loved to do so, his arms were strong and well formed, I like when he hugged me, it was so strong and I liked the aroma, I know they just like mine, we are for each other, not that I fear I have is that I love is right, and it would be foolish not to love, it's perfect, well maybe it was time to lose my virginity.

Was about to speak when he interrupted.

-No, bay you should wait for a perfect moment.

-I said nothing.

-Know what you're thinking.

-Can't read my mind I can sometime just me.

-So not need to know you and no.

-Well as I know.

-Only pas without thinking.

My brother arrived late and after a few minutes came Hewett, Alan finally left, the next day I went out Monica, went into towns, had to leave the house, along the way will contain what happened in the night, she just laughed at me but I remembered that she was pregnant and will erase the smile, during the course of about two hours each block where I passed looked shops watched porn ads was irony or something, or I was waiting traumatizing for my sex, she made fun of me but I finally distracted on purchases, arriving as expected, she was went straight to the baby clothing store, many clothes look what we would have wanted to buy all, but she had not said anything to my brother, but still did not hesitate to buy some clothes white color, of course we would have to hide and would be in my room, since my brother always snooping, but we still see each store things we would be undergoing, she watched baby clothes I was getting nervous, but she was still euphoric.

We went to eat ice cream and then we went home, since the phones stop ringing and almost were coming to get us, leave baby clothes Carolina home and then we went to our own, where we waited the three boys, concerned although we had warned them, were like caged lions.

-Take long.

-Well, we were having fun and time just passes.

-Guys that brought us. Hewett commented

-Nothing. While putting anything on the couch

-That bad, we worried and you did not bring me anything.

-Do not be impatient.

-Impatient course not. While watching the bags

-Waiting.

-Okay.

The good thing that we know well, Alan will bring a new mystery book just out and knew that I had not, my brother brought him new sneakers and shoe fanatic was, he liked a lot, as well Hewett a child to a, we brought new video games that ultimately enjoyed all.

Knew it would look and it was a good idea we left baby gifts Carolina home, but wanted to tell my brother did not dare, after our visits that week at the monastery for training, we learned that we all knew and tried more carefully, but knew that Adriel did not know, and she wanted to train, the good thing was that she is strong and was only day, she had things to do with his sister at school, but nevertheless had to take care and was exhausted more than before.

Spent the week faster than we could imagine, a very late summer, there were only a couple of weeks, we were still without news, the school was over and everyone was grabbing vacation plans, we did not wanted to go on vacation, the situation was tense, not knowing any news.

Look at Monica and made a rare look that really have to tell my brother, his gaze was obvious approval, I think that seeing all those baby clothes made reconsider, not left he sat on the couch.

-Adriel. We all stood in silence

-Love happened?

-Was fun to go with Sarah to the store... look much clothing and more than... babies, you think of the babies?

-They are awesome, cut and funny.

-Funny.

-If you look at you nephew is great funny and terrible but a good child.

-And if you had one you would.

-Spoil him and more if it is as Marcos.

-Not going to let him do whatever he wants.

-Why not.

-That has to behave well and if it's a girl.

-If a girl would like you cute strawberry and passion for fashion.

-If true but I would like to have something from you, also if it is a girl or boy if that matters.

While he would say that she touched the stomach and watched, looked at her a bit but did not took much interest.

-Clear that no matter if is a girl or boy, I would want much.

-Well, we will be parents soon, I have five weeks and I'm happy.

He smiled a little and she looked furious, on what had taken as joke, it was not his intention to be bothered.

-Is serious? Fainted my brother

-That is not true is a joke.

We look and really had fainted, slow one now, did not wake up, Monica is upset, went to the kitchen took some ice cubes and place them on his face and chest that was discovered, it will jump up and look laughing.

-And my husband thinks of this?

React and hug and passionate kiss, awkward me and gave me envy, Alan took my hand and smiled at me, then let go to Monica and gave a shout of joy.

-And since when you know.

-A week ago.

-That and not tell me. Why?

-Is that thought there'd be so happy?

-That, kidding I am the happiest in the world. Kissed her again

-We have to buy man things. And made me laugh Leave them alone.

The Third to Overcome Together

Finally after much thought, I got the call of a school companion.

-Hello I hope you are not so busy and say yes, and we will not go anywhere some of us, and we know you never leave.

-Happens, detours stop fooling Jenny?

-Good we rent a couple o cabins on Lake Ditroy and wanted you and Hewett and clear you brother, your friends if you want.

-I do not know when it will go.

-This weekend, would be there weeks, one week in June and two of July.

-Course it would be nice to celebrate the independence day at the lake with light and everything.

-Well… if will go.

-Say if I will think about and I tell the boys, I speak on Thursday.

-While I expect.

Knew my brother and Hewett would love but was no sure that Alan would agree to let us go, so maybe invite him and convince him to let us go, if only we would go a couple o weeks but it was enough, my last days out were terrible.

My brother and I left the job, had a lot of work, Alan us not had more important things to do and also showed that if he could do what we put, us anything.

The next day we left early from work and headed to the monastery, we had to prepare more.

-Hi guys.

They were all on the patio enjoying the afternoon sun, we were missing only my brother and I, we joined and then sated our training, only a difference, Monica just looked this time, my brother talked to her and made her understand, it was crazy train with us, and she accepted, she had to take care of the baby, but still was close for anything, and all the pampered like a crystal doll as delicate, but she did not like that idea, if felt silly.

She was so good it did not seem pregnant, until seemed that this already had almost two months and was still just as thin as before, was totally different from his sister Carolina that her stomach was huge, from the beginning and it bothered her that soon be left of clothes and was coming down frustrated, I hope that does not happen the same to my friend one more month, as it would inevitably stop her weight gain, we headed to the dining room and after a while.

-Sarah already you commented to my brother of lake.

-Are you talking about?

-And we do not treat me like a fool, Jenny also spoke to me, I knew you not would you say.

-I have not said anything, and then I will.

-Well, I do want to go and you will convince us to let go, you will.

-I can't, how would you do I?

-I do not know but you have to do, I do not have fun since we left to skate, and I'm dying to have fun.

Stepped back in time and remembered those moments indeed strangers that I had fun too, and then I remembered that it had submitted some of my past, and did know how Alan had made to go away, even so was happy that had happened and I have not had the opportunity to ask as he did.

-Well I will but with a condition.

-Clearly it is? Said very discouraged

-I want to know how you Brother Richard conventional he left.

-Are you sure you want to know.

-If it does not want to know.

-Well, I thought you did not care.

-Not that it matters much, just was curious.

-Well, I'll tell you but did you know about me… why not you ask my brother.

-I will of course not.

-Well, just convinced him it was a mistake to lose everything because of a misunderstanding.

-Continues.

-Has a son and brother made him see things that would lose everything if I kept here, and would not allow you to do damage and would end up in jail, and his son would suffer by their absence and I think he understood everything and went without putting any resistance.

-And knew they had a son.

-In fact it is a girl, and we investigate whether we knew all about.

-While it was not hard to convince.

-Clearly adores his daughter Samantha.

-Her name is Samantha.

-If really cute.

-If once told him that this was a name that I would like to put one of my daughters.

-He remembered, wait one of your daughters.

-If I would like to have several naughty.

-Waiting for my brother to know.

-I'll say no.

-Good bud will not tell, but the…

-But he that.

-He says he is terrified of the idea of having children.

-Does not want, and Monica was the problem and it turns out I would have the same.

-Not that, is that if he dread the idea of being a father, but it would be fascinating to see his face.

-You say.

-If you and he already…

-That, of course not, I never… I stay silent

-Actually kidding, but you nerve already have almost twenty.

-Shut Hewett.

-I'm ready.

Take a sip juice, had made a mistake in saying, I do not explain and he understood perfectly.

-No, of course not, shall be him.

-And if you do not want.

-What you mean.

-And if he dare not, I mean you're the daughter of his former lover and if not…

-Silent and not say it.

-I'm just saying that if I could.

-Not you dream.

-Already forgot about the night that slept with you.

-No, but not the same.

-Please know that I mean something.

-Anything and do not look at me like, well clear that good kisser.

-And what is the problem.

-I love your brother.

-I only speak of passion only.

-Not clear that it does is dementia.

-Friend is not sex.

-Silent.

His offer was strange he was very charismatic tempting and daring to comparison of his brother, who was sometimes something cold and grumpy, but very sexy and I loved, but his brother filled my head things with his voice so beautiful and exciting, although they have almost the same you that you brother are totally different, we were still laughing in spite of their stuff, it was fun and I had a good time with me to laugh.

-Well, my offer still stands and is seriously.

-Yeah right.

-Then convince him to let us go to the lake.

-If offered sex and maybe convince him.

-I would like to see that.

-Pervert.

-That would be great three who cares.

-These crazy wise.

-I know why you like me, no.

Between their madness was true, I like your fool and his jokes are good, although his brother is angry understands and does not judge, and Alan only wants the best for him.

-Since when you're not with someone Hewett.

-I have to tell you.

-If you have to.

-Good, do not remember I've been so busy that I had time.

-Brain affecting you knows.

-Can be.

-These insane.

-If you love me as you say. He kept flirting with

-And what happens to my friend Pilar?

-She is cute but as you say we're both insane, can you imagine what would happen together.

-If I think so.

-I want someone special as well as yourself for my brother, and for you, someone like you. My face change

-Already you are of him, and understand, I mean I want someone different, Pilar is cut but not are to each other.

-This seriously amazing.

-Just do not make fun.

-Of course not, you'll find it someday.

-I hope, get older.

-If as if that could happen.

-Nobody can know Sarah, but if I want someone special, and want everything.

-Clear what will happen just be patient and you know I do not think that bothers Pilar have sex with you, she does not like long relations, would not mind.

-If it is true just what I need.

-While your brother will convince us to go.

-Only that we will all, if he says that if we do not let go alone.

-Well, it's that or stay all summer punished.

-While I accept that, provided out of here.

-Tell him this afternoon.

-Look at his face, her look is priceless.

-Are you talking about?

-This infuriated by our conversation I know.

-If it can be but do you like mad, no.

-Clearly if but feel that taking revenge, so you should go with.

-No, it was very obvious, let them.

-Not ever.

-Please?

-Not beg.

-Please?

-Well, we will.

Alan we approach that was with Elmo and Andrew, made a face but did not take importance.

-Hey guys a friend spoke to us and invited us in Ditroy-Lake this weekend, but three weeks, we wanted to know if we let go Alan.

Everyone put weird face.

-Would have to go all out. Elmo said

-Course, we will also invite you.

All look to Alan pleading with his eyes.

-Well go to the lake… provided you not do something stupid.

-Promise to be good.

-If you tell your brother Sarah.

-Okay Hewett.

-These annoying Alan, Jenny spoke to me this morning I was not hiding.

-Of course I'm not mad.

Elmo and Andrew left did not want to listen; I take the hand and do not reject it but was very distant, well I have to go home and my brother leave with Monica, who had brought Hewett and had to ask him take me or Hewett, but that would make things worse.

-In that case you can take me home, please be last time and the car will use more you gave and I will not have to ask this favor.

Grit the teeth and walked, do not pulled but I had the feeling that he wanted to do, that was one of the things that bothered me, it was strange but I was not afraid, I lower my gaze for a second, but the noticed.

-First I want to go home right.

-Yeah right.

And went to his house to get to it as paresis very cold as before and uninhabited, a comparison of the wedding day, everything was returning to be turned off and no light, entered his house, he head to is books, I stayed in the room all lit it imagining, walked around the house, my footsteps were heard as usual, could not yet be as silent as the, finally joined me after half an hour, or even follow, knew that she liked to be alone, I was back in the living room and sitting on the couch, was placed next to me.

-I can hug you and kiss you.

-Why always questions?

-What if you bother, do not want that.

-Well you can hug me. Was silent

-Know that if.

I felt his kiss colder, somewhat distant.

-Not have to be jealous of Hewett. Sing

-I'm not perhaps as looked in my mind.

-I know you do not need to know what you're thinking and you're wrong.

-If maybe.

-If maybe.

-He is your brother and I will not bother you, but it's very nice to be near him and just want you to lean.

-I support him despite never understanding like you.

-If it is true and that bothers you, think that we are irrational.

-If you sometimes want to be like him. I laugh

-Kidding I think he wants to be like you and you say you want to be like.

-That would want to be like me.

-Why do not you ask him?

-I later.

-Not have to be jealous of him, I love you.

-You like my bother.

-And who does not, its fun.

-If is true.

-Well you can take me home Alan.

-Sorry not be like him.

-Do not have that enough is enough and do not have to behave that way, you know that I love you and it it's because we've been together since sorry.

-That is not why.

-Then what happens to you, maybe should I go home, I speak to Hewett passing though my.

Lowered his face and gulped; I know this would put it seriously but I had to react, he listed his face, look and hug me.

-I'm a fool indeed.

-Something.

-You stay with me, have much time we're not together.

-Sure.

-My brother really wants to be like me.

-In a way yes, but ask him and you want him to be like you.

Kissing him without saying more and was better than before, I was more relaxed.

-Thanks for letting us go to the lake the pass well.

-I hope so.

I fell asleep on the couch, was very comfortable, he stayed with me, the weekend arrived very quickly, this time pack more things and since we would go more we rent a few cabins that were not aside from each other so, the only that would not go would be the teacher and Samara, would be left waiting for news of his friend Ernesto who was tracking anything, as we had a ball magic to tell us where will be the devil and Rosalba witch and his friends Hokon and were sure that we got rid of them, well not all, was feeling.

My brother went with Monica, I was alone in the yellow car and Hewett went apart as would presume his new blue sports car, Dylan and the others would arrive the next day, Alan did not want to push it out with me that day, the view of the trip was fabulous and the parade of cars and the truck that was yellow like the car, the truck even more modified and sportier, with loud music and dark glass like those of the three cars, suddenly joined Andrew and Elmo and green in a car just as extravagant or more than mine, did not even know was coming back but not expected would leave us alone for a day. But their laughter could see in the rearview mirror, also smiled because I knew they were happy to leave the monastery like all.

Arrived at the Ditroy Lake and we expected our classmates at school, astonished by the cars, we parked and opened the doors of the cars at the same time, all got along colorful clothes, I wore a white sundress with flowers on the bottom no to flashy, Monica were shorts and whit pregnant blouse, and boys shorts and t-shirts stuck to their skin, leaving your muscles show, because I had not realized that my brother had changed so quickly was stronger and muscles.

Jenny and other girls were left with their mounts open without disguise, and had not seen Alan and others, would stay just as exited, Andrew was very handsome too, with clear green eyes like a cat, and Elmo had his hazel eyes, Jenny approached us to give us the welcome all guests, she never imagined we would come and I did not returned the call.

-Sarah hello good that came.

-If, you know invited other friends but will come tomorrow I hope do not mind.

-Who they are. Say what are the names of two of them?

-To true, sorry, he is Andrew and Elmo.

-Cute gladly.

-The pleasure is mine. While biting her lip

-I hope you do not mind we came Sarah invited us.

-Of course not, welcome.

-Sarah is gorgeous, so are all your friends.

-Lately if and I was saying that will come more friends.

-Okay, only how many will be, do not think... are comfortable all the two cabins.

-Do not worry as we rented some.

-Seriously.

-If in the end we rented four sisters Monica and Pilar wanted to come too, but not bothered much, they will be on their side of the cabin.

-Okay, will comes more handsome guys.

-Course.

-And their names.

-That?

-If I would like to know them.

-Curran, Alan and Dylan may be come William.

-Curran is not a good name.

-I know but it's great, just Dylan married.

-And what about Alan.

-He is my boyfriend.

-Good and these two.

Pointing out to Andrew and Elmo looking

-Single and ready.

-Well have some fun, and tell me how is the.

-Who?

-Your boyfriend.

-Well is cute, I like her blue eyes, a bit like Hewett, tomorrow waits. The party was ready and at their best, as it was near the lake shore, the boys went into the water, me and Monica stayed with Jenny but then she was gone, Monic did not want to get in the water so I stayed with her, walked a while in I lakeshore and then just dipped out feet in the water, while we listened to music, who'd bet that even be heard underwater, which we mentioned about would be, boy or girl and who would put him name but we came to nothing.

Afternoon came too fast guys finally came out of the water to eat, things started to go down the car since nearly all go along in the truck, except the clothing.

-Help them girls.

-Cleary if Hewett.

-From where you came.

-That Sarah, you know I'm always near you I lose one second you do crazy things and my bother killed me.

-Course, well helps us.

Then the guys watched and helped, my brother moved the truck closer to the cabin so we would not work and cost us was better, enter at last, was great very comfortable, there we would run four and Alan when morning came, his sister and another alongside Dylan, Curran and then Elmo, Samara would come the next week, and could not stand the idea of staying, and it was not fair to leave her, and the other would occupy Yasmin, her husband of Carolina, Pilar and Sonia, and next did not know who it was and was and smallest than the others, maybe only if a case, Elmo and Andrew occupied the other, and then when she got Samara, I expected that William too.

Accommodate finished everything and chose bedrooms, back to the party on the lake, the music is towards stronger as we approached, I was Hewett arm and clear my brother wearing Monica's hand at the end to get to and separate from the, my brother and Monica dancing, Jenny approached me, her boyfriend was elsewhere.

-That envy.

-Why?

-You tell them anything without the help not left alone for moment.

-If they are very cute with us.

-If it appears the Hewett's more than that.

-No, is the brother of my boyfriend, not what you think.

-Good, just saying.

-He is very cute but he is just my friend.

-Yeah right I wish I have a friend like that.

-And your boyfriend what.

-He is with his friends look beyond this; I wish it was as Hewett.

-You like Hewett.

-It looked cute and his eyes are amazing.

-If you expect to be those of his brother are identical.

-Serious?

-Of course, the perfect.

-And that is not here.

-Has something to do, but tomorrow will be here.

-I present them.

-Clear that if.

-Sarah let's go dance.

-I'll be back, Jenny.

-Course friends.

I stated dancing with Hewett.

-I hear the last thing said Jenny, of talking?

-She thinks we have something.

-Have something.

-Yes, we are friends.

-If it is true, but if I like you and you know.

-Not continues with this.

-Course but it's true. Keep on dancing

-A question, what is your favorite fruit.

-Why?

-Just one question that I don't know and do not think is the strawberries.

-If I like but I love kiwi and fig, are my favorites.

-Kiwi, almost like my name.

-If true.

-Rather a point in my favor.

Made me laugh and kept dancing, it was late I was exhausted, my bother almost all came and bed, Andrew was the first and then my brother and that Monica is tired faster.

-We go.

-Clear I am tired.

Walked to the cabin and everything is silent, we said goodbye, kiss me on the forehead and ran to his room, and then I to mine, when dawned went out to walk, then return to the cabin, and were having breakfast.

-Alan spoke to arrive at noon.

-Well, we're doing today.

-I have an idea, let's climb the volcano.

-That? Andrew his gaze was serious.

-Is seriously true.

-If.

-Know that I will be able to go.

-Clearly, if you can go and wait downstairs.

-No, I bore too much.

-You will be with my bother.

-If, like me bore you.

-While you wait downstairs and then go for us in the helicopter.

Adriel made derisive laughter

-Know that I dread the idea.

-Did not know.

-Okay I will Andrew wait to all at the top, and who fly.

-Clearly do not know really, well Curran it will, Alan would say but I do not want to lose the walk, is fan of heights.

-Alan can fly.

-Yes, you did not know Sarah

-Now!

We prepare to go and then we all went out with Jenny, at noon came the others.

Jenny was left worse than yesterday when paraded the five sports cars and convertibles, I remain surprised similarly, the teacher William came with them and Vanessa with the, the second blue car just like Hewett was Alan, in the third purple Kalinda and Dylan, Samara fourth one was pink and the fifth strangers, well I had seen in our training, but did not know their names, and were everyone equally handsome with his tousled hair color black as night.

-They are your friends.

-If they are. Well down at the same time

-I want to be you friend, I present them.

-Clear.

-Waiting give me an attack, first of the second car is perfect as well as in my dreams, his hair is fabulous, if you will.

-Well do not faint calm.

Walk with them while everyone else looked to all sides, and Jenny grabbed my arm, I approached Alan looked wonderful with her white shirt glowing skin with the sun and shorts.

-Hello girls. Alan greeting

-Hello. Silly voice she said

-Alan she is Jenny.

-Is Alan?

-Yes.

-Pleasure.

-Equally.

She looked at me, others came, the teacher and other guys.

-They are friends I hope do not mind. Alan asked

-Of course not. Jenny replied

-Hello. They all said

-They are Johnny, Tony and Miguel.

-Alan introduced them, and answer as if began to know.

-Hello. Salute

-Sarah overwhelmed me.

-Indeed.

-Curran and where it is. Ask

-He brings the helicopter, is back at the request of Andrew.

-Has them speak.

-A Helicopter. Jenny said while laughing nervously

-If we're going to climb the volcano.

-Want to join us.

-I have never climbed anything.

-Two of us, but we'll be fine, trust us.

-Yeah well, I have to think.

-Well, but we are going in the middle hour.

-So fast, do not they plan?

-Already planned everything.

-Seriously.

-If we will have fun.

-I tell my friends I'll go with you right back, I need to bring.

-Alan.

-Johnny brings anything you need for one more.

-Right back.

She went to tell his boyfriend is not yet up by ever drink the night before.

-Hi Sarah as has been happening.

-Okay but better now that you got.

Smiled and kissed me quickly took my hand.

-Hello teacher would not know what would come.

-Clear that I would lose the excursion to the volcano.

-Already knew.

-Andrew told me well and I knew I could not resist.

-Well and will fit everyone in the helicopter.

-If different.

I did not ask them anything is strange.

-Sarah.

-If Jenny.

-The accompanied them.

-Great, you will go with Hewett.

-Monica going as well.

-Clear that her come. Alan answered Jenny

-Sorry did not mean it to sound is form.

-Okay.

Samara was with Andrew and went to the rocky slopes of the volcano, the parade car was amazing, and not one would lose the excursion, were fans of extreme sports.

-And she knows all of us looked very interested.

-So no know, just surprised cars and singular appearance, all are very handsome, that to me equally surprised just as her, they are all fabulous and you know, but she likes you Alan.

-If I understand.

-Understand.

-No wrong, I understand that we are disrobing and disturb you.

-Of course you do perhaps you have not looked. He smiled.

-That disturbs me more.

-I'm glad you feel that way.

-Torture truth.

-Revenge.

We arrived and all the cars, the helicopter arrived with Curran, the largest was the common almost like those used by the government.

-Your friend Ernesto. I said to Alan

-Is only a loan for the vacation?

-Great I like it.

-I go first; see you at the top guys. Monica said

-I thought you had panic.

-Who would have this fear?

We prepare, my brother was with us and swam clear helicopter, who brought radios had good signal everywhere even in the volcano.

-Ernesto equal.

-Not friend, these are of us, we only use the satellite of Ernesto.

-Is that right Alan?

-Clear Miguel is right.

-And he knows it.

-Course he know.

-Sarah you friends give me chills.

-Fear not, they are great.

-It too much to be true.

-If the same thing I thing.

Took things all ready

-Indeed have everything ready Sarah.

-I told you Jenny.

Each walked with our backpacks something heavy but it was a slow journey and hopped that it would hold Jenny, roads all together, we find a stone barrier that is where the backpacks came into play with ropes and rappelling harnesses, Kalinda and Samara helped us since they were experts.

-Frightened.

-Slightly. Discussed the two

-Well, be fun.

We had three groups one of Hewett, Samara, Jenny and Tony, the second was the teacher Vanessa, Dylan and Kalinda, the last, Alan, Johnny, Miguel and I, was more fun and I was not hard up as I had expected, even so it was strange, follow up which it was nervous was Jenny who continually slipped, wise and rocks were falling near Tony and she swallowed hard, but did not mattered knew it would be that way and easily dodged as it was like all of us, she must go with Monica, but not offered it so she said nothing and continued with us, but it was very awkward would fall, so would I if I had not spent so much with the boys and I had trained and have given me a heart attack of fear just like the one she gave at times, and looked tired but was still.

-Sarah this do for fun.

-No girls sometime we go skiing hobbies easy. <<Commented the teacher.

-Girl, how many years you have?

-Only 25.

-Clear I am a girl I have 22.

-You have no idea. All laugh

-Well and you've accompanied your Sarah.

-No, it's the first time and hopefully not the last. Sounded the phone whole the helicopter was passing.

-Monica so she had something to do tomorrow and that she can do.

-And it is.

-The jet skis.

-Cool. Hewett said

-And smile Monica of this recording. The salute

-Well and you thing Alan.

-Vote. But all raise our hand less Jenny

-Not like the jet skis Jenny. I said

-Yean right but not if it has my vote.

-Cleary, if while you're on our side. Hewett said

-Then clear.

-While we all agree.

-How many ask?

-They say guys.

-To order 20 Jenny's friends can use.

-Well teacher.

-Curran orders 20 to Ernesto and have insurance.

-20.

-If you say that you want to test the prototype CIA towards the said they were fast.

-Well, some favorite color.

-Black.

-CIA. Ask Jenny

-Not ask. I answered

-Ok…

Got up at last, almost dark, Monica was waiting in the top along with Curran, Hewett helped bring things Jenny and also Miguel a while each, only ate energy bars on the road and we had no hunger, thirst only, on top getting sunlight was amazing.

-Get use to a view like this.

-Jenny's true we all get used.

But came and shot at the ground despite Alan's hand took and led her ugly places, I said nothing because it was my idea, Hewett takes their stuff.

-We must return.

-If in a couple of hours Jenny.

-In a few of hours why?

-We must appreciate the view at dust.

-That there will be.

-And girls will see it. Replied the teacher

Monica was eating a fruit salad, which we will, Curran took good enough for all, the night was falling and about nine in the evening, the best in the world, sitting on the volcano with a warm campfire watch a comet pass.

-Alan saw him.

-A comet.

-If.

-Wait a little more.

-Wait.

Pass one more.

-Make a wish if you pass another.

-I like. Jenny said

-Monica it's time you turn it on camera.

-Sure, that.

-Children will know already.

Alan took my hand and kissed me on the cheek.

-Enjoy it is to fascinate.

-And I'm enjoying it.

All was silent for a minute, but I spend nothing, Jenny settle into one of the stones and the others started to talk and then the unexpected.

-I told you, only you had to wait.

-Knew.

-Clear why we are here there is only one chance.

Hugged him around his neck and kissed him on the cheek, but we were all excited but more me, Monica and Jenny.

-Really going on. Monica wonder

-If love is real and I'm just like you.

And was a fantasy come true, a dream that never imagined would happen, a meteor shower it takes half an hour, Monica left the camber at its base to appreciate the view, if when the sun blushed was wonderful this was better, my heart was racing so fast, with emotion, an event like this is impossible happens, last look at the top of a mountain.

-Quiet does not want to confuse you with a star.

-You know I'm like a star Alan.

-Are better than a star to you I can touch and kiss.

Kiss me tenderly and almost always did, no matter the looks, Hewett until I hit a bump on the back and hear you loud, everyone turned, finally finished the show and the cold was stronger.

-Guys have to go back.

-Yeah, well let's go. Said the teacher

-Where this Curran.

-Sitting back here.

-You do there.

-Resting, it's up to Alan take.

-That?

-I do great.

Got out and took me with him ahead.

-Put on your headphones… you want to fly.

-Of course not.

-Is easy.

-If as no.

-Well look at and then you do.

-Not ever.

Then tell me how everything works push some buttons told me if I remembered the end, but had no intentions of doing it again, the helicopter landed on where we left the cars and then go off, but someone had to take him back.

-Tony you take my car.

-Clearly, if friend.

-I'm going to Tony. But he takes my hand

-No, of course not, you're going with me.

-Okay.

I went up where the first time, but did not let me took me in his arms and I went up for me to take off.

-Are crazy you want to die.

-Of course not.

-And I do.

-Already taught you remember but hopes to stay away guys do not want any accidents…

-Well now as it is already on you just have to take off.

-Is all.

-If that's all, just calm down.

-I can't do is crazy.

-Clear this is crazy, so you do it.

-Well here we go.

Made strange noises and laughed like crazy achieve mocked off, just did what he told me.

-And now I do.

-Well fallow them.

-Which like?

-With controls.

-Ha-ha.

The followers a little nervous, but he was on the of my almost grabbing everything, but could have been easier since around the volcano had a huge lake, the only thing wrong was that we had to turn around to go with the cars and who had everything and was more interesting than just go down and have could well past us, but Curran was late, but I was happy as it was great view, but was still terrified.

-Have insurance this thing.

-Of course not.

-What?

-Is CIA and given we are proving is one of the easiest to fly, that agency would want to insurance.

-That the easiest, joking, has many buttons.

-If you learn to fly and survive you and be approved.

-If it does not arrive in pieces.

-If hope not, the good thing is that there parachute to one side in case.

-That you're crazy, wanted you had fun but this, this is crazy.

-I like the strange.

-Ha-ha.

Was still making fun of me and I did not remove the hands from the controls, the small flip a cry of emotion, Alan was still laughing.

-You had to land are almost there.

-I will not I'm terrified.

-You have to or out of gas.

-Not true.

-If it is.

-Where it landed.

-In the lake.

-And I said that your brother was crazy, you're worse than.

-If we are brothers before wad fun us this way.

-And when you became bores and then fun.

-Then I tell you, it's time to land.

-I can't.

-If you can, and do not close your eyes, low controls slowly and decreases the velocities.

-I do not let go of the controls, we're down do not move, just quiet.

-What's that sound?

-Nothing still, missing a few meters. Closed my eyes

-Sarah opens your eyes we are in the water. Breathe and opened.

-Sarah quiet, we're fine, just released controls, drops them.

I heard that the cars were approaching, the lights looked around but did not release the controls, Alan finally pulling them out and was on his side to the dock, rather a small wooden bridge that I thought would destroy, and he low and he extended his hand.

-Let go see already finish everything.

I gave him my hand but did not take any step, was still terrified Hewett and my brother came and help, I was like rock but in the end down and I hugged my brother.

-Great Sarah did wonderful. Say Hewett

-Corse did great, that's my sister.

Then he let go and I did not felt my body was still shaking, just before falling Alan reached me, and laughed at me and my brother.

-You dropped friend.

-That is not true Tony.

-Still dizzy honey.

-I'm terrified Alan.

-You did great.

-Where we're going.

-To the cabin, these pale, pale are also others.

-I do not mean that, that will make?

-Your classmates have a party; I think to stay a while.

-Yes, you will go?

-No, I want to be with you.

-While I like and can put me down.

-Are you sure?

-Yes.

But I could not stand up my legs would not respond and returned to carry me, walked in and I lay down in the room.

-Well, the helicopter passed the test.

-Kidding.

-Of course not.

-Know was fabulous and frightening.

-Clear it is, and it is best to not have to jump.

-That funny.

-I'll bring some ginger expected you will feel better.

Return very quickly with ginger and take it, I like the taste, then say a while I felt better, and we exchanged glances and kiss me whit the kiss passionate and seductive as always left me sighing again and asking for one more, clearly could not withstand and ask for another, he turned to me one more bat before that smiled clearly and sly blue eyes looked at me and I to him and then the kiss.

After that, leaned back beside me as always and I fell asleep in his arms faster than I would have imagined, I just remember his blue eyes staring at me.

As always the breakfast was ready on a small table and he was gone, the end came out, everyone was outside the sound of the voices were enough, and everyone was excited about the helicopter, trying to convince Alan to give then a ride in the.

Jenny was with them and would not let go of Alan and Hewett, Curran was the one who took them for a walk, gave only around the volcano, seen was the first in line to get with them, the good was that Alan will not go, heavens was angry that my companion's chat with class, will you come for me to talk to his brother, but do not believe her if she flirted, ran his hand touching her hair and did not move, she had a according to litter in her hair, but no, it has never inconvenient, is as fanatical to the perfection of her body and his hair more.

-Good morning Sarah.

-Hewett scared me. I elbowed him in the ribs

-Woke up late girl.

-If I think I was tired.

-Look already has competition.

-Of course not, she has a boyfriend.

-And that he is a fool and my brother is not.

-If true.

-My offer still stands…honey.

-No be necessary.

-But do not know if the way you want.

-But could change if you wanted.

-Do not start, do not ruin a vacation I hope not the last.

-If still no news.
-Not one.
-Nothing.

Breathe deeply and hug to cheer me, in that Jenny turned and looked at us, knocked on Alan's arm to announced that we were behind them, turned to sing, while Hewett laughed, she looked angry but that does not erase his smile, they are came laughing and she flirted, he looked great as always and smiling at me, but he keep is smile Hewett mocking and wise why.

-Good morning friend.

It was not really my friend just classmates.

-Hi Jenny.
-You coming with us for a ride in the helicopter.
-No, I think not, last night was enough to pilot it.
-Might do it again. Hewett said
-If I could but will on another occasion.
-If you better go and area going up. Hewett said
-If it will be better to climb.

Alan as she watched his beautiful eyes, ignored in an instant but then react.

-No thanks see you I have something to do.

While she flirted dismissed, Hewett approached me to my ear.

-I will go I will keep alloyed a little. I gestured grateful.
-Hewett has fun.
-Know not think it's so funny, he's done hundreds of time, the fun quick passes. Alan said
-I was just wanted to tell him.

And stated to walk behind me, with step country and he match with me.

-Why not go with her, also bores you fly.
-I prefer to fly.
-Yeah sure is more exciting.
-Clear that if it was better last night and you pilot.
-You had fun on my last night.
-Course was fun.

But was still being indifferent to him.

-The jet skis came in a little longer, you want to do.

-Nothing just walking.

-Okay walk.

-Not have to be with me, you can go to have fun.

-Clear if and also I have to be when get the truck, and then have fun.

Kept walking, the sun was great although it was strong, I loved it but I felt uncomfortable.

-Are okay Sarah.

Sarah told me now, and not girl, gnashing of teeth he could hear them, took my arm and stopped me.

-That's wrong.

-Nothing.

-Know not lie.

Hug me by the waist and carried me, he turned around to go back, we walked along the lake, and throw some stones in the lake, and bounced away almost to the other side.

-Try it.

Take a small flat stone as underside plate and launch water rolling down left right and then sink down.

-Have strength but so is not.

We get closer to the water, it huts bad step on a stone and slide, but to keep from falling I took the shirt buggering the buttons and have no time to react and fell with me in the lake, although it was on the shore and the water was warm was worse because it hurts a little, the hug me around the waist to help.

-Are you okay girl. I smiled

-Of course not, I'm wet.

-I, we are want to swim a bit and we're here.

-Bring pants is uncomfortable.

-If it is true.

He threw water on my face.

-So. I did the same

-Get out you jet skis arrived.

-If we are going.

I took my hand and we went, he took his shirt wet and without buttons, I run out of breath beside him, never seen him without a shirt, I gestured to myself while was returning to take my hand and in the other his shirt wet, walk, and flamboyant truck comes with a logo dangerous cargo.

-Just in time.

-If.

Hewett jumped off the helicopter, the cry was heard in spite of the noise, came out of the water and goes to us.

-Imagine that you've already done?

-Yes but higher.

-They finally got the jet skis, racing brother.

-Clear that if.

-That happened to you guys?

-Not jump from a helicopter that is.

-You should is great.

-Then maybe.

-I need to change.

-Not want to see de jet skis.

-Clearly yes, but I feel uncomfortable wet.

-Hewett.

-Yes brother.

-I'll go with Sarah care of them down and anyone touching them until I returned.

-Not waiting.

-Nobody touches.

This time the was change but stayed shirtless, put on a short of thinner for the sun to dry it fast, white with blue as his eyes, I wore a short white and yellow somewhat longer because was my favorite color, I do not look good but I felt as well.

-Ready.

-Yes.

Hands as always, we faster or maybe not enough, the helicopter was already in the water.

Tony and his friends were in the water with jet skis Kalinda, Dylan, Elmo, Curran, Andrew and even my brother Monica strapped to his waist, less Hewett, the teacher had one too.

-I told you.

-As if I could stop.

-So I thought, and how many sent.

-Only fifteen.

-God since…

-Well Sarah wants one for you or you will go with me.

-And let your brother beat you, I shall gain them.

-So it spoken Sarah.

-Left over one, somebody already asked you for.

-Course, Jenny and her boyfriend the abuser.

-Abuser.

-Course treats others badly and humiliates them.

-I know, we play the race and then I'm going with you, Samara with Hewett, Kalinda and Dylan, and left over three more, and would be four for them.

-Is right.

-Clear that if. I said

-Sarah ready.

-No.

-Great win them all.

-Dream my brother.

-Clear that not Hewett remember the last I will win.

-So the rivalry.

-Good start already. Alan radius rang.

-That's ready for us comes first wins.

-To three?

-Why not.

Samara counted, only splashing water left behind, of course we were all even, but the continuing competence of siblings was obvious they slashed each other, while our spectators shouted with emotion to see fourteen black colored jet skis and all of them beautiful figures because until Samara and Kalinda they were very beautiful, wearing only a short and other small and rest exposed, with only that, I was the strange in all this, at that time all his perfect hair and stunning bodies.

Stirred water too, since some of those who were in it came to shore, and we were a danger, we occupied the entire lake and it was huge, we're all having a great time, Samara and Tony went forward and was still Alan and Hewett, that were still competing, fighting with the water, sorry you can't use our powers said Miguel, then be a fair race, the teacher who caught them, I guess he wanted to win, seeing accelerate all, good that does not bring concealed weapons, but I prefer not to touch any buttons.

The who sped to the finish, looked into my brother and Monica with a big smile, Alan and Hewett went ahead and we were not far from them, if we accelerate more and the first to reach the goal was Dylan, water jump with Monica and completely get wet and we all go on purpose, I think Hewett and Alan were draws, then all at about the same time, we turned around and met my brother, and said who had won but do not was agreed draw, all shouted with excitement, as they left each one by hand, and then we went and led the four jet skis like as we had said, they use two by two.

Jenny and her boyfriend in one together and some more of those who were there, who had humiliated Jenny's boyfriend, Hewett leave use them, while down Alan gave another turn alone.

-Do not go with me.

-No, I'll go with you brother.

-If… guys do not touch any buttons, remember as I commented Jenny are barrowed and I do not have enough to pay them, whether that be careful, if not already they will pay, will be responsible.

-And you if you have to pay them, the race got were dangerous and could almost swear he would destroy them.

Said Jenny boyfriend

-If I have enough to pay for the helicopter that is there so be careful.

All made fun of him and went is best and the others followed him, I guess it was his turn to lose.

-Were not you a little hard on you speech?

-The Sarah annoys me is a fool.

-If true and you had to mention the money.

-Clear I have never a chance to shine.

-Show off.

-If and see Jenny also looks.

-Clear.

-That, look your bathing suit and all the girls are the same way, except you, that's wrong.

-If then, we have more time I can wait to see you naked.

-Shut up you hears Samara.

-And that is the truth, if you look great if you imagine.

-I just can't imagine.

-Clearly you see all the time.

-If suppose.

-And think of you.

-To pervert.

-Well it's a question.

-If I guess right.

-Just well.

-Yeah, you think of Jenny.

-Well has nothing to see, is very thin, no nothing.

-No nothing.

-If you look at your legs, you're…

-Me that.

-Want to continue.

-Do not think so.

-While I will continue imagining like my brother.

-What?

-Yes, he also thinks like me.

-You talk about my body.

-Why not, my brother and loses the breathing when he sees you perhaps think I do not think.

-I had not thought of.

-Well do not do it, do not tell him I told you.

-Clearly not say we talk about sex and my body, your fantasies yours, are you crazy.

-Yes, and I have reason.

-You do not.

-I've never really seen in a mirror.

-Everyday I look in the mirror and I fell the same way.

-No silly I mean, you're sexy and you have everything but they and besides, your face is bold, your flirt smile as if the flirtatious to all and that leaves us frozen.

-I do not do it on purpose, my smile is natural.

-Yes but too provocative. I laugh

-You see what I mean; anyone would think that I flirt.

-Do not think my smile if flirty, I'll have to let laugh.

-If you do then it would be you, even if you will be a little flirtations smile.

-So you think.

-Course that I imagine with you smile out of the lake in swimsuit. I almost choked gulped when I heard

-That is normal am a man, and I'm sure Alan thinks like I do, and I hope it happens before we you promise.

-Promises that you'll see in swimsuit.

-Not crazy, but I'll think maybe if I'm jealous of Jenny flirting with Alan.

-Well, think of Jenny and prove that she did not have much.

-If you're crazy.

-Your equal you are, you're jealous of her and knowing that my brother loves you and does not look at her for a second.

-But you started I was comfortable and came told me that I had competition.

-Should have seen your face when you look together, I just wanted to check.

-It'll pay.

-If you like, hit me.

I gave him a kiss on the cheek and a huge smile as I took off my shirt in his face that could almost touch me, my hair was falling on my shoulders when I untied, he ran out of breath and I smiled with my flirtatious smile provocative as he would say.

-I was not wrong, it was better than I thought.

-And waits to remove the short.

-Come on!

-Then, I have to go with Alan.

I close he mouth with my nails and another kiss on the cheek, as I walked away with a big smile, walk to where Alan, as if by magic he expected, as if I called, Hewett froze for a second and then followed me to go with Samara.

-Hello Alan.

-Hi girl and that smile.

-Just amused me.

-I see.

-You mind if I drive the Jet Ski.

-Of course not.

-Tanks.

While to answer me back is toward giving way and placed his hands or my hips uncovered, it was not necessary it never is would fall, was motioning for Hewett to see, I put the dark glasses and daring me to see more, and was placed in his, turning my face and kissed me, with your kiss that said she is mine, and I of her, and then we went, reach to see Samara laugh at Hewett, and also look at Jenny stay with almost blank eyes and her boyfriend drooling.

-He deserved it.

-Are you taking about Alan?

-Do not lie, I heard everything, forgetting to turn off you radio.

I keep quiet, after I turn off the engine away from the Jet Ski; only hear the sound of water.

-You heard everything.

-If everything is right and you're beautiful not to be jealous of Jenny.

-Yeah well, you need not be jealous of you brother.

-I am not, in any case I have reason to be and you do not.

-Because she flirts you.

-Like you my brother. He was right

-What was his offer?

-Really want to know.

-Clear.

-Okay and he knows not been with anyone and you do not think you'll do, mortified you know that I am the daughter of my mother.

He laughed

-Sorry that last sentence sounded strange, continuous.

-And do not you dare think, and he pointed.

-And what do you think.

-Do not think anything, I'm not interested.

-No interested?

-No.

-Not interested in his offer, oh I do not want.

-Seriously do not want.

-Cleary yes but is your decision.

-Kidding.

-No.

-Do not bother me say you do not mind me being with you brother, I can be with it, and then go with you, gone crazy.

-No would you be with me, you'll have to decide.

-I hope this conversation erase from mind.

-Why?

-You know I love you Alan and I have not thought about the issued that you said would happen only between the two without thinking.

-It is true sorry.

I turn to him face to face, the Jet Ski was comfortable and started to kiss me, do not happen on a jet ski, thought as he felt his touch on my back.

-Clearly not happen on the Jet Ski and not today.

-You said, just what I thought. Was silent and did not answer.

-How do you know?

-Just happen, your thought got into my head.

-Since when you do.

-Only sometimes but do not bother.

-That as seen.

-Nothing does look thus.

-Tell me.

-Only when you are mad, to know that sometimes I do not understand your behavior thus easier.

-That's private.

-Do not bother.

-You know what else; I want the truth or enter into your mind.

-Anything, just that you were angry at Jenny and you love me.

-I said I love you.

-Yes but not what bothers you.

-Think so. Was true that did not bother me

-I know I will not do it again unless you let me.

-Okay not do it again or I will do the same.

-Well, I can another kiss. Fell a bit but allowed

-Hewett and really deserved it, just one more question.

-Which Alan.

-You take off the front of the shorts. I smiled coquettishly

-No, I take away in front of you.

The swallow saliva and stay pale for a second.

-What if you heard everything he said your brother, you know he said you imagine the same as him.

-Well actually yes, but I have more imagination than him, my dream is better than of him.

-Tell me.

-Is my dream and I will not tell you?

Turned on the Jet Ski and turn me to drive again, he liked to put his hands on my hips and waist, kissed me on the neck and left with the others.

-Having fun.

Told me in the ear affectionately and gave me tickle that made me shrink the shoulder and shake.

-Clearly yes. I yell

Spend much time in the water, Hewett was still challenging his brother and ties were always in the background either wanted to win, that was my impression, the teacher was not in the water, ready to another of the guys who were happy, then Samara got bored and jumped into the water to swim to shore, Jenny and her boyfriend had to get out so that others could use them and was not very happy her boyfriend, she went swimming it was very good the truly, Tony time passed and Hewett played races with, my brother left to Monica on the shore, and was a little dizzy, but my brother followed, he joined the race Hewett and Elmo, played three against three, Tony joined him Miguel and Jonny, career watched them since now we expected we would see we were your goal and that team the won.

-Cheat.

-I think if.

Sometimes slightly used their power to not notice anyone, but it was obvious that agitated the water, unlike us we used not vest all the other guys had to use them, that was one of the rules if not they could not use, had to agree, Kalinda also swam to shore and Monica accompany Samara, enjoying the sun and a lemonade next, that I was craving.

-Who won?

-All are good, but I think you brother will lose.

-That, so good.

-Yes but he is the only one who would not cheat.

-If then maybe fair.

-If so, jet skis bring their tricks and maybe just use them.

-Like what?

-Have to wait.

-Then I want lemonade.

-Of course I like.

-We will let the Jet Ski to Jenny.

-Not.

-Why?

-This is different.

-Different.

-If not bring weapons and the conferring on them.

-Only yours.

-No, the six that are there and the Andrew.

-Eight are different, why do not you borrow.

-Exact, can be dangerous.

-And Dylan and teacher.

-No, those are normal but faster.

-Without weapons.

-To whether it is.

-Almost come.

-If you get ready.

Using his powers were coming and first to cross was Tony used his magic almost upon arrival, water slashed us, then crossed for a few seconds Hewett and Elmo, then brother and the other boys.

-Good all we cheated.

-Seem that if.

Were super-wet and before going for the lemonade as they approached Alan water threw them all, and went so fast, we hear your radio.

-Yes.

-Buy you think you escaped waits.

-On another occasion Johnny.

-Much time.

-Used you power.

-Just a little bit girls, you have used yours.

-No, you said I was dangerous and I think even I fear.

-If I'm terrified.

-Of course you are, I can kiss you and let yourself unconscious and stay with your memories.

-Sure you can but you will not.

-How are you so sure?

-Because you love me. Accelerated more than in other cases, even more than that when competed with Hewett

-Sure you have won.

-Clear I'm more than all of them, but do not tell them.

-Clear that they know it.

We did not stop until we get close to the shore where they were Monica her sister and her cousin, the splashed on purpose with jet ski, they hit a cry of annoyance he just threw a smile and turned off the jet ski.

-We got here.

-Swim.

-Curse is very close, afraid to get wet.

-Of course not.

Was released into the water and getting wet with her hands and face, I jumped against him and caught me in his arms, and dropped in the water, in itself was already wet, but if it felt strange and colder than what I thought, but I get used very fast, swam to where the girls were drinking lemonade, of course we take one I die of thirst, but not enough, take two bottles of unflavored water.

-Calm do not think take the bottle.

Made me laugh and I came out of his mouth water, he fell to Alan above as it was very close to my.

-Sorry.

-And hydrating you, go to the water.

-Okay.

We play in the water for long, but the swimming races play was better than me, the more enduring underwater breathing, watched our friends left but the jet skis to the hand it to him and throw themselves into the water to join us, the only one who let the jet ski so that others will use was Dylan and early return to us, but not enter at the water sat with his wife Kalinda a while, then went by balloon volleyball and made teams play, of course we were winning, the only one who not was the teacher and do not ask where it was.

-That you all play well.

-We had practiced this.

-I imagine, but I am very clumsy.

-You do well.

-As if.

-If you do well.

-Well the only thing I like about all this is to be near you and mare where when you carry me in your arms.

-Something. And took me in his arms to one more kiss

-The kiss was extra.

When he said that his brother hit him with the ball and I let go, stick a cry and everyone laughed at one point I thought it could not get out of the water but he react and take me in a second.

-I'm sorry, are you okay?

-Yeah sure, just a second.

-Those who wish, what happened.

-I enter the water with my mount open and I took me some water, but I'll be fine.

-Sure.

-Clear, we're done with them.

-Is good idea.

-Who will bet to make it more interesting?

-What they want. Answer Elmo

-We met, Johnny, Andrew, Miguel and us.

-Such their cars. Andrew said I look weird.

-That! I like to Hewett.

-Something else. Ask

-Well that such a collection of weapons. Andrew commented

-Great I do not have a collection of weapons. Laughed

-Is true.

-Any other ideas.

-Can't be simple. I said

-Clearly if, that is simple.

-And if I choose something less exaggerated.

-You want girl.

-Well, we have not bought lights for July 4th if they lose to come down and then fetch them, but which are enough we can use the lake.

-Good is not what we think but it is good idea. Miguel answered

-If true. Johnny said

-Well ok.

All agreed with my idea was simpler, we told the idea and accepted, but expected something more different, but they knew it had been my idea, not questions anything really, if are needed the lights, after that terrifying part because if terrifies me on second, I felt drown, we continue to play this time Alan will come knocking at his brother, several times and also I played better and beating range to hit a couple of occasions, eventually they we win, they will have to go shopping, then ate out of the water with the girls, after they took as jet skis closer to the smallest cabin, where they stayed Miguel and his friends, in the end all three were brethren, rightly so the resemblance between then, when they returned and we had music and Jenny and her boyfriend that Hewett did not like the distance still heard the sound of the jet skis, but it was late, were reached the day, Monica went to sleep I was tired and the teacher had the difficult task of picking up the jet skis, they understood if they wanted to use the next day, at the end we all left, the time flew by usual, Monica's sister would arrive on July 3, who come very fast, the kids already have list lights across the lake but near the volcano.

The little Marcos get happy with her aunt and my brother, then he ask Alan to give him a ride on the jet ski, from him that he liked more, seemed to me all the same but he wanted that, unfortunately occupy all jet ski that day, but at the other end and had used all week, Carolina dared to use one for herself, her husband one more, like Pilar and Yasmine, Sonia not clamed with her husband, was left without one, so that went up with me for a while, but then pass it on to Tony she was happy, I think he likes a lot.

The little Marcos was happy with Alan that spoiled him and let him drive; his parents did not bother because Caro knew he was in good hands, better than in her or her husband, everything was perfect racing clear that we are playing the last two arrived was Carolina and Pilar, Hewett though that would be with her but no, the was alone.

-Hewett happened to Pilar?

-Anything, just want to have fun alone.

-Alone.

-Good to you without one above, I can see that we are bothering about you, so is she.

-And not endure it.

-Exactly.

-Little stand it.

-If true, I'd rather be alone or with you.

-You spend well with everyone even with you brother.

-Clearly, if it is my brother and you're funny.

-I know.

I throw water on her face wearing something of my power, had leaned watching them do.

-Or that if war.

-Just reach.

Clear that all looked he, could not reach me, this week was better know which buttons to play, I win in turn, clearly flouted said I cheated by starting first, play more and I also win, as said war, also use water as a defense but I won, followed mooching turn off the motor the jet ski for while.

-Well done girl.

-Thanks Alan, you have fun Marcos.

-Clear your boyfriend is very good.

-As you know he's my boyfriend.

-He told me.

-To the told you.

-If it says you're special.

-To, you are also special little one.

-He said the same thing.

-Than you believe us.

-If he said that he would teach me some trick.

-Some tricks that he said.

-If. He laughed

-I have already hungry Alan want to go with my mom.

-And I take it if you want.

-No, I do, this it is my copilot, and back.

-Do not delay.

-I will not I have to tell you.

-While I wait.

Not long in letting Marcos but before he came he asked the jet ski of Carolina, one of the guys who had pleased him well Hewett, but did not know it was disturbing, back taking to someone and I knew it was Dylan and Kalinda.

-Happens it's all right.

-So these guys just want to gave a turn to some girls and digested that if, you can spend with me.

-I can't, we will give the Dylan.

-Oh.

-Well come here with me.

-With taste you'll go to the end of the world.

He took my hand and I just came through with Dylan and Kalinda, Dylan is way to mine and took her, hers Kalinda gave the boys and went with her husband.

-You wanted to tell me Alan, something happens.

-Not only wanted to ask something, but see turn around and see me.

He took the waist and was so fast and I do not hurt.

-You're scaring me.

-Do not panic everything is fine, it's just an observation.

-And what it I'm misbehaving.

-Too well, you know look around.

-Yes.

-You see.

-My friends, the girls sunbathing.

-Well and the girls as they look.

-That.

-Just say.

-Look fabulous, you like. It made him laugh

-Somewhat more of them.

-Are nearly naked like that too. Turned to laugh

-Happens?

-Just think about it more.

-I do not understand and no make me jump into the lake. Hug me as if I were really to throw.

-Let go, I'll no throw.

-Are you sure.

-Yes, but tell me what you want.

-Yeah well I want you to consider something, do not bother when you take you blouse the day you were angry with my brother, you looked great, there's nothing you grief, just do it without fear.

-Mind my clothes.

-Of course not, but I think it bother your body.

-Maybe, but you know what I think.

-True, but I think you should be ashamed to give you no shame.

-Let's not talk about that.

-Of course.

I turned and I handle the jet ski, he hesitate to hug but he did, I was comfortable but did not comment anything, except that I was hungry like all, he left me on the shore and on me, and it was not necessary to leave the jet ski away, which grab the boys knew.

-Hi guys. Said expensive

-Hello.

-Will eat something.

-If I have hunger.

Alan went with Marcos to play, I was very quiet all the time, and he ate the same way.

-Sarah happens.

-As Carolina.

-If you are well.

-To it.

Pass a bit more and se retuned close.

-I can sit.

-Yeah right.

-Is that we are not friends, well what we are but not as with Monica, friend but if you want to talk, look who were you and him talking in the distance, discussed.

-No.

-Good, I do not want to get, sorry.

-Not wait. I grabbed her arm

-Well, want to tell me.

-It's just that…tell me what you think of my clothes.

-Discussed that.

-But you think.

-That is cute.

-That's all.

-Clearly if girl and you look great, you have a huge rear.

-That's the problem, he says that I'm ashamed my body, so I do not dress like the girls aver there.

-Good you have it.

-If I do.

-I think its panic.

-Panic.

-If you are beautiful and a spectacular body, if I had it would be up and naked. Clearly I laughed

-But no, look I'm not like before and you are perfect, you have nothing to fear.

-If so thinks Alan and Hewett.

-Hewett.

-I know what you think, but just my friend.

-You need not fair, uncovers and do not think he wants something else, just wants to show you off.

-Something else.

-If you look different, jus want you to feel comfortable, not filthy mind.

-Filthy.

-If he love you, and I's not Jenny asks you that.

-As you know.

-Well I'm a woman and Monica said.

-Clear.

-Just think about it, you do not have to do it if you don't want.

-Tanks.

-Anytime.

-You could wear.

-Do not bring anything.

-Clear that if I had considered but I dare not.

-Well, I can help you find something for tomorrow.

-If well, a while.

-Yes, but that stays in your room.

-Yes, but nothing happens.

-Know.

-Know.

-Cleary if I told you, he's different and...

-Monica told you.

-No, my husband.

-What.

-He talks to him once that.

-Tell me.

-No, you have to trust in him and in you.

-Okay.

-I have to go with Marcos, lately many questions and I think that will not lie, that worries me.

-You're right.

-Go with them.

-Walked and laughed she's nice; when we arrived the little Marcos asked things.

-I told you. Turned to laugh

-Guys doing.

-Alan tells me who the jet skis are.

-And you know who they are.

-If your friend Ernesto CIA and I want to be like him.

-As Ernesto.

-Not as Alan.

-Why?

-Has many friends and all things lend.

-Want to give you things?

-If and I want to be like Alan to have a very cute girlfriend like you.

-Like me.

-Yeah, you're cute, and I also want your house, your car and... Approached me and whispered in my ear.

-With his powers.

-Or told you that.

-If he says I'm like him.

-Well you better let you go to play, and do not worries, when you grow up you will have all that, but you need to study.

-You studied Alan.

-If buddy, study law and criminology and other things.

-I will study science.

-Well, it's funny my brother study that thing it might help.

-Thanks Alan then talked goodbye, bye beautiful.

-That said that to me, you teach.

-I nothing really did not say that. I bush

-Is tremendous indeed, you say all that.

-Very smart.

-And he has powers.

-I can feel it's true, but it is still very small.

-As you know.

-Good it's in is blood, Monica have them and it is likely that the same.

-Or good he'll be happy but not so much Carolina.

Spend the afternoon and ended the day, the next morning we woke up very early, the phone.

-Hello Gregory.

He spoke and stood up very quickly and hung up the phone.

-Something happens.

-Was a friend, says Hokon planning something.

-You know it is.

-No but he says it's dangerous, we have to tell others.

-Clear I accompanied them.

About that knock on the door he opened it was Carolina; forget that would come not a good time.

-See you in a while.

Give me a quick kiss on the cheek and left but salute Carolina.

-Something happens.

-Nothing serious I think he has to go with the boys and their sister.

-Are you ready?

-If I think.

Chose the right cloths, it did not take much, just a little, I wanted to go with them, after Carolina went out and seek it out to Monica, but it was not, I left immediately, but did not know where they would, walk Kalinda's cabin but before arriving I found Hewett.

-Wow these fabulous.

-What, thank you, where they are.

-In the cabin of Tony.

-Okay let.

-Not have to go and ended, they soon leave.

-And what happened.

-The same you know.

-Is the same.

-The teacher will go to the monastery in the helicopter.

-Be fine.

-Yes, he needs to investigate what Alan's friend said.

-Gregory.

-You know.

-No, but listen to your brother say his name, he said.

-Not much but we have to be alert, William had left to think that we're back and or not come here looking for us, but we will remain vigilant.

-They are looking for us, but they know where we live that there is no.

-Because the angel's mountain is protected, we are safe beyond.

-But Rosalba entered and Kokon.

-She yes, but they can no longer after that you sent to the shadows, became demons but are not as strong since you killed one and we need a demon, so they look for when we are away from the mountain.

-We go.

-Of course not, Alan talks to Ernesto at this time, he warns us there is movement.

-As will know.

-We are different our energy is denser and how we will know when someone arrives here, well its satellite, and also he will send some of his friends in the CIA and FBI to help us.

-Know.

-Not have to know.

-Clear terrorism alert.

-And you learn.

-And we do.

-Fun going swimming.

-Are you serious?

-If we can't do anything, but wait and Dylan are checking the lights for the night, and all will have to continue as usual.

-I can't do that.

-You have to, are your friends and Marcos, we have to pretend.

-Is true, then swim.

-Come on.

-If I prefer to wait your brother.

-While we wait on the lake.

As we walked I felt a lump in the throat, wanting to mourn melancholy, thinking that would destroy everything that our moment of happiness ended again.

They were all in the water, the other guys friends Jenny used the jet skis, but we were using us were empty, we had no desire to use them, Alan hug me from behind.

-You will swim.

-Not think so, only looked.

-That huts.

-That.

-Look at you these very cute.

-I think not.

-Of course not you saw in the mirror, Carolina help you

-If that.

-Did a good job, I like you clothes; I like color, matches my eyes. Made me laugh, he knew, what ought to know, that I loved her eyes.

-Are comfortable with the clothes.

-Forget truth that I stated this; I was more worried about you.

-And I explain my brother, we can only wait.

-That always sends him.

-I do not, it is offered and if I send my sister I think do not agree.

-I get along with her.

-Yes but not enough.

-May be true.

-I gave reason to, and well swim.

-Maybe then, we go with Carolina.

-To?

-I want to make sure it will be alright.

-Clear but Monica and your brother will be with them all day, whatever we warn; Pilan and Jazmine Samara care for them, and Sonia and her husband Curran will do it, three of us we take care of the kids of the jet skis, Elmo and Dylan at the edge of the volcano took a jet ski pretending to be in charge all day on the lights, Andrew is responsible to care for, like shore and Tony another, they soon come for the jet skis, the same way and could use weapons if necessary, and Johnny will come in a while we help with the kids in the water and the other civilian review.

-We have to have fun.

-If, I wait in the water.

-But.

Direct the water ran out, it was early I wonder if we have to spend all day in the water, but finally I approached the shore I took off my scarf waist and I enter the water, wore my hair down, walks slowly with them, and watched with silly face.

-Hewett mouth shut. Alan said

-You do not talk.

-Shut up.

-I had reason.

-If.

-You were right? I asked and smiled

-Not even to have noticed.

-True.

He embraces the rich and felt his could hands on my body, and I realized that I had to react wearing suit that day, when I realize what separates me, I went further into the water, that not look at me.

-React and friend, is a nice blue color as my eyes.

-As your eyes.

-If friend and no longer have to hide, my dreams are realize.

-That?

-Hewett leave her alone, you wished you had not, enough.

-But she does not know.

-Brother enough or I send with Pilar.

-I callus continues swimming. And swim away

-Of who speaks?

-Is that inadvertently solved the day you.

-As.

-You stay alone with you tiny bathing suit and you take off your scarf in from of us, with a coy smile and was very provocative.

-It was not my intention.

-I know my brother would like the water was frozen at this time.

-And you.

-I well, not be enough these divine.

I smiled and kissed him with much love, took my waist and lifted me.

-No words to describe this moment girl, was perfect.

-It can be better.

-Best I will have to get away from you.

-Really kidding.

-It wanted, but do not worry I'll be fine, just do not kiss me.

-That.

-Yes please.

-And if I do.

-Will not want to know.

-I think not.

Swam for a while and then we got on the jet skis, we had one each and we remained more apart than together, all we brought a few small appliances in the ears and we listened to each other, and they made jokes to pass the time, not how many times reviewed the detonators for the lights, everything was perfect and went well because I could not return, I left the water on occasion stop watch as were my friends, and I had warned my brother and Monica, not had them, were afraid but cooperated very well and even Marcos, who wanted to be with Alan in the water he understood it was dangerous but is a child and Alan so were pleased to give him a turns and then returned it, on to questions and as always the answer with the truth, and not on bit scared, that child is very strong, wise just like all of us, but when he finds Carolina will not make you any grace, but apparently it just understands the future of your child and would support at all times, but we hoped that everything changed and he did not live with what we now step noon and arrived the three in the afternoon, Ernesto had sent more than we were thought, help us with the people at the entrance checking everything, was a great help, and many knew that they would have lights on the lake and would be enough to if not rented many cabins that only went to the park with his family to spend the day, there were many people.

-I'm tired of spinning, I can go with Caro. All were silent.

-Friend if you can come with us. Said Monica

-I can Alan.

-Okay but do not do anything foolish.

-Of course not everything will be fine, plus you can hear everything we say.

-True brother I can go with it too, and I got bored and sun burns me.

-No, you stay and the sun no problem not do nothing, do not exaggerate.

-Good I had to try.

-Yeah right.

-As you let it, just because it s cute and smiles you convince you.

-Clear that convinces him, is his weakness. Said Samara

-Guys enough.

-Alan does not bother what else we can do. Johnny

-Put attention to demons.

-If on that as we kill. Asked Michael

-Still not sure, the last Sarah kills them.

-Alan then she will do it again.

-No, this time look the other way, not letting this alone.

-If we can't. This time Jonathan

-Doubt you buddy.

-Would not, but you're not able and stronger than us.

-But together we can, and it's dangerous for her to use them, many people.

-I can control myself. I said

-Of course not, I will not let you, and is the last thing told.

-Sister he's right, do not have to be alone, you know.

-Finally someone supports me.

-I like brother.

-Thanks Hewett.

-I also think the same friend. Elmo said

-I think we all understand but you have control over is dangerous, leave it to us this time, we are more prepared.

-Only one condition Dylan.

-Which it precious.

-If you need help I'll help and let me do it, if I can help I will not let anything happen to them for being fools.

-Is a good point but Alan decides.

-We'll see.

-Yeah right. Miguel said

-Enough guys do not fight the rest of the day.

-Is true girl, sorry.

-See continues enjoying the rest of the day.

-Clear that if.

Monica did not respond anything to our discussion because it was close to his sisters, take the place of Kalinda and she mine, to get to it I gave him a big hug, and it was worse for her family and she could not help because she was pregnant, the good thing was we did not have to hide from her sisters, and they were aware of all the dangers, the little Marcos was tires was a child, I took him bed, I almost slept together with me, but the voices of the boys kept me awake and alert, remained silent the last hour, just listening.

-Tock, tock.

I opened the door and was Alan.

-Something happens.

-If something happened and I had told you did not have to go see it, but it became too time no see and hear.

-Shut Dylan.

I kiss him, he could not say a word more and the guys were laughing on the other side, until Monica laughed listen to Carolina told her that tell the joke, and it looked like it had been crazy for talking to herself and laugh alone, but it was only joke they know what was bringing.

-You are going to end and let it breathe. Elmo said, but we were still kissing.

-Leave it as cute, rally has to return this evening, and have worked to do.

-In a while I am with you Elmo takes it easy. Everyone laughed

-Calm down your friend.

We parted when Marcos was moved, so we were waking up, we approach the silent but this sound asleep, we sat on the couch next to the bed and hugged me and I fell asleep.

-Little girl awake.

-What happened?

-You slept that happened.

-And Marcos.

-Okay with his parents when awakened Monica came by.

-Let me sleep. Hear voices laughing

-Friend anyone could you woke up, we talk, cry, talk about you but it was as if you are dead never woke up, and also snore.

-No true Tony.

-Clear that if, and it is best that we have recorded.

-Or if it is. Said Hewett

-If you were fast asleep girl.

-Has happened.

-Nothing as usual.

-Hey I'm good I can continue helping them.

-If we.

-Just give me a few seconds to change.

-Brother I can take you place. While others laughed

-Not, and will leave too.

-Do not be mean.

-Shut up and guys are crazy or desperate. Samara said

-Desperate. Mention Tony

-Stop laughing, I know all of you are equal.

-Of course not.

-Yeah well that's your Hewett, not you wanted to be in the place of your brother. Increased teasing

-Enough all, Alan outside only be a couple of minutes.

-Take all you want cute.

-Enough Tony left it alone.

-If boss.

-Never change.

-No, I think not.

I quickly got a new bikini and black short and a blouse something stuck something small, cute and output was very fast.

-Are you ready?

-If let's go.

-I like your blouse. Laughter again

-I would not like to know what you guys think seriously not. Monica told them, but we know what they think.

-Be better not.

Had walked back to the girls, it was more tense as time passed, I could see it in the eyes of all present, Jenny came to know of us had seen him all day, and it was a bad idea embers close.

-Hello Jenny.

-Hi Sarah wanted to know if it had nothing else to do, we will have a party after the lights, kindly Ref your friends, just do it.

-Do not know.

-No, it's fine when you can.

Alan followed him flirting and laughter against me plus the Hewett they kept.

-Alan can tell you brother invited.

-Will know clear what.

-And others can also go.

-If we tell.

She returned it along the way but return.

-Alan.

-Yes Jenny.

-What time will the lights.

-Well I'm not sure I have to ask Elmo they will know more.

-Yeah well if you know please let me know. Lighten her hand and pursed her eyes.

-By the way that you have pretty eyes.

Monica all laughed even as he knew that was what I liked about it and it had not been said, and she was saying it just like that, was still squeezing his hand, he did not say anything but everyone realized, Monica approached.

-Calm you shall break his hand.

-I'm sorry Alan. More laughter

-Calm friend I'll take her. Samara said

-Everything is fine no problem.

-Of course not, but look at her she's hot. Johnny

-Is true that outfit leaves nothing to the imagination. Elmo

-I'm in for good. Johnny

-Has a boyfriend, boys.

-I'm not jealous, and also that does not stop her for wanting to be with Alan.

-Of course not. Hewett

-As you know they wear are just across the lake.

-Friend these binoculars I can see everything and even you wear under that small black shorts, you look to sexy.

Alan watches him swallow and had a lump in his throat; I was clutching my hand tightly.

-Seriously you can do that.

-Unfortunately if.

-That thing away from me and my friends.

-Clearly, if there are other views around us.

-Enough boys, what they are not the time to play concentrate, remember that it is not a game.

All were silent by the voice of Alan something hard and strong since it did not do anything last grace and I also, continued talking about the girls but not me, so I'm glad we walked a bit more and started getting dark and Alan's cell phone rang, the good that we could hear.

-Hello Ernesto.

-Came with you in an hour, our satellite indicates a higher energy approaching from the south.

-The devil perhaps.

My stomach turned I felt more frustrated than before approaching the hour of our death again and in public, that's the worst innocent people.

-I fear that my friend, luck it was time.

-Thanks Ernesto.

-We will do. Ask

-You'll have to stay with Monica, Hewett returns you stay with it, you came with us Adriel grab your jet ski and go with Elmo, Samara and Kalinda with Elmo, Jonny get out all the boys of the water, take their jet skis, you have three minutes, and then come to the shore with Sarah and my brother, it's up to protect this side the three, others stay where you are, I'm going with Elmo as they approach your hand, we must stop them before they arrive, the Hewett inform you the teacher.

-Wait I want to go with you.

-No, you have to take care of everyone here, please you can.

He was very fast, even left to say another word, took the jet ski and disappeared in the dark, just look at the light of the jet ski on the other side, and there was no one in the water and people began to gather in the shore with chairs and blankets, waiting for the lights, that was what they expected and we demons, Monica and the others arrived and were close, but we could do, just watched, our eyes changed drastically and the others knew, Carolina held her Marcos and Monica gave her not to go because Ernesto's friends look after our backs, all were armed it was that no one noticed, she looked and stood motionless, just gulped and took my hand to her husband and his sister look, I continued listening for the small headset in my hate.

-Elmo that teacher news.

-Comes in three minutes.

Three minutes just hear the sound of the helicopter flying overhead lower than before, but silent, it was not so outrageous; it was a relief that the CIA provided was perfect.

-Guys are about ten but the demon in the front row, I feel it arrived in less than twenty minutes.

-We ready teacher.

-Clear I will land near you before they arrive.

-Yes.

-I want to do the same with you, do not let the devil between and do harm to people, you watch him.

-Like I can do that but I can fight you on your side.

-No, you have to be more concentrated, many people who have to care, including the family of Monica.

She looked at me sadly and said nothing but that look great.

-Okay.

-We'll be fine, take care of you four, and not come unless you tell them guys.

-Of course brother. Hewett hug me.

-We'll be fine, they can, and you can. Mention Hewett

-We can.

Johnny said and laughed at the small twister, but quickly disappeared when the sound of the helicopter did not hear more.

-Come get ready, I'll be in seconds.

-Of course teacher.

-Well as are all.

-Nervous, as we have.

-Three minutes.

-Okay Dylan begins with the lights.

-Sure Alan.

To hear the first sound of the lights the people shut, and the noise I could not hear anything but the three minutes had passed and did not know if they were ok, hand tighten Hewett and I returned the squeeze.

-Are well Sarah is you turn.

-Clear.

Around the edge of a mantle rose to gigantic that no noise whatsoever, just five feet down into the lake, but still did not hear the voices of the boys, the lights went out slowly.

-Are okay, as hell Hokon arrived, but not the demon that came out of the abyss.

-As you know.

-I listen to.

-As I do not.

-Sarah concentrates, just so you can.

-Monica listeners.

-Not.

I close my eyes and concentrated, my anxiety was so great that finally hear, but it was not nice, just listened to the voices of the boys rather hallow cries.

-Hewett.

-We cannot go until say it Alan.

-But.

-Sarah I feel the same way, but he knows what it does.

Marcos was impatient, Carolina had to lower it, and approached beside me and Hewett, was happy for the lights that had just five minutes, and it would take half an hour.

-Andrew, Tony come help.

-Of course Alan arrived in a minute.

For me it was the longest minute of my life, but heard that they got, had not used their power till this moment I heard speak in Latin, like in the practice knew what was happening but could not see anything, suddenly felt like something hit the barrier, try to make it as best I could, creating it even stronger than the last one had since I was three feet away from us on the water, a small moan escaped me.

-That was.

-I think the demons are in the water.

-As.

-Alan so if we wanted on this side, knew that some could come.

-Are demons.

-Well, shadows I believe, as did the other demon.

-I can't see anything.

-Me neither, but feel like they want to cross.

-Yes, I do.

-Still do not lose focus.

-That is what you want the devil to people.

-If that's what I think, imagine that people are scared and bad, what more would you like the devil, his strength would increase.

-Wants the evil and fear of people.

-That seems.

-We will do to help.

-Sarah stay where this do not even think.

-But Alan.

I heard him scream, I wanted to go to him, but like, I could not run on water and help they had all the Jet Ski on their side.

-Since we can't see the shadows if they are pretty close.

-Your mirror is reflecting in water and therefore can't see the other side.

-What?

-Seems that we can only see the firework that's weird.

-Dylan they do not touches the burdens of the lights.

-I got this.

-Alan passing?

-I can't answer I'm kind of busy. I look Hewett.

-I think we want to blow to pieces.

My heart sped up, the small Marcos all to hear our side, pulled my by the arm and too me, I could see what was happening, I look at him and smiled.

-Clearly if you're right little one.

-Sarah happens, I want to know. Hewett

-Marcos has an idea.

-It is.

-Just wait.

-Reperio ire repipi reportus niteo illi lacus-us visus visibilis. (Is the brightness of the lake an let me see do visible)

Hewett he understood every word I had said and put attention, darkness exchanged for a different one, as if the full moon, something that only our eyes could see, apparently Marcos also the tremor, not leave your hand but look at the fear in his eyes and I felt like mine.

-Be brave.

I said as we watched the shadows trying to catch us, we could see across the lake, as our friends were fighting, and Dylan away to one of the Hokon of detonators, the little Marcos sight of anguish, take it in my arms.

-Thanks for everything, you're right Alan, are special little one, you did very well but you have to be brave for your mom your dad and your.

-And for you.

-If at all, watch them feed on our fear must be happy.

-If I can do it.

-Well, what if you kiss your mommy fell that you love her.

-Yeah right.

-Hewett.

-Understand.

He carry with Carolina, was very helpful, he recalled what Alan had said, and as the light helped, only had to utter the correct way.

-Hewett something bad happened.

-Carolina will be fine now, Marcos help us and has a mission.

-What you mean.

-He has to make them happy, Monica will be better than this with you, we can see what is happening bit you do not and this affects, and they will be fine listening to Marcos.

-If I have to make you happy.

-I have to go back, Monica will be with you, she will tell us anything.

-Thanks Hewett.

-Monic anytime.

-Alan can see us.

-If it works fur us too. Alan

-Johnny can cross the mirror and finish with the shadows.

-I do not know is dangerous and if it gets any.

-Johnny you will be fine, go with him Hewett.

-I will let them in, but not let out.

-Are sure Sarah.

-Clear, but only one chance Hewett.

-Well you let us know.

-Just something, as they enter will go into the water.

-Just watch.

-Well, come now… wait.

-Happens it's all right.

-Alan thinks it's a good idea that they go alone.

-No, but I need to do so, I'll catch you later.

-One more thing.

-That.

-Do not bother.

-Hurry.

-Know where is the devil?

-No not yet.

-Luck guys…now.

Ran in front of me, was like a wind across the lake, not even water slashed one bit, ran very strong on water in the blink of an eye, used their power over water and light, but was estrange the shadows they disappeared but felt the same force as if they were the same amount of shadows trying to cross the mirror.

-Hewett is not working go back.

-We can't, we need to end them, just missing some more.

-Return something is not right.

-Girl occurring?

Though far I look and look back at me, was like so understand my silence, my anguish, gradually shadows they made one, leaving Hewett and Johnny disoriented.

-I know where the devil is.

-What?

-This in front of me.

Alan ran over the water like faster than the same Jet Ski, but it was impossible to get his brother and friend.

-Hello Sarah.

The he referred to me without approaching the boys.

-Alan why not arrives?

-I can't go.

-That.

Look the devil.

-Princess I also have the power to create barriers and you beloved could not save them.

Like they did not do anything imagine he wanted something more than talk and kill.

-You propose.

-Sarah does not. Alan shouted

-Intelligent.

They could not move, a second free had them in their hands.

-Let them, you want?

He would stare at humans and around me, turn and look at the little Marcos with fear, I smiled, the recalled what I had said, not to be afraid.

-I want something obviously.

-Never.

I yelled as the pain of the boys increased and across the lake looked like Alan tried to enter, while he was detained by Petula one of the Hokon who was now a demon.

-Alan me.

-Sarah does not.

-Are dying do not leave you and wants the little Marcos.

Monica heard the cry, and the cry of all Hewett even to bear the pain.

-Who the hell are you, you want of a child.

-Asmadeo.

-You Asmodeo the demon of evil and death.

-So, are you knows me?

-Enough.

Everyone knows that demon face and worst of all, he was sent to abyss for San Rafael, I shuddered just thinking about it, not know what to do.

-Why you want the child?

-Obviously is special.

-For what you want?

-The return to life I'm still dead and his blood was returned, I am able to enter heaven, when Cirrus will open it.

Surprises us at every moment as the blood of and innocent can give life to evil and open paths to the unknown.

-Marcos. Monica scream, I felt his hand on my side.

-Do not move Monica be fine.

I bent down to him, look and understand the problem in which we were, his mom it had arranged a crystal he had found a while, take it out of his pocket and put in my hand.

-It's heart?

-The angel San Rafael.

-The angel.

-Is you crystal he said what you borrow, you give energy to higher levels, is of the.

-You know how it works.

-He said you know.

-Remember what I said about your mom.

-If I have to give her another kiss.

-Clear that if.

I murmured something in his ear.

-Are ready.

-Yes.

Place your crystal on my neck and he was with his mom.

-Alan I'm sorry.

-Will you do, not work.

-Asmadeo I have another offer for you.

-Which is cute?

-I go in and you let them go.

-I want the child not you.

-My blood is as pure as that of the child and you know it.

-No Sarah.

-I love you Alan.

I felt someone's hand on my back and turn.

-Jenny you do here.

Often heard repeating his name in my ears

-Just wanted to know if it will go the party.

-Not a good time.

See his bewilderment in his eyes.

-Just wanted to know if it will go to the party.

-Alan is look across the lake and arrives in a while more, then pick up the trash, you can expect it in the other shore, and look him I speak.

Remove the phone and talk since simulates knew he was listening.

-Hello Jenny wants to date you, no problem for me, see you on the other side…of course.

-Said.

-If you look when it's over.

-Are you sure of what you say.

-Yes I'll not be around to bother you, I promise, you can go to the.

-Sarah you do girl.

-But maybe you'll have to go maybe arrives earlier.

-Thanks bye.

She was happy and maybe would be true; I do no will be at a time.

-Sarah you did.

-Alan sorry.

-Good princes accept you deal.

-Let them go first.

-Of course come closer.

Dubious approach me I sank into the water, but not.

-Sarah stops.

-I will not let them die.

Crossing my own mirror and followed by protecting people from the other side.

-Let them.

-Clearly yes, but do not believe in what I see, we are not complete.

Alan finished the other side with the devil, and ran toward us look like devil let him in, but only to him, but before coming to me let him immobile.

-Change of plans I want a guarantee princess.

I said nothing the boys attacked the demon, but did not do anything, throw them against the water that seemed hard as a rock, I was among them and leave in peace.

-Let them go.

The lift and were behind me.

-Are brilliant so fear you think you're a compromise a monster as they think of me.

-Never think thus of her. Hewett scream

-I think that you but what about the other.

Were silent, the lights of the fireworks still brightly illuminating the lake on occasion, but no one saw, all were struggling with our enemies and even though they won, the devil was more powerful than us, Dylan killed another demon over the Hekon there was only one of which was difficult to eliminate, where we were headed, just stay on the shore Miguel controlling lights detonators, but still failed to get closer than they wanted, just as I put a mirror so that the devil does not go through, he did the same with the boys, Alan still did not move and the pain increased.

-If you love me you'll have to come get me.

-Well, so be it.

-aqua-ae. (Water)

But he stopped her, that does not stop me, that boys helped me, not stopped and need to leave free Alan and let others enter, and there were only about five minutes to finish the great spectacle of lights, and ended our distraction, fought with him and would not say it was easy, all three at the same time use the same trick.

-Barathr-ium aqua-ae. (Watery abyss) The devil cry and Alan was free.

-Welcome friend.

-Thanks guys.

-Are right Alan.

-Sarah.

-That, I know what I do.

-Then tell us that we do not know.

The devil stay in our swirling water, take the hand of Alan and Hewett, and gave them my idea, in fact I made into my thoughts.

-If it works I support her brother.

-I want to know that they speak.

-Alan when entering helps me tell others.

-Of course if girl.

Jonny touch I said same thing to them, Alan joined us just as we, and glass broke just enough for them to enter, the demon broke free sending us to the water to the four, and let go a laugh terrifying, on the shore look Marcos I knew who was still watching us, I waved and he understood.

-I still like princes, a scary thing but you blood is as pure as the same God.

And others were near ready to attack but Alan stopped them, I fight with the devil to give them time to tell our plan, he broke the mouth and bleed a little, stayed in his hand and savor while I was on the floor at his feet, in my ear heard the voice of Hewett holding Alan to not get close to me.

-They delight in your blood is pure truth imagine that will all together.

I got up and stepped back to get close to the boys.

-If I have idea and will be the only drop you'll have me, or anyone else who is near, do not hurt anyone ever.

-So you think you will be of us.

-But not today, and you'll be not to see.

Marcos towards his works, kiss his mom comforting hand and taking it to her and even stranger, Carolina took her husband's and Monica's, the stranger took that of her child and the child of his mother, and she and her daughter should all be were holding hands, making one yourself, full of faith and hope, the angel's greatest weapon against death, against the devil, is the love and light, while the last firework deafening sound, came out the more grandiose light that always united an entire nation, red color and blue, with the stars more white than ever, that reflected the same stars of heaven, all shouted with joy and jubilation, with the glow of the flag, take the hand of my beloved and Hewett, behind us the others did the same.

-Asmadeo you're wrong, I'm not like you, I am not a danger and they love me, and we're friends, something you forget as being among the shadows, and never will know what it's like, to have you soul dead, without feeling full of hatred and resentment.

-On fides-fidei is-ea amoris amplior-ius amplius. (Whit faith and love bigger purest)

As I said that the devil tried to immobilize us, I thought more about what I had said and to receive the love of all hearts around me and in the laughter of little Marcos, look at it while doing bigger and more intense the swirl of water crystallized as diamond like a star, he could not get closer to me, was lost between the water shattered into millions of drops in the purest element of life, what is a vital resource for living the demon took liquid water instead seemed frozen and shattered was falling back strongly into the abyss, and matching them with the water of the lake where who seemed frozen at our feet, water as diamond vanishes in our presence, turning everything to calm, I fell to the ground a little dizzy touching the crystal that gave me Marcos, to remind me that the most powerful weapon of San Rafael was the love and light, and the crystal reminds us the pure of life and innocence of a child.

-Are you okay?

-If I looks and you.

-Well you do not look at all well.

-If I'm right.

-No, you're bleeding from your nose.

-What happened friend. Wonder Tony

-I'm fine, just that was more energy than before.

-Come going with Miguel.

He was with the other side of the river, with the lights and he had finished, Alan took me in his arms running on water, like the others, all came to the shore in seconds, stay more dizzy than before, but I recovered quickly.

-Guys are right, great Sarah you were fantastic girl.

Did not answer I did not have words, and Alan did not go me down, drink water bottle Elmo he had with the last one, but I would die of thirst.

-If you love the water, take as desperate.

Everyone laughed but I like the water, I recover but said nothing I was comfortable in his arms.

-We lost the lights.

-Adriel true.

-No, of course not. Elmo said

-Leave the best for last.

Put the cable into the detonator and the sky is full of light for three minutes straight, looked at Alan and lights made me look his eyes glowing.

-Already can put me down I'm fine.

Under me before finished the lights, and my brother and Hewett warmly hug too, then the others, even Kalinda and Samara were happy not to let their brothers die.

-Well done girl.

-We owe to Marcos is a very special child.

-Finally let me help without getting angry with me.

Hug me till the end of the show, the boys were given a red flare to each, to indicate that the lights had finished, we hear the cheers and screams, even in spite of the distance, and knew that only a few people are in the place if not all we were friends, then up all the things the helicopter, and the teacher went and come back on the jet ski to the other side, even with the flares on, to get all greeted with applause, as heroes without them knowing we saved their lives, celebrated as if they did, and greeted us all and without thinking we were all smiling and happy.

-Are happy Alan.

-Sure we are alive.

-Well, I remember that Jenny waits.

-That's your problem Sarah, you told him not me.

-You wanted to be happy or throw me into the lake.

-I'll help you brother.

-No, I work out.

-Then go to the party.

-If we go to the party with them.

-Brilliant. Johnny cry

My brother run where was Monica, who was cheerful as we listened and cried at the same time, and listen to Marcos asking for us.

-Go with them.

-Clear that if.

Arrived fast and Alan stretched hands to carry him, he was happy was his friend, hug Monica and Caro thanked us.

-Caro hero you son reminded us many things.

I was saying as he handed his crystal, put it in your packet.

-A big applause for Marcos.

Others were already on our side, applauding the little Marcos, he was happy.

-Good thing Marcos bedtime. Said his mom

-Five minutes more. All laugh

-No, it's time.

-Okay…

-Alan can teach me to fly the helicopter.

-Clear that if you teach tomorrow but mom leaves you.

-If Mommy if.

-Clear but its bedtime.

We said goodbye to Marcos and others.

-Good and the party. Hewett reminded us

-Clear go.

We all go including Monica.

-Will you do with Jenny, if you want to go with you, I promise.

-Hewett go with I take care of everything.

-Okay.

-Girl jealous.

-Of course not. Everyone laughed

Forget that they could hear, no one had removed the ear speaker, only Alan, I do not listen more, then I take it away, did not want to hear what he would said to Jenny.

-Kidding, do not want to hear.

-Of course not.

-Invite her to dance.

-I said I did not want to know.

-It is difficult to know, look beyond are dancing.

-And if it is nothing, not even invited to dance.

-Dance friend.

-Not.

-Please.

-Dances with Pilar, she's more than ready.

-I know, but I want to dance with you lovely.

-Later.

-I'll have to wait.

-Happens to Marcos, it is normal to think that way.

-What you mean.

-Apparently has powers like us thought that we had to grow.

-Depends.

-Depends on?

-Some until they are teenagers or in your case until we met, we always the me have had from children, by we've always know, and in the place of Marcos this near us, and is like us is not strange for us Alan that answers you questions.

-Understand will be more prepared than scared, but is too for a child.

-True.

-If you're the same, you were not a normal child, whether now you behave as such, want to have fun.

-Something.

-Well let's have fun, let's dance.

-Clear that if.

Danced a while we had fun, and the device had been removed of the ear like everyone, had not see Alan, did not know if he kept dancing with Jenny or what, but I was okay with Hewett and would come when I had to everything was fine I think.

-Where is your brother Hewett?

-I guess in the room with Jenny, do not you think.

-Not funny.

-Clearly not, well a bit, my offer still.

-I'm serious, where this Alan.

-As I know friend, do not bother you know it's like a ghost.

-If true.

Continued dancing but do not stop think about what Hewett said, but he was an irresistible offer to be with Jenny as she is cute.

-Stop worrying he'll be fine.

Big hug me and I get burned where the drinks, gave me a bottle of water he grabbed another and drink then he had to laugh.

-He's fine and not with Jenny, he dance like two pieces only talk to her and left.

-Know where.

-If not complicated, remember that he promised Marcos that will teach him to fly the helicopter, will I talk to the teacher and brought him, then took him back because the teacher did not want to stay, if not long in coming. I gave him a kiss on the cheek

-Thanks friend.

-Forever, keep on dancing.

-While go.

-Not so fast brother, my turn.

-That, I told Alan falter more.

-I did my best.

-Make amends you.

-As Sarah.

-With a kiss.

I gave him another kiss on the cheek, more intense than the other, with a hug smile, and we went dancing, Alan also smiled mockingly.

-Miss me girl.

-Not really.

-Seriously.

-Clearly I missed a lot.

-I miss you too, but I had to do something.

-know, and she happened to Jenny.

-Dance will be fine just talked and it was all.

-Was it.

-If that's what you promised, it was your idea, not mine.

-And leave you to if like it.

-Clear is cute, understood quickly.

-Cute huh. I said sarcastically

-Marcos will teach morning to fly.

-Do not think it's too small.

-Yes but it promised.

-Fulfill all that promise.

-Clear that if.

-Good in this case promise that you will be with me.

-Is easy although not I promised will never be away from you.

Keep on dancing and see that Samara danced with Andrew, it was rare never had looked together.

-Having fun your cousin.

-It seems are longtime friends.

-Already all clear.

-If that I believe, because in reality I am the last to find out what happens.

-Can be.

-If true can be not only.

-It's because you're so foolish never obeyed.

-Look if you want but situations change at a time and my head tells me it acts, I only what I have to do.

-If maybe, and everything you do has been good, we've saved many times at all, and therefore have many admirers.

-Yeah right, I just know your brother.

-Good that such Jonny to the like you.

-I have more problems, right.

-No, I told you he likes you nothing else, it's hard to haven you around you smile just because they like coquettishly.

-Not my intention is a form of greeting from me.

-If you are, you are only mine.

-Of course.

To Knowing More

Marcos is happy in the helicopter with Alan, and he accompanied his fader leave to use some buttons, after several laps but decided not to go with them, Marcos insisted that had more turns and of course I indulged.

-Hi Johnny.

-Hello Sarah how it goes.

Totally nervous rose when he saw me, he was checking one of the Jet Ski, had used the Jenny and her boyfriend.

-The decomposed.

-I fear that we will have to return it.

-Ernesto hope not bothers about that.

-No, understand and if it have insurance at the side of the helicopter.

-Great, there will be no problems.

-If it is very good to know after we've been through, it's a good thing.

I felt silly and looked the same, do not know what else to say.

-If the good news is welcome at this time.

-Will not go with Alan.

-No, he has committed.

-If Marcos is great.

-True.

-Good I have to climb the Jet Ski in the truck.

-I can accompany you.

-Course, provided you do not have problems.

-Do not believe me you will have.
-While go.
-I can teach you to handle it.
-Rally?
-Yes why not.
-Clear look at the speeds, you need to pull the truck and the brake pedal, then release the brake and accelerate slowly, care with people, and only if go reverse, whether it calmly.

I did what he said, but trailed off not one if not several times.

-One more try.

This time not was shut down but sped up to more, and stop when the truck suddenly shuddered, and pasted a cry, he was dying of laughter because it was enjoying watching me suffer, and I was nervous.

-Could with the helicopter and you can with the truck, it's a shame.
-I think I prefer the helicopter.

He got out of the truck, be silent but I did not move, suddenly Johnny was still next to me with the door open.

-Go the other side look and learn.

I shut down the truck alone but was afraid to jump again, leave the steering wheel, hands to help me move to another seat, he smiled, it lit quickly, place it just behind the Jet Ski, near the lake in just three seconds, and I would have gone to the lake, as it was down.

-Are great too fast.
-Hurry.
-That.
-If you learn your, turn him back to the parking.
-No, I think not even said a word.
-I said watch and learn, as he had done did not work.
-Can repeat. He laughed
-You're funny.
-Thus.
-Clear, Hewett rightly having fun with you, he's right.
-If fun of me.
-And who is not three demons you faced and you can't with a truck.
-Different.

-Fear gives you a truck more than a demon.

-On second thought I think so. Turned to laugh

-That gave me nerves, you learned quickly?

-No, actually shock the first time I try it, but I kept on.

-A point for you.

-Yeah, well we're going up the jet skis.

-The jet skis.

-Id they broke more than one.

-More than one.

-If, the four who used more, and will not bring my repair tool.

-Know repair.

-Yes, but you do Ernesto will be happy.

-Know him.

-If we study tighter mechanical and criminology, the same year than Hewett.

-The three were together.

-If you did not know.

-I do not ask much.

-I see.

I wonder how many careers have indeed Hewett.

-Johnny few careers you?

-I just those two.

-And your brothers.

-Have the same plus a.

-And it is.

-Botanical.

-Study plants.

-So is a mystery many of them, and they are fascinated, you must be interested since studying medicine and part of it is composed of plants.

-Is true but not a lot about plants, just that I like roses and flowers, but I'm allergic.

Turned to laugh and cut a small white flower of the grass.

-Is for you to take care of her well.

-Clear thank you, the conservers in my favorite book.

Laughed again, we put four jet skis damaged the truck, I help him, I was no poor fund, others looked at us without believe it, but I did not care.

-Are you ready?

-For.

-To operate the truck.

-I do not want more ridicule.

-Probably not.

-Of course not.

-Well, I will do it, come on.

Turned up with although he was not far from the parking lot, this time put more attention to it than to the noticed.

-You'll do well with practice.

-You think.

-Cleary, if I promise to teach you.

-Well, I'll take it into consideration, only where we will get a truck.

-Is easy I'll take care of that.

-Clearly, if everything is easier with you.

-I think so.

-I hope so.

We left the truck and walked a while, he told me about it and some things he likes to do.

-I feel kind of weird that guys can't use the jet skis.

-Feel guilt.

-Something like.

-Well is their fault because they did not listen and we occupy the other, and Hewett's no very happy, because it thinks its Jenny's boyfriend broke down purpose.

-And what do you think.

-Professional opinion, I think I like him.

-Then it is true. Gestured

Went with his brothers, his smile was strangely similar, smiling all three equally.

-Miguel, as fish go.

-He is very bad, not wearing one but I already I have three.

-Only three.

-Friend is difficult, it takes patience.

-And that is what you have.

-Some I have not.

-And by that fishing?

-Being patience clear.

-I can try also need to work on it.

-If of course.

I got a fishing rod purple color, as if they knew that I would appear his brothers were nice.

-Have here as fishing.

-Two hours. Said Tony

-Only two and three fish. All laugh

-Can overcome it.

-Could.

-Without cheating.

Snuggles, was a bench where we could be four, rather broad, a little weird but I was very comfortable likewise had cinnamon cushions.

-Plan to be much sitting right here.

-So is. Said Miguel

Had a good time, enjoying the sun the four, and had spent the last five minutes watching the water without moving.

-Girl wake is moving.

-Not true only water.

-Notes not unlike that been as much time watching the water, Got up quickly.

-And I do.

-Return it slowly so slowly that.

-Slowly escaped.

Looked like it had intentions to take my fishing pole and do it, but they let me do it, and I was excited by the fish chose my fishing rod and not theirs, we were laughing and finally came out, the fish was bigger than theirs, I was happy about that.

-I'm better than you found it encompasses all three of you.

-No, you cheated.

-Of course not.

-Lie.

-Tony told me liar.

-Clear… not.

Place it in a tray large, we thought filling, Alan joined us and we caught a lot more than you expected, the laughter and looks happy, continued but eventually returned them to the lake, as it only we remove stress, and take good care of them until we gave them worms, we overran and of course I think I was lucky win.

-Beginner's luck. I told them

-Clearly, if friend. Tony said

-And you won.

-Alan did not bet anything.

-That bad.

-Why.

-That nobody had ever won.

-It's true you're the first, we're pretty good. Tony

-But not today.

-Are lucky. Miguel said

-If so it seems, want something to drink.

-Clear and something to eat.

-Well, we should not let go of food.

-Too late.

We met with the others at sunset, the sun is shining reddish huge as usual, but we had peace and we were still together.

-Hi Andrew, you do, this very lonely.

-Just thinking.

-I can accompany you.

-Clear.

-And well if you think I know.

The sigh was little astonished at my question.

-Well, just think of my brother I miss him

-So sorry it is terrible.

Is terrible and if I thought of Rosalba's proposal, in joining her, I know my brother fight until the last moment no to, and I was not as strong for thinking even for a moment... you know he enjoyed the sunset, the warm days was sat like this to talk and laugh at ourselves, and it is gone.

I felt a lump in my throat stronger than before, I could not say a word of comfort, and stronger than the he was, his sorrow finished inside.

-Not your fault and humans make mistakes but we are still good, only we were wrong.

-Your brother is right.

-In that?

-Have always believed that we all have more goodness than evil, and if you're wrong.

-I'm right with you, despite the pain that you have in your heart you always do the right thing no matter how hard it is and that is very brave.

Our sighed the two.

-Are great so it's so nice to be close to you, doing not blame Hewett for that.

-Not detach from me.

-Clear, and in truth I'm better.

-Maybe you just need to talk.

-I talked to everyone and never felt better.

-Good I'm special and I say you have to be happy and smile.

-Yes of course it is. And began to laugh

-See I have reason.

-Despite everything you've been right all though we bother to speak.

-Annoy, bother them say I've done well and prefer to think that I'm wrong.

-If, it's always the other way, are you the one that always saves us, supposedly we will have to protect, prevent Cirrus get caught or his demons, but it is always backwards and wonder how you do it.

-I wonder the same thing; you know who he is Cirrus.

-No, I wish I knew. Only sigh as always.

-Tanks Sarah.

-Were only a few words.

-Not only that, I thanks as it should when you went by the three.

-All bothered, but I had to go.

-If and thanks.

-Only thanks I deserve more than just thanks.

-Yes, but could be.

-A big smile.

-Clear that if.

-You are very honest and not afraid to say what you feel I admire.

-Admire that.

-By honest people I know are not so.

-Are good friends.

-Clear that if, very good friends.

-Life is rare, something we all thought you were arrogant, impulsive, a girl capricious and conceited.

-And you think now.

-If you're conceited.

No hold the desire to laugh.

You're still cute and whimsical, but we know you're great, and only want to help; your intention is good more than many that I know.

-Clear.

-Just say you're great.

-Are cool.

-Continue to pray for a few long minutes, Alan came and sat next to me.

-Good job.

Said in my ear, as he devoted a smile and his breath caressing my neck, making me swallow so good it felt to be close to the.

-I see you have fun.

-If your girlfriend is divine.

-Of course it is.

Saying that and giving me a kiss on the cheek, Hewett joined us and jokes were immediate, not where he got so many, it was always a different one.

-You should have comedian.

-Have said the same thing but does not like the fame. Laugh all enjoying the last rays of sun.

-Think we get out of that.

-We all hope so. Andrew replied

-We do about it.

-Keep looking for them and stop them.

-And if we can.

-Clear that if.

-Good because we destroyed three demons, we can with some humans.

-I worry; I will not kill anyone again.

-Again.

-If you forgot to send to the shadows to Hokon, and all that is normal for you.

-No, not like us, but are they or us, and cared not kill us.

-Girl true, not just for us, if not all, remember that if get to heaven do not think their plans with the earth are good, everything we know will end.

-I understand but still am difficult.

Others heard our last conversation as they approached us more.

-Be with you. Tony said

We got everyone to observe at the view silently, only a few laughs of Marcos, Samara I do a wide smile and then direct his gaze to Andrew, I take my beloved hand and the pressed it slightly.

The water remains calm as most people had returned to their jobs; the jet skis were all unoccupied and had no intentions of using them, and the helicopter stay in the shore and us watching and enjoying the beauty of life before the end.

Did not want to think of an ending or a farewell, and we were not ready for that, but this time was unique, all gathered there silently embraced or holding hands, saying goodbye to the look, just pass saliva and not a word came out, and I guess none of us.

-Everything will be fine as long as we're together, we're family.

-Hewett clears that if we are family!

Jonny replied calm voice and their eyes on the water, and all support him with our eyes, I had more than a few companions in battle, more than just friends, no, we were more than that, we all brothers family.

The Return Home

Take long to collect all of the cabins, Curran took the helicopter to the monastery, one of the CIA came to pick up the truck with the jet ski, Jenny and her friends would be left one more week said goodbye to them and each one we went on our cars, now looked more extravagant since we all went together in a row, Alan had a new passenger, Marcos sin that had made very good friends.

Getting off the volcano all cars went together but on reaching the highway was difficult, they like the speed and as always competed, did not lose the opportunity, I wanted to see who came first to the monastery, but they were not the only ones who are amused we all included, even father of Marcos, Curran was watching us from the helicopter, not resisted to have a view of competition, we use the same equipment in the ears, so Curran warned us about the traffic or if we would find some police descended the speed.

-This time if I shall gain them all.

-As if it were possible. Tony said

-Remember it's true, the last time we play were the last Hewett.

-But they cheated Tony does not count.

-Rather you can't drive.

-And who won. Marcos wonder's daddy

-William.

-The teacher will win, well we won them all.

-His car was fast.

A voice suddenly intervened in communications, if only I had listened to a few times I recognized.

-You guys think you're doing.
-I think you know my friend. Johnny answered
-Will cause a disaster.
-I do not, everything is under control.
-Alan does not be childish.
-Perhaps because you forgot how were you doing the same?
-No, but is past.
-Better say that you are envious.
-Of course not.
-Well, let us only this once.
-Until Mr. Hecher is involved in this, shame that goes in last place.
-Apology, drive a minivan, is difficult.
-And I believe that if, well end his career.
-Ernesto you should be with us misses you.
-To win again you Johnny.
-That was long ago, be different.
-Not upload their video to internet.
-Video.
-Sure miss as you think I know.
-Satellite.
-Curran it is sending to my computer.
-Great we make copies. Hewett said
-I do not want another disaster like the one that caused the last time Sarah.
-I.
-If you when you end up with Alan hammer.
-Knows to end the cars sir, I promise nothing happened.
-Everyone knows Sarah.
-Caro. Ernesto answered her
-Okay, do not make the arrest the police, no will help you this time, I will leave you to punished.
-Clearly not a friend. The interference end
-Know we would leave right Alan.
-Have fun watching us.
-As is Marcos.

-More than happy.

Finally conclude the race, the first to reach the exit of the car track won, and he won as in other things was Alan was obvious, them Jonny and the last was daddy Marcos.

We reached the mountain of angel clipper noise could heard in most of the house, children playing with water of sprinklers all enjoying the summer, children running with great frenzy in the park, completely ignoring past events.

I think that would be best, the world is not prepared to deal with the destruction, at a magnitude of disbelief, closed to the unknown, to which we have to face, fear of reality, we disconcerting the thought of the unknown.

We split each one head to go home, Alan took Marcos with his parents and then return with us, Monica and I prepare a delicious dinner, she had improved a lot in the kitchen, and the best thing was that she did not have nausea by pregnancy was great, it looked perfect, was his gaze that changed, a penetrating look happy fill of life.

-You think to fix quarter over the house.

-For.

-Good because you will have a wife and bay, will need at last one quarter.

-We can arrange that occupied Monica.

-No far from yours.

-She's right buddy.

-And you propose.

-Well home remodeling.

-If required.

Monica had to go get an ultrasound next Thursday, but we accompany all let us in, only my brother and she entered, but anything would warn us, wait for more than an hour and finally came.

-How are you? Ask all at once

-I'm well more than good.

The doctor went along with them.

-Are lucky to have so many friends.

-If I have luck.

We all sat down but she insisted on going outside that she had to take a breath and went.

-Well to show us the ultrasound.

-Yes but first I have to tell them that...

-You're fine, we distress that.

-Here is a picture for each, but not see them wait.

-Ok.

-Well two.

-Two photos, I have only one. She laughed

-Hewett no two babies.

We were surprised and said nothing did not we thought.

-Not true, as two. Returned to say Hewett

-If you look at them are two, have two kids, well baby.

All the while we embrace but we had to take turns, the boys were euphoric, were happy.

Also congratulate my brother was happy.

-Congratulations brother, I'll have two nephews that well.

-I'm terrified Sarah.

-Is normal, well be both.

-And if I can't with all this, the babies and the end of the world.

-Not the end of the world.

-You know what I mean, I have fear that something happens to me and let alone with two babies.

-Nothing will happen, we all with you to care for them.

-Tanks you sister but I'm terrified.

-Well do not show it, smile. Hug him again.

Because Monica did not know what would have, we wait to paint the bedroom, my brother was happy and very well we passed by buying things for babies, but did not know they were most white checked it, Alan studied architecture and help us remodel the house to welcome the new baby, one built another room next to theirs with your bedroom entrance to the baby, term ends July and almost August, late September and will know that my nephews.

The day was hot as usual in August, but that day in particular we were at 105 degrees, the sun was hallucinating at that level people, but it was a perfect setting to test our endurance.

In September go back to school and was very close, and yet we had not news of the witch.

Finish our training and take water as desperate, thirst was tremendous and I was out of breath, it was the worst of all training, preferred to snow the sun burning my back at the time, but remember that when you want to heat cold and hot weather we want something cold, is to it ironic, we are never satisfied.

As the last days Monica just watched and amused us, then they left, I turned alone around by the monastery, because I love the view, as fabulous as ever, felt to be on top of the world.

-Hi girl enjoys it.

-At every moment.

-I have something to show.

-And if it is.

-Some history.

-History.

-If is that you will love.

-Already think so.

I took my hand as always, had the chapter, and the collection of ancient bells already were doing at the far left of the monastery, next to the was metal ladder which was permitted only to authorized persons, as it was private.

-I have never come down to this place, you feel this good.

-Clear that if more than good, you fascinated.

Pulled out a small wooden box with red padding inside and a key on it, walked down the stairs to the pavement for a couple of minutes, direct to a home that had never entered, is take out the key and opened the door that he had only small window, opened and he heard a squeak, everything was dark, the light lit on the walls were several paintings unknown.

-Alan secret museum.

-If a museum treasures are stored.

-Treasures.

-If some would say strange relics or a collection…

-For me are treasures of the year 988.

-Long.

-Yes, I'll give you a private tour, very few have entered.

-Already think so.

He turned off the light when passing the corridor, and it another in the next room.

A picture of the image of the Virgin Mary caught my attention, was made of precious stones, and did not know that stones were.

-Is of the year 1664.

-God is fabulous.

-Is the original box the only one of its kind, each gemstone is original.

On a shelf was a box apparently not longer than the palm of my hand, covered with red silk, grab it and on put in my hands yet to discover it was chunky, very carefully he remove the silk.

My eyes were wide open as spheres, my first release inaccuracies was that scared me, but only gave it a passing after the beholder.

-One hand.

-If not any.

-In really, real hand?

-Clear you be lying.

He had no reason to lie for; the box was made of solid gold weighing so much, and with walls to watch, kept even gold rings and diamond to his fingers something disturbing for my taste.

-You know who is?

-Is a saint,1446.

Place it back in your hands and put it in place, then it was not very big book below pictures of saints, all original years ago, hundreds of years and some more resent or it seemed, care was perfect but he gave that were very old but well preserved.

-Books are as old as the pictures. I said

-There are all… this for example was the first year missal was in Russian Orthodoxy 988

-Russian.

-Clear that if.

The opened it and put it on a special shelf that used to read when officiating a Mass.

-Know Russian.

-A little, but this book is hard to understand, is Old Russian.

He opened book on a chapter that contained the missal of the day today, according to Alan.

-True?

-Yeah right.

-Pity that no Russian Orthodox to confirm. He laughed and hill and take another book.

-This is history.

-That history.

-Russia and this one talks about the crusades.

-Ho.

-Continue.

-Are okay.

-Yeah, well a book is better than a hand.

-There are more.

-No more hands.

-If something.

Was something covered with more silk on a shelf, this time bigger, uncapped it and took a step as the last time, he was behind me and hug me back even when, watch the object.

-I'm serious, you're scaring me.

-Not everything is real, but contains much of the.

-A mommy.

-Not anyone.

-Is another saint.

-Well you better let him rest.

Alan silk retuned to put in place had so many things to do but it was strange.

-Offspring are Russian.

-No, but at this point in the monastery come from many places. Turn off the light and headed to the other side of the room, behind the small pillar boxes were taped to the wall, with glass windows.

-All are real.

-All, each of them belongs to a saint.

-More mummified human bones.

-Yes but we still have one of each saint existing in the world.

-As obtained.

-I'm not sure.

Continue to another room, this one contained the way they dressed that time the Russian people, and some that used in our era.

-Are cute.

He turned off the light and continued to the next room, then looked all at around I thought we finished.

-There below.

-Even more.

-Yes.

Narrow down the stairs made of stone, and the walls were pictures with stories.

-The Russian alphabet.

-Of course.

Continued to see more stuff, this time on stories Orthodox Russians, who did not even know it was that but it was fabulous,

-This is privet but it is real.

-Everything is real in this place…

-Are some real clothes in the corner is the blanket with which they covered the face of Jesus Christ the son of God.

-But not the original true.

He looked at me and smiled, showing me more things followed after that we come back up; he took another key something strange.

-These are replicas of the church of the Crusades and this is the proof of the Vatican Pope signed by him Juan Pablo II which certifies that all we have is real and we can have it.

-I have a legal and church Vatican knows.

-Course we're friends.

-Of course.

-Ones I have, the more bones.

-Not only stories.

-Well tell me you favorite.

-I'll tell you a short story, she is Sister Maria de Jesus de Agreda.

-A long name.

-Danica like yours.

-Certain.

-She is of Agreda.

-I get it.

-1627-1656, she wrote about the Mother of God, I call his work, "Mystical city of God" published in 1970, and also hag gifts specials.

-Understand.

-This is my favorite story.

-His smile was promising, going to another box that was on the wall.

-She is Santa Maria.

-Many Marias. It interrupted

As a young man fell in love, but then his religion was persecuted, and had to leave his beloved to be safe, time passed and was still waiting to see their loved, only knew each other for newsletters but days passed before they arrived, but rather months, the time step, she wait him day and night, his love will never end for both, so the wait was greater than the distance that time, but there are tragedies, he died before he could see again, clear that the pain was terrible, it was still young, became a nun and recalled his love for the rest of his life, imagining that someday they would see, that he stays away but close to it.

-How sad never to be seen again.

-If very sad, but his love was so pure, if they were marred but never lived together, and she was always a virgin.

-Even more amazing.

Left the private museum and took another turn for the monastery, and then we left the restaurant, he was my brother and the rest, lived beyond as usual, Miguel talked with Pilar, and Andrew with Hewett.

Even in the evenings we served food to homeless people, and Mr. Robles was with us on occasion, and he knew of our extracurricular tasks, he also pointed.

Alan I'm sacred to pass no news.

-Is true all is calm.

-Ernesto has something new.

-No nothing.

-We will ready.

-Clear that if.

Already in the house started to make a cheesecake because Monica had craving for it, and I was tired when standing more, my brother helped me.

-How you feel friend.

-Well, but I'm worried like everyone.

-Will take care of you know?

-I'm upset than I can't help.

-If I also am.

Made her laugh and hit me with his elbow in my rib, and if hurt me.

-Good it true a lot you help us and you know but you better not, I want you watch these babies.

-Clear that care.

-And not think about it, you need to be clam.

-If.

-What do you think you'll have?

-I do not know, whatever will be fine, but they are healthy.

-Clear but know the guys and bet, some that will be girls and others boys.

-You gambled.

-Of course not.

-But Hewett and your spouse if.

-If bet if lost Hewett will give your car and if he wins you'll put your name on one of the children.

-Friend will be terrible.

-I hope they are girls, seeing it well.

-And if it is the case already thought of a name.

-I like Kimberly and Evelyn.

-I like cute names like.

-And if not, well apparently one that Hewett will remedy and the other being Edwin.

-That cute.

-I like them all but we have to wait a few weeks more.

-If that anguish, I think we all more nervous that you Monica.

-If it appears and you will not know that, and the chamber to a not ready I thought about painting it white for now, I hate him so gloomy.

-We help.

-We can't start work tomorrow.

-If clear and dry when we get started to put things.

-Yes.

The good things was that the furniture was of mahogany as the two cots, only maskers were missing it but would not be so difficult, after knowing they were babies.

Cheese dessert was ready and she did not expect much for it to cool, in itself loved and pregnant more, and it was best not worried about their weight, and passed it great, every day looked more beautiful.

Started painting the baby's room, my brother and I but room was not big enough, as Hewett and Alan help arrived, than other moments arrived Andrew, Tony, Johnny and Elmo, and ended too quickly.

-I have an idea as to Monica's likes my brother house why do not we put some gold in their children.

-Would be good but we have no gold paint.

-No problem Andrew and I will by whatever is needed, you put everything together finish, Alan has some changes.

-Well, why not.

-Only one problem.

-Which Hewett.

-Monica.

-Than with her.

-If a surprise should go.

-Adriel why not takes her with her sister and stay there.

-I have to stay with them.

-Whether if it will be a surprise for both.

-Okay, and how long finish.

-Hopefully at sunset.

-Adriel, clear we will notify you. Said Elmo

-Good.

Everyone left we were just Alan and me, because at the end they came up with other.

But it was worse for us because we had to clean, to ensure that we had reached more reinforcements arrived Samara and Kalinda along with Dylan, put music to all that was, Hewett clear idea of this.

-And well they have in mind; she does not want anything extravagant.

-Be something simple, just special.

-Okay.

Put stars on the ceiling a crystal chandelier, the gold was put across the shore, and she wanted white leave it that way, brought something with Ernesto managed to dry the wall and get the smell of paint, settle furniture and Andrew had brought toys and necessities for the little ones, only missing by buying the car seat and strollers for color.

Staying fine, but we wanted it to be better, Monica thought it would be too much, not all children of the world could enjoy family and amenities like this.

Alan made it look elegant with necessities and it was great, she will love it.

Finally finished was not as hard as when we knew they were a little exchange, Hewett finally spoke to my brother Adriel.

-How long arrived.

-I just go him, take abut twenty minutes.

In what we wait we watched the room, Alan took my hand and smiled as usual and he knew that I loved, at the other and Dylan kissed Kalinda and I to the hidden, began to feel somewhat uncomfortable, but not others, it seemed they were accustomed.

I think it was not hard to know; apparently the thrill of Monica for their babies she had been began to think about it, and despite the danger that we could with the newcomers and she might think that despite the situation could be happiness, some little one in his life.

-You might be uncle.

-It seems.

-And think.

-It's a bad idea.

-And you think of having children.

-I'm not ready.

Tighten his hand but made no move whatsoever, clear that I did not think about having children, but if one day, but he had reason was not ready, you hear the sound of the truck at the entrance, and all keep composure, as Adriel knew what he had to do, just take her to see how it had been painting.

She just walked in, the light on crystal chandelier was enough light like a sun, and obscured but not enough, nobody said a word not a surprise, just wait.

-Well, I'm somewhat surprised I thought it would be just white.

-That is all. Hewett said surprised as all

-Course, is what coming thinking; just imagine the white room is everything but this.

Remained silent I think a bit disappointed, my brother neither believed what he heard and said nothing, worse observe a couple of tears on his face and sat in the char and started swinging it like a scolded girl.

-It's just like I wanted, so life with so much light.

-I love great guys. Said my brother

-You did not know love. She asked

He knelt beside her; of course it was not a surprise to them.

-Thanks friends, I would do without you.

Monica stood up and hugged Alan and them my even crying.

-No done. Johnny said

-There is more.

-Course, what happened when day and want to sleep. He gave a small the control in his hand.

-What is this?

-Good press the yellow button.

When squeezed, on the large double window rolled down a curtain as steel, but not heavy so it could handle, white color simulating the wall as if there were no windows.

-One bedroom armored.

I said quietly that only I could hear.

-Sarah light off.

Johnny sent me to me, as it was closer to the light switch, but there was more than one, I knew what the light was, Alan had told me.

The room had to be completely dark but it was so lit up the ceiling and walls, like a terrarium with stars and everything was fabulous, but do not support the idea gave me envy.

-Johnny could sleep with all this and I never will do it either.

-Good can turn off some lights and just let the stars are in the ceiling.

Was great, luckily only the stars when the light was returning was as if none of it existed.

-Is fabulous now I'll sleep with them all the time.

All laughed but she was right, the room was great, and there were many details as they had done all the work and of course not charge anything.

-I too like friend's thanks for being with us.

-For that is the family.

I hugged her again, and then she went to hug the other.

-Thanks Kalinda.

-I had fun.

-And the best of all is that we all gifts and clothing for the pleasure to accommodate to you friend.

-Thanks but you closet is huge missing me more things.

-Clear a lot, but we'll have to wait to know that.

-One clear Hewett this. Said Hewett

-Girl brother will think that you'll see.

-Kalinda clearly not.

-Monica you should have one for each person, we will fight for them. Said Dylan.

-Well I think it is time for you to star my friends. Color change but do not answer.

-If it's time.

All left the room and left alone.

Thanks guys told everyone and they just laughed.

-Can give us some good desserts that you made.

-Clearly, if Johnny.

After that, time step and the continued anguish, strained eyes did not change, the time reflected anxiety as the days passed, his friend Ernesto had not new.

Everything belongs silent as a ghost when we went to the monastery, and do not even ask, is that whatever they would say me.

The End is Near

Ran through the woods back to the monastery, thinking what will be our end, with a melancholy wanting lie to me that everything will be fine, the worse my heart I can't lie, is that we may fail this battle, we may already be in the end.

William received a call that Ernesto had fresh news, and was still running not only for exercise, but to think each person each plant looked around me, and even looked at one another tourist visiting the place, nevertheless had that fight, one reason why we live, it was strange, but which we have opportunity, they are as strong as us and maybe be more, finally arrives with William who was waiting in the doorway, had already finished running.

-William.

-Hello Alan and these better.

-No, still the same, that I have news.

-Well Ernesto found the castle of Cirrus.

-Well you better go before we catch them all.

-Not wise because we know it's a trap.

-Yes but that option we have.

And that had happened while running back but the heart even if I kept pace, about to jump out of my chest.

-You propose.

-Wait.

-And expect too much there to discuss it with the rest.

-Wait a little more.

-Both.

-Just a couple of days, while Ernesto tells us how many are.

-Not will know.

-Not approach.

-Well just a couple of days.

Leave the place but I was immediately to my bother about this, and he agreed with me, afraid it was too risky, and it was very risky and not just my decision it not all.

In that case we would expect, walk slowly did the same like Sarah contemplate everything around me as was saying Marcos, looking around the world, the cold air hit my face but did not felt too strong, I finally got on my car and went to Sarah the restaurant, but I do not found her, had gone to the library, would not go after her, if that wait outside in the park but where I could see.

Step over an hour and she finally came out, walk fast before she left but Jenny with her, then do not come near me, because the girl confused and did not want another headache, wait until they wear off and then she returned to the restaurant, I had left the car in front, she looked at him and asked for me I guess, that came back, this time I was across the street, she saw and walked towards me.

The look, sometimes I can't forget his gaze I dare not do, not what happens I want to get away from her but I can't, sometimes I keep dreaming about her, it's hard to be around her but is more difficult to be away, everything has change lately, she's my reason to continue, she smiled coyly as usual, stop worrying about the future, just enjoy every moment this close, it was so easy to love her so much and so rare that just happened.

-Hello, Are you doing?

-Girl watching you.

-Just that?

-If, came here.

-Clear that if.

The subtly embrace much love, I had not realize that I had never been so afraid of losing her, hey my reason, I just wanted to be near each time.

-Alan everything is fine.

-Yeah right, walk.

-Yes.

Take her by the hand and I love the softness, roads down the street-aimlessly, circling only because what we had done before she did not ask, and do not question where it was since I already know and also I guess she already knew.

-You know I love you girl.

-If it is, just do not say often.

-Yes but do not forget that I love you.

-Never forget it and less now that you repeated twice.

Melancholy felt as if I was attacked from behind without mercy, she was right I do often; his words hurt me, just swallow saliva as a in precious previous occasions, had already dark so we went back, waiting to close the restaurant, she left in his car and I fallowed.

Entered his house, my brother was already there eating nachos his favorites and watching a horror movie.

-Hello brother.

-Hi Hewett, comfortable?

-Course you know this is my home.

-Yeah right.

He was happy that he had invited to live when he wanted to, and had no problems that he accept, and that made him missing a family, and I'm not opposed, but would be in place, despite the things he was happy lived every moment as if it were the last, I sat next to him and gave me their nachos.

-Are delicious.

-Alan wants something more because I do.

He went to the kitchen listening to the bag of chips falling into a bowl that seemingly had no end, the noise term and the layman with a huge bowl of nachos for everyone and lemon sodas, I eat very strange but accompany, like ate Monica, stirring all the food lately, which is not a normal person would eat, but their status was understandable, she clutched her stomach and her husband did the same to her.

-Why like horror movies?

-Look at all but apparently when we get a horror love you join us.
-Serious!
-If you chose Monica today.
-Seriously.
-Hamm.
-Alan something happens.
-No, nothing.

Continue watching TV, then leave Monica and her husband, and was running more than my brother fell asleep on the couch, I plug it with a blanket, he was like a child.

-He's great.
-True.
-As it does, look at this so comfortable that I envy.
-If it happens to me girl.
-You stay to sleep.
-Yes, and you want to go.
-If I think if I wait in my room.
-If well.

Wait to put on his pajamas and then enter, listening to music very low but clearly heard, leaned back and everything trembled within me, but I lay down beside her.

-Girl misses you so much today.
-I always miss you.
-I would like to live with me.
-Like?
-Yeah well not only is it wrong to say.
-You will like to live with me.
-Clear that if.
-Well, stay with me here.
-I can't.
-Well I can't go with you, Monica needs me.
-Yeah sure, just ask if you would like to live with me.
-Clear that if.
-Well I hope someday happen.
-I like.

She leaned back against my chest as usual but this time not slept.

-Know something.

Deep breath did not want to tell the truth yet.

-Girl not yet but do not think that everything will be fine.

-I will trust you always do Alan.

It was becoming more difficult to answer, I straightened and look in to his eyes and she smiled, I slowly stroked her cheek, she sighed and me too.

-And if we had no enough time.

-Girl you're talking about.

-And if all really ended.

-Everything will be fine.

-Worse if not, I can ask you something.

Feared to hear your question I do not want promises.

-It would.

-Could… well I want to be with you I've thought a lot and not today but want you to be, well you understand.

Everything inside me wanted to say that if, each kisses me so passionately gave me to continue, the worse it was not right and neither this time.

-Well, girl promise to make love, love you till the end. She smiled seductively before I finished my comment.

-Promise.

-Clearly if. Sigh girl you test all my senses, I like what you do love me more, I will I promise.

I was saying this while stroking.

-But I will after this is all over, he'll get through this all.

-But.

-Listen, I am one hundred percent sure love you, you have no idea how much it costs me to be near you, I desire to have you is burning me, the warmth of your skin, the taste of you kisses, all provokes me… is very provocative your offer, I will when it's over.

She hugged me tightly and kissed me, which I felt my body was burning even more, like I was inside a volcano was completely in flames, his body was burning, I felt that I cut breathing, his body had me right where she wanted, was causing me know what she was thinking, I wanted to lose myself in your body fill with passion, dying to be with her and I am suffering, but she would not stop kissing me, touching me, was cruel and very passionate, but full of pain I did not want it to be the bye.

I continued motionless until she separated from me, hugged her tightly to my chest and kiss her on the forehead, I knew that was not enough, but she understands.

-If life allows us together.

It was not my intention, but a tear rolled down her cheek, the kiss one again, his kiss was different with anguish and was still crying, hugged her hard again, wrapping her in my arms like a girl, increased pain finally fell silent again but could hear soft sobs for preventing her mourn, clung to me hard like a farewell.

-Sarah I promise a moonlit under the star at the edge of the sea, promise to love you until the last day of my existence, but it promises to wait.

She looked me back.

-Wait that this is not goodbye.

One more kiss on her cheek made her smile again, regrets not is better for her wanted to please but not this way.

-You better sleep, you stay.

-Clearly if unless you ask otherwise.

-Of course I want you to stay.

Be accommodated and slept soundly as usual, when she woke up I was still at his side.

-Not sleep again true.

-I could not sleep.

-You need to rest, you know I will ask the day off and stay here. Not questioned and that was what I wanted, until the last

moment of her, outside her room listen to the voice of Adriel awakening to my brother, the shower was heard guess it was my brother.

-Well, I have to do something for breakfast. Went out and Monica was in the kitchen.

-Monica hello how are you.

-Good Alan and you, you look terrible happened.

-Did not sleep. Sarah replied

-Friend you should learn something from your brother.

-Would be helpful.

-Kidding he has no trouble sleeping.

-Of course not, is a child yet.

-Speak friend Jenny said she had questions about something yesterday, you talk.

-Later, you'll do friend. Sarah asked her friend

-I have not much to do, I have to go a single class and go with Carolina and I think that's all.

-And when you have the next ultrasound.

-Friend on Friday.

-I accompanied them.

-No ever want to go my sister and I will not bother because they fell rejected, and left no help much.

-If you talk to my brother.

-Clear that if and agree.

-Sure it'll be fine.

-Clear what could happen?

-Do not say, give me chills to hear that.

-Do not tell.

They are preparing breakfast, I wanted to help but preferred to just watch them, it was strange how much they waned, it was like sister, my brother went out and the first thing he did was put his hand into the food.

-Delicious girls, never I'll go from here.

Not upset then that I think he always did to not but I gave a look of disagreement.

-We leave it like you company, it is a good friend. Said Monica

I did not say anything just smiled, and my brother made fun of me, not made me laugh, and patted me back Adriel.

-Leave it is in your home and your equal.

-Thank you.

I think I missed my brother, and that he lived with me, and suddenly just come to live with Adriel, though I asked him to look after them, did not imagine this.

-Really miss him.

Monica I wonder as if had read the mind.

-If something.

-Good come live with us, marry with Sarah.

I had no words to answer, and they did not even try out, she walked without saying anything, I notice my reaction surprised, not scare me or anything, but I had thought and less live with them, I felt strange, they got along so well, and my is difficult for me to be like them.

-Alan joins us for breakfast.

I still did not move until Monica came for me.

-I regret the comment; it was not my intention to upset you.

-Think she wants to marry me.

-Kidding, look at her she love you and you to it.

-I had not thought about getting married, only belong to her forever.

-Works if it kills me to say it, you love is too crazy.

-As.

-I love my husband but not as you love yourselves.

-As.

Do not get me wrong I love him too but you is more than love, is a connection that no one ever will break it, a love so pure, are strangers, it's hard to say they are, or as is his love, eat breakfast.

-Of course.

Television was on, had breakfast and it was weird because it always would disappear before breakfast with them, turn off my phone did not want to receive calls, I knew all I had to know, it was not necessary to take it ignited, it was nice to be them, the last time was Christmas, and already has more than half a year that way, school talked, his task, the restaurant but less of past events, for more harder than were, were nevertheless happy.

-Stay at home all day Alan.

-That seems Monica why.

-Just saying.

Finished breakfast and everyone picked the left, the Adriel had classes, I had to go to the restaurant, was still working there, so nice time was over, but they were doing all mornings, as was normal but I enjoyed them and to every moment, it looked in their eyes with joy, this feeling and this time never letting go.

Sarah's phone rang.

-Hello.

Walked away from me to speak and not be able to hear who it was but did not take long to hang up, approached me.

Jenny wanted to know if it was done with the task, but I said no, and not go to school today.

-Do not need you to stay if you want you can go.

-I know is not necessary but I want to stay send it by mail and there will be problem.

-Are you sure?

-Course I'm sure.

Expected to say that really, did not want to go but it was my decision, if he changed his mind had to accept.

-We do.

-As.

-Alan if you do, you want to stay all day at home or want to go that although you do not find sleep, I do not want.

-True.

-Well I prepare you can take your brother's clothes clean and we can go wherever you want.

She went to her room and I course I change; only my brother would charge her clothes, left the house I my car, it was harder to hold her hand and I felt a complete fool by side, and after night I was not sure what would happen then, to some air since September began.

-Already been a year we met, and everything changed, before he had lost a day's work, but instead my brother got married and every happen in a year.

-One year.

Had no mood to celebrate and she wanted nothing of her birthday and we all agreed, not even mentioned it, well I do but without gift was just a kiss and was it.

-One year if you believe.

As if also believe I have always known, just that she was referring to something else, her phone rang, she talk a lot.

-Yeah right.

She put weird face.

-Monica told you true… okay I do not think that bothers…see you Carolina.

She hung up and took a deep breath; hope it's not bad news, since I still did not turn on my phone.

-Carolina wants a favor I hope not bother… just had no choice, wants us to care to Marcos…all day she has something important to do.

-No problems.

-We are on.

-Yeah right.

-I'm sorry but it bothers you go by.

-Of course not, Marcos is great.

-I think the same thing.

-Plans that will change with it.

-I have an idea.

-If it is a good idea.

-Better than leaving it to ignite the house itself.

Went for the child, I do not mind being with him, I reminded myself, until his gestures with his arms crossed and mouth sideways when he was angry, it's fun to see it that way and remember my childhood, arrived and was preparing his backpack with things, it seemed very heavy.

-Hello Alan, hi Sarah.

-You carry in you backpack.

-I'm a spy and carry dangerous things.

Think about dangerous, he is dangerous but apparently there is nothing to stop him.

-And who spy on.

-Not yet but we will be together.

-Clear that if, I took the backpack agrees.

-I can take the hand of you girlfriend.

I bent down to him with a huge smile.

-Have to ask her like a gentleman.

-As I do.

I approached him I murmured in his ear, he approached her.

-Hello lady could take her hand walk to the car. She smiled.

-Clearly if gentleman

Took her hand and walked to the door together with Carolina and I behind her.

-Marcos you behave.

Caro said as she bent and gave him a kiss on the cheek.

-If Mommy.

Sarah opened the door to go up but did not.

-Alan she has to go up fist, I have to open the door and she goes and then I.

-Good this time I can help you. I opened the door to Sarah.

-My lady.

As she stretched her hand and she was still playing, but I liked it, in realities all the time I did, not stretched hand but if you opened the door always.

Marcos then went up not only leave to carry him secure the belt, which cost me more work his special chair for car, close the door and went up.

-Anan are very gentlemanly, we can come to your house to play the spy.

-I have another idea.

-Better than you house.

-Even better.

-That is better than you house.

-Good one spy headquarters.

-If a spy headquarters.

He scream all the way, the good who likes the music that got along and sing some of them, Sarah laughed at me because she enjoy my face when Marcos scream the first time, and I get scared and I deviate one seconds of the road, I thought something had happened but he was excited.

We took him to the monastery as promised I would have her room spy, be let back into the control room; monitors were still turned on even by Ernesto call, which not enough for Marcos made us to play with.

-You promised you Alan.

-Good, you plan Marcos.

-William can spy you and me.

-Only the two.

-Of course while we surprised Sarah distracts.

-Well, I will go to distract the teacher will not be problem.

She left because their toys were not real we gave one of our own and of the course knew use, Andrew joined us.

-Andrew can go forward and we back.

-You sent me as bait.

-Good is a plan.

-I motioned to help us.

-Okay I'm coming.

-Alan you know fight.

-That slightly.

-Good can't catch the bad guys without a fight.

-Alan hi's right you have to fight with the teacher.

Andrew was still laughing could hear everything, and that kept Marcos press the button to talk, I just hop Sarah told William what happened.

-Andrew found them.

-If friend, are near the angel.

According to us were quite silent, well actually I do, but he could not clear that it is a child, finally got near them back, and Andrew the front, appeared first and Marcos ran to them, I had to catch up could not wait.

-Gentlemen are in serious trouble, they have to surrender.

Told Marcos while running towards them and showered a toy detective plate.

-Alan help me partner.

-If you do what he says?

-Resisting arrest, well my friend will give them a beating.

-I want you to try.

William approached Marcos and look in his eyes intentions to catch, as it was a game that did not hurt him, but if I go not take chances to attack it, and knew I would do it smiled, but not away from the child away and uploads it was harder that way, it passes from one side to another, so you will not come any blow.

Test was a strange thing, he took it very seriously, whether they just pass Sarah and she took but little thought that he would fall.

-Andrew same me she is bad catch it.

I got distracted a second to look at him, and Andrew tries to take it off and fought, but also was difficult for her, take it off and put it behind his back, was a good move, she did not want to shovel if William took the child and gave it to me, and she fought with me and it was fun, and not much for the child stopped, Andrew and William were still fighting at the request of Marcos, the fluttering leaves in the air, it was a game, take Sarah's arm and place it next to me and she kissed me.

-Yak, disgusting. She smiled

-That passing friend, she is cute even if it the enemy. Hear her cry, William it had taken off my back.

-Win, and I have the boy. William said

-It is not cheating Sarah distracted.

-Good in war all is fair.

-Ok as, William me down.

-Clear buddy.

He approached Sarah and gave her a kiss on the cheek.

-And that for that Marcos.

-Well, by Alan only.

All laughed and she returned the kiss to the little one.

-Alan.

-Yes.

-I said you had a dog, where is.

-This at my sister.

-We can go see him.

-Well do not know.

-Please.

-If not I know it. Sarah said

-Well we can talk to Kalinda brings me to my house and we can play with.

-Yes.

I talk to my sister and we went to my house she was when we arrived, just when I stopped the little one shot out the car and Sarah scared behind him.

-Like Marcos.

-Clear is fabulous.

-Fabulous, is bigger than you Marcos, does not scare you.

-Sarah of course not, does be a girl.

I could not hold my laughter in your comment, the little one petting the dog while it was still holding Kalinda because he was still young less than a year old, was not ready in its entirety but an excellent dog, we have brought much but still had to be careful with it, everyone loved.

-Its color is very nice I like it. Said Sarah

My dog was a Rottweiler colored brick, was very big for his age and his weight was fine, we know that they are dangerous and if someone neglects it shatter, so do not take it out, was very dangerous, and just as it was for us we able to control.

-What is the mane of your pet?

-Lucky.

-I take the name you give it to me Alan.

-Do not think your mother would seem like a good idea.

-I might faint. Said Sarah

-Is very nice.

-Thanks.

-I see that Dylan likes.

-If you feel it is of him.

-Good, cares it's almost him.

-I guess so.

Spend another while watching the dog, play around with it, and was very playful in my opinion was a good dog.

-Time to go, get you home buddy.

-I can stay with you Alan.

-I think you cannot, your mom needs you must take care.

-But promise me play another day, we have to beat William.

-Cleary I promise.

-Well ok, come on.

-Kalinda goodbye.

-Goodbye Marcos.

Took the child to the home of Carolina, along the way he fell asleep already running and if we had brought that likes to run, but got tired and it was late, it off the car in the arms and take up his bed and we did not want to wake, Sarah under his things and put the radios we use to play with as a gift from me, when he woke up and wanted to talk to me he could do it, of course was very small cell to carry would give his mother a heart attack if I gift one.

-Thanks for caring guys thank you.

-No problems really enjoyed us.

-Gave no problems.

-Clearly not very obedient.

-Well just listens to you friend. Said his father

-Well I think that he loves to play.

-No, I think you aware at all, so you hear more than me.

-Not my intention.

-Of course not, I'm glad you are a friend, parents are to call them the attention and clear that you tolerate it and no problem with that, by the way you gave the volcano already premiere.

-And well liked.

-Clear just had to share another lamp in his room.

-I feel it may be more aware due.

-Do not apologize thus, and of course it was a perfect gift keeps him busy, when we are, and it's better than playing electrics, remember their birthday it was worse after up to hide the tool point.

-Understand.

-Do not stay to diner with us.

-I think another day.

-Another day will be good friend and thinks again.

We said goodbye to them and take Sarah to her house, I was just Hewett and Monica as Adriel would have to keep working, we wait to arrived for dinner as I had told him what I had done, he just said it was more fun than his, and I had to do the task and Sarah, got to do it, Monica had already finished his, when arrive Adriel had dinner, then I turned on my phone, and my heart sped up the thought that tomorrow we will tell them what happened, decide among all to do.

-You stay with me tonight.

I signed not know if it would be a good idea.

-I promise to be good I promise.

-Okay I'll stay.

-Too well.

Clean the entire kitchen, after cleaning and watch TV, because they did not complete the task, and we were helping Adriel, I did not help, because after the first time they asked me, I refused and no longer asked again, between them they helped but not all study the same thing, had some classes together, finally ended and they went away, this time was my brother and he was tired very rare in, they were the first to go, but I understand then we and they well guess too.

-Was trap, Marcos is right.

-What you mean.

-The kiss that is.

-Was not cheating it was just momentum is everything.

-Just that.

-Clear I do not resist kissing you.

-Yes but was trap and as Marcos said I want a rematch.

-You sound like your brother, when he loses with you.

-I think if.

Agreed to play with Marcos without cheating, after that I was tired, so I guess I fell asleep.

-How was your day love?

-Very well and Adriel yours.

-I'm exhausted.

-Good we rest.

-Clear that if Moni.

-Miss me.

-Know love is a century one day without your, of course I messed you, do not look at all day, and every minute I thought of you and in the babies.

-Clear that if it is, I am indispensable to you.

-So you think.

I hugged and kissed as usual, if I messed I find it eternal being away from her but at the end of the day is a reward because the force of love makes me capable in anything, even expected, for which she will be her my beautiful angel.

Life is a crossroads and a maze full of mystery and false starts, hard to escape it, just as it is difficult to escape the fate.

A light fell from the sky as if the same sun, looked bloody my hands, it was the end of my heart, the lady who had so persecuted showed his face at last, secrets are revealed but not what they seem, there are more keys…

Walked near the light to the girl…finally ended the anguish she was saying, the blood will be shed as sacrifice, the truth will be revealed and my waiting rewarded, no more pain, no more mysteries, it was time to choose the path, the moment of truth.

That detective that never was lost a single case aware that it would be the first on your list, but I would give up because my knowledge was greater than before, then understanding the blood along with the mystery box now knew its contents, a key that would have the door to God, only opens with a heart, in spite of all keys you need a heart and the mysterious lady had found the end.

The maze was still being endless maze, and we can't win this time, light as the sun itself would disappear into it in the wrong people and everything would destroy.

-Love awake.

I felt a warm kiss on the cheek was Monica that I woke up; my dream was so real like my fear.

-What time it is.

-Not later than seven o'clock.

She looked at me with a worried look.

-Love anything happens.

Do not know, just that Alan told us all we had to go to the monastery this morning had something to say.

-Advance you something.

-Nothing.

-My sister and Hewett where they are.

-Already left, only we miss us.

We prepared and went to the monastery, but was still the anguish of my dream, and I dreamed that when something bad is about to happen.

-Adriel something happens.

-No honey, just think about the urge to go to the monastery, and not beyond that in the house, that worries me.

-If I think the same.

I took my hand, just a few minutes later we were already in the monastery, the fluttering leaves and the chill of the morning was strong, this time we use the elevator because Monica did not went to tire more, had almost five months and her stomach had grown this mouth but as they were two I think was normal.

-Are okay sweetie.

-Clearly, if.

Did not want her to get involved in that but had to know, but I was terrified at the idea of leaving her alone, walked to where the monitors were, they were all assemble, including some who before had accompanied us, had to be something serious for such reunion.

-Hello.

-Hi.

Salute to all, Alan was with teacher William, and Sarah approached us worried like everyone.

-Passing sister.

-I'm not sure those were expecting, but I do not think that is a good thing.

-It so it seems.

-How you feel today Monica.

-Good friend hungry.

-Did not eat anything.

-Not give me time.

-I will go to the cafeteria to get you something.

-Can you bring me a cupcake?

She yelled when my sister was leaving all looked, my sister followed and not long in returning.

-Need to watch more friend, you have to eat.

-If I do and you know just today thanks friend.

-Eat.

My sister brought a chair, if were friends and her pregnancy were more together than ever, that I liked a lot, helped me take care of where I was not around, and if she did not Carolina.

-Are better friend.

-Clearly, if these babies really like chocolate.

-Like the mother.

-True that it.

The wait was terrible not they expected we all sat anxiously.

-This is about Cirrus know where is.

We all started in silence for your comment so direct, I shuddered and I knew what it meant, and see my sister and looked just as distraught as everyone else.

-And they plan to do. Miguel wonder

-We must stop them before it's too late. Andrew replied

-So I think expecting Alan.

-The approval of all of us.

-I think we all support you Alan. Tony said

-And well they have planed. Elmo wonder

-Go this weekend for them, since no accurate but Ernesto nears know how we face.

-Ernesto it will help us. Samara wonder

-Clear that if also concerns the same.

-Alan, Are you sure it's the best? Ask my sister

-We have no choice or wait they catch us.

-Know how many are. Johnny this time

-About two hundred but we know it may be more.

-Then too and you know it and some are just as they as strong as us. Said Dylan

-Proposed.

I wonder why consult us all if only they always order and that's it, but if something happens.

-We have not choice anyway because we will face it either today or tomorrow. Said the teacher

-Know well that we can't lie, we risk too much to go there, it could be a trap rather it is, we should know that anything can happen.

-While I agree brother.

-Thanks Hewett, someone else.

All agreed, except my sister and Monica who wanted to go, we would not allow Kalinda and Samara would be left with them, nor they welcome the idea.

-Male chauvinist. Monica said quietly but listens

-Monica is not that but look at you risking your children.

-Teacher course not sorry.

The reason he had never would leave to participle in this final battle, we did not know really what we faced, also would be useless as if was, we would have to take care of her and would be a hindrance, luckily she cannot know what I think, as my sister, or I sleep on the couch this day.

We were not working we were all in the monastery, and we would have to train harder than before, as the days go fast, but not wanted, and had to talk to Alan, we had a break and went with Monica.

-You mast cancel your appointment on Thursday I do not think its wise.

-I want to go will be fine also go with my sister and you know that this felt for not include much.

-Yeah but I still think it is not a good idea.

-Everything will be fine.

Continue practicing after the break.

-Must put attention because it will be difficult, the temptation will be very strong.

-Teacher temptation.

Elroy ask one present I our decision, we will clear this time.

-Look if they manage to open heaven will be asked to accompany them, since you're powerful and you will want to join.

-Try that does not happen. Said him

-Well guys is all for now, have to eat and we'll see you again tomorrow.

All did out greeting of respect and we separated, my sister was with Monica like Alan, arrived as they were closer than me.

-We leave Adriel.

-You feel bad Monica.

-No, just ask.

-In a bit more, we can talk please Alan.

-Clear and girls back.

We separated from them.

-Adriel passing.

-Is about a dream I had and it and had even before I met you.

-Concerned.

-The future.

I told him my dream from start to finish.

-Are sure it was her.

-Completely.

-Know how many keys are there.

-Appear to be five but I'm not sure as it was a dream.

-Your sister knows.

-Only the first dreams but no sense today.

-Know which the keys are.

-Just that it's the blue star and heart, but she has them all.

-We have a problem.

-I think so yes.

-I'll have to talk to the teacher can go home with Monica anything I notice.

-See you later Alan.

Walk quickly after that Adriel and his wife left, accompanied me Sarah.

-Alan thought that you had already gone.

-New news William.

-Happened.

-I toll the same as Adriel had talked about their dreams.

-We must wait a little, you know about Gregory.

-Still nothing, I fear that I may discover.

-I hope to God not.

Take Sarah's hand and said goodbye to the teacher William.

-That true.

-If that fear your brother is not wrong.

-As you know.

-Just know.

-And passing the keys.

-Wait a bit, however and everything is planed, anything well be ready.

-The girl of the dreams of my brother really is Rosalba.

-If that fear.

-That rare.

At that moment I felt something strange but maybe it was nothing.

-You stay with us.

-I think this time I would like you to stay in my house, and I have things to do.

-But I need things I have to work tomorrow.

-I take for them and then went back.

-Okay.

Arrived for his stuff

-Alan and what happened with I said.

Monica was something serious I guess you already knew.

-Will follow all the same, we will be alert and when the time I will let you know.

Sarah hurried with their things.

-Not remain here friends.

-I have things to do, I need to find out more about the keys and information is at my house, but Hewett will be with you and any developments warn us.

-Of course see you tomorrow.

We left the house but they and Sarah had the sad look to if I assumed there to be wanted to go with me, got to my house I headed to my books take place in a few the black briefcase large enough, the wheels helped by the weight.

-Happens you're traveling.

-No, go back to you house, I think that I have enough to read and my brother can help me.

-Return you sure?

-Know you're not comfortable leaving them alone and to be honest I'm not either.

-I fell better if we return.

-I thought that.

Around more since it would be necessary to open the door all was quiet, there was no sign of them, and Sarah talk frightened, and they went out of their rooms quickly.

-Sarah is all right. Adriel wonder

-If you are fine.

-Clear what happens?

-I just do not see them and thought that something had happened.

-We are good and returning sister.

She sighed and said nothing, whether I answer.

-We will be better all together and brought some books to search. Hewett opened the briefcase and pulled out the first book as it was in Latin, and knew would be of much help.

-There is something we can read us for help. Monica said

-Clearly there are some that you can check.

Carefully place all because some were very old, we set out to read, as if was not a long, the first books contained no more than what we already knew.

-Are sure you'll find something in these old books.

-If they are old Moni and contain our past are invaluable.

-She did not respond, soon fell asleep was tired.

-I do not think stamina to read a book more, as my head is killing me. Adriel comment

-You can go to rest.

He took his wife, but we still, but Sarah does not stand since it fell asleep in the early morning.

-Is a waste of time brother found nothing!

-Still looking for we can find something.

He fell asleep, my frustration grew with every passing second and could not find a solution, and if there is not, because Rosalba have all the keys, and can open the kingdom of heaven will be possible, God will allow it or if Sarah is right and it is a war between men and she thinks that way, by not allowing us to obtain the help of an angel, because God gave us our powers to change the wickedness of man.

Watched while they slept comfortable in the uncomfortable sofas, and wanted better a bed, sighed deeply, and I lay down next to my brother because he used the couch largest, followed with my reading but this did not take me to anything, it was all becoming me confusing and overwhelming, what would happen with the truth, and it was just a myth that the heaven could open the heart, I do not think a single necklace can opened the heaven, there must be something more, I do not think Sarah powers are thanks to that as we all have and do not need any of that, but I do know perhaps his mother transfer some power to it when she sacrifice that day for us, maybe the blue star has power in it too, since seek Cirrus and get to the point of kidnapped Monica, one chapter that nobody wants to remember.

Forget what matters most and cling to what is not possible.

The day was warm, but very rare dense air, she looked at me with his eyes told me goodbye, I could not stop and she had planned it that way, her husband wanted her power to live forever so, trust you at my best friend, and he replied, only a life and mine is better than hers, but before she can take her off life with a dagger really beautiful, that there was ever seen, she prepared enchantment, to die and was immortal, no, cry the hard but it was too late, she holding hands of their children protecting them, took his life and I could not help, the only thing memory of her it is huge smile before the end of his life, and retuning my life, and asking me to take care of those two lives.

-Awaken both needs to wake up too late.

-That where I am.

-At living room.

Alan and Hewett finally woke up and could not help laughing, and they were very well embraced sleeping, nobody would believe me if I told, reacted quickly and woke up, but not before I take their pair of photographs, just so someone would believe.

-How cut they look.

-That's like Monica. Hewett wonder

-A camera.

-And you do with it?

-Evidence only that my friend.

-Were not able certain.

-No what you mean.

-Monica gives me back that.

-Ever.

-Where is Sarah? Alan asked

-Working.

-What time it is.

-Nearly four p.m. friend.

-Is cerium. Hewett said

-Clear, Sarah asked me not to do it, but its late guys, good come and eat.

-No, I have to go…Monica tanks.

-Alan was not a request already served if you eat, and do not make me angry.

They ate with me and even if I was hungry Alan dissembled, after he was suppose to see Sarah, Hewett stayed with me, do not leave me alone and spend all day eating candy and I accompanied his as it seemed to me similarly.

-You will be worse if you keep eating so many cupcakes.

-Look who's talking!

-Well, I am not going up in weight, but eat a lot.

-Presumed.

He laughed at me since before it was the same and did not raise much weight.

-These will be excited to know that the babes.

-Clear that if, I want to know to keep buying more clothes.

-Shopping fascinated you.

-And who does not.

-I am also excited because one of them takes my name.

-I hope not, you name is terrible.

-How bad is your mommy, right Hewett?

Being referred to the babies and they moved a little, and was startled by that, I was too close to notice it.

-Okay something happened.

In a tone of voice alarmed, I could not help but smile and pursed mouth.

-Moved only normal I think he likes you voice.

-As you know.

-Well according to the studies react to sounds, or perhaps uncomfortable.

-Ok I prefer the first option.

-I like.

My husband finally came and Sarah, but Alan did not come with them, we were greeting and my husband gave me a warm kiss as always, followed Hewett eating and my sister in law and my husband joined him.

-And Alan. Ask them

-Friend at home has more books to read I guess.

I'm glad to read at home, I could not read one more were too, my head ached.

-Back later.

-I do not think we'll see tomorrow in the afternoon.

-As you sure you want to go to the doctor Monica.

-If sure love.

-Well do not change your mind I can do and what if I accompanied them.

-No, you have to go to school and then to work, I'll go with my sister.

-You will not change your mind.

-No.

-I accompanied them you Monica.

-No.

Not change his mind, because I promised my sister that would leave to join me, if only go with Carolina and my nephew, when my appointment came.

Was cold bundle up me very well and went with my sister and then headed to the clinic, was almost empty, only the receptionist who behaved somewhat strange, as annoying.

-I have an appointment.

-Take only a couple of minutes.

She called us as promised, Marcos entered first because it ran, but in a second and not listen, walked and we expect a nurse who had not ever looked, I guess new.

-Follow me.

-Sorry did not look at a child.

-Yeah right, and are in the room.

Caro and I followed slowly and she stepped forward a little in taking my time, but still not listens to Marcos and was too weird as it was very mischievous.

-Continue the room waiting already.

Opened the door first, look at my sister with a look of horror, and looked at that image she had been unable to clear my head back again, she was with my nephew Rosalba gunpoint and my sister had but someone knew.

-Let my family.

-Clear that there is a guarantee for you to join us.

-I will go just let the go.

-Not.

My anguish was terrible already I could not do anything was at risk my sister, my nephew and my children equally, had no choice but knew this cold end badly.

-I have another option.

-No cute.

-They will realize that I do not return.

-That's the idea.

-What you mean.

-I wanted them to come for you and especially Sarah and Alan, they are the other keys I need.

-Let go of the child and my sister.

-Clear that no friend.

-You are no my friend witch.

She just laughed and spent gun to another of his companions, and pulled a dagger from his boot which certainly are cute, approached me, spent his dagger through my stomach and gasped, then she laughed cynically.

-Well go with you.

-I hope to walk.

-Let my son please.

My sister asked her heartbroken but she just scoffed, walked out behind the clinic and were upgraded to the same van that had kidnapped me the first time.

-Sister will be fine I promise.

She just sighed and hugged his son, a couple of tears rolled down her cheek as she kissed him, I could not avoid a few tears also rolled against my will.

My phone rang it was my husband, she took it and looked at it, let keep ringing and then look at me.

-If you speak again say that all is well and falter a bit more. The phone rang again.

-Hello.

-You know that we love.

-Not yet delay a little much patients.

-Want me to go.

-No. Hard voice answered

-Okay.

-They call me I have to go.

-Goodbye. Hung up without say more

-Well, until I convinced my dear.

Carolina took my hand for me to calm down but not work at all.

-Something more you talk to your sister in law Sarah and I'll say if for you want me to go the clinic.

As she said that held the dagger between his lips with a smile of evil end snatched my nephew.

-I will.

-So I thought.

-Hello it's all right. Sarah wonder

-Clearly just want you to come for me.

-Something wrong.

-Of course not, I'm just a little dizzy is all.

-And Carolina.

-Her… this here but wanted you to come.

-Well, I'm with you in fifteen minutes.

-That you'll do.

-Nothing I can not hurt her not yet.

Vision was blurry and I was getting nauseous.

When the phone rang this exited, I knew that my friend would have, I headed to the clinic and his car was parked, I seemed nothing out of the ordinary, park mine at the other end and I get off, were a couple of people in the surroundings, walked to the clinic but something told me to go Monica first car, check it out the window and everything seemed strange but normal, in a second I felt something on my back not painful.

-Do not move just listen.

One of the guys put his phone in my ear.

-Sarah helps us.

-Marcos goes where are you?

After that change voice discreetly.

-If you want them back, goes with the boys in his car without scandal.

The call came down, they drooped the phone, have them all and they said, obeyed his order and went with them even blindfolded me, they had no intention of hiding, did not speak at any time, and of course do not ask and did not care, I just wanted to get to my destination and was all.

Traveled for more than two hours we entered the forest by a paved road, outrigger leaves the road and were still tumbling more, watching the woods pass another long time…the front of the black truck was covered in leaves and, in the distance over the tops of the trees looked some stone buildings, as we approached was more remarkable, a castle too old I'd say.

At the entrance two people one of them was the witch knew perfectly Rosalba, the following figure not recognized, the car went into the place, and stopped, opened the door I had no intentions of fighting them so no excuses down, were placed each of my side by guarding or rather if to escape.

Had no intention of that and I wanted to see my friends, we walked, the place was cold and wet as what Monica had described in his terrifying kidnapping, we walked opened a couple of doors creaking, apparently was a dining room or was that way, and would weigh it was a dance hall of the mansion like Alan, but this had terrible curtains, light did not come much longer everything was closed and the lights off.

-Welcome girl.

Listen to someone's voice but his silhouette old man showed something else, was younger than his voice was even and Rosalba side, just wanted to hold her in my hands and beat him up and it would not be able to kill despite everything.

-Get closer more.

-That's what they want.

-I just need your help dear.

Man said hoarsely something and some difficulty speaking.

-Where are my friends?

-Are well, in one of the rooms.

Did not reflect light like her and us, remained hiding in the shadows.

-That's what you really want.

-Clear some of your blood.

Wise and even ask for the wanted.

-Know what you do.

-Clear that if.

-That.

-Well I want to live forever.

-And take possession of the world.

-The smiled very little since it was hard.

-Not only the world if not the entire universe girl want.

-Not think you're capable of running the universe. He angry replied.

-Clearly, if established that you and I can.

-At cost of so much pain.

-Clear I want power and do not mind the pain when I'm gone and suffered too.

-Well that's life is suffering and learning.

-Not have to be that way, you can come with us.

-Never would.

-You have nothing here.

-I have a pretty happy life.

-So… next to you beloved Alan that just follows you because you have resemblance to his beloved Lucy.

-That's not true.

-If you say so.

-Not only what I have him.

-So your brother abandonment you marry your friend.

-You're wrong even more.

-So you tell yourself.

-Think what you want, it's your problem not mine.

-Well, we will have your blood anyway because you gave voluntarily.

-You're wrong again.

-We'll see, of course I will ask to see your friends.

-If you want my help to just take me with them.

-Smart girl, I see that Alan compare you to her, are really the same, believe or not.

-Who are you that you know both their lives?

-I'm an old friend.

-I see if I believe about old.

He enraged at the word old, Rosalba so fast approached and slapped me, not even moved a little and I did not ding any of pain, which the more enraged, and was about to give me one more when the talk will stop her, I smiled and she walked away even more furious.

-Rossi will have you chance.

-Enjoy it, I think witch.

I turned to smile this time she did not listen to my mockery.

-Really believe that will be able to open the heaven.

-Clearly, it we will.

-I do not think you're not a Gad.

-You either know dear but you are close to that to that, a daughter of God and as granted you so much power.

-Then you fear.

-Of course not.

-Then you never get away with it, since God trust me to stop you.

-We'll see.

-Well lose and you know it.

-You're not the only one who visited us know honey, your beloved Alan is invited too and will make to open the portal company.

-He will not help you.

-For you may even die, like last time shame that was late for both.

-Are you talking about?

-Not know that girl.

-But your gonna tell me true.

-Yes, but we'll leave it for later.

-Why wait.

-For most, if not create pain.

-Clearly if, what more could you want.

-My girl eternal life, and do not forget those invited.

-Ever.

-Enough, take her away.

-Alone brother.

Clear that what Rossi are equally cruel brothers.

-Take her with them.

-Of course Cirrus.

-You're wrong you're not the emperor of the sun, if not rather an abomination.

She returned to hit, this time louder, achievement to bleed from the mouth, this time she smiles but did not remain so as it spat the blood on his blouse that looked like new.

-It'll pay.

-Well see if you can.

-Rosalba enough…takes her enough.

Bodyguards led me through the halls to a locked room opened it and threw me in like an old rag and fell to the ground.

-Sarah!

Monica cry immediately recognized it, I got up quickly and looks and with me, shall also was Carolina and Marcos.

-Are good girls?

-It these bleeding friend.

-Happened. Wonder Carolina

-An incident with Rosalba witch.

-It as staying.

-Good… not even touch, but stay angry.

-Pity I can't kick it myself.

-Friend I'll do for you when it comes time.

Marcos was playing with toys wearing the backpack that we care of the day; I guess that did not represent any danger to them.

-I regret what happened is my fault again.

-If it's your fault this not to let you accompany them, but do not worry we'll be fine.

Little blood clean from my mouth in the bathroom, where there was only one small window, try to find a way out but it was obvious that that there was no some, I was spinning in the room like Carolina, Monica was in bed and Marcos with toys noiselessly usual comprehended the situation, chattering the door was the witch with a girl enter her arms, she put her in bed because remained asleep and affectionately sheltered, it was hard to imagine that she felt tenderness for the little girl, I guess was his prisoner for bringing with us.

Hear a noise of some wheels in the hallway, entered a lady with a cart of food, while he witch went without saying a word, the lady came out and the door close behind there, do not even try out for that as far as we would come as Monica pregnant and with two children.

-I can eat something mommy.

Carolina looked at me as she treats the girl I'd like to think not harm to the child.

-If you can eat Marcos.

-We all die Sarah.

-Cleary not a friend and eat all looks delicious.

-If love eat too. Monica said

Monica said as he took a bread basket, and take one every one, the small one is move a little to fit, did not seem to have more than three years.

-Know who is?

-Monica does not know, but I want to know.

Did not eat more than bread he had taken, was desperate was still hanging around the room, getting dark and the little girl awoke up crying, I stayed watching her and approached her Caro comforting but not achieving much, I approached her.

-Hello sweetness you're hungry.

-Slightly.

We gave him to choose the food and ate very well.

-I miss to my daddy.

-Me too. Said Marcos

-As your name little one. Ask Caro

She did not answer Marcos shared some toys with her.

The small dried up and fell asleep, Carolina lay near his son and Monica girl side but I could not sleep was still just hanging around.

The courage that felt at that moment was too, but did not show it, sometimes we suppress our emotions, as we thought so we will more protected, but in reality we are drowning in them by keep them.

Nevertheless was hoping to get out of all this, I watched my friends sleeping, felt a lump in my throat just thinking about the future of my family, since everything was uncertain, was still hanging around, just heard the sound of the very mild voices out there and some hurried steps, but could not see anything, my anxiety grew and I could not do anything, I just waited for the arrival of the guys who would looking for us right now.

You would think my beloved at this time was only one second of carelessness and pass this miss him kisses.

-Friend what time it is.

-Dawn.

-Not sleep.

-I can't.

-Have to get some sleep.

-Will try your still sleeping.

Monica began to mourn I approached bed and sat next to her, hugged her until she fell asleep again, I could not bear the pain already hut to my brother, she felt guilty for all, was a sister to me and even against my life would care if necessary.

Sighed as her crying but was still slept, put my hand on her stomach and her children move apparently were distressed with the mother, I closed my eyes already almost dawn, but I managed not mourn, and I kept thinking who was that girl, round short black hair, light brown skin as if tanned, poor creature she was doing in this place.

Was ready as all day when I hear the phone ringing.

-If.

-Alan is Monica and my sister with you?

-I did not think to would be in the restaurant at this time.

-Monica spoke to Sarah that was to bring, but I've been calling and did not answer and even Carolina not to come home.

-I go to the clinic right away, see you there.

Hang up, take the motorcycle and went out hurriedly, in the way the talk to others and we were to see in the clinic, come too fast, all arrived at the same time, except Adriel already waiting for us, even let me park the bake and approached him.

-And ask no one to see.

-Is silly because their cars are here.

-Speak not check the cars. William said

-Adriel wait do not move.

-But.

-Please! Hewett has extensive experience as Johnny.

He did not move I approached Sarah car and looked normal.

-You fond brother.

-Nothing in Sarah's car… let the Monica.

Johnny said and found on the side of the car of Monica, Sarah's keys.

-Is what I think it is? Asked

-Johnny took them? Hewett said

-If so it seems when Sarah's looking surprised. Johnny replied Adriel approached me.

-Alan happened.

-Fear took them away.

Took the hands on his head and looked at all directions and he could not do otherwise, clenched lips and hit a cry of agony.

-Take along the cars to my house we will be there, and Samara go with Adriel.

-Course cousin.

I can't leave her for a second, he is in trouble, is silly there was to fear so many people, and we were wrong, as usual we arrived all.

-William will do. Samara wonder

-Go get them.

Got get them said Adriel distressed, I just gulped because he had won the phrase, of course I support him would go for them.

-I'll go with you friend. I said

-No wise friend and that we will be waiting.

-Are you talking about William, go for them.

-In that the phone rang, we all sat in silence.

-Is Sarah.

-Hello.

-Hello dear.

Froze on without saying a word, I remove the phone and did not resist at.

-Where you are.

-I think you already knew here I will wait.

-Know we will fight.

-Clearly show us you best love.

-Leave then out of this.

-Never.

-You do not want that you are not this way.

-You do not know me.

-Let them go. Command him

-I not been clearly seen by them, I hope expect tomorrow.

She hung up the phone and scourged with anger, left me paralyzed and swallowing.

-You owe bother Adriel cell.

Had not reacted that it was my phone, but it was late and it was shattered, since he had retuned that had been given, no matter mucho I think I'll give one much better.

-I'm sorry friend then I'll get well.

-I would have done the same.

-We have to go there is no other option.

-Yes, you have to prepare. William said the teacher

-We need to like to Ernesto send us some help.

Mention my brother and he was right, they all went to the monastery, I would reach then.

-Adriel we bring back. Hewett said

-You say to Mr. Hacher.

-Is true I had forgotten.

-I notice you just send someone to care.

-Alan clears that if I take care of that.

Everyone left, I call the father of Marcos was somewhat difficult for everyone, the worst thing was that I could not go to her house, I said gently as possible but like all blight, wanted to go but I suggested that it was the best, to leave us to ourselves, as we did not wanted to risk the same way.

His voice cracking at last accept, I sighed in sadness and not know what to say.

Come into my house and think for a while, walk through the halls that made me too small, and as Rosalba knows we know where they are.

Be Better to Deal with the Past

Walked among the books recalling the times when I was with Sarah, and that's right we wanted to help and never understand her, she's in trouble, it is also our fault, the house was silent, as always but now it was worse, I went to the piano room so I walked, just touch a couple of seconds, I get up and go hands on making noise, I was furious with myself, the sound was heard throughout the house echoed through the silence and how big it was, was still walking and arrives to the private library, remembered Christmas, new year rather, I brought her to this place, that day I asked her to be my girlfriend in the middle of the road, was strange as a second things changes.

-She gave me something.

That silly and been and read so much looking for answers, finding nothing and maybe I have in front of me.

I said out laud as I pulled the box that had my name, I had never opened not want face the past as it was very painful, take the box in my hands took a few turns on the desk as I look at something decentralized, I dared not open.

-That nonsense.

While slowly opened it, inside was just a note, place the box on the desk in the background was a nice ring that I thought was lost.

Smiled and take it, this ring I give it away in the form of friendship to Lucy, she willingly accept without question, she knew it meant something else and yet I accept it.

-Finally opened the sheet. Alan dear:

Like magic really does not come from any medallion, lucky charm or object, but it comes from the heart. Is the strongest weapon and strong and powerful that it is beyond our comprehension, just have to believe in it without much effort they will get.

You will be reading just because I give you my daughter, as was this box which could only opened by photographs necklace with the heart that one day give me was she only will have because you give to her, and unfortunately will be in danger.

Lost heart legend is true, just focusing on the wrong heart, because as I said the magic does not come from objects.

I always knew why the sacrifice to save my children, and my good friend, and that my death was proved necessary before, well, I knew Patrick betray us, had long suspected it, just be safe with my decision, as we pursue at all time, just be safe that way and false leads that I made myself believe, my brother heart was broken to hear, but was strong at all times while at your side.

Never regret what happened that was my destination nonetheless even though was only friends. Awaits a real love at some point, to heal the past and heal the wounds.

Just remember that the real magic comes from the heart, and life comes from God.

Fold the paper, and I knew exactly what she wanted to say, I left in a hurry from the house, heading to the monastery, at last between what he wanted.

Coming to the monastery all geared up, many guys who accompanied us were seminarians who were being trained by William, many of them were too young, they were feeling prepared but I could not say the same for me, walk among them seriously, just looked at me with a look of concern because they did not want to die.

After passing them I found my friends, Adriel was the first to see me, and I approached.

-What the keys are, and it is only one.

-Like you said friend?

-If Johnny I know which is.

-And well spoken. Wonder Adriel

-Is the heart of you sister.

All were silent but looking to Adriel.

-Are you sure?

-If I am.

-Then we hat to avoid.

-Are you sure that is the heart of Sarah's brother, not something else?

-I fear that.

My voice broke with so much like pain.

-Are ready guys, one last training day today, tomorrow and face a battle to the death my friends, as I had mentioned in our previous training we have to be brave to everything that we wait in that place.

-Yes teacher.

Adriel teacher patted his shoulder, those guys go to practice.

-Alan.

-Yes William.

-Did not warn your of this to Ernesto perhaps you can make your.

-Clear friend.

I went straight to the phone inside; I take it and check its privet line as always.

-There are problems friend!

-Alan what kind of problems?

-Have the girls.

-As such a thing happened?

-An oversight.

-What are your plans?

-Go get them.

-Is crazy.

-Is best, we need some of your men.

-The mission guy.

-Do not let it die Sarah.

-I know you love her friend but not our priority.

-Believe me that if Ernesto.

-Continuous kid.

-If she dies well be the end of us all.

-She is the key, right.

-So is a friend.

-I'm so sorry.

-Send help.

-It clear that if, where.

-You know friend and I want in the dawn, I want you around as we arrive.

-Okay, good luck.

-Thank you.

-Not fail you.

-Know.

Communication are short, was the end of the conversation.

-Everything is ready William.

-Well get ready.

Was more than ready but was referring to was ready for the worst, his eyes were of trouble, was growing cold in the afternoon evening, I had a whole night without sleep, checking everything and turning in the monastery, was not the only one awake most hanging around the place, came down I heard a car approaching, it parked, two men are close to me, the recognized right away was Mr. Hacher and William set to watch.

-You doing here.

-I'll go with you obviously want to or not.

-Know is not possible.

-The only way to stop me be dead, and dare you not to kill me.

-Is my family, I need to go with them.

I looked into his eyes filled with pain, but I could not allow it to be.

-Sorry not possible.

-Know I can do it kid.

-I do not doubt you bet will be something more to protect.

-Think I'm a nuisance.

-I did not mean that.

-Then let me go.

-No, his wife would not be very happy.

-And you think I'm.

-Guess not.

-Imagine that.

-Is that not everyone feels the same way.

-But you will go right.

I sighed before answering.

-We just want to protect, since they could use it more for it.

-Friend please let me go, let me protect my family, and if ever I look again, is this is my last chance.

-We'll bring them back.

Some were close by watching our discussion shouts.

-Alan begs you, let me go.

-Alan.

The teacher yelled at me, loudly.

-If teacher.

-Anger with us.

-That.

-If he's right, maybe he has no chance to see them.

-I absolutely refuse to that end.

I said I would not be willing to lose to anybody, especially a child innocent.

-Nobody wants that end but we have to contemplate it.

-I do but I keep refusing.

-Withdraw all is time to leave.

-William thanks for letting me go.

-Disastrous hopefully not my decision.

-Will not.

-Well let's go.

Disagree but drought had choice, he wanted to be near his family, like Adriel and I and even the others, it had won the affection of the girls.

-Sarah wakes.

I jumped up, and Monica was awake and also Carolina.

-Are fine.

-If but something happens friend.

-By which you say it.

-Have stopped spinning.

-So that's weird. Carolina said

-And I believe that if they have overnight laps.

-Boys would arrive for us.

-Maybe yes.

-Sarah will do.

-Just wait.

Cool my face in the bathroom and then came out, the kids woke up and the small girls was still sad, hear several steps closer to the door, case would be alone and not tried to leave, but it well be useless because we would not like to escape, the last time we went to a place we did not go very far, as it was not so hard to take them all home, only we would move a bit and we caught.

The door opened slowly, and I close my first and stand in front of the girls, the children were sitting on the edge of the bed.

-Good morning.

-There's nothing good.

-It clears that if at least if for me.

-Witch want?

-Need to get this, in a couple of minutes someone will come for you.

-Will not go anywhere without them.

-Well in a couple of minutes will come for you. She left the box on the bed.

-Your better use it as if for you own good and theirs.

-Who is the little one?

-You'll know soon.

She came out and the doors closed behind her, Monica opened the box.

-Wow.

-Little one happens?

-Is pretty as princes.

-My son is right.

I approached the box and saw a white dress with pink ribbons, seem like girl, Monica it out.

-What a shame that I do not have, if not me if I would put.

-Monica.

-That's cute.

-I did not will use it, apparently they are living in the past, and it's cute but looks at it.

-You will make us friend or damage.

-If Sarah and want to go with my son home.

Did not want to disappoint them, but I would not be so sure that we would return to home.

I finally put it on, come with some really beautiful shoes, the door open this time turned three people were coming.

-It's time to walk girls.

-One of them approached me smelling my neck; I did not move an inch.

-The smell good.

-Know.

-Are sincere good maybe a little longer for now walks and takes the girl in your arms, I hate children?

Follow them though the halls I carried the girl in my arms, she clung tightly to my neck, so I tore the heart, did not even know his name, and said nothing and not we pressed, Marcos was the hand of his mother very quietly, but was not, we were returned to the ballroom, which used it as a dining room, several were assembled like a family, the witch got up and called us to the table, but I pretend no sit motionless stay.

-Came closer dear, I want you to meet someone.

They pushed me against, the girl still did not look, but I was very familiar to the silhouette, my friends sat at the table and Marcos began to eat some fruit, the estranger raised his gaze.

-Your.

-Good to see you already know, well and knew, said the man, with the voice of an old man.

-Sarah I'm sorry.

The little girl listening to his voice straightened and looked at him smiling and happy.

-Daddy. She cried

He arms stretched but not have it stopped, and did not resist, sing, the little Samanta was her.

-What is he doing here?

-Well we had to push you more.

-You did Richard?

-Nothing, not even know what I do here!

-Let them go all you got me here.

-Of course not, they are part of this.

Kindly man said that I find equally pathetic, while my stomach was writhing in anguish, more and more innocents people who would die because of me.

-But sit beloved breakfast.

I sat down and put the girl to my side, but I just bumble orange juice, which was in a silver cup, like everything on the table was of silver, the room was more enlightened than the day before, this time the old man's voice was allowed to see, it was familiar, but it was impossible, it was like the age of Alan, maybe that's why he know, strange it was her voice, but maybe that was not immortal and appeared to be for souls tortured and taken away his power to stay alive.

-Almost time dear, your friends are on their way.

-Will not come.

-Clear that if I talk to Alan and your brother.

Rosalba said enthusiastically as if they had won the war, maybe if she had everything under control until now, my hear hoped that would not end badly, they could get out of this my friends, like this girl my ex-boyfriend Richard daughter, one more question doing here and where his wife, well that's tow questions, the firs was obvious would press me, but had me scared, so had the small and his mother did not know.

Someone entered and hurried beside the man called Cirrus.

-Are here sir.

-How well the show began.

I guess it was my friends, my family; my heart sped up even more.

-Get our special guest.

-If he is, we do.

-Stop we will leave in a little longer.

-Clearly, if sir.

Unfortunately one that we thought we would be on our side it was not, we had betrayed, Mr. Anselmo was sitting at the other end of the table, look displeased, wanting to say something, but I hold, along with him was a younger man, who was talking with him, and was somewhat aloof with Mr. Anselmo, did not pay much attention.

-Gregory.

-Yes sir.

-Can you please bring my coat?

Recognized the name immediately, Alan's old friend, I felt more relieved, but obviously not react as would endanger not, Alan and I trust in also I have to do it, he brought his black cape and put it next to Cirrus and returned to your seat.

Cirrus was still very carefree eating witch like her sister and everyone else, for being here inside I guess they are important and their expression was familiar with brightness as the teacher of William I guess they are immortal, finally finished eating the old man.

-Come with me dear.

Richard got up and ran with her daughter, this time not stop him.

-Look at the balcony.

I had not approached any balcony from the day that I fell from the balcony in Vegas.

-Do not be shy look down there.

I finally approached, put his hands on the rail and tighten hard, as if to demolish, but it was impossible I only managed to ache the image was scary down there, a war against my feet, scope to distinguish some guys fighting with soldiers from Cirrus.

-Stop them you already have me.

-No, I need some sacrifices, and as they came voluntarily, that counts as such.

He had reason my friends were sacrificing for me, I wanted to throw it from the balcony, too bad had my friends pointing a very sharp sword.

-Look well-loved in the center.

-Do not see anything leaves cover everything.

-aer-is.

Stirred the leaves and the center remain clear.

-In that place you go sweetheart.

-I think not.

-Good you'll do voluntarily.

-How can you be so sure?

-Say it is your future and you will.

-To be see.

-Thy will sacrifice yourself and you will.

-To be seen.

-You sacrificed yourself for them.

-Sarah does not, he will kill us anyway.

Richard in a strangle voice cry, and hugging her daughter, was the most sensible and sincere than that in years, did not trust him, but was very honest with presence of his daughter.

-He is right killing us anyway.

-Promise not to. He paused.

-Not you.

-Your word is not worth as endangering may innocent to satisfy your ego and you beauty something unstoppable.

-You are beautiful and if you do not want to be forever with you loved Alan, who remained in the same way.

-Not at this cost rather die.

-Good it will make the sacrifice you will die by the.

I totally changed my words picture as that was to sacrifice my soul for all and he would win, but who would not do if it is for save his family.

Ernesto had sent us help was as well trained as my friends, did not need weapons to defeat.

-And well you think girl on brilliant plan.

-No work.

-Clear that if.

He had drawn a six-pointed star with the name of six angels, the most powerful of creation which defend the kingdom of God.

-Enslave the angels legs preinstalled.

-Bingo that smart, you're just like you mother.

-Do not you dare even to name it, and no do it, not up out of the heaven.

-No continued discussing the end you will make it.

The names of the angels were at each corner and one in a her heart...Rafael, Gabriel at the north end, south Hanel, northwest Cassel, east castile, western Camael and a the southern end Uriel.

Cirrus kept me on the balcony looking around the battle that was beyond low, since by more they tried some in spite of everything perished, friends or enemies, some were already injured, I could not see Alan or my brother, maybe they were in the forest, as also heard some yelling in this immense place, it was gloomy at night but day was gorgeous.

-Almost time dear.

I look puzzled, while felt the wind in my face and into my hair flaying as she wore the dress because it was long, I stand the cold it.

-Rosalba children bring them in.

-No.

Shouted the four at the same time, but they ignored us, and look between struggles with Carolina and Richard, and I could not get me that if I did one of the bodyguards Monica slit her throat, just tighten my hands tightly and swallow saliva as many times before, Carolina looked at me with pain and I her helplessly.

-Please let go will do what you ask.

-Just in case you regret.

-Not have to be this way girl, only because I do not trust you as happened before.

What he meant to before.

-What will happen to those three?

-Will be in the balcony watching and if you fail they die.

-And that you let the children down.

-Good there's someone down there who wants to see the little one, and if the child is not with her mother, not the girl will be with his father.

Marcos kissed his mom and said he loved her, my soul was torn and I could not help a tear this time.

-I promise I will care.

-Ha.

Rosalba witch growled and wanted to destroy it but had to children.

-Walk.

-I get carried away children.

-Okay... Rosalba give it.

Take the girl in my arms and Marcos take it from his hand, at that time made me as light as the wind and with only one arm held her and not let go of Marcos, look at my friend and told them goodbye look, Caro was shattered, cold walk through the halls until reaching the huge wooden door, which when opened slowly creaked.

-Get ready dear, do not do stupid things.

I look with a gesture of contempt, to fully open the door and went out first and Cirrus and Rosalba behind me, I stopped to see so much pain and -agony scope to look at Hewett and did the same and them, after seeing one to one of my friends, look far away the father of Marcos, Mr. Hacher, stands by Alan, almost close to the trees, trying to get us, but it impeded.

Mr. Hacher was not so bad and Alan protected them too, how it is possible have brought him, Caro was dying in agony as his son.

-You like the view.

-Are crummy.

He mocked and nobody approached us as their guardsmen had come to protect them, so it was almost impossible, they stayed close to me.

-You better look.

He made a hand signal and quickly came several people as shadow, deep purple coat, placing in center of each corner jugs, knew every well what they contained, and it was an invocation of heavenly angels, my agony was growing.

-Cirrus reconsiders not know what you do, what is at stake.

-Course that what is at stake my life is ending.

-That is your destiny.

-Of course not, I refuse to accept it.

-I likewise to imprison them.

-So my second plan, you or the kids, they are as pure as you and his blood will serve me.

-Are sick.

-If I have thirst for power.

He said with no remorse, nor surprisingly his eyes were evil, and I've always believed that there is good in all people and that was about to change, he would be the first thing that has no remedy.

I looked at Alan approach close to me, but follow without looking at my brother maybe was still in the trees but it was frustrating not to see them.

-Walking girl is almost time.

Finally enter the middle of the circle, he came back to make a sing, perhaps pass one minutes, Alan was closer to me, but outside the star, I guess Cirrus had allowed him o get so closer, and then look at my brother in the blink of an eye next to him, I tried to move but it was useless, I watched my friends on the balcony totally anguished.

-Alan.

Pronounce his name softly as a whisper, but he hears it and looked at me with anguish like my brother that reaches his eyes look, Marcos stretched his hand towards him.

-Everything will be alright little one.

-I want to go with him.

It look but he ignored him because they kept attacking, but Marcos insisted much, Alan then stretched his hand, I let with concern but did, he placed it on his back like in the game of detectives, said that would hold hard, suddenly all my friends were about men fighting with purple coats braking the defense of the witch and the elderly.

-Have problems witch.

-Think so.

I went out of the star and ran towards her, the heels and the dress is not impeded me move, passing the little girl on my back, I said that would hold strongly, she managed to understand quickly, we fought, I with them more difficult than her by girl, the power that had used it and cold stop hers, by fading as the wind was going only to the sides of my body, scope to look at Alan approaching Cirrus.

-Are you, is impossible.

-That I should be dead.

Alan did not answer and without thinking he attacked with great fury, after five minutes, a pair of hooded the witch helped her to and she stepped back, I was closer to Hewett.

-Hello Sarah.

-Hello my friend.

-Who is the girl?

-Is the daughter of Richard.

-Are you serious, where are they?

-On the balcony inside the guarded not by how many actually.

-Give me the child.

-I promised to look after me.

-Sarah trusts me please.

-You do?

-Give it to me.

-Little one everything will be fine, but you have to go with him. She was saying that no head.

-Will take you to your daddy dear.

She reached out her hand and difficult step in what we were still defending, I covered when it away from me, the girl gave Miguel and for a reason I did not understand, Elmo had Marcos and some more were at his side, they were some guys seminarians, black pants and white necklace on the neck of the shirt, some if knew, entered and closed behind them, I was not sure what was happening but it should be a plan, but we left out, well were protecting girls and children that was fabulous.

Spent about four minutes more an eternity at that time, heard a cry in the air was a person tumbling by the balcony, my expression change a little Elmo and the rest were with my friends, was an immense comfort.

Try to go a little further to see was happening, and look everyone in the balcony, Caro had in his arms to Marcos and his daughter Richard, but Carolina's anguish did not end, and her husband stays down with us, they would have gotten along with the children, but only had a chance, and was too far away but his eyes were less distress that before,

Gregory was with them as reflected in his eyed, Alan thanked him with her eyes, Cirrus knew what was happening, he remove a friend, but no all betrayed us, not his friend of Alan.

My brother was getting closer to me like Alan, the teacher, Jonny and Hewett had not entered the castle, stood near me too, everyone around me protecting me, was something strange because in a moment did not fight nobody, I was just standing in the circle made of friends.

-Something is not right.

-If you die the heaven opens.

Said teacher William but I already knew, and only works if I sacrifice myself, it seems that part knew not, since they did not try to kill me, if not my friends and I would use to sacrifice.

-Not hurt me can't kill me.

-Are you talking about Sarah?

Sing, at the other end purple coats men guarding Cirrus and I could not see him, but I knew what his thought, so much blood as possible. The star burned oil vases and water stations, and that they wanted enclose the angels needed the power of some of them, and the first water from each station was a piece of heaven as pure as my heart.

-Alan.

I said and I hold his hand as we only had a moment.

-To open the heaven I have to kill myself, sacrificing myself for you, so he brought all to push me, it's a trap, never wanted to kill me.

He looked at me silly but he believed just like all.

-So speak which you Alan, she wanted to come.

-Achieving what we're all here.

-True.

Maybe they were safe but not quite, Cirrus had a plan and it was separate us as it was easier that way, which had the husband of Carolina and we were cold from distress, and we could not defend it, Mr. Anselmo was near them with a huge smile, mocking, Alan looked at him coldly almost killing him with the look.

-You should not bring.

-I said the same thing.

He threw a look of fury at William and wise it was his idea.

-Which side you're.

I said something mocking smile, he did not bother but if swallowed, ought to listen to Alan.

-Too late. Said Hewett

Cirrus came out from his guard, as everything was calm again and we were still without moving, had raised Rosalba witch, approached the star, placed the blue star necklace, I still thought it was a silly name, since it was purple but put in the center, the earth trembled one second necklace was introduced into the soil, not completely in a kind of lock inserted in the middle right in the center of the star.

-Believed it was not a key. Alan Said

-You're wrong a key, a relic that has to power to create and destroy and should you decide Alan, I thought that was what we had to protect.

Well is really not, but I thought that if, and I still think.

-Is one of many, and power is what Alan said, and can be used for many things, even for an angel to kill, destroy or just catch. Said the witch

-Alan friend of mine… you by this gentleman. Cirrus saidTighten it tight and do not let him take a step.

-That's what they want.

Finally released him and I understood what I wanted, look at my beloved; he took my face looked at me and kissed my forehead.

-Is that you have to go.

Cirrus and turned back to walk a little, but stopped before reaching them.

-Let go first.

-Course, walking.

Gave a push to Mr. Hacher the way to us placed next to William, with a look of shame, which approached him, that infuriated me more because I play very pleased and kissed him quickly in the mouth, but Alan not corresponded so I feel really angry, and wanted to go to beat that could not bear the thought of losing him blatantly made fun of me.

-Dear just like before.

-Friend once we are in the same situation.

-My friend died long ago.

-Clear that if he died I am no longer the same as before.

-Neither do I.

-If I see... you want the daughter of my beloved Lucy.

I look at Alan bewildered and knew not that it was, I suppose that suffering is part of the old spoke, and did not want to know the truth, it was too much as to what happened, and to hear more bad news, because I do not think they are good.

-Not tell you truth.

-Of course not, who would know that you're alive and you want to destroy your blood.

I was more confused than before, his blood was crazy, who is your blood, Alan may already wanted to destroy him but he gave his parents had died old my anguish was more overwhelming and my question again, but did not want to know.

-Good cute he's right, as you told how your mother died.

-Do not you dare shut Cirrus.

That if it was something I wanted to know, since I was not sure of anything, but it seems to be more painful because Alan did not want me to know, and maybe it would be better that way, but it would be so painful to not know.

-Well dear is a short story.

Short, it would be so bad for not knowing.

-Like I said she died by Alan cute.

-By him.

-If she sacrificed herself to save him and give him all his power to it, so it is almost as strong as you.

-What you mean with almost all its power.

He remained silent since he had not reckoned with my question and would not answer.

-If tell what you mean, or do I keep with the story.

Well Alan wanted to know or not, he looked knew that I expect an answer.

-He removes the power to your mother until she realized...

I agreed with her, better Alan than this wicked man, as kill her in the end anyway.

-Was her decision, but wanted his power, and had me killed, his power save me.

-See his power was a strong as yours now did not have to keep sterling the hearths of some immortal.

-He cheating us he was immortal when ever has been.

-Alan said this and I understand, he wanted his life... but as it is slowly stealing?

-Who are your?

-Is true not know who I am. He paused and looked at Alan

-Well who are you?

-My name is Patrick.

My head was spinning, could not be the same Patrick mother's life, but that explained, as he did slowly, was close to the, my pain grew and my eyes met Alan, who was still guarded by the witch with a dagger in the throat, in the photos that look did not look like it is now was better in the pictures this gentleman could not be my father.

-Not true lie he never would do something like that.

-Yeah well I never import it, less you.

My heart is full of pain he could not be so cruel, as it can cause so much pain, my heart races with more intensity, and could not stop looking at Alan as he said nothing, but maybe he was right it was better not to know the truth, he was protecting from pain, preferred to me know that he was good and not the person who tried to kill us, and killed his own wife, his gaze was Alan pain, I guess he did not want us to know of it, maybe that was part of his promise.

-You are a damn and curse the hour when my mother met you, you are not my father.

My bother said it with such fury and pain tears welled up in my eyes I could not stop them; he was just as confused as me.

-Thank you son like me.

-How dare you compare me with you, you are a despicable person that has no value.

-I'm glad your courage gives me more strength. Cirrus said. My brother wanting it launched against murder, but it was useless he was stronger than my brother, not his son was stopped, my brother stayed near Alan who was still inside the star.

-Get up boy.

-Witch want the locket as it is the heart that wanted no.

-Do not try to fool us you know it's your heart that we want, not that useless stuff you have there, the heart just shine in the hands of your choice, your heart is the brightness, and had the courage to save your friend, and we had to check, always knew what we knew, are you the key her, not the thing around your neck girl silly.

I had to try because now the two were in the star, and we continued with more distress than before, I remember my brother's dream in which he said that I was the key to all this, he was right, too bad I do not understand his dream, I better listen more often.

-It good to have Adriel.

He was furious but did not attempt anything or so I thought the witch attacked, but Alan did not move as some guns pointed to our friends, and the father of Marcos.

-You are a cowered as ever Cirrus and ever you'll be what you want.

-Just in case you think I care what you think, because you never consider a friend, use you just like Lucy.

Alan hit a terrifying scream of anger, while in the blink of an eye witch dagger hurt my brother, without thinking ran to his side that was what she wanted but was too late to stop, but just before entering the huge star I stopped, but my brother was on his knees before her.

-No.

I heard the cry of Monica in the balcony, raise your gaze and held it Elmo because for a moment I thought it would throw, just as I, was a common reaction.

-ado-ere, add Idi, abditus, escuton is ea angelous caelestis caelistus operio, apertum caelum ita immobilize-e angelus is. (Put away the shields of the angels from the heaven sky, the heaven opened and the angels immobilized)

-Enough do not follow what you do not know.

She took his dagger and made a cut on his right wrist and accomplishment that the blood ran towards the star, would not come since the last time I could not get out of it, it would happen the same.

-You have no choice.

-Why him?

-He is part of keys as their blood is pure like you.

-And Alan.

-He has his part in the same way as you.

-You mean.

-Their blood will stop as it has something evil in it, and we check the day he let out the demons, his blood will stop the angels.

-Are crazy you have no idea what you mean.

-Clearly, if all is for the greater good.

She did the same with Alan after all was to force.

-I hope that God will punish you and you do not let your soul live.

She laughed at my words, finally heave what they want, and it was not proved necessary to keep fighting against them, look around at my friends, they got the massage, Rosalba also left the star, and looking the old insane.

I enter the star as they hoped, up to Alan and my brother.

-I will only if they leave, already have the blood they need, is a fair deal.

-They can leave.

-Sarah do not you know that's not right.

-I know beloved but it is necessary.

While I caressed him in his face, and will not let me alone.

-Do not say that, your death is not necessary.

-Not to let die.

-They kill as anyway.

-They need more than my heart to open the door.

-Are you talking about?

Hugged him and told the hearing.

-Remember that to enter heaven their blood must be pure, said the devil, he will have to take my blood before I sacrifice myself, and do not leave.

-As you will.

-Trust me; remember what happened to the demon in Las Vegas. I let go and laughed.

-Out already.

-Ever.

Did not want to leave since that time I fought myself with the devil, not including, this time would be the same, would not let them perish, did not wanted to go, I was worried about that, and I had no choice but to push the two using my power some air, sorry about that but I want friends outside.

The two went smoothly so I'm glad a little, entered first the witch had no intention of letting her be in this place, I put my defensive position and she was surprised, and did not expected, Hewett cover his wounds with his shirt and tie them nicely not to continue bleeding, since it was something serious but not enough to kill them, I'm glad they are out, whether my brother can be happy next to Monica and my nephews beloved, that they would be safe if I managed to stop all this, even scared my heart knew what he was doing.

-Not believe that would not fight.

-Well, be a pleasure.

The pleasure will be mine, she started the attack and he was furious but my soul was calm, use what was around the star in the vases, the fire was very promising, and spite of being immortal she does not have enough power as I, was something strange she could not touch any item of the star, it was rare I guess I did not have a heart so pure, and above had killed and taken away their power to some people.

-You surrender witch.

-Never.

The heart quicken every moment, I remembered that they can remove the power to the people, but of course, I smiled.

-Are you sure you do Rosalba, you think everything is good?

She did not answer but I doubt it, an opportunity will touches its heart and take it its power, it displeases me but I had to, to comparison of them that I would not do it killed even think there's good in her.

-Enjoy the rest of your life I hope to be good, you have another chance.

She fell to the ground and all were puzzled Hewett jump within like her, came like nothing.

-She'll be fine by himself, he is unconscious, get her out of her.

He took and carried in his arms, Cirrus yell but did not move from his place, Hewett put on the floor next to them, and not lost sight.

-You want my blood.

I took the dagger from Rosalba and slowly cut my wrist, the same as the early had a prior mark, very quickly gushed blood and took my arm and take it, but take it away from him, he would not let that have the strength.

Leaves turned a deep red as fire and rattled around me, my heart was burning like hell, everything revolved around me in slow motion as… them on a TV, I could see the gestures of my friends around me, leaves not stop spinning and tears of my friends were rolling down her cheeks intensely, reflecting the worst pain of his life, the agony of knowing that they would lose their lives, her face erased all hope, until mine was lost in a moment, I planned not feel so much sadness and pain, not only the blood was falling on the star and captured the angels around me, always agony in life as it is complicated.

I put a small crystal barrier around me, as it was so small it was not working to maintain it, it would not let anyone enter, was even stronger than before, and could control it, or so I thought.

A ling fell from the sky and did not know exactly what it was, but it as of a violet or light purple, I could not explain that feeling of peace in my heart, but was still accelerated, the crystal as stronger as diamond as usual, worked perfectly around the stat, not letting anyone in or out, despite the intense light.

Cirrus followers wanted to go with him, and weighing the gate of heaven was opened, but I was no entirely sure, whenever they wanted to get some pain felt, my friends took notice and tried to stop.

-Let them enter they will come with me.

-No you will go alone.

The bother and try to get close to me, but he did not achieve because he did not have the same power than I, would not let them to approach me and take my power and more of my blood.

The vases were empty and fire off since had used in the fight with Roslaba, and there was no angel caught before I bleed on the star, and he understood in a second.

-Is impossible you can't, that is not written in the legend.

-Legend, this is not a game, not a legend is reality.

Seemed a warm summer day, the leaves were still on a pure red because all my energy was at its maximum but did not hurt anyone.

-You'll have to leave alone.

-You come with me.

-Of course not.

Manifested around us some different colored lights crystal clear, so pure that could feel it in my heart.

-I forgive you for what you did, but the punishment will be given by God, since you want to go with, I guess he will allow, his angels are free and you do not control anything.

-Not return them to the heaven, close the door.

-Is too late, my blood keeps falling, and your blood is as pure now as mine, so you fell fear.

-I'm your father did not let me die.

-It's time to get back; your time is over in this place long ago.

-Not want to go, not my time, you will pay.

-Already pay to know that you've hated me all your life, and not living a family because of you, but I also love a lot more than you imagine, that you did not see beyond that you destroy your ego, you power ambition was bigger than you and you have to answer.

-Stop the angels, daughter. His words hurt me.

-No father, this is a matter of heaven and not of men, the war among men finished at this point, since you want it so.

I thought it was true that men always had to resolve their differences, because we caused our problems ourselves, war was among men, is our problem.

Lights surrounded him he screamed in fury and despite everything my heart felt pain as he was my father, for more bad it was, but really forgive.

Alan pushed to Mr. Anselmo to the glittering lights; he was screaming with pain that causes his expression reflected this.

They became side with the six lights, which imprisoned, imagine that they were the six angels in the kingdom of the Lord, because what we had trapped a few moments ago, did not even know it would work.

They returned to heaven where they belonged and clear that I continued here, but did not know what was going on, the color purple was completed, the ended warm day, but around me the leaves were still spinning.

The Stories Never Really End, Always Star One When You Think It's The End. Why?

(By the love i feel about you)

-Stop is over.

Did not understand the words I had my eyes closed and felt a few tears trickle.

-Stop, let go in, you kill your own.

Finally opened them and looked at him it was Alan, but did not know what was going on, the leaves had not been calm, the weather was still turning slowly, look to the balcony my brother was with Monica and others.

-I can't, have to go please.

-Will not leave you, you can stop.

The crystal did not break, because he could not get in and did not know who to stop it, although it was more small that the lake was more powerful and had not controlled it as past, he was right, I had no control of my power and was dangerous but it was too late for that, the leaves of the trees around.

-Try Sarah.

-I try but do not work.

I could not leave the star could move but not enough; I calmed a bit and started down the fluttering of leaves, he was at my side.

-Well done girl you can.

I looked around but had not changed much, as all were still looking somewhat puzzled.

-Must leave all, and move out. Alan shouted at them

-But brother.

Said at the same time the two Kalinda and Hewett, my brother was nearby and Monica and the others put his hand on the crystal and could not enter.

-Alan passing?

-Have to go, you can't stop, it's too much power for you, you took the Cirrus and it was too and that he took the many innocents.

-As possible.

-When he took you blood become pure and you took his power.

-I think not.

-To whether it is as difficult as it may seem.

-I'm bad like.

-Course not dear, you're too good to be bad.

-Well you have to go, get out of here.

I turned to everyone and look with a smile.

-This is my fate; have to go, do it please.

I put my hand on the crystal where my brother had his and I said goodbye to him, and see the belly of Monica and said goodbye to them, my brother finally took the hand and walked away.

-Adriel no, we have to get her out here it is my friend, is you sister.

-Know, and that's what she wants, you save yourself and nephews, though it hurts me we gotta go.

She sent me a kiss with his hand and walked away with my brother, and everyone followed him slowly, Marcos sends me a kiss imitating his aunt, and gave a big smile, was happy with his parents.

Finally all left, there was only Hewett.

-Not have worked.

-Of course not, I love you both; we'll the see the other side friend, an idea of how to get you brother out of here.

-No, it was hard to let it enter… do not let go.

-But if I want to come out.

-Do not believe it is part of you and you of him are to each other.

-Hewett… take care friend.

-If I'd better go now.

-If goodbye.

-Goodbye brother.

-Hewett bye, be good with Kalinda.

-Clear if.

He went, did not return at any time, disappeared into the forest like everyone else, the pain I had say goodbye filled my whole being, could not say a word and did not want Alan to be with me, I could not believe what had happened, but I was glad to know that everyone was fine.

-Sarah.

After one second very softly I answered.

-Love you should not be, this should not happen.

-Will not leave you alone.

I turned to him with big smile and he returned it.

-Why do not you being inside hurt?

-Because you do not want to hurt me I guess.

-As you get in?

-You let me… look at all your energy is concentrated here in and it's better like that, as being outside all probably will die.

I let out a sigh and hugged him.

-I have fear.

-Perhaps it is our destiny and we must accept it.

-I know but still I have fear.

-Also I have fear, but I'm with you.

-You should not enter.

-When least expected and I found you I will not let alone girl.

-And I, who did not believe in fairy tales and I'm in one.

-Just not all end up as expected.

-There anything I can do.

-No, nothing Sarah.

-I can get you out of here if I try.

He took on my hand and looked into my eyes, I could see them he was very happy with me, and I try to get him out of here.

-You may smile a little girl.

He smiled, and for so many words, if that was enough for both, also smiled as he wanted him and hug me too hard, only know hi's my paradise and I'm glad that crossed my path beyond he will be in my soul forever, I found my love.

-Always you, you're my destination, never move away from you, I'll… with you beyond life we'll be together, you are the angel of my soul; you were always, forever the two for eternity.

He was right, we were one for all eternity, that no matter what happened, my life is perfect, that matters if it ends this way, since I have what I want, I have love.

The leaves that were red as fire still hovering at my side, spinning wildly and could not stop them, this time it was quiet but even so achieve stop them.

-You owe me a night under the moon on the beach, remember.

-I remember it clean that love, I promised.

-And promised that everything would be fine.

-If you hear… but everything went well we're together, I do not want a life without you.

-I do to stop this, as I end up with this power?

-I want you to understand that I love you and no matter what happens I'll always be by you side.

He without saying anything more intensely kisses me like the first time, even better, but it was a worse situation I felt that my power diminished, I could not stop kissing him, was so sweet and was able to listen to your heart, I now seemed slower than before, did not want to see thoughts but I went impossible to stop.

But could not stop crying, he was absorbing some of my energy, and instead of help was killing him, remembered every moment with me every touch every smile I devote, and even the night to provoke it, felt the heat that felt in his heart to close to me, his love was beyond this world, do not let it enter my mind but did not stop, he embrace with all his might, leaves dampened her fire color was more prolonged kiss that existed beyond.

Did not want him to die but it was useless, do not it, that's the point that you die and I stay alive, you're my relief, my life is broken into pieces without you I'll die if you're not next to me that is what matters, I do not want a lifetime of loneliness, it is not fair let you go, no explanation to say what I feel, he heard my thoughts.

Still had the knife in my possession, and not would leave him to die, every time I have been in danger he has to save me, my life with him was divine, my heart had revived when he was nearby, I did know it.

Let my soul look, I loved him too much I needed to be with him, but not this way, everything around me shone I knew that the mirror had been broken, could almost swear you hear as was breaking into pieces, his heart was beating with difficulty, achieve separate, and with a slight shove it tighten on me, do not would hurt more.

-meus-a-un amoris. (My love)

I said and I devote a sincere smile in the end I would sacrifice for my beloved, the dagger was stuck in my heart would end with my life, because it had so much power not to die quickly, the heart slowly stopped.

-Not.

I heard him screaming relentlessly, but he could do nothing, and everything was done, a love that was gone, all that was once at last it's over finally, I was just comfortable with dying beside him, near him, all he gave me was more than a gift from the heavens and I think God for having known.

My body went a blue glow; perhaps because it was my favorite color, the trees shook the earth shook, and my heart was about to stop, the foundation of the castle collapsed, the light covered us protected us from the rubble, as a perfect blast was falling just behind us, I smiled last breath, with my flirtatious smile as everyone thought.

-Did not have to do it.

He took my hand and I even with the dagger in my heartfelt blood run, I knew that everything was done I felt an immense peace; he took my hand and kissed me on my forehead.

-You are right not worth living without you. Could not answer could only smile.

-Silly girl, I've lived a long time but you're just a girl, you live a long way.

He rolled a couple of tears that hurt me in the soul; I tighten the hand to comfort but not enough, the sky was beautiful blue as his eyes, was my greatest happiness and close my eyes.

I left with the last look of him over me, with the color of his eyes in my memory, and everything around me was blue like the sky.

Not know what to do; I was just there with her, looking at the close of his eyes, watching the light escaping from his body, the dagger still embedded in his heart, the blood-stained dress dripping inside the star, take the dagger from her body, she still had on my holding the body motionless, to come my end since I've lived long enough and not letting go well it's time to let her go but I would go with her, the way up to now had been too, was exhausted at this point I was giving up or perhaps needed some help from heaven, did not had to lose my faith, I remember that was the purpose of his sacrifice.

-Stop you think you do.

-Hewett.

-What are you doing?

-I want to go with her.

-Not know what you're saying.

He removes the dagger from my hand, and approached her for a pulse.

-Is still alive just very weak, as is possible since it went through his heart with this.

He placed the hand on her wounds but was aware of what was happening.

-She will die.

He touched my shoulder comforting me.

-If she did not hold out.

-Are you doing here?

-Said we do here.

All were back at least our closer friends, Elmo, William, Johnny, my sister and Dylan, my cousin Samara, Curran, I could not understand what was happening, Adriel and Monica of the hand, but only they, as followers of Cirrus escaped when he vanished, the feared to be the next, just we stayed with Rosalba as she was unconscious, I guess that Hewett sending with our friends.

-Why returning?

-Because everything is different now.

-Different, are you talking about William.

-The explosion in the distance looked was not normal, as it was blue like the sky, the illusion only saw us as it was.

-You say William.

-She finally opened the door to heaven, and who sacrificed himself to save you, as it was written.

-It not happened before.

-Not only were the angels.

-If the heavens opened as we close?

-Only opened for a short time I think since everything is back to normal.

-You think.

-Have another explanation, everything is quiet.

-Very quiet.

Adriel was close to his sister, looking inconsolable, holding her hand, she only had a few minutes or seconds of life, maybe if he understood what happened, she opened the heaven, I would have let go, but it was later, I did not understand she reacted to her voice with just a slight smile.

-We can take her to a hospital.

-It is too late.

-Any chance.

All just watched, and Monica cried for her friend, like his brother and I inconsolable tears we only had drowned, the sky was so blue very bright as she liked, God is good if you think it is his fate accept, one as pure white light low, was in front of me, it was just the silhouette of a person.

-You are?

All looked puzzled like I was crazy and was talking to myself, I guess he was mad and I sow hallucinations.

-I am the Holy Spirit.

-Is impossible.

-Of course not, come down from heaven.

-Only I see.

-Whether it is, only you.

-Why?

-You asked.

-Asked you to come.

-You asked his fate shall be on it.

-You take her with you.

-What do you think she wants more? Look all around me.

-Hear it right.

-If brother.

-She wants to be always by your side, but does not want you dead. Said the Holy Spirit which gradually became visible to others a very pure blush white light.

-I suppose.

-And you want.

-Leave it with us.

Adriel replied the spirit is turned towards him and looked at him, but Adriel never looked down, I knew what I was asking.

-Are willing to change the destination.

-Why are you here then spirit? I said word to cut.

-Know that when… when Jesus Christ and Maria I came for them to open up the heaven.

-You come for her?

-Not seem to let her true.

-If she has to go, okay I accept that.

-I do not accept. Adriel said

-There is a way to save her? Ask the spirit

-If God wishes is likely that if.

-And how to know.

-There is a way.

-Mention already please.

-Are willing to lose his immortality for her.

-Please explain.

-If all you give a little of your heart, the part that is immortal and if God willing she will live.

-She will be immortal and we do not.

Kalinda wonder and made a look in disagreement and disappointment, and had lived long enough and it was time to have the last life.

-No, of course not, only give enough strength to live and grow.

-I give my immortality.

Monica said with great enthusiasm.

-And I alike. Said his brother

-Are sure of this.

-Equally clear that I would give my immortality to save her.

-I do not think it's enough.

-Give you mine as well.

Hewett and Andrew said after that Elmo said the same and Johnny.

-I just give my immortality. Curran said, Miguel and Tonny.

-I hope it's good enough guys are ready.

-Wait, gives mine too.

Dylan was responding, he just looked at Kalinda and gives her a huge smile.

-Is time dear I have lived long enough and I've been happy with you, but she's just a girl who began to live, and gave us life will change hers.

-While a more kids, good decision.

The spirit approached with Sarah and watch, and watch Hewett had the dagger, the hand stretched and my brother gave.

-Waiting spirit, I offer mine too.

-Are you sure Kalinda, because you can be immortal and never die, you can also live with me in heaven was still open.

-Is a pretty nice offer spirit.

My sister paused, I could not believe what he was thinking, she could go with the spirit, her husband look like all decentralized.

-Thanks for everything.

-Took the hand of her husband and gave him a smile.

-And well.

-If I want do…

All did not nod of disapproval.

Please let me finish, if I want to give my immortality to Sarah, is how much she loves my brother, and thank her for saving us, and never would live without Dylan, I would do the same like her, she deserves to be with my brother.

-Keep in mind that God's decision not mine let her live, the will decide what is best, if she dies anyway you lose their immortality, are sure to do so.

-Yes.

We all said in unison at the same time we all our heart, at least I do and his brother, and my and Monica, was too much to ask at all, but it was our turn to show that we loved too, since she has made everything for us, always to save.

-Are ready.

-Clear.

-Note that we have to accept wholeheartedly.

-Are ready. Kalinda said

-Well, take the dagger together.

-A question that I could not save her as Lucy did with me.

-Alan boy too strong, and had the heart enough to save you, like hers.

-So one is not enough.

-So is.

We look, he knew what he was doing, all come to him, and we held the dagger, one hand over the other, he said the words that not one understood, seemed Latin but it was not because not understanding what he said, somehow some of us came a spark of light in our hearts slowly, and was introduced in the dagger was still holding in the same way.

Was ready to grow old with her if had to if allowed and it was just like that, would die faster to be mortal, she will remain in my heart for all eternity beyond the distance beyond death.

The light of our hearts was to end in the dagger everything completely, after that the spirit touch Sarah in her heart, this brightness ten times more than ours and pounded but this did not wake up, did not move a bit, my hearth felt so much pain, my heartfelt much pain, the light faded completely, she stopped bleeding, the wound close but did not move at all, try to calm me down as I was warned if she die.

-Is all that I can do, my job ended.

-That's it.

Adriel said sadly.

Before he left he put the dagger in the palm of his hand, turning and truing elevate disappeared.

-That's it guys, the heaven closes when I entered it his sacrifice was appreciated.

He lift up to the heaven an disappeared, the fall back, it was rare all change, the sky back to a point of something gray white clouds as evening come, then the change was for him the blue sky, he was hire and was the favorite color Sarah.

I was still holding her in my arms, I could not believe it not been with me, all ducked the look and could not believe anyone, even my brother was sad, touched me back as to comfort, but that would not work.

-We must go.

William said, I woke up with her in my arms, a bloody dress like my left hand, tried to walk but I could not move I had forgotten it was in the star and it was difficult for her to leave.

But is dead as can't go out, not letting this place not this way; she felt heavier every moment.

-Alan passing?

-I can't move.

-No joke man. Miguel said

-No joke I can't move.

They went back and looked at me in amazement.

-Is impossible. Hewett said

-I think so to friend. Johnny replied

-If we do not let out Alan.

-That is not dead. Samara said

All froze as it was true, his heart had been stopped.

-Maybe she has to stay in this place man.

-No letting Elmo.

-And then I do not want to leave her.

Adriel his brother said, but all were silent as so many times before, all remain strange, every second we lived something new and different, a challenge to life, and every challenge is to more complicated at every turn, as if we had something to deal with, something that ever ended.

I still with her in my arms, and standing in the middle of the star with the hart full throttle and could not move, I just wanted to be with her, but I had no the dagger on my property, and that the spirit that the spirit had gone.

In seconds was returning to his heart is light, this time more intense that before along with the star, blinding brightness locked us that never before had bothered, so to now, all eyes were covered, I thought that I would stay reaping, because I can't cover mine, I'd never hurt light, but this time I did, at the moment the light wavered, only hearing voices as a very sweet whisper.

-Who are they?

-As you know, he the left with you.

-He.

-Our father, we are all grateful to Sarah.

-Thanks, why I can't watch, just listen.

-No one can see we are spirits, not bodies we can only come to earth as humans if our father allows it, this is a great honor for you as we are listening.

-Clearly it is an honor to be in his presence.

-The Holy Spirit gave them an option and accepts our father, the immortality of you in exchange for her life.

-I thought that did not work.

-Can take longer and need our help too, since his hearts is too impaired.

The earth trembled slightly but did not move even a centimeter from my place, the voices disappeared and the light became more intense, covered it to her and in a second the light disappeared into his body and then rose into the heaven, and all was as quiet as before, listen to you hear beating slowly my joy was greater, had wanted to scream but I was not the only one since I earn Hewett idea and was the first to scream, followed by all other.

-That was great. I guess all heart.

-So is brother.

I said with a huge smile and I was happy but still had a strange feeling, I did not know if I could leave the star at this time, Sarah's brother approached her, look at her with a big smile.

-That scared me sister.

I do not listen to him but he was right, it was a terrible shock.

-We'd better go home and do not want to be in this place.

-Clearly, if Adriel.

Heisted on e second and I was not sure I could move, but finally took a deep breath and took the first step, I finally move and I'm glad, at last come out from the star, Hewett smiled and looked on, I turn and he pulled the necklace from the star and had not difficultly in it out, the win was rushing like a whirlwind around.

-Things are still rare.

-I think so Hewett.

When the wind finally calmed down and opened our eyes was like nothing had happened, it was a beautiful forest covered with trees, not a traced of shattered stone castle under our feet, all covered with leaves and soil, the star had disappeared, it was magic or simply erasing nature God reestablished everything bad that had happened, the smell of nature was fabulous just like my dear Sarah.

-The surprises never end.

-Life is a surprise.

Commented Hewett and Miguel, I supported them, life is a surprise, although the scenery was beautiful we had to leave, we started walking in the forest, since we had left the car same distance off the highway, we walked very fast almost as if us run.

-Wait a second is not supposed that we are not immortal, for we walk as if we were.

-Good question Hewett as ever.

-And good I say.

All wanted to have an answer, but not had.

-aer-is. (Air)

Hewett attempt with a tree and this was strongly moved; he hit a shout of excitement.

-Is great to not lose our power fiends, even what we have.

Others tried and even Monica and we all had, I was not sure of doing and I stayed away, almost go the trucks and kept walking, I wanted to come to my house and sit down Sarah who was still unconscious, others followed me happy we did not lose its power even thought they lost their immortality.

-Where is Marcos and others?

-Send them to the monastery, like the girl and her father; we have to talk to them.

-I do not think there is problem with my family. Monica replied smiling.

-She's right. Said Adriel

-If we know but talk about Richard.

The teacher was right; I just hope that Richard did not trouble.

-Talk with him and understand.

-And Gregory.

-This with them, okay and grateful to be back with us.

-And I'm glad that we missed.

-If, regrets not helping us more.

-Not their fault.

-Of course not.

All we got, this time take the Hummer because it was completely rebuilt and better arming, for any complications, and the last time we did need, the boys took Hummers this time for the return for Monica was more comfortable than the other jeep we brought, only missing one and guess what for the girl and used his father, we went, diving the Hummer Hewett while I was with Sarah in the back, my fingers went through his hair and his face, watching his breathing.

My brother looked at us in the rearview mirror a huge smile, but I ignored, I know that smile was about to make a joke, seeing my reaction repented and followed just laughing and driving, take us long to get to my house, the car stopped I did not move for a few seconds, Hewett on and opened the door.

-I help you brother.

-Clear that if.

He took Sarah in his arms and went out, the others cars arrived at the time, parked and turned off the engines, all they come out to us approaching, Sarah his brother was the first Sarah approached, wanting to hold her.

-As is she?

-Okay but remains unconscious.

My brother and I answered simultaneously.

-Want her friend. Hewett said

-No, you take her in as it will be the last time you let Alan do it. Everyone laughed because Adriel not mistaken, but I had no reason to not let him help since he was as concerned as all.

-If I carried her into.

He said mockingly, all went behind him, until my sister Kalinda was with us was very strange that she cared about Sarah but it did for me and Dylan, but that for her, Hewett's leaned back on the bed and stepped back, shaking his head in disagreement.

-Going brother?

-I still feel the same.

For a moment I thought he was just as attracted to her as ever.

-Alike! I said

-If I do not feel different is as if we had not lost immortality, I feel the same.

-Feel as you thought.

-I don't know, as they lack something of me, a hand a laugh something but not, I fell complete and it is fascinating.

-I feel the same.

Kalinda said, while we all watched.

-Someone has an explanation.

-We are all alike, maybe that was our destination because we have complied with our purpose.

-All will be peace on earth teacher.

-And in the heaven Hewett, also the heaven is clam.

-But not in peace, right. Elmo wonder

-There will always be some bad stalking heaven and earth. I replied to Elmo, all sighs.

-Good but by the time everything will be fine and will have to leave all of the room.

-Why? I ask Monica

-Look at her, looks awful must be changed.

Without another word, to look all bloody white dress that did not help, all came out, by more impossible it seem Kalinda stayed with Monica as she was pregnant to do the job alone, could have gone as Samara could do it but stayed, it took a while, in the living room was spinning as far as ended, when his brother finally left her bother quickly came before me, he was closer to the door, waiting at the window where she uses to read was close without interfering with each other, and all the others were doing the same.

-How long it will stays this way?

-Do not know.

He gave her a kiss on the forehead and got up, then went with his wife.

-We have to go talk to Richard. I look at William.

-Curran and I'll go get it.

-Thanks friend.

All retired to the bedroom finally leaving me alone with her, some went to the outside, and my brother and Monica to eat and watch television and they had become customary, Andrew and Samara were in the library, then listened to playing with his powers the others kids, happy to still have, I too cheerful for that.

Was sitting at the bottom of the bed, not leave her alone for even a second, it seemed statue did not move anything, just know that going on in his mind, she remembered death, and when she awoke from his consciousness but it was hard to tell, my anxiety was decreased but not as quiet as she was not aware, and until it opens its eyes would not fail to worry.

Never love someone some intensely, and the pain of leaving him alone disturbed me because I did not want to let go, even when dead, I wanted to have with me, the fear of not having him around me in the other world made me feel scared, I felt lonely I was missing something in my heart, I clung to him, though I knew that was not possible, something wanted me to forget about it, but his memory take it so strong in my heart that was beating likely gone, the only thing I looked at was the blue sky, it was the only thing my eyes behold.

Far away heard his voice calling me, would not let me out, I felt close but could not see him because I was dead, not only heard his voice if not my brother also he asking loudly come back, the Hewett to the same, and even more surprised to hear the voice of Kalinda, nor let me go, and then all at once, as in chorus was wonderful is feeling, I close my eyes and I felt better they always remind me, I closed my hand and squeezed hard, took a breath and opened my eyes.

-Sarah, how are you?

The first thing I saw were these blue eyes, wonder if I'm dead I cannot see those eyes, maybe it was a figment of my mind that I betrayed.

-We miss you girl.

-I will miss you more.

I replied to the voice, not sure what was happening, fits my head and it was a very comfortable pillow.

-The pillow is comfortable.

Laughing voices heard, gradually my sight revealed more details of her face.

-These better?

-Are you part of my heaven?

-Clear and your part of mine, you're my heaven.

I approached him and hugged him regardless of whether or not a mirage, but the heat so real, it was real the sound of his heart and breathing were the same as I remembered.

-Girl how you feel.

-In the clouds or in heaven rather, I'm in heaven. Do not get away from your body.

-No, you are in my house, sorry is not heaven but maybe a little closer.

-What is amiss?

Asked puzzled because it looked like it was at the home of Alan and was hugging him, did not want it to be a dream, my sorrow follow in the wake of the, and react I'm dead.

-What happens? I asked again

-Are alive and you're in my house.

-Is a game.

I let go and stepped back was scared, he placed his hands on my face.

-Look at me I'm cute, Alan is not a dream, not in heaven just in my house, you're not dead, you're just confused.

Then I felt a pain in my arm and touch.

-Is because you've been a few days unconscious, only serum.

-Look at me, calm everything will be fine.

Hug to comfort me but was not sure what sure what happened, were heard loud voices, entered the room.

-Wake up!

-Were Johnny and Elmo, looked very happy to see me and I see them, I smiled.

-Miss that smile flirtatious friend. I turned to smile.

-I'm seriously here.

He smiled and hugged my tightly.

-Alan recalls care no longer immortal and can hurt.

Elmo smiled and Alan grumbled, but if it was real no matter who was not immortal, as long as I were with them, hug him tighter than ever, and I felt the pain of the needle in my hand and made a slight moan.

-Waiting let's take that.

Alan it off gently and the guys were not moving even a centimeter, were very attentive to what Alan towards as monitor it, and almost wanting to do them more when I winced when removing the needle.

-Pain is good you remember you're alive. Johnny comment.

-Thanks, good to know.

Wanted to get up after that but I felt a little weak and not try it again they were not moving, and I smiled to Alan looked at me and then at them had the face of silly, and then feel uncomfortable.

-Well I'll tell the others woke.

-Wait everyone is well.

-Luckily, we're all good friend. Elmo said.

-Tank you.

-Johnny is right Sarah. Said Alan

-And my bother and Monica.

-Were outside playing with the leaves look like Hewett children.

-As he is. Excellent Elmo answer

-Do not tell them I want to go see them.

-Of course.

Left the room but did not leave the house, did not hear any noise.

-Are you sure you want to leave.

-Course, only I have to change.

-Clearly have clothes there at the button of the bed and these clean Kalinda and Samara bathed you.

Remains somewhat surprised and look weird, really did not want to know who, it was aimed to answer.

-Say no more, just as last time.

-Half weeks.

-So that I missed.

-Then I tell you.

If it will be better after and wanted to go see the others, the get up this time was better and accustomed to the reality and happy for not having died, that was another question that I'm not dead, I look off but not for that reason I would change and did not come out.

-You mind leaving.

He looked at me not wanting to move, just motioned towards the door with his hand and took a single step.

-You serious!

-Clear that serious.

Finally came out and close the door, I quickly change, my hair was braided, in put a coat and went out the room, he do not waited outside the door, walk across the room to the exit and before leaving I heard many voices laughing, the best known was that of my brother and Hewett mocking Alan.

-Not change.

Hesitate a second to open the door, take a breath and finally opened, it was a perfect scenario, Marcos recognized Hewett running behind, reach around to see the little one black hair.

-Richard.

I said to myself, as I walked but did not see, the little ones playing in the leaves with the boy, down a couple of steps and see my brother out from among the trees with a ball of football, it went to Andrew and Marcos, thought it was cold everyone was playing, comments so the kids seem to still smiled, per a second thought no one was looking at me, but I was wrong, everyone turned and down all the steps towards them, I beat my brother Hewett to reach me, we hugged too hard, almost had waned to mourn but he did not it stand, jus his voice broke.

-As I missed sister.

Actually for me it was only a short time, of course I missed them because I thought... I thought that I would never see them again, that was part of my pain.

-I thought that I'd not see you again brother.

-I thought the same thing.

-Let me hold her, take off your kid.

Hewett shoved my brother did not bother, Hewett hug me more sensitive that my brother, as if I were to break.

-That rich smell Sarah.

-Do not change anything.

-You know me.

-Friend.

-Monica Are you okay?

I was pleased to see her, and her stomach looked bigger, hugged her gently, as Hewett he had done with me, but she squeezed me, Alan approached me.

-Someone wants to say hello, let her through.

Marcos was bringing the hand to the girl, I look Alan.

-Okay, she did not was taken off of you always take books, but can't read and speak little tells the story with the pictures.

-She was reading.

-Clear, as Marcos.

She came and takes in my arms, Marcos pulled my pants and bent over him and embraces with great affection.

-Children I love very much.

-Alike us.

Marcos said and went to play, and then others hugged me as much as they had waited.

-Where is Richard?

-He is with William at the monastery.

-And Caro.

-Happy.

-Where it is.

-Okay, let us changer to Marcos.

-I'm glad.

-I'm glad you're back girl.

-As it was.

-That…

-Where you were, you remember.

-Really nothing, just did not want to let you go and hear the voice of all of you sad about my loss, and it was blue, my eyes just looked blue.

-Well you are right.

-Do not let me out, and if we are all sad for you and together trying to bring you back.

-If I died.

-A while if.

He told me all that I missed being in the afterlife, every detail of what happened, but I knew he was hiding something.

-If there is something more.

-Nothing.

-No think that's all, do not grateful for the angels save me, there's something else you do not mean.

-If there is something more.

I like his honesty and was not good to lie.

-We are all mortal.

-Like, why?

-Good to bring all offered that little part of us, that your heart continues to beat.

My hearts is paralyzed with fair and were no immortal for me.

-I thank you, but I'm not happy with their decision.

-All want this life, we grow old.

-Getting old.

-We enjoy our last life.

-Should not do it, you should leave me there.

Was furious at his decision, I put them in danger and now we do.

-Sarah is happy this way, and we did not lose our power, we all agreed not to let you go.

-All?

-If all, none of us is immortal, my sister agreed.

-That's my memory, she wanting me not, it was real then.

-We hear.

-Was more like to hear your thoughts your feelings?

-That they did, why you did it?

-"By the love I feel about you"

My heart sped up more than usual, I was totally out of control was full of emotion.

-I love you too.

He took my hand, walked after looking at all happy playing around us, everything was better, he took my face in his warm hands and sighed, it was beautiful to see her eyes once again.

-Miss you so much girl; alone could not survive…

-I agree with that, I would have done the same.

-You did, you saved us all.

-And would do it again.

-Endanger you ever again, I promise.

-My days are better with you right.

-My body was raised, you know that I took among my heart when you went you left me alone, I was dying of pain, do not think I could live without you, I was just waiting for you to wake up, and all the time I thought that would be the end, you'd go and were leaving, never ever scare me like that.

-Never.

I replied with trembling voice, I missed hem a lot, because he said everything my heart had been thinking. The two was afraid of being separated, just knowing the damage that causes desolation, was tearing us our heart, bug hug me and I to him, then accompanied by a kiss as many times before and always so passionate. I missed his kisses his heat, we locked into our eyes and continue enjoying the sunset, "and if so many words if a glance is enough"

The Dreams Are Forever

Characters

Sarah Danica: (Hebrew) "princess"

Adriel: (Hebrew) "of God's majesty."

Carolina: (Latin) "little and womanly"

Marcos: (Latin) "Warlike"

Sonia: (Greek) "wisdom"

Monica: (Latin) "advisor"

Pilar: (Spanish) "religious"

Jasmine (Persian) "Jasmine flower"

Alan: (Irish Gaelic) "handsome; cheerful"

Hewett: (Old French German) "little and intelligent"

Kalinda: (Sanskrit) "sun"

Samara: (Hebrew) "ruled by god"

Dylan: (Old Welsh) "from the sea"

Curran: (Irish Gaelic) "Hero"

Elmo: (Italian) "helmet; protector"

William: (Old German) "determined guardian"

Andrew: (Greek) "strong, manly"

Ancelmo: (Old German) "divine warrior"

Tonny: (Latin) "priceless"

Johnny: (Hebrew) "god is gracious"

Miguel: (Hebrew) "How is the lord?"

Gregory: (Latin) "watchman' watchful"

Richard: (Old German) "powerful ruler"

Samantha: (Aramaic) "listener"

Hugo: (Old English) "intelligence"

Ernesto: (Old English) "earnest" Mr. Hacher.

Elroy: (Old French) "king" Messrs Gonzalez.

Jonathan: (Hebrew) "gift"

Jenny: (Welsh) "white fair"

Vanessa: Literal. Invented by Jonathan Swift.

Serapfina: (Hebrew) "burning ardent"

Kira: (Persian) "sun" Peter:(Greek) "rock"

The angels: Rapfael, Gabriel, Castiel, Miguel, Uriel, Camael, Haniel

Bad characters

Cirrus: (Persian) "sun emperor"

Rosalba: (Latin) "white rose"

Donovan: (Irish Gaelic) "brave dark man"

Petula: (Latin) "seeker"

Duff: (Celtic) "dark"

Lowell: (Old French) "wolf"

Opfelia: (Greek) "snake"

Tansy: (Greek) "immortal"

Patrick: (Latin) "nobleman"